EVERY SIDE
BETRAYED

MICHELE JEAN-EDWARDS

Book Cover Design by Twenty4hrdesign

Book Design by HMDpublishing

Conundrum written by Michelle Jean-Edwards

Dedication

This book is dedicated to my parents, Peggy and Harold, who I lost way too soon. I'm grateful for the years that I had with you, but my heart is a little less full without you. Mom, you provided me with the skills to put my thoughts into words that I hope others will enjoy. Dad, you were a laugh a minute that I hope conveyed in my story.

Contents

Acknowledgement

Without the love and support of my family, this book wouldn't be possible. My husband has been so supportive throughout this process. There were times when I'm sure I drove him crazy with the changes and revisions, but throughout it all, he's been my rock. I'm thankful for my son understanding in his five-year old way that writing this book is important. I'm extremely thankful for other extended family and friends who have supported me through this journey.

I want to personally thank people that supported me while writing this book by reading the many versions I produced. Dr. Pamela Gill Franklin provided valuable feedback. Mrs. Lydia Lay imparted so much insight to help me bring clarity to the characters. My husband provided a valuable male's perspective and content editing.

Ian Mars edited several versions of the book to help maintain the integrity and content of the story. Tremika Massey contributed to design the cover. I'm thankful to Twenty4hrdesign who brought my vision of the cover to life. Their help has been invaluable, and their snippets of wisdom have been instrumental while I crafted the story from Lauryn's point-of-view. I would like to thank hmdgfx with book formatting and self-publishing assistance. I'm thankful for Cynthia Gibbs' words of wisdom regarding "kill words" and over usage of them. These tips have been instrumental in drafting the best book that I can offer the masses. I'm thankful to Cover-2-Cover and Ivy Readers book clubs for providing valuable insight from a reader's perspective.

I'm also thankful for you, the readers, who chose to support me by purchasing this book and going on this journey with me as we learn more about the characters that sometimes we'll love and hate throughout the story. I know that you didn't have to purchase or borrow this book to read, but I'm grateful you did. So, grab a glass of wine or whatever your beverage of choice is when reading while I take you on a journey beginning with Lauryn Davidson's life.

Note to readers: There have been some changes to original publication. The integrity of the story remains the same, but some of the errors were corrected. Some of the character names have changed to better fit with the story. I hope you enjoy the book.

Prologue

Everyone in the location dressed to impress or simply to the nines. Some would call it the crème de la crème or in laymen's terms a black-tie affair. No one stood out. The crowd blended perfectly. Excitement and chatter filled the room. Those who normally didn't speak to each other made small talk as they all waited for the big event, the annual awards presentations. The holiday affair turned out to be the best one yet. He spotted her. The one he searched for all evening. The only one who could make his blood go hot and simultaneously cold at her sight. He couldn't help but notice she wore a dress that made women envious, but made men want to bed her. Surrounding her were other pretentious upper echelon who craved praise. He eased close enough to overhear her every word without being detected.

"Jackson," she whispered, "I'm nervous about the award. What if I don't win? What if I do? I don't think I can get up there and speak in front of this entire audience. I'm shaking and perspiring. Why did I wear a dress where every sweat stain could be seen? Can you tell if I'm sweating like a pig? It seems like I'm going through early menopause, hot flashes and all."

"Sweetheart, not that I can tell. Raise your arms."

"This is probably not the place for that."

"Well, you're not sweating anywhere I can see. Put your hands in mine," She handed them to him, and he rubbed them. "No, sweat. It's all in your head, baby. You'll be fine. Just imagine the audience is naked."

"That doesn't work."

"I heard it does," he laughed.

"Kim," Lauryn spoke to the woman sitting adjacent to her. "Do you mind going to the ladies' room with me? I need a female's perspective."

"Sure, girl. Caleb, I'll be right back. Can you get me some more of that bread, boo? It's kind of good for a WP event."

"I got you, sweetness," replied Caleb.

He had an urge to follow the ladies to the bathroom, but that would probably seem super creepy, and he wasn't a creep. He considered himself to be a gentleman. For one moment, Lauryn stared right at him and didn't acknowledge his presence. He didn't know if he should be upset or glad that she didn't recognize him. She would make getting intel easy if she's oblivious to his existence. He contemplated returning to the bar where he could remain incognito. Rational thoughts prevailed, and he made his way back to the bar.

He avoided some rambling guy who spoke to anyone that would give him a moment of their time. He didn't favor chitchat. He knew he must at this type of event. Being standoffish would cause him unwanted attention. He didn't want to seem weird or like he didn't belong. He knew he had no choice. He had to blend into the crowd. He only wanted to keep an eye on her. What's her game plan for the night? Would she make a fool of herself when she gave her speech? He looked forward to seeing that.

He had to learn as much as possible about her. He needed every bit of ammunition to achieve his goal. It wouldn't be difficult once he examined what she chose to wear to the event. If he happened to feel any kind of way about spying on her, he didn't anymore. If she had the gall to wear something that could pose as a negligee in public, why should he care about diving into the depths of her soul?

No one outside of him and those close to her knew her secret. From the outside looking in, she appeared confident and self-assured. He knew that she was scared shitless about presenting herself before the entire room. He still couldn't discern why she wore that dress. It was too revealing for someone sweating over speaking in public. He couldn't take his eyes off her when she returned from the bathroom. He wondered if she really did have a wet spot under her arms.

"Girl, you're going to be fine," Kim said. "The room loves you."

"Girl, stop. No one here loves me with the exception of you guys and Jackson."

"You're crazy. Everyone's staring at you. You own this room, girl."

"I do not. No one's staring at me. It's probably you. You're the redhead vixen."

"You're oblivious to your appeal. That's good. Do you, and you'll be great when you speak tonight. I'm going to get a shot of tequila to calm your nerves."

"I don't know..."

"One shot won't hurt you."

They stood right next to him ordering shots, and he swung around in the opposite direction. He wanted to eavesdrop on them without being obvious.

"Two shots of Patron Silver, please," Kim ordered.

"Right away, ma'am."

When the bartender returned with the two shots, Kim placed them directly in front of Lauryn.

"These are yours, mama."

"Uh un, you're taking shots with me."

"You need your nerves calm, and one won't be enough. You need to chill. You're too nervous and shaky right now. Trust me and take the shots."

"Alright, but if I'm a bumbling idiot up there, it's all on you, missy."

"I'll take all the blame. Now, as we said on the yard, 'Shots! Shots! Shots!'"

Lauryn downed the shot, licked the salt, and sucked the lemon like a pro. She drank both, and it seemed to mellow her out a bit. She joined her friends at her table. She mesmerized him. He noticed others were staring at her, too. Beautiful women filled the room, and none of them compared to her. She somehow made the other women pale in comparison. She exuded a sex appeal that couldn't be denied. He didn't want to be drawn to her. He didn't want to feel anything. His body tingled peering at her, and he knew she had the advantage, even if she didn't realize she did. Her dress left nothing for the imagination. She appeared to be nude under it. The way the dress fit didn't allow for panty lines. The bartender gave him a nod to indicate he acknowledged his presence.

"I'll be with you in just a minute," the bartender said.

"I'm in no hurry," he replied.

"What would you like to drink, sir?" the bartender asked after a few minutes.

"Rum and Coke."

"Okay, I will be right back with it."

He glanced at her again, and he couldn't turn away. This irked him. He had to hate her. He couldn't be attracted to her. He couldn't dare to have any emotion for her other than hatred. She meant nothing to him. She couldn't ever mean anything to him. He must remain objective. She wasn't perfect. Far from it. She must be using her body to advance her career. Her lack of decorum provided as much evidence he needed to confirm it. Everything about this outfit reminded him of a woman of the night and not becoming of someone who had pride in herself. She appeared to be nothing more than a high-class hooker.

This angered him immensely. His blood boiled. He found himself imagining, no, needing, to know what lie beneath her dress. He could imagine how soft and silky her skin would be. He couldn't control his body. It wanted her now. He always got what he wanted. As he contemplated storming back towards her seat, someone started speaking at the podium to make an announcement.

"Well," the announcer started, "this has been a well fought out year, and we've been able to bring in double the amount of new accounts. To round out the awards for the evening, I would like to recognize a key player in making things happen for us. She's been with our little company for over seven years. It's hard to believe it's only been seven years. She's been kickass since she joined us. Without further ado, I'll announce the senior project manager of the year, Miss Lauryn Davidson. Lauryn, please join me at the stage to receive your award and to say a few words."

Lauryn appeared nervous as she reached for her date to kiss him. He didn't like seeing her kiss the guy. Why did they have to embrace longer than the recommended 15 seconds? This bugged him tremendously. Lauryn flashed a brilliant and dazzling smile, probably to psych herself out, before she rose from her seat to sashay center stage. He noticed her every movement. A smirk appeared on his face as he followed her stride.

Her confidence could be felt with every movement she took. He figured she used every step, glance, and whisper to her advantage. Tonight, she would shine, and she proved him right as she owned the room. A bright light zoomed in on her, and he could see every curve and angle of her body. This affected him in an uncomfortable way in his lower region.

"That's one attractive woman. Her man's very lucky," the bartender said.

"Yea, she's beautiful. Lucky guy indeed," he replied. He didn't like the bartender's comment, but he couldn't deny her attractiveness at all.

To be the most sought-after person in the room presented its own set of problems. Despite his judgment, a little part of him swelled with pride. Scratch that. He detested the fact men wanted to do nasty stuff to her. It didn't matter if the men were white, black, green, or purple. Any man breathing knew she owned her sexiness tonight.

She reached the stage, and her heel caught on something. She stumbled forward into the arms of the announcer.

They fell back into an awkward position, and he yelled, "Whoa, little filly. I got you. Are you alright?"

"I'm good. Thanks for catching me from falling."

"No problem at all," he made sure she didn't need further assistance before saying, "Welcome our own Lauryn Davidson to accept the award of senior project manager of the year."

People applauded, but he wasn't sure if it was to hear her speech, or the fact that weird announcer got to feel her up. He smiled at her like a guppy. He didn't help her out of generosity.

"Umm, yea. I don't know what to say," Lauryn began nervously, "Umm. I'm truly honored and pleased to be presented umm this award this evening. Umm, to my colleagues, I owe my greatest debt of gratitude. I think umm. You're responsible for me receiving this award. I couldn't achieve any of it without you. Umm... those who have supported me with each engagement, thank you. Umm... to my family and friends, thanks for your support and love, this is for you, too. Umm... To my one and only, Jackson, thanks so much, baby. Umm... I couldn't do this without you having my back. Umm...there have been many trials and struggles, umm... but I've learned a tremendous amount through the adversity I've faced."

He couldn't listen to the rest of it. He imagined the volume suddenly being cut off. He couldn't bear to hear anymore after the words, "the people who supported and loved her." He hated hearing her say, "my one and only, Jackson..." That irritated him the most. How much longer would she speak? He didn't have a clue. He wanted her done. He didn't want to hear anything else.

Someone tapped his shoulder to momentarily distract him from the highlight of the evening. He couldn't imagine who would tap him at this event since he didn't work with this group, nor did he particularly socialize with anyone in this crowd. He turned around trying desperately to hide his growing annoyance at this interruption only to learn someone had tapped his shoulder by accident. It happened to be an inebriated woman who appeared to be three sheets to the wind with more than a few hours left before the event would end.

"I'm sorry," she said. "I thought you were someone I knew."

"No worries. These things happen," he responded.

"Well, this could be a happy coincidence instead. You want to buy me another?" she asked while tapping on her empty glass.

"No, I really shouldn't. I'm waiting on my girlfriend to return from the ladies' room."

"My apologies," she turns to leave and suddenly changes her mind. "If you want to have a little fun, she doesn't have to know." She winked and turned to leave.

The drunk lady would probably land in some rando's bed wondering how she got there the next day. Nope, he didn't want any part of that. He wanted to fully concentrate on the woman of the hour. The woman who had everyone hanging on her every word, and what a tantalizing mouth she had. He wondered briefly what her kiss would be like.

She glided back to her table gleaming full of excitement and joy. She only saw Jackson, her boyfriend. That was disappointing. His mood changed drastically when he observed her man caress her back. This enraged him. He dropped his glass of rum and Coke, and the crash could be heard throughout the room.

He turned away before anyone could comment about the drink. The room suddenly filled with music and laughter. He noticed that Lauryn and her boyfriend hit the dance floor. She appeared to be tipsy. "What a lightweight," he thought. He could definitely use that to his advantage one day. She didn't do anything embarrassing, but he could tell her boyfriend held her up. Before drinking, she seemed very uptight and high strung. Now, she let loose like nobody's business. The DJ played the "Wobble" by V.I.C, and he used this opportunity to get close to her. He maneuvered himself right behind her to have the perfect view while he engaged with the music. Lauryn didn't disappoint him at all when she displayed how she could "get in there." This event turned out to be less stuffy than expected, and he ended the night with a smile on his face.

CHAPTER 1
Lauryn
(Two years ago - 2014)

"Bang Bang by Jesse J, Nicki Minaj, and Ariana Grande blares loudly in the room. I love this song! It absolutely gets me hype. I'm very tempted to get up and dance with how excited I am to face the day. I don't need the alarm. I probably should've shut it off since my nerves wouldn't allow me to sleep soundly. I couldn't contain my sentiment about the day ahead. I eagerly hit the stop button. I normally would hit snooze at least two times. I like my sleep.

Today will be huge for me. Gazing over at my sexy man lying next to me, I can't help but smile. I wish I had enough time for a morning quickie, but sadly it won't happen today. What a shame! There isn't such a thing as a quickie with this stallion anyway. With torn emotions, I begrudgingly rise slightly. It's not like there's an alternative. I shake off the urge to ease my sexual tension by moving out of the bed. I'm meeting with the C-suite to show them I'm the right person for senior project manager. I'll deliver value for the organization in this key position. I'm in it to win it for sure. I only wish I could get a double W with some bedroom action. No one could deny my day would start off with the perfect "bang."

It's time to focus. First step, secure the senior project manager position followed by a junior partnership during my twenties. My ultimate goal is to secure the CEO position by the time I'm forty. This may appear to be an unlikely goal for an African American woman in a white male dominated field. This may be the case if it's anyone other than me, Lauryn Christina Davidson. It's time to change the flavor of the good old boys' club. What a sweet, sweet day this will be for this organization! Enough of this dreaming about what's to come; it's time to get this promotion. It's time for my daily positive affirmations to keep my mind right.

(You got this girl! You're strong! You're bright! You're a winner! You make a difference at the firm! They need you! This job is yours! Go wow them!)

Waltzing into the closet to choose the perfect outfit for the day is step two. This shouldn't be a difficult choice. The question of the day is, "What power suit indicates, 'You're our next senior project manager?'" Eyeing the black pantsuit with a power pink chemise is the most logical choice. The power pink chemise could add the right amount of stature, but this is a good old boy's network. Why am I debating this? This outfit is perfect. I'll exude the right amount of power, strength, and confidence wearing this.

It can't be forgotten I'm a black woman trying to make it in a majority white male-owned and operated firm. The assimilation I do to fit in is real. In the past, I would've straightened my naturally curly hair. Fortunately, today, it isn't as intimidating since Thomason's daughter has similar hair as mine. He once asked to place his hands in my hair. It's not all that shocking he wanted to put his grubby hands in my hair. He surprised me by mentioning my hair reminded him of his daughter's. He stared at me in a very creepy way. I'm weary around him. He doesn't seem to be imagining his daughter when he wants to run his fingers in my hair. Needless to say, I steer clear of him.

I dress in my suit and choose the perfect accessories. First, I slip into the quintessential pair of Christian Louboutins prior to applying my natural makeup to perfectly cap off my appearance. Finishing with a simple silver watch and a string of pearls leaves me appearing completely polished. Taking one last glance in the full-length mirror, my image reflects confidence. I blow a kiss and glance at my watch to gage the time. I look good, and I got this. There is time to stop for coffee and properly wish my gorgeous boyfriend goodbye.

Strolling near the bed right now as Jackson rouses awake is a risk I'm willing to take. Stretching his arms and yawning only proved how handsome he is. He's too sexy for words, and he doesn't have to work hard to achieve it either. I'm not going to lie. I'm somewhat jealous. I have to hit the gym every day to maintain my body. Seeing his sculpted chest is extremely dangerous since the sheets barely cover his lower half. Revealing any other body part would make getting to work on time a challenge. Noticing the outline of his long legs and the bulge between them makes me tingle. Another naughty thought enters my mind since he isn't wearing anything under those sheets. Yea, he's always in the buff, and it drives me crazy.

"Hey, Angel," he declares as he reaches for me. "You're beautiful, baby. I want to take a bite. Why don't you come back to bed and let me give you some good luck today?"

"Babe, I wish I had time. I could use some of your good luck," I flirt. "I didn't sleep well. I tossed and turned quite a bit."

"I'm sorry you didn't sleep well, but you got this!"

"Thanks, babe. Now, I have to get out of here."

"You just want to get coffee," he smirks at me, "You aren't fooling me."

"You know me so well, baby."

"Well, let me brush my teeth. I need a goodbye kiss."

Not wasting a moment, he rushes to the bathroom prior to returning to caress me from behind. This could be trouble if I don't leave soon. He kisses me softly on my neck and turns me around to face him. His kisses reach my jaw and claims my slightly opened lips for the taking. He thrusts his tongue into my mouth very sensually, and I moan from the pleasure. I taste his minted fresh mouth with each swirl of our tongues. We kiss for several minutes, and I move away breathlessly.

"You're starting trouble now. I need to get to work. Why don't we plan to celebrate tonight?"

"Done. All I'll need is your sexy body for this celebration, preferably naked," he remarks continuing to gaze at me seductively.

"Deal," I proclaim as I come towards him to get another kiss. "That's for the luck you mentioned."

He smacks me on my tail and utters, "Umm, yea, luck. Now, I need to get ready for work, too."

"I'm extremely happy to have you in my corner. Thanks for all your support, babe. See you tonight."

The offices are in the metroplex area of Nashville. The office building is quite impressive, and it's generally extremely busy. This is a consultant firm, and most of the firm travels. The headquarters is a place for people to work while in town or in between assignments. In anticipation of entering, I freshen my lipstick. Those kisses with Jackson this morning left my lipstick smeared.

Going into work today, I'm on top of the world. Everything is going right. I'm getting this promotion today. I have the love of a wonderful man. I have the best friends a girl can ask to have. As predicted, the presentation is going well. Eugene Upshaw, one of the founders of the company, is sitting in on my presentation. It's nerve racking to have such an esteemed member of the C-suite listening to me, but I'm pretty confident my nervousness didn't show. Mr. Upshaw approaches me to discuss something.

"Lauryn, exceptional job. You're truly a rising star within the organization," Mr. Upshaw comments.

Smiling like a schoolgirl with her first crush, it's great to hear Mr. Upshaw compliment my work.

"Thank you, Mr. Upshaw. Your encouraging words make me want to work even harder."

"Your work ethic and drive have been admirable and everything we want at this organization. It's a thrill and honor to have you join my team, Lauryn. You'll go far within this organization."

"I'm honored, Mr. Upshaw. I'll continue to do my best to always make you proud of me."

"I'll certainly hold you to that, but you'll always make me proud. You've only shown the best judgment. Keep up the great work, Lauryn."

As Mr. Upshaw leaves, I could only beam. My future will be absolutely wonderful. I'm excited about the new challenges I'll face. Now, attaining all of my goals appear plausible. It doesn't matter what people think. I'll be the future CEO of this organization. I'm making the right connections to fulfill my long-term dreams. I'm joining Upshaw's team. This is extremely exciting. He's the force behind this firm's success. I'll have access to the right accounts to make a difference. I'll also have the right visibility within the firm. I'm ecstatic to start this new role. Sure, there'll be more work demands with this job. I'm not concerned. I'll have it all! My daydreaming over the endless possibilities of my career and future with Jackson is interrupted when my phone vibrates with a text message. It's Asia, my best friend.

Asia: Hey Lola, U want to go to lunch?

Me: Yea, let's do it. I have a lot to celebrate today.

Asia calls me Lola, and she has all our friends calling me the nickname. She started calling me Lola during our freshman year. She said Lauryn's too formal, and I needed a nickname to suit me. For some reason, she wanted to call me Lola to jazz up my name. We've been BFFs since freshman year. We're meeting at a restaurant near my job since I have a busy afternoon. I'm pretty sure she wants to discuss Cedric.

Asia isn't facing facts about him. She's the only one making compromises with her on and off relationship with Cedric. He wants to string her along just enough to prevent her from falling for anyone else, but he isn't willing to commit to a relationship with her. This isn't something Asia wants to discuss. I'm trying to be as supportive as possible. I don't care for Cedric at all. He isn't any better than any of Asia's exes honestly. She sure can pick them. Every one of them has treated her like garbage, and she deserves better. I enter the restaurant, and Asia's already seated.

"Hey, girl," I greet and give her a hug.

"Hey, lady. What are we celebrating? Did you get the promotion?"

"Yes, we're celebrating the promotion. Plus, Jackson and I have made the big move in our relationship. We live together now."

Asia's face droops with sadness. My relationship status with Jackson isn't helping. Her rocky relationship with Cedric is more than likely in the forefront of her mind. I don't want to rub my happiness in her face. I'll steer clear of my relationship with Jackson.

"I'm sorry, Asia. I didn't mean to shove my happiness in your face. I understand things haven't been good with Cedric."

"No, don't you ever hide your happiness from me. I'm happy Jackson makes you happy. I'm sure he'll make tonight special for you."

"Yea, I'm tremendously lucky. How will you handle things with Cedric?"

"He's a fuckboy, but I love him, girl. He'll eventually figure out this is what he wants," she comments by moving her hands around her body with extra dramatic emphasis.

"He's definitely a fuckboy. He should appreciate all you have to offer, but you need to love you, girl. He's a man, and another one will pop up sooner or later. Get a better one."

"Girl, he does phenomenal things to me in and out of the bedroom."

"You would focus on his sexual bravado. He has to offer you more than some good loving, girl."

"I hear you, but sometimes it's hard to refuse him. I've tried repeatedly to end things, and he sweettalks me back to the bedroom."

"You have to end things with him in a public place and absolutely not at home. You need to ghost him for a minute, and he'll leave you alone."

"Damn, girl. You have this down to a tee. Is this your future exit strategy?"

"Nah, I have no need to exit. My man is amazing, and he loves the hell out of me."

"Well, don't ever take him for granted. Having a man love you the right way isn't easy to come by. I'm a witness, girl. Cedric isn't the first wrong mistake I've made."

"We won't speak about your past mistakes. Since you've been messing around with Cedric for all this time, it shouldn't be a surprise about what he really wants. If you're okay with not being in a committed relationship, do you. I have a sneaky suspicion you don't want casual anymore. You deserve better. Get out of this thing with him, and demand something better."

"You're right girl. How did you get to be this smart in the game of love?"

"Well, I don't like to brag, but I took a psychology class in college. It focused on relationships and connections. I could be a pseudo couple's counselor if I opted to work with people. I laugh."

This is not something I could seriously do. I don't want any parts of other people's problems. When it comes to helping my friends, I'm down. I don't have any intentions of dissecting the issues of the "Molly and Coopers of the world." Molly and Cooper are the types who complain all of the time about each other, but they shouldn't be in a relationship. They don't want to face the facts, and they're better alone than with each other. Someone else should deal with those problems. For the rest of the lunch, we catch up about mutual friends, our respective jobs, and our future vacation plans.

I'm restless at work after meeting up with Asia. The constant search for the clock is driving me crazy. I want to get out of here, but the second hand keeps dragging. As much as I love what I do, I want to get home and start the real celebration. This is one of those rare times I'm leaving work about an hour early. I deserve this reprieve. I want to surprise Jackson, but it'll probably be him surprising me tonight.

When I finally make it home and open the door, the living room is setup with candlelight and roses. I'm blown away by this romantic scene. The transformation of this space is nothing short of fabulous. Jackson never ceases to amaze me. He strolls over to me. I'm literally transfixed where I'm standing. He beams and embraces me. He gently tilts my head to engulf me into a kiss. I'm under his spell, and I didn't notice the door shut behind me. We begin kissing with abandonment until I break away for a breath to lean against his chest.

"There's one thing I don't like here. It doesn't work with my plan tonight," he whispers into my ear.

"Yea? What?" I ask.

"You and all of these clothes," he leers, "I recall telling you I wanted you naked."

"Well, I'll certainly accommodate your wish," I tease as I gently push him away in an attempt to undress. This isn't something I normally do, but I want him to see me bare all for him. I start my sexy striptease by removing my jacket and my pants. Jackson scrutinizes my show with a very pleased expression on his face.

"No, that's my job now," he announces as he removes my chemise.

"I can do it so much better. Something you won't forget."

"You're perfect. The sexiest woman alive. I love examining your every motion, but this is taking too long. You still have on too much. I'm in control now."

He tugs me close and sensually kisses me. I don't know how he did it, but all my clothing had been removed.

"Why am I the only one lacking garments?"

"Well, what do you want to do about it?"

"You'll see," I reply as I draw him towards me and rip off his shirt hastily. I jerk the buttons on his pants and unzip the zipper faster than he expects.

"Someone is anxious and ready for this."

"You have no idea."

"Well, let's not wait any longer," he states as he carries me upstairs to the bedroom where rose petals lay all around.

He's kissing and touching me generously as we land on the bed. Every part of me is experiencing a warm desire anticipating us making love soon. I want him more than anything, and I'm caught up in the sensation of him. Every nerve in my body is starving for him. As we kiss, he reaches over to grab a condom from the nightstand. He doesn't miss a beat with his tongue in my mouth while his hands roam my entire body. I'm moaning from the pleasure of his embrace and kisses in my most sensitive areas. My body craves everything he's offering, and I want to explore his body as well. My discovery yields special surprises. He doesn't stop engaging with my most intimate parts. My body is exploding with the ultimate amount of pleasure. I'm anticipating what will come next.

He rolls on his back, and he asks me to ride him. This is my favorite position, and I'm ready to give him the good stuff. Before long, we're both losing control and moving in synch with one another. I am powerful. I'm the only one able to provide him this much pleasure. He's screaming out my name, and this is the sweet spot of our love making.

He doesn't want things to end. His eyes stem with hunger emitting something more. Something tells me he won't be coming (not yet anyway). He flips me so fast I thought he could be a magician. He maneuvers me into doggy style. He doesn't hesitate to pump in and out of me with an acute amount of power. We finally come simultaneously before collapsing on the bed. He kisses me on my back prior to turning me to face him. He cups my face and tongues me with passion resembling a never-ending flame. He releases me, and he faces me with more desire than I've ever seen.

"I love you, Angel. You were amazing."

"I love you so much, babe. Thank you for this celebration."

"Oh, this isn't your celebration."

"This isn't?"

"No, this beautiful experience made both of us happy. I made you a delicious and delectable meal. Hungry?"

"Famished. The workout you provided gave me quite an appetite."

"Good, you're going to love the food. I made your favorites: lobster and shrimp pasta. You're going to need fuel and energy for rounds two and three."

"Someone is confident," I joke.

"Well, I'm hoping to have a trifecta tonight. That's not being too confident, is it?" he asks innocently.

"You spoil me, and I'll be ready for the trifecta, baby. It's not being too confident. In fact, it could be more than three."

"Now, who's confident?"

"When it's a fact, is it really being too confident?"

We put on t-shirts and go to eat the amazing meal he prepared. It's an aphrodisiac for me. The passion growing in between my legs is on fire. I can't wait to get back to our bed. I tease him by eating my pasta seductively.

"Hmm, you're being super sexy with the food right now, Angel."

"Am I?" I ask innocently. "I didn't realize that I was doing anything differently?"

"Well, you seem like you're ready for round two."

"Do I?"

He smirks, "You playin' with me now."

"What if I am? What will you do about it?"

We usually make love to music. It's sort of our thing. We couldn't set the mood earlier since we were hasty. We have the whole night ahead of us. I sashay to my phone and connect it to the Bluetooth to play perfect music for the scene, "Your Mine" by Mariah Carey.

This song is made for lovers. Making love to him knowing he's all mine makes me want to be bold and go for what I know. I want him more than anything right now, and I can't wait to have him. He jumps and comes over to lift me. I'm laughing nonstop as he leads me back to the bedroom where we'll spend the entire night making love.

I didn't get much sleep last night. I don't need to explain why. I'm calling into work. I'm exhausted. We're both playing hooky. This isn't like me in spite of this being the right choice. My happiness has transcended the mediocrity of normality, and I need to be with him today.

"Baby, since I'm skipping work for you, how do you plan on making this worth my while?"

"Oh, you don't think I'll make this worth it for you to skip. What are you missing? Some data analytics or problem-solving blah blah blah stuff you do all day?"

"I still haven't learned how yet," I emphasis sarcastically.

"Angel, I'm better at showing you than anything. Just know I'll rock your world today."

"Well, all talk, and no action makes Jackson a man short on delivery."

"I'll show you 'no action,'" he grins.

He rushes towards me and brings me into his arms. For a minute, I'm not sure what he's going to do with me. I sense the hunger in his eyes only I can satiate. That may sound super cocky, but I have special skills. We spend the day making love, and it's magical. I'm in heaven, and I can't imagine how things could get any better. I have the job and man of my dreams. He's beyond supportive and constantly inspiring me to do and be my best. I'm fortunate to have his love. We lazily lounge around all day.

"Thank you for convincing me to play hooky with you today."

"I would've convinced you one way or another anyway."

"Is that right?"

"Damn right. My lady doesn't get promoted every day. It's my duty to worship her entire body until she's fully satisfied."

"Well, you took your job seriously. You have earned top scores for your performance."

"Top? Do I get an A? I'm an overachiever. If I didn't get an A, I'll do everything I need to do to get one. I'll do some extra credit or make-up classes. Just tell me, and it's done."

"You'll definitely get an A+"

This is a new day. I'm exhausted. I wouldn't mind a rinse and repeat of yesterday's actions. Who knew having sex all day would make me exhausted like I ran a marathon? Well, if I ever run one, I'll do a comparison. My body is somewhat sore, but I'm down for more. The huge grin on Jackson's face mesmerizes me. I doubt he'll complain about having a sexaholic girlfriend.

"Morning, baby. You ready to go again?" I leer at him seductively.

"Good morning, Angel. You want the next round now?"

"I'm not shy about going after what I want," I caress his thigh and wait for a reaction.

"I thought you would never ask."

He reaches to grab a condom but comes up empty. "Damn, baby we've been getting too busy. I'm out of condoms. I need to go to the store."

He's anxious and prepares to leave. I grab his arm to stop him from leaving.

"No, baby you don't."

"What do you mean? You want to have sex without a condom?"

"I've been meaning to tell you I have an IUD now. I love you and you love me. We trust each other, right?"

"There is no one else for me."

"Me either. Now, come back to bed and give me what I've been desperate for since sunrise."

He chuckles, "You make me feel so wanted."

"You're wanted. Right here, right now."

He doesn't hesitate to give me what I need and want. Well, in sexaholic fashion, we do what we do best. I never imagined sex with Jackson could get any better. Making love to him without a condom is everything all at once. The emotions and the volcanic eruption I experience catapult anything and everything. It's like the best kept secret in time. He makes me feel in ways words can't express. I won't diminish what's happening between us a simple happenstance. This is the best sex I've ever had. Sex with Jackson is always earth-shattering, but this right here is what makes galaxies. He'll never have to ask me for extra credit again. He's breaking the bank with these strokes.

We both cry out in synch with one another. I love this more than I ever thought I would. Coming down from the mountain top, my breath is slow, and I need to sleep. I don't want to close my eyes, but I do. Boy, my body is weighted like I ran about ten 100-meter dashes. If my celebrations are always like this, I'll never go to work. I'm exhausted, and I could go back to sleep, but I'm not. I want to get out and do something since we've been in bed for a day. I give into sleep for what seems like two seconds but it's more like an hour. I wake and stretch my arms out to realize Jackson is staring at me. He beams at me in a way that makes my entire body tingle with anticipation.

"Your smile makes me weak and under your control."

"I'll never use my power for evil...only good," he remarks as he pulls me near and into his arms.

"What do you want to do today?"

"Hmm, I'm unsure. What do you want to do?"

"As much as I love you ravishing my body, it's time for us to get out into the real world."

"Ravish your body, huh?"

"That's what you took from everything I said?"

"Well, when it comes to sex, I kind of have a one-track mind."

"Well, I'm going to need you to think about some non-sexual stuff with me." I lift his chin to gaze into my eyes instead of my naked breasts.

"Well, we could shower and then get some breakfast. I would cook for you, but I want to get out in the world and show-off my super smart and independent, boss moves making woman. After breakfast, I have a surprise for you. I want you to know how proud I am of you."

"I love you."

"I love you more, Angel."

We spend the day doing some of our favorite things. We have breakfast at the best omelet and pancake place in the city. We go to Centennial Park to walk around and hold hands the entire time. We later spend the afternoon going to a double matinee show (an action movie for both of us and a chick flick because he loves me). As we leave the theater, our stomachs growl. Dinner is calling.

"You want to do something reckless, Angel?"

"Without a doubt."

"Let's go to the burger joint with like a million calories and have burgers with shakes."

"You're right. This is reckless. But I'm game. Let's do it. We burned a million calories these last few days."

"We did, didn't we?"

"I love being here with you. I wish —"

"I know, baby. I wish we had this every day, too. I don't take it for granted that we don't. That's why I take advantage of every moment we have alone. Every moment with you is precious."

"Aww, I'm touched. You're everything I could ever want in a mate. Thanks for being mine."

"No need to thank me for something that's a given."

"What's a given? You'd be mine."

"I'm yours. Always and forever."

The waitress took her time getting to us, but I'm still pondering what to choose. I narrow it down to a slow roasted burger with all the toppings and gourmet fries or an Around the World burger with sweet potato fries. I go with the roasted burger, gourmet fries, and a Kiss Your Mama milkshake. It's an adult French vanilla shake with rum. Yum. This combo is the best around, and I savor each bite of this juicy goodness.

"You got something on your face," Jackson grins as he wipes my mouth with a napkin. "You're such a messy eater. I can't take you anywhere."

"Well, I can leave."

"You know, I'll take your messing eating, and the rest of your flaws any time, Angel."

"You better," I utter with fake anger.

"Always and forever, baby."

He gives me a PDA appropriate kiss since I'm not really into getting down and heavy in public. I cheese at him like a girl with her first crush. I'm enjoying building a life with him.

CHAPTER 2
Lauryn Present (2016)

"Work" by Rihanna blasts from my phone alerting me it's time to wake up. This song always makes me pumped and ready to go. I arise quickly, and I'm more alert than I should be on a few hours of sleep. I'm not sure if I set my alarm for the right time. Peering hard at the clock, my panic increases by the second. I set it for the wrong time. I'm going to be late. I better hurry.

I'm cognizant and considerate that my baby is lying next to me, so that I don't wake him. I need to leave for work immediately. Being late isn't an option today. It's time to get dressed. It's imperative I arrive at the office prior to everyone else. I'm in and out of the shower in less than ten minutes. This isn't common for me. I dress in a hurry in a standard power suit accentuating my assets in just the right way: classy and slightly sexy. Looking good should never be a burden.

I rush to kiss Jackson on the cheek, grab my favorite Louis Vuitton purse, and dash out of the door. I jump into my Jaguar F-Type and rev the engine to go. I'm reminiscing about the day I purchased it. It's hard to believe it's been two years already. I deserved the fat bonus I received, and I rewarded myself with the car. I'd been saving for many years, and I bought the car with cash, my first big purchase. It's a beautiful, satellite gray metallic color. I'm driving faster than I need to drive, but I love to drive fast. I'm slightly nervous about today.

I'm there by 7:45 AM and ready to seize the day. Walking into my office, I stress wondering if I need to view this presentation one more time. I have nearly 20 minutes to peruse this bad boy. I'm fairly positive I'll kill this presentation to secure the promotion. Reflecting for a moment about what's to come, I smile about the possibilities. I have a few minutes to check my email. Right away, I glance at an email from HR, and it has a star indicating it's important. I don't want to bother with it, but it states it's important.

The email read: *Lauryn Davidson, we regrettably inform you, as of today, you will no longer be an employee at the firm.* My whole body collapses. I'm not comprehending what's going on! They're firing me? On what grounds? All my performance feedbacks have exceeded expectations. I'm one of the few black women who kills it here on a regular basis! How cowardly of this firm to send an email! Who do I need to speak with to get a better understanding? I can't even believe this shit right now. I should be promoted not fired today!

In the last two years alone, I've brought in and managed accounts exceeding $50 million. This financial quarter alone, a whopping $30 million. I'm on track to exceed this amount. How am I the one that's being "laid-off?" Out of all ten senior project managers, I rank #1 in account management. How could this be happening? I won PM of the year just a few months ago! What's wrong here? Does it make sense to lay off the top earner in the firm? Only idiots operate like this.

Stanton, Thomason, and Upshaw. The firm's better known as STU. STU has been considered the place to work in consulting for new college graduates. Everyone I knew who wanted to be a consultant wanted to work at STU. They flew me out to their headquarters and put me in a penthouse suite for the three-day interview process. The process included going out to clubs, bars, and hanging out with other recruits who were graduating. Everyone understood STU's policy evolved around working hard and playing even harder. What early 20 something wouldn't find this appealing? I certainly did.

Maybe all the money STU threw away on recruiting and last-minute travel should be evaluated instead of me losing my job today. There's no telling how much money STU wastes on recruitment trips, expensive bonuses, travel, and every other thing under the sun. STU saved some money moving the headquarters to Nashville from Boston. They're recruiting more local and regional candidates, but I guess it hasn't made the impact needed.

In total, I have seven years with the firm including my internship during college. My trajectory from intern to senior project manager is generally unheard of in seven years at this firm. My boss, Michael, enters my office as I reflect on my career. I trust Michael, and he goes all out for me. There's no way he had anything to do with these shenanigans. I doubt he had much of a voice in this decision. Michael is one of the few black men in upper management at STU. He doesn't really have the power and influence he should.

"Lauryn, I wanted to get to you first. I wanted to be the one to break the news."

"You're too late, Michael. What's going on here?"

"Lauryn, the company has been losing money on most fronts. We've lost some major accounts. I —"

"Not any of my accounts," I interrupt.

"That's true. The partners recognize your talent, but there have been quite a few financial issues lately. The C-suite has decided to eliminate the senior project manager and the junior partnership roles. They didn't believe you would accept a demotion. These decisions are above my pay grade. If I were at the table, you'd be staying."

"I'm positive you would've done things differently, Michael. I don't blame you. You don't operate like this."

"Thank you. I want you to know you're a valued employee, and I'll write any references you need. I influenced what I could. I pressed for you to have two years of severance pay and the bonuses you normally would receive each of those years. I got it for you. I'm losing my best employee. That's the least we could do for you."

Two years pay plus the bonuses will definitely give me some time to field my options. The economy is decent. It shouldn't take long to land something else. I find it strange they'll pay me the same monies as if I'm still employed here but keeping me onboard doesn't work for them. I've had numerous offers through the years, but like a dummy I loyally stayed here. I tried to make the most impact and career gains. I can't believe how naïve I've been. They're paying me back royally. They're basically firing me for reasons I don't quite get.

"Lauryn, a lot of people are being laid off today. At my count, it's around 40 people being let go. No one's getting the same amount of severance as you. There'll be about ten people demoted to management consultants. This is just the beginning. It goes without saying you didn't hear any of this from me."

"Of course, Michael. You can trust me. Will you stick around much longer?"

"I'm doing what I need to do to prepare for my next move."

"Thanks, Michael, for your honesty. I appreciate you looking out for me and fighting for my paper. You've always been forthright and straight with me. I'm grateful you were my manager."

After my conversation with Michael, I sit still for a moment to ponder. I pack the few personal items that'll fit in one small box. I developed some key strategies I'll take with me, especially the pitch I would've given today. I peruse my office one more time, and I only recognize STU awards and mementos around the office. Yep, right in the trash those things will go. They're worthless to me now. It's like I'm sleepwalking. Could this really be happening? All my sacrifices and hard work plummet down the drain with the force of a tsunami.

How did I not see this coming? I have to get out of here. I'm like the crazy girl who's hanging around long after her boyfriend dumps her. I need to have words with some people before I leave this establishment for the last time. Now, I have to find Tony and Kim. I hope neither one of them got canned. Tony's a brother, and we've commiserated many nights about STU. I consider Tony my work husband. I'll miss him a lot. The only other person I'm tight with is Kim. She's mad funny and crazy. I love working on projects with her. Tony's working in his cube. He doesn't travel and works on local projects. His eyes avoid mine, and he's very solemn.

"Tony, it's okay. You don't have to pretend like you don't know they laid me off."

"Lauryn, I don't get this. You kill it here."

"Have you seen Kim? Is she safe?"

"She's in Massachusetts on a project."

"Whew, I was worried they may have let both of you guys go. It's only a few of us here. What would that say about the firm if they're letting all of us go?"

"I'm nervous. It's a matter of time for me. If they got rid of you, someone who brings in banks and banks of money, what will happen to me? I better get my resume together. This is all a bunch of BS."

"I said the same thing. Apparently, the firm's having financial difficulties. They won't solve anything by letting key people go. It's no longer my problem, though. You may have some time, but I wouldn't trust they won't gun the project managers and management consultants next. You need to be prepared. I have a feeling this is just the beginning."

"I trust nothing. If their mouths are moving, lies spew out. It took me a really long time to confide in you. I wouldn't be surprised if the plan would be to get rid of all of us. My plan is to be out in three months or less. I hope I have the time to find something worthwhile."

"Yea, it took about a year for you to REALLY talk to me. You were a hard nut to crack for sure. You're the best work hubby ever. Tony, I'll miss you. I hope you connect with me soon."

"Hey, work wifey, I'm gonna miss you, too. We have to have lunch if your man doesn't mind."

"We're good. He's cool, and he knows you're my boy."

"Take care and keep in touch. Tell me when you land somewhere."

"The same goes for you. I need to hear from you."

When I finally leave, I'm slightly somber. I'm going to miss my true homies here at STU. I have a suspicion this goodbye will be it for us. Who really keeps in touch with old work friends? I hope my theory isn't true since Tony and Kim are good friends, and they both need this job. I'm sad I didn't get to tell Kim goodbye face to face, but I'll call her soon. I acknowledge a few other friends on my way out, and I wish them well.

Driving to a destination unknown, my first day at the firm comes to mind. No longer the intern, I would be an analyst ready to learn and make an impact. Being 22 years old and fresh out of school, the challenge I accepted allowed me to tackle this whole different world as a working woman. I became a management consultant within six months of hard work. I had an extreme amount of confidence this career with a lot of travel would be worth it in the end.

I wanted to achieve the pinnacle of success within my profession, and I trusted this was the right path to get what I wanted. Trusting in myself worked as planned. Well, until it didn't. I navigated my career into avenues I couldn't imagine when I began at the firm. Not a lot of young black women achieved what I did at STU. Working hard came at ease at first. At the time, I lived to work. I didn't have a man since Isaac dumped me during my last year in college. Work turned out to be my solace until I met Jackson.

I credit STU for providing me with vital work experience and offering me the chance to shine. When one door closes, another one opens. This door closing is probably for the best. Seven long years at this firm is like 15 years in other organizations. Tireless work weeks to prove I have what it takes seem pointless now. My loyalty to this firm isn't appreciated or valued. With my credentials in engineering and management, I will bounce back in due time. I'll give myself a few days to collect my emotions before I figure out what my next move is.

My personal life has suffered from working all these hours. Jackson has been exceedingly supportive especially if I had to cancel plans with him because of work. We've been together for a little over three years, and we've lived together for two. My relationship is the one bright spot in my life. He's my everything, but I'm too embarrassed to face him. With the promotions in the past, he's gone all out to adorn me with affection and attention. He'll do his best to console me. I don't want to burden him with this just yet. It's his off day, and one of us deserves to be happy.

Part of me wants to call him now for reassurance, but it wouldn't be fair to put all of this on him. Plus, it's humiliating to admit I lost my job. The job I put above everything and sacrificed so much. I left him high and dry more times that I'm able to count for this job. Luckily, I don't live paycheck to paycheck.

Maybe I'll go to the gym. I always keep some gym clothes in my car. Kickboxing will change my mood. With the morning I've had, I really want to take it out on the punching bag. Torturing myself for 30 minutes sounds like a great idea to me. With every punch on the bag, I'll visualize punching someone's face at STU. This brings me unimaginable joy. I notice Alex, my favorite trainer, is here, and he'll bring it.

"Hey, Lauryn, you okay? You don't seem like your cute and adorable self today. Well, you're still cute," Alex greets me with a wink.

"I'm actually not great, Alex. I don't really want to get into that right now, okay? I need to pound something."

"Pound away, sweetheart. I know what it's like to have a bad day. I'll work you out extra hard."

"That's what I need."

Alex isn't giving me any mercy or breaks. He's making me perform every complex variation of each exercise in every round. It's a HIIT workout with a burpee at the end of each round. It doesn't hurt the gym is nearly empty. In fact, it's a plus. I'm able to receive one-on-one training in every round. As sadistic as this sounds, I appreciate the attention I'm getting. It really helps to beat on something. My mood is better now that the workout is done. My stomach growls, and it reminds me I haven't eaten anything all day. I'm starving! I need fuel. I stop by a local juicer for a protein drink.

I need my sanctuary and my man. I want his arms around me to help me deal with the shock of the day. I'm happy Jackson is off work today. I hope he's home. I just want to crawl into bed and his arms following a shower of course. I'll probably eat a gallon of ice cream and sleep for the rest of the day. This won't solve all my problems, but this is what I need right now. On the bright side, I certainly won't miss living in hotels.

I love my home too much, and now I'll enjoy it. My parents gifted me the condo in college. I've owned the place for eight years. I'm incredibly appreciative for the head start my parents were able to give me with the condo and my trust fund. I wanted to prove my worth at least to myself. My parents inspired me to achieve greatness. I hope they won't be disappointed in me for losing my job. I won't tell them about this right away. How am I gonna tell my parents I got laid off?

I'll focus on my relationship wholly now. We've been a part too much because of my job. I'm looking forward to seeing him on the regular. We'll discuss our future which includes getting married, selling the condo to buy a home of our own, and most definitely kids. Jackson wants all these things, but I may have given him the impression that the timing isn't right for me. At least, STU is no longer a burden for us. This layoff helps me to put things into perspective. I want a future with Jackson. I want to become his wife.

Right now, a long soak and drinking a bottle of wine is calling my name. It's still kind of early to drink wine, but I'm sure it's five o'clock somewhere. I'll hit a gallon of ice cream. Call it a meal for champions. I rarely do anything obsessive with food. Well, today is a new day, and I'll throw caution to the wind. I'll work out to make sure I don't get too chunky. Today, I'll wallow in the pain of losing the only job I've had in my adult life.

All the sacrifices I've made in the name of STU roll through my mind. I want to put those images on pause. Better yet, on delete, but I'm finding this difficult to do. I did too much work for nothing. How could STU treat me this way! I gave the company everything, and what do I have to show for it? I should stop. Belaboring this issue won't change anything. This isn't doing me any good. I'm obsessing about what I could've done differently. The answer is nothing.

In the elevator, I try to will my thoughts in a different direction other than my shitty day. This day once riddled with promise turned out to be a complete failure. The excitement generated through my body a few hours ago no longer had a spark to survive. When I open the door at home, there's the old school song, "Make it Last Forever" by Keith Sweat booming through Jackson's sound system. As much as I'm not in the mood, I guess I could be. It could get my mind off my horrible day, but how did he know I would be home right now? I haven't called him.

Jackson's name is on the tip of my tongue when suddenly a woman moans and yells out, "Yes, baby, don't stop!" Who's that? Am I hearing things? Something in my mind wants it to be the TV. Maybe Jackson is watching porn. I'm not a prude, and I know he partakes in a little sometimes. Hell, I do, too. I've observed some good porn on occasion. It tends to get lonely on the road. Idris Vy, my vibrator, has been getting it in on the road when I miss the real thing.

My senses are on high alert as I slowly ascend the stairs to my bedroom. The door is wide open. Jackson and a woman, who I don't see very well, are completely naked in our bed. My heart breaks, and my ability to breathe is gone. I don't recognize the scream from my mouth, but I know it's me. What the hell is going on in here?

The noise reverberates like some sort of wounded animal. They don't budge. What kind of sex did they have to make them unconscious? As much as I want to cry my eyes out, it would have to wait until another time. I have to deal with this now. They still don't stir. I march into the bathroom and grab a jug of cold water to dump on them. It's not like I need these sheets anymore anyway.

I scream, "What in the hell? In my house, how dare you?!!! The blatant disrespect! Get out!!"

They both jump in horror, and I recognize the woman. It couldn't be her, but it is. My best friend, Asia, is fucking my boyfriend in my bed. I didn't comprehend a word coming out of their lying mouths. I only observe their lips moving at a frenzied beat. It's like I'm in a trance, and everything is foggy. This won't stop me from taking necessary action.

"This is some bullshit. Both of you get out of my house!" I yell.

They appear to be in a daze. They didn't seem to comprehend their surroundings. Is this real? Am I crazy? Is this all an illusion? I close my eyes and open them. No illusion. They're still here. I want to hit them. After a moment, they realize I mean business. They put their clothes on fast. I run to Jackson's closet and drag out some clothes to throw at him.

"Get out and don't come back tomorrow. I can't with you. I'm not doing this. Get out!!!"

"Angel —"

I scream, "I don't want to hear it! Don't you dare call me 'Angel' again! You lost that privilege the second you slipped in between her legs. How could you do this to me? Both of you? I fucking hate you both!"

"Lola —" Asia utters between tears.

"You, either. No more 'Lola.' Get out now!!! Don't make me hurt you!!"

"Baby, please —"

"Both of you disrespected me, and you're despicable. How do you explain this and with my best friend? Asia, how could you betray me like this? Nope, don't need to know. You did what you did. Now go!"

I'm thankful they're leaving. If I have to call the police, I will. As soon as I'm certain they've left, I start ripping the sheets off the bed. I throw them into the large garbage can in the kitchen. What a day! Losing my job stirred emotions of inadequacy that have been long buried, but it's clearly not the worst thing to happen today. Who did I hurt in a past life to deserve this? This is my sanctuary. How could he disrespect me like this? Did we share anything real in our relationship? I'm suddenly nauseous and throwing up in the bathroom.

Did I enter the Twilight Zone? I contemplated marrying him. How long has he been with her? They must hate me to stoop to the level of doing this to me in my house. I grab a bottle of wine and a gallon of ice cream. I don't imagine I'll feel any better, but I want to be numb. I want to be devoid of any sensory or emotion. Nothing at all. I try to force myself not to cry. Once I start crying, I won't be able to stop.

They don't deserve my tears, and I'm not successful in holding them at bay. I'm drinking straight out of the bottle. Yea, it's not lady-like, but this hasn't been a lady-like type of day. I don't even remember finishing the bottle. I'm disappointed there isn't a drop more of wine for me to guzzle. I scramble back to the kitchen in search of another bottle. I smile because there's another two, and for once today, something is going right.

As much as I don't want to dissect every second of my life right now, drunk me misses Jackson more than sober me would like to admit. He's not only the man I love; he's genuinely my friend. He's supported all my hopes and dreams. He brightens my days all the time. Well, he used to change my perspective in a brighter way. Who is going to fill his shoes now? I have no one. Why is my life a cesspool of despair?

How did this even develop between them? What am I missing? How could the two people I trusted the most betray me? He didn't like my job much. He told me he could wait for things to be better for us. Did he mean he could wait? He never complained about my job. I guess it's ironic now since I don't work there anymore. If I were here more, would he have been in bed with her? I'm not sure. I guess life is really a bitch sometimes. That's what I don't get.

I'm definitely drunk right now. Tears flow down my face, and I don't have the power to stop them. I'm howling with an awful gut-wrenching noise one makes when crying. I'm pretty sure I have very ugly tears flowing all on my face. The pain is like a dagger in my heart. I have no idea how long this pain will last, but I'm drinking to completely forget today. Music is blaring in the hallway that makes my mood sour even more. The voices I hear are Lisa Lisa and Cult Jam singing "All Cried Out."

Why would this damn song be playing right now? Did the universe have an inkling my world would shatter before my own eyes? Is someone in on this cruel joke known as my day? I would love to rewind this day and start over. This time I swear I won't make the same mistakes. My head plummets to cry some more.

I drink several glasses of wine to discover my eyes resemble a raccoon ('cause I laid my mascara thicker than usual this morning). I face myself in the mirror. I look like a dragged through some shit version of myself.

What did I expect drinking an exorbitant amount red and white wines? The tears don't help my overall appearance one bit. Why am I concentrating on my outward facade? My ex-boyfriend and ex-best friend were sharing more than saliva just a few hours ago. I don't care about the frivolity of it all.

I'm not thinking clearly, and I only want to drink. I crave to be devoid of any emotions. Numb to a world full of hurt. The wine is gone, and this disappoints me. I have no other choice but to change my choice of alcohol. Drinking the pain away is not the cure. It'll only a delay the pain. I know this. I'll worry about pain later. I'm an empty shell of myself. I've lost everything that meant anything to me. Why would he go to bed with her? It's hard for me to even comprehend how they got close. Nothing about them being together makes sense to me.

I probably resemble a serial killer with all the fantasies I have about them right now. An episode of *Snapped* is what I need. It will either get my mind off my problems or make me want to murder those two. Don't worry, peanut gallery, I'm not murdering anyone. I love myself too much to end everything good in my life by murdering them.

I hate them, but I don't hate them more than I love myself. Shout out to those who love themselves!!! These sadistic women commit murder most of the time because of greed. If it isn't greed, it's infidelity which points to greed as well. You have to be some kind of evil to kill someone in cold blood.

I'm certain there isn't anything out there to get me out of this funk. Watching TV would be a waste of time, and it's not going to help me. I argue with myself to forget this notion of vegging out in front of the TV. I get into a few mindless shows, and now I find myself binging *Schitt's Creek*, and it's hella funny. This has been just the trick I needed to not worry about my predicament. I love how David gives everyone the "you're dumb as shit look," when something idiotic is said. I'm sarcastic, and I love sarcastic comedies.

Before long, I'm hysterically laughing at the episode where Johnny Rose notices the sign for the town and loses his shit. The fact that the locals couldn't see what that sign displayed. I'm laughing too hard. I have to go the bathroom. Amid all the sadness there is joy. After several more episodes, I dredge to my temporary bed to attempt to get some sleep. After some time, I dose off.

"Hey, baby," Jackson glances at me with his adorable smile, "I missed you."

"I missed you, too."

"Why don't you show me how much?"

"What? You don't think I'll be able to demonstrate my emotions. You underestimate me."

"Never! Come here and give me the good stuff."

"You need to work for it," I joke.

"Oh, I'll work for it, alright."

I run away, but I don't get far. Jackson is a sprinter by nature and superfast. He slips his arms around me and throws me on his shoulder in one swoop.

"Now, I got you were I want you. You're all mine, baby. I don't expect any interruptions for the next 24 hours."

"Only 24?"

"Well, that's all you'll give me before you leave me, again."

"Well, you better make the most of your 24."

"You think I won't. You'll be calling out my name in seven different languages before all's said and done."

"I only know three languages, smartie pants."

"The other four aren't recognizable, but you'll call it out none the less."

"You're very cocky today."

"Come again?"

"You're very cocky today."

"I'm about to show you cocky."

He doesn't lose any time disrobing me and demonstrating how he'll make me call out his name in the seven possibly fake languages. I won't lie. At one point, I spoke in an inaudible tone because English, French, and Italian evaded me.

"How is that for me keeping my word?" he asks assuredly.

"Mon amour tu étais explosif," I remark in French, "mon cœur désire." (My love, you were explosive, and my heart's desire.)

"As much as I love for you to speak French to me, I'm too spent to try and decipher what you're saying, Angel."

"Vuoi amarmi di nuovo?" I switch to speaking in Italian just to throw him. "Ti amerò a lungo." (You want to love me again. I love you long time.)

"Two can play that game, sister," he jokes, "Te haré el amor hasta que no puedas pensar en nada más que en mí. Estarás desprovisto de pensamientos," he speaks in Spanish to get back at me. (I'll make love to you until you can't think of anything else but me. You'll be devoid of thoughts.)

"Comment oses-tu parler espagnol quand je te romance en français et en Italien?" I respond in French. (How dare you speak Spanish when I'm romancing you in French and Italian?)

"No cariño. Estoy hablando el lenguaje del amor," he responds still speaking Spanish. (No sweetheart. I'm speaking the language of love.)

We go back and forth like this until we both surrender and fall into each other's arms again. He kisses me passionately remembering there's no need for us to fuss and fight in foreign languages when the universal non-speaking language is working for us. My body feels weightless as I melt into his arms. I snuggle against his well-defined chest. He's not bulky nor is he thin. He has the perfect body. Lean and defined. If there is such a thing as a 10-pack, he has one. There isn't an ounce of fat on his fine ass body. His long legs exude strength and power as he walks and does other things that having strong legs compliments. The feature I love the most about him would be his eyes. I swear he does things to me when he stares into my soul. Not only do I get weak in the knees, I'm also susceptible to his every whim and desire. Most of the time his desires coincide with mine. We're a perfect match.

He's doing his other favorite pastime when I join him on the floor in front of the big screen. It's our modest media room. We like it. He's playing Call of Duty, and I'm not a huge fan. I'll play it, but it's not my jam. I love Mortal Kombat, and he's fully aware of that. I give him the "it's on" expression, and he knows it's about to go down.

"You want some of this?" he mocks me.

"What's there to want? You already loss, son."

"Let's see if you can back that up with action."

We both get in our battle stances. We're serious about our gaming. I'm positive he'll pick either Scorpion or Raiden. How can he be serious about the game if he doesn't stick with a character? I'm always Kitana, and I play to win.

"Let's do this, baby," I yell.

"Loser has to grant the winner whatever he wants."

"You're fairly certain it'll be you."

"Hmm, more than 75% certain."

"Well, game on."

We jump right into round one. He chooses Scorpion. He comes out aggressively with kicks and punches. I counter back with several kicks, jumps and punches. He then goes for his signature special move, the spear (Spear: Back, Back, Low Punch. Teleport Punch: Down, Back, High Punch. Leg Takedown: Forward, Down, Back Low Kick. Air Throw: Block in the air and yells "Get over here."). He takes some of my energy when he does this move. I gain it back quickly and counter with my signature move, the kiss of death (Hold low kick, forward, forward, down, forward, and release low kick.) His energy goes down. We're back and forth like this until he gets me one last time with the spear special, and he takes round one. I win round two, but sadly I lose round three making him the winner. I don't need his ego boosted any more than it already is. The only way to work this now is to be humble. Humility makes others mirror the same behavior.

"Ok, so you won. What do you want?"

"Only you, babe. Come to me."

I'm in my happy place in this world where Jackson never betrayed me. I don't want to leave it. I'm interrupted by some annoying noise. It's banging like a foghorn in my ears. I rise up suddenly unaware of my surroundings not wanting to leave the façade I created for myself. I sweep the room where I acknowledge the truth about what I've confronted. The life I had with Jackson doesn't exist anymore. Unfortunately, my happy place isn't reality. It's time for me to face a new reality where love no longer lives here. I'll miss him, but I know we aren't meant to be together. My heart is slowly breaking. Each second, minute, and hour it breaks more.

I grab the bottle of Tequila and gulp a healthy swig. I rummage through the kitchen looking for lime. I don't find any. I can't drink Tequila without lime and salt. That's unheard of, isn't it? I need to go to the store and get the lime. It's a little shop that sells fruit and other stuff in walking distance, I think. It can't be farther than a few blocks. What direction is it? I'm horrible at navigating directions and maps. I pick up my phone to Google this place, but I don't remember the name. I type nearest fruit shop and hope to get the right result. There's a place called Fruit and More not too far from here, about 1.2 miles. I can do that in a few minutes and be back here in time for my own little happy hour. I can't sit in here any longer. These memories make me want to scream. I throw on some sweats and go for a walk. Yea, it's late, but I don't care. I'm drunker than

I realized. The sidewalk is swaying under my feet. I bumped into something. Is it a person?

"Watch it!" he yelled at me.

"Sorreeey!!" I slur back.

"You need to take your drunk ass home."

"You need to stop talking to me. I bump...bumped into you. Not a crime, asshole. Plus, I apolo... apol... I said I was sorry."

I continue in the opposite direction of my place. I can't stay there another minute. Why do people react like fucking assholes just because someone made a mistake and bumped into them? Is he fragile like a piece of China? Jeez, get a life!! It's not like I did it on purpose. Wait, who cares? Where am I going? What am I doing out here? I must look confused because an old lady chooses to approach me next.

"Young lady, are you okay?"

"No, I'm not. I'm not," I cry out and suddenly I feel the urge to break into song. I don't sing, but in a time of desperation and being more than slightly inebriated, I go for it. I don't care that I sound more like a hyena in heat. I'm so off tune, but I don't have a bother in the world. All I want right now is to sing my blues away. In pure diva fashion, I put on my performance face and keep singing like I sound like a Tony winner rather than a shrieking donkey.

"You're no Beyoncé, so leave singing 'Irreplaceable' to her," someone yells.

"Well, neither are you. I can dance like her, though."

I attempt to do a dance move and nearly fall on my ass. I keep going like I'm not drunk. I don't care. I'm feeling myself right now. I imagine I'm dancing like an Alvin Ailey's dancer with poise and finesse rather than an unbalanced drunk girl moving around to her own beat. Sometimes, I really should ignore the image in my head claiming I'm killin' it. Truth be told. I'm not.

"You're still no Beyoncé! Leave the singing and dancing to her," someone else yells.

"Boo, boo!" I yell back.

"You may be cute but leave singing to the professionals. Don't even try karaoke. You suck!!"

"I hate you!" I cry out, "I hate you, Jackson."

"Oh, dear," the old lady says with concern, "You may want to sit down for a minute. Maybe, I can have my grandson call you one of those what-chathings. Ustart. I'm not sure what the name is. Something to get you back home."

"Thank you, for your concern. I'm not far from home. I can make it on my own." I'm still crying.

"I don't think you should be alone," she says, "Jimmy, walk this girl home."

"Ma'am, I don't think that's nec —"

I couldn't finish my statement. I frantically move to the side of the road to vomit. I feel like I'm upchucking for an eternity. Someone is holding my hair back from my face as I let it fly. I know when I wake up tomorrow I'll be so embarrassed of how I acted today, but for now I'm in complete ignorant denial. In the end, I let Jimmy walk me back to my condo's entrance, and I didn't have any limes. That's probably for the best since I didn't need any more Tequila.

CHAPTER 3
Interloper

"Wicked" by Future played in the background as he grooved to the beat. This song resonated so well with him. It summed up how he felt about everything. He'd been told his whole life he was wicked, so he figured he'd live up to their expectations and prove those haters right. They had one thing wrong about him, though. He did amount to something unlike their hurtful words and wishes on his life. He'd become quite successful by pulling himself up with his bootstraps.

His plan worked like a charm. Hard work and planning were the bedrock to achievements. He would never get enough of patting himself on the back. If he didn't communicate "good job," who would? He didn't want to get too far ahead by high fiving himself because his work had only just begun. The plan still had a long way to go before his true objective had been met. He stared at the front of the building from an obscure vantage point. He had a great line of vision of the front door to the stairs leading to the parking area. He stood close enough to hear and see everything and everyone coming out of the building this way. He hoped he didn't have to wait too long to see the shining star of STU fall to the bottom. It appeared today wasn't Lauryn Davidson's lucky day at all. He shouldn't have to wait long.

She should've been informed she no longer worked at STU. What he would've given to be a fly on the wall when she learned this shocking news! As he pondered about how everything went down, his heart began to beat wildly, and his pants bulged out in the crotch area. He couldn't be getting hard from her unfortunate turn of events. Why did the thought make him hornier? He turned away for a second to make sure his little friend didn't cause any shock and awe from anyone who may happen to catch him in this state. He'd never hated anyone as much as he hated her, Lauryn Davidson. He nearly missed her, and he would have if she didn't stop to talk to someone who called her name.

"Lauryn," the person yelled out, "Where are you going, chica?"

"Leslie, hey," Lauryn responded with a distraught appearance, "I guess you haven't heard. I no longer work here."

"What! You quit?"

"I wish it had been as simple as that. No, I got laid off a few hours ago."

"Wait a minute! What you say, girl? Come correct. Stop joking," Leslie pantomime's repeat.

"No, it happened. STU laid me off today."

"What in the holy hell is wrong with them? You have to be the best f'ing senior project manager here. Who gone replace you? Name somebody. The rest of those MF's don't know a got durn thing. You know, I'm hot. They got me cussing up in here."

"Well, I guess your form of cussing anyway," Lauryn chuckles.

"How can you laugh at a time like this, lady? What are you going to do?"

"If I don't laugh, I would probably cry. This company doesn't deserve my tears. Not after all my hard work and dedication to wind up laid-off. Nah, I laugh in times of trouble. I have no idea what I'm going to do. If I had any inclination this mess would happen, I would've bounced a long time ago. It's not like I didn't have options in the past. I hate I never took a chance on myself."

"What do you mean you never took a chance on yourself?"

"I could've been poached from here a while ago, but I wanted to stay and grow my career. What kind of dumb shit is that? Sorry, Leslie I shouldn't have cussed. I didn't mean any disrespect. I simply can't believe my circumstances."

"Don't worry about cussing! You're human. You have a right to be upset and express yourself. I'm nervous about going in there. They could be laying me off as we speak."

"I would say don't worry about it, but I don't know for sure. I heard senior PMs and junior partners are the only ones impacted today. It may not be a concern now, but I would have my ducks in a row moving forward."

"Thanks for the heads-up, Lauryn. I wish you the best, and I know a company will swoop you up right away. Someone with your talent will not be unemployed long."

He couldn't help himself. He had to disagree with the alluring woman speaking with Lauryn. She resembled an angel on earth to him with her chestnut-colored skin and dark brown thick hair flowing down her back. She dressed rather demurely and conservative just like he preferred. Lauryn reminded him of a harlot with her breast poking out of her chemise. Why did he backtrack to Lauryn when the lovely Leslie stood a mere ten feet away? He could deal with Lauryn later. Leslie and Lauryn went their separate ways, and he took the opportunity to catch up with Leslie before she entered the building. He made sure Lauryn turned the corner and headed towards her car before he presented himself to Leslie. She appeared to be enjoying time outside before going back into the office. His day continued to get better and better.

"Why hello, lovely lady." he smiled pleasantly.

"Who me?"

"Do you see another lovely lady here?" He made sure to check to see if she wore any rings on her left-hand ring finger. He nearly cheered when he saw it was unadorned, and there weren't any ring lines either. "Score," he thought as he brought on the charm.

"Ok, how can I help you, sir?"

"I couldn't help but notice you and your beauty. You're distracting me from a meeting I have with Arthur Thomason." He made sure to drop a line with one of the key owner's names, so Leslie wouldn't have a reason to question why he'd be here.

"I can't be the one distracting you from meeting anyone. I could get in deep trouble."

"There'll be no trouble on your end. You haven't done anything unless you could be blamed for being the most beautiful woman around."

"Thank you."

"Are you available for lunch? I'll just move my appointment with Arthur. Hold on." He didn't wait for her reply and dialed a phone number. "Arthur, something came up. I'll swing by this afternoon." There was a pause before he spoke again, "See you then." He turned to Leslie, "You ready to go."

"Nope."

"Why not?" he figured she didn't feel him like that, and he grew disappointed.

"I don't dine with men I don't know. Especially, when I don't know their names."

"Easily remedied," he replied, and his mood instantly changed for the better.

CHAPTER 4
Lauryn

Waking this morning with a massive hangover is making me question my choices. It appeared like a good idea at the time to drink all those bottles of wine. I'm sure I mixed some tequila shots in there, too, at some point. I had a real party of one last night. More like an extreme pity party. I want to drink some more to get Jackson out of my mind, but it's only a temporary reprieve. He'll come back in full force once I get sober. That's what I'm dealing with now. Reminiscing about how we started and how things have changed for the worst. How did we get to a place where he would cheat on me with my best friend? He couldn't love me at all. In fact, does he loathe me? The depth of his betrayal fills me with resentment and hatred.

The memories flood my brain. I met him at a party, and his confidence turned me on. He had the right amount of swag. It drew me in immediately. Not to mention his body made me shake. He defined fineness, and he didn't have a blemish on his handsome face. I hate to remember our good times. I refuse to remember all the times love just made sense. I won't play this scene over in my mind. I don't want to daydream about a time where love rotated on its axis for him and me. Replaying our story is devastating. I want to forget it.

Our physical, mental, and emotional connection were more than I'd ever experienced in a short amount of time. Everything happened at lightning speed with us. We went from dating casually to becoming a couple in a matter of weeks. I felt something deeper and stronger than I had with Isaac, my first love. We were fascinated by the same things and had very similar interests. We simply enjoyed being together. What could have gone wrong?

We've had deep discussions about the plight of Black America. We were both spurred to action from events which ended in wrong doings against young black men and women. Jackson and I had deep discussions about the plight of the black man and the Black Lives Matter movement. With the recent death of a young black man in Florida, true sides of America were revealed. I still can't believe America's elite and not so elite, couldn't view this event as murder. The constant questions about what the young man did, and his history bugged me. Why was he strolling in this neighborhood after hours? Why did he fight the coward with a gun? This infuriated us both. Why did this coward have a right to defend himself and the kid didn't? The prosecutors never portrayed the minor's story well.

What about his fear? What about the fact a potential predator could have been following him?

There've been too many escalated incidences of police violence that ended in the death of black lives. People always have something to voice about the victims as if they were asking to be killed in these seemingly non-threatening events. Why is it the people of color always have to be concerned if we will return home if encountered by the police? Why did it matter what victims did to cause their deaths? Didn't they deserve due process and to face the consequences in the court of law versus the judge and jury of the police?

Our relationship exemplified ease. This is how we were for quite a while at least prior to my work schedule changing. He supported the changes I faced at work. I would always anticipate spending time with him most evenings and on the weekends. I loved him and wanted us to spend more time together. Who am I kidding? I still love him. That's why this hurts too damn much.

We were on top of the world when we began living together. It would pick me up to spot him when I came home from traveling. Did something change without my knowledge? He never complained even if work became very demanding. We were happy last week. At least, that's my impression. Am I imagining our life together? Do I need to evaluate everything between us? Were we like smoke and mirrors? "Fuck him!"

My heart is broken beyond repair. We were supposed to get married and have kids. I believed my life would change following the promotion I didn't get. Realistically, though, would things really have changed at work? Were we doomed to end no matter what? As my career started to gain traction with more travel and bigger accounts, the more time we didn't have together. Would things have been different if I worked in town? We were absolutely happier when I traveled seldomly.

He was always my number one fan. Is there something I just didn't detect? How did he and Asia start hooking up? She isn't even his type nor is he hers. She'd always comments how Jackson and I were like two sides of a coin. She'd imply we liked the same geeky stuff (outdoor life and poetry). We also shared a love for dancing, video games, and movies. It could've been all bullshit to throw me off. Have they been fucking around this entire time? Could this have been a slow and painful death of our relationship until they were caught? I'm not sure what drove him into her arms. I won't be blamed for his poor decision making. I'm still confused about them. "What did I do? Nothing! Fuck him! I didn't cheat!"

Jackson has a type with characteristics a lot like mine. I remember vaguely noticing him on the yard with quite a few fair-skinned chicks. I never called him on it. He loves a honey toned woman with long hair. I find it hard to believe Jackson even wants Asia. I'm not saying Asia isn't beautiful, but she's totally opposite of his standard type. He would swear he's attracted to all flavors of the brown color spectrum, but I'm fully aware that he prefers the lighter honey dew. I guess types can change. His certainly seemed to change. Maybe Asia is an outlier, his purple unicorn, and he couldn't help falling for her. That shit burns me up.

There are other things that's throwing me off with them. He had a proclivity to stroke my hair in and out of bed. Sometimes, just sitting on the couch he would wound his fingers in my hair gently caressing it. Asia preferred her hair in a short, layered bob. He is an ass man, too. Not to throw shade, but she's lacking in the rear. This is surface stuff, I know. None of this makes for longevity in a relationship. This has me stumped. I never would have pegged my man and my best friend together ever. This breaks all kinds of codes. Did girl code mean anything to her or him? With all the fucked up in the head dudes out there, what made her go after mine? What made him fuck my best friend?

Subsequently, Jackson desperately wanted to create this new video game. He used to work in gaming, and he really didn't want to work in the hospital. He complained to me about it all the time. I couldn't help with any aspect of the development because work always took me away. I suggested Asia assist him since she taught English, and he needed someone to help him write the copy. Could I have been the catalyst that hooked them up?

They spent quite a bit of time together. It didn't bother me. I never suspected a thing. Nothing seemed strange or different. I remember Asia started to kick it with this dude, AJ. She said Jackson acted as her wing man. Did AJ even exist? Was he thrown in the mix to throw me off their scent? How long have they been making a fool of me?

Maybe I didn't want to see it. Maybe they were right in my face, and I would've been too distracted with work to notice. Since I traveled a lot, I made it easy for them. I do remember calling Jackson on FaceTime and Asia being there. I didn't give this a second thought. They were working together with some long hours. Now, I wonder if they were intimate prior to or after my call. I don't recall much about it honestly. Were they acting cagey then? Did they ever give me any clues? Now, I'm questioning everything between them.

Jackson said Asia's vibe was very cool, and he could have conversations with her. Even later, nothing appeared amiss between them. He started relying on her more. She listened to him. I'm a firm believer that men and women can be friends and coexist. Am I wrong? "Hell yea, I am. They were fucking!" He'd been on edge lately. I assumed work had him in a mood. He never liked working at the hospital since Klockinout, his previous employer, folded. They didn't appreciate him at Van Hogen. I encouraged him to go after what he wanted. "I don't give a fuck about his work situation now!"

This whole thing has really got me flabbergasted. I don't know why, and it's bugging me. I never could've imagined they hated me, but I guess I was wrong. I fucking hate them, too. Didn't I deserve the dignity of a conversation to end our relationship instead of finding him in bed with the girl I called my best friend? How will I get past this? I'm not sure I ever will. My heart is completely broken, and I have to figure out what's next for me. I'll be guarded moving forward.

The next few days things don't get better. Tears continued to flow abundantly. I could probably build my on lake. My mood is dismal and funky right now. Could you blame me? This is the first time in my whole life is such a mess. No job or boyfriend. My phone has been blowing up with calls from Jackson and Asia. I refuse to deal with them. Not now. I sent them straight to voicemail. What is there to discuss? I don't want to spend another day in pajamas with an appearance from hell. They're probably having a good laugh at my expense, and I'm sitting around looking like a hobo. Nope. No more. Not today. It's time to reclaim at least a small portion of my life.

Well, at least I stopped drinking. Gazing in the mirror, the face staring back couldn't be recognized. Hollowed eyes without any glimmer of happiness reflect back. This isn't a surprise, but my overall style isn't public worthy. I need to put on some makeup to appear human. Oddly enough, I think a single person dance party could cause my mood to change. I turn on some jams and Drake's "One Dance" blares from the speakers. The beat is so catchy that I start stomping my feet in tune with the bass in the song. Unlike last night, my dance groove is back to avenge my embarrassment. I jump up probably a little too fast because the room begins to spin just enough for me to be off balance and fall to the couch. I grab my head instantly because I feel a migraine coming.

I don't want to spend the day in bed with a migraine, and I've done enough wallowing with my very own pity party. The time for me to get a grip on things is now, but how do I do it when everything I've known is a lie. My mood has to change for the better, and it does when Rihanna's "Pour It Up" comes on next. While grooving from Drake to Rihanna, I start to feel like myself again. Music uplifts me and changes my mood.

Unfortunately, reality sets in, and I get a cramp in my neck. Not allowing myself to sleep in the bed I shared with Jackson is taking its toll on me. I haven't slept well these last few days. I've avoided my bedroom and spent most nights on either the couch or in one of the guest bedrooms.

The bed isn't bad, but it's not my bed. It's more like a hotel bed. I always find it hard to sleep in those. Today, all this ends. It's time to reclaim my life. It's time to get his stuff out and reclaim my home. Jackson is calling me again. What did he think would happen? Doesn't he understand there isn't any coming back from what he did to me? What could he mention? Does he imagine I shouldn't believe my lying eyes? I don't want to concern myself with his issues. Part of me is interested in what he could possibly have to convey, so I pick up, and I regret it immediately.

"Hello," I note angrily.

"Angel," he begins.

"No, don't you dare call me, Angel. What in the hell do you want? Why are you constantly calling me?"

"What I did was unforgiveable, but baby I want to try and make amends with you. I don't even know how it happened if I'm being honest."

"What do you mean? It's called you stuck your did somewhere it didn't belong, specifically, in her vagina. How in the fuck do you propose you make amends?"

"Baby, I didn't do it. I promise I wouldn't do that to you. I just need you back."

"Ok, I'm supposed to forget I found you naked in bed with her because you didn't do it." I'm being completely crude, but what will be accomplished with this bullshit apology?

"I love you," he whispers very softly. I barely recognize what he's said.

"Please, that's bullshit. You don't do what you did if you ever loved me. The only question I have for you is why? Sorry, I have two. Why cheat and why her?"

"Angel, I didn't do it. I can't explain how it looks."

"How would there ever be a reasonable explanation for you doing the unimaginable with Asia? You had a choice, and you made the easy one, Jackson."

"No, not an easy choice. I don't remember making a choice."

"What do you mean you don't remember? Don't try to play like you have amnesia," I warn him.

"I'm not. I don't remember her coming by the house."

"Stop with the lies, Jackson."

"Ok, it's my problem that I don't have any recollection of anything before I saw you shooting daggers at me with your eyes?"

"Well, I don't care. What did you expect me to do? You had sex with my best friend in our bed."

"I don't want her. I never have. It hurts my heart knowing that you're hurt."

"Your heart? Tell me this. If I hadn't caught you, would you have confessed this to me?" Jackson paused without uttering a word.

"Your silence is my answer. You're only sorry now because you got caught."

"But babe..."

"Jackson, I question our entire relationship now. I don't think you ever loved me. If you did, this wouldn't have happened. We would have discussed our issues prior to any of this happening."

"Don't question my love or our relationship. I love you."

"You've some nerve letting love come out your mouth. What happened to you being the man I love? The man I love would never hurt me the way you did. You're not the man I thought you were."

"I'm still that man."

"Please, just stop. Do you care that you're hurting me?"

"I don't want to hurt you. I'm sorry. I won't force things."

"I got to go. I need you gone."

"No, wait. How do you want to handle me getting my stuff?"

"Well, it's funny you're calling about your stuff. I'm packing your things shortly."

"You don't have to do it. I'll pack my stuff."

"No, you won't. I don't want to see you. I'll text a time and date for you to retrieve your things." I hang up.

Getting off the phone with Jackson has motivated me to get his stuff out of here. The nerve of him calling me. I only just stopped crying over this bullshit. I can't with him. I search around the house, and it's devoid of any shipping boxes. I jump in the shower and dress in gym shorts, a tank top, and tennis shoes. I emerge from the house after being fully immersed in hibernation mode for several days.

I hope I don't run into anyone. I don't want to chat or go into the events of this week. No such luck. I arrive at the store and run right smack into Jeremy, who works here. He's always helpful to me. I've completed several home projects in the past. Jeremy has always provided me with the right recommendations and suggestions.

"Hi Lauryn, how are you today?" Jeremy asks.

"I'm doing well," I reply. **(I hope Jeremy doesn't ask too many questions.)**

"How may I help you find what you need today?"

"No need. I'm only getting some boxes. I got it."

"Ok, you have a great day."

Moving away from Jeremy, I sense him staring at me. His co-worker remarks, "Don't stare too hard Jeremy. She's like a ten and you're five on a good day."

Jeremy replies, "What you talking about, man? She's a great person and a loyal customer."

With a slight jolt of confidence, I go to the aisle with the moving products and choose six large boxes. Jackson doesn't have any major appliances. He only has some clothes, shoes, video games, and knick-knacks. These boxes should accommodate his stuff. I head back home. I'm glad there is too much to do to be angry. I choose to haphazardly throw his clothes into boxes, and this makes the experience somewhat therapeutic. It's kind of like shooting hoops in a box. The gray cashmere sweater I love catches my eye for a moment. I recall how good he looks in this sweater. A single tear drops on my cheek.

That's one of things I love about him. He's never confused about what to wear to any function, casual or dressy. He would be fine as hell wearing a t-shirt and jeans or a suit. It really didn't matter. Remembering anything about his body isn't healthy right now. I refuse to get caught fantasizing about our happier times. Maybe one day I'll be able to remember the good times, but not today. Pondering about him is just dangerous. This could make me soft and provide him with a way back to me. Nope, not going to happen. After I finish packing the master bedroom and bathroom, I plod throughout the house to search for any other of Jackson's items. The media room mostly contains his stuff. Everything ranging from video game consoles, video games, movies, computers, and music collections. I'm going to miss our video game battles. **(Nope, don't do it. Affirm positive beliefs.)**

For some reason, he still owned DVDs, CDs, and vinyl records. He tends to like tangible items. He would comment that digital music didn't capture the same essence as vinyl records. I would joke with him about coming of age in the wrong decade. I smile sadly. Again, memories creeping on me like a zit before a romantic date. I'm not a vindictive person. I could've thrown these items into the boxes and not worry about the damage. Better yet, I could throw it all away like he did us. What good would it do? It wouldn't make anything better in the end, and I don't want to go back and forth with Jackson following this week.

Jackson and Asia together makes me want to vomit. I may consider having the place cleansed with sage. Leslie, my hippy and lovable friend from work, swears by cleansing out bad mojo out of your space. I've never believed in cleaning out bad spirits or mojo per se, but at this point what could it hurt. I've had my share of bad mojo this week, haven't I?

I've gone through the entire house, and I'm positive I've packed all his things. Glancing around the room at his stuff packed, I lose it. The tears rain down like a waterfall. I told myself I wouldn't cry anymore, but damn it, how could I not? We recently celebrated our three-year anniversary. Three years of my life dedicated to him. I never cheated on him. Yes, this last year I worked more than I should've. I didn't desert him. I never once betrayed him with anyone else.

Yea, sure, we didn't have as much sex since I traveled with work, but he got his. When we were together, he got my total attention. I tried to make up any lost time. I guess he missed the emotional connection of the day-to-day we used to share. Being on the road, things could be distracting since often times the companies STU consulted lacked organization. Did he have the right to step out on me because of some BS at work? What if he traveled for work? Wouldn't he expect me to hold it down and wait for him? Men travel for work all the time. The little woman is expected to wait patiently for him to return.

Fuck this. I'm not blaming myself for his lack of commitment and betrayal with my best friend. I'm done. I must get myself together to end this now. I give Jesse, the doorman, a call to inquire if Jackson's boxes could be left downstairs for him to retrieve. He's disabling Jackson's key FOB for entry and updating mine. He's also removing Asia from the approved visitor's list. I'm sending Jackson a text with instructions to retrieve his stuff. I'm considering blocking him now.

Moving on from the man who I love with everything I am, is proving to be very difficult. Now, it's time to reconfigure my dreams, and the plan for my life. I guess the lesson I learned is stop trying to plan my life. I need to be okay if something doesn't go according to my plan. The dream job turned out to be not such a dream. Why does it seem like I was thrown out like yesterday's trash? My personal life is a waste dump not worth discussing. How will these events change the trajectory of my life? I won't be as trusting as I've been. Any future mates/friends of mine will suffer from excitis.

(Excitis is the crime committed by ex-boyfriends and ex-friends. At least I still believe in love. They didn't take this from me.)

I believe I'll recover from all of this in time. I still love him, but I don't trust him. I'm uncertain if my love for him will ever die. If I'm going to be with someone, I must trust them completely. We won't work. I don't care how much I love him. Trust is hard to regain once it's gone. I won't sit around crying about this anymore. People love to comment about relationship failures. One my favorites is, "If you aren't pleasing him in the bedroom, he'll find it somewhere else."

In this patriarchal world, the woman is always to blame when it comes to deficiencies in the bedroom, but honestly, we didn't have a bedroom issue. He never left my presence unsatisfied. That's a guarantee. When I arrived home, he wanted me immediately and the entire weekend. He never sent me away. I guess he could've wanted me and her. Nevertheless, it's over now. I have to keep it moving and try to be optimistic about my future.

My head is going to literally explode if I have to be reminded of Jackson and Asia's dalliance again. I always saw us as the couple who would have it all. Marriage, family, and careers we love. Staring into his eyes, I saw not only my future, but I saw the past and what brought us together. I guess we weren't real. I should've paid closer attention. I would've noticed our glass was clearly shattered. We weren't built on a strong foundation. We were built on unstable cracks doomed to ultimately fail. We weren't built for the long haul. We were only meant to comfort and console each other for a moment in time.

CHAPTER 5
Lauryn

ackson is an anomaly and not who he purported to be when we first met. That's very clear to me now, but what about Asia? How does a "best friend" engage in naked Olympics with her best friend's boyfriend? How does this happen in her best friend's bed? Only a skank would do something like this. In a way, I blame myself for not having the best judge of character here. How did I allow myself to believe in them?

This is obviously an opportunity for improvement for me gaging my trust meter. I guess the friendship we cultivated for the last 10 years didn't mean a damn thing to her. I don't understand her at all. She didn't even like guys like Jackson. She prefers the ghetto type, gold-teeth and all. How could she do this if this was only a fling? I wonder if she did something like this with Isaac, too. She might just go after what's mine. At this point, I wouldn't put anything past her. I'm not absolving Jackson for his part in this in anyway. He did his dirt, and I won't ever forgive him for his betrayal, but Asia betrayed me, too. I won't forgive her either.

The old school song, "Friends" by Whodini, comes to mind. It reminds me of times during my Saturday morning cleaning ritual with my parents where they would play these songs. There are no truer words spoken than the lyrics in that Whodini song. That begs the question. What is a friend? If someone said Asia and I would no longer be friends, I would call them a lie. Well, the joke's on me. Friends don't do what she did to me.

Could I've been fooled all these years? She's had her issues. No one is immune to issues. Her problems generally were self-contained and only affected her because she made poor choices. Those choices never impacted me personally, but as a friend I wanted the best for her. Asia simply lacks self-awareness and confidence. This annoyed me. I often encouraged her to love herself more. In no way did I intend for her to love my man. Geez, is this my fault? Did I hand him to her on a silver platter with a side of gumbo?

Unfortunately, I'm examining and evaluating everything with a fine-tooth comb to dissect where I went wrong. How could I trust her and not figure out this subterfuge right under my nose? What's wrong with me? What other signs have I missed? Asia and I have been friends since freshman year in college. We eventually became best friends. We pledged the same sorority. We were roommates, and we clicked instantly. I had her back through thick and thin. She needed my help a lot, and I didn't mind helping. She was my girl...my best friend.

Asia didn't have a lot of confidence in college. She saw herself as too tall and lanky. She didn't believe guys were feeling her, especially following the head game Mack played on her. He damn near ruined her life. I figured out that her judgment with men needed some major adjustments. I learned about it the minute she started dating him. He demanded to be called Maxton. He wanted to sound respectable. Ha, that wasn't happening. I personally always called him Mack to piss him off. He was an asshole, and I didn't care if he got mad.

He understood when to turn off the jerk and become charismatic. I guess that's how he fooled her. In reality, Mack loved to dominate and beat her. What a class act. What a true prince. He took his royal time to hit her in areas that weren't easily discovered. She didn't have a clue how to get out of her abusive relationship. I'm not sure if she really wanted out. She would constantly make excuses for him, but the tide changed thankfully. He put her in the hospital, and she finally decided enough was enough and chose herself. She didn't do it for the reasons you would think. She finally resolved to end things as soon as she learned he cheated on her, too. I didn't believe she would leave him alone. She marched away without turning back.

The summer after freshman year, my parents bought me the condo downtown. Asia moved in with me. Being in a condo with security, he didn't have access to Asia anymore. He eventually got over her. I believe he got bored and left the school. I didn't see him much after sophomore year. Good riddance. He was scum and treated her like the bottom of his shoe. Asia's betrayal hurts me more than Jackson's. We'd been through so much, and I trusted her like she was my sister. Since I'm the only child, my true friends are like family to me. Asia had it rough since we met. Not only did she endure the horrible relationship with Mack, she also suffered a major loss when her brother, her rock, died in a terrible car accident the fall semester of our sophomore year.

I got the impression Asia wouldn't make it through school following the accident where Anthony was killed. He drove his normal route from work as a car hit him from behind and pushed his car into a lake. Months later a body was recovered from the lake. Asia's mom called her to inform her about the accident. She let out a violent scream which lasted for at least two hours. She received all incompletes in her classes. She repeated the courses the following semester due to the tragic loss her family suffered. She spent the rest of the semester at home with her family.

Asia returned to school, and a big part of her died with her brother. Some of her light and essence would never return. I noticed her differences, but she put on a front for others. Anthony and Asia were close as two siblings could be. They were only one year a part, and they called each other every day. I'm positive Asia didn't tell Anthony about Mack. Anthony would've made sure Mack never laid hands on another woman. He was very protective of his sister.

I never shared with Asia my feelings for Anthony nor my view of his sexiness. If he wasn't my best friend's brother, I would have pursued him for sure. He used to flirt with me. I would flirt right back. We kissed a few times. Those kisses left me breathless, but we both knew we couldn't take it further. He didn't want his younger sister's friendship to be destroyed, and I agreed with him. We just shared a few glances and some kisses.

I cried silent tears in Asia's presence, but those tears became much louder in her absence. Anthony's death hurt me deeply. I went to Humboldt, Tennessee, Asia's hometown, for the funeral, to support her and provide a shoulder of support. I tried to be the rock she needed. I barely notice the knock on my door until suddenly there's a bang and someone shouting out.

"Ms. Davidson, this is Larry with building maintenance."

I answer the door quickly. Larry makes several trips to retrieve the boxes. I tip him and fall back on my couch exhausted. I text Jackson he should get his stuff by Saturday. I ask him to respect me and not reach out to me anymore. I truly hope he honors my wishes. My next priority is to inform Asia this friendship is done. The only way to end this is an old school letter.

Dear Asia,

We've been friends since freshman year. I never would've believed you would betray me with Jackson. I had your back. I was there for you numerous times. I did what friends do, especially best friends. I helped you during the Mack mess. You didn't have the self-confidence or love yourself enough to comprehend you deserved better. I guess you never really learned to love yourself. If you did, there's no way you would resort to sleeping with Jackson. I don't have any words about how you should have kept your hands to yourself. A true best friend wouldn't have hurt me the way you have. You betrayed our friendship and everything we built over the years.

You remember graduating and not being able to find a job? I helped you out financially until you were able to find work and support yourself. You're aware of all of this, but I had to state it. I'm unclear about your motivation. How could you do this to me...to us? I sure hope Jackson is worth it. You've definitely lost my friendship. There isn't any way to recover what you've destroyed.

This friendship is forever irreparable and destined for the trash dump. You've violated the girl code without a care in the world. Chicks before dicks should've been your motto. If anyone had told me last week you and I would no longer be friends, I would have called them a bald face liar. They would be mistaken. "Asia and I are homies. We're ride or die friends. There is nothing she would ever do to hurt me and vice versa." I was extremely wrong about you. You've broken my heart irrevocably, and there isn't any coming back from the damage you've inflicted in my life.

All I want to ask is this: "Was it worth it?" Did our friendship ever mean anything to you? What did I ever do to you to deserve this treatment? Obviously, I've been blind when it comes to our friendship. I never would've fathom this would happen. I'm not sure what drove you two together, but I hope you're both as miserable as you've made me. This will be our last correspondence. Don't try to text, call, or come to my house. There's actually no point in doing so. Someone once said, "Some people come into your life for a reason, a season, or a lifetime." I thought you were a lifetime. It appears you were only meant to be in my life a season.

Lauryn

I put the letter in the mail drop in the hall and go back home. I take a nice long bath followed by a nap. Sleep doesn't come easy. I get up and make some decor changes. It's time to get rid of my master bedroom suite. I won't ever be able to unsee them in bed together. It's like it's on a constant loop. I need to start fresh tomorrow beginning with new bedroom furniture and finding my purpose. Things could only ascend from here, right? I hit rock bottom without having a substance abuse problem. Why do I want to create a ten-step program for those recovering from a cheating boyfriend and best friend?

+ *Don't trust a hoe*

+ *Don't trust a fuckboy who falls in love too quickly*

+ *Don't make hoes your friends*

+ *Don't trust a hoe with keys to your place*

+ *Don't let a fuckboy live with you*

+ *Don't give your heart to a fuckboy*

+ *Repeat the first quote ten times until it sticks*

+ *Repeat the second quote 20 times until it sticks*

+ *Circle back to the first one because it didn't stick*

+ *Circle back to the second one and don't forget it.*

The little pep talk lightened my mood if only for a minute. I'm going stir crazy being in this house. I don't want to encounter any people either. I have to get out of here. I change into some workout clothes and debate if I want to go on a long run or punch something. Punching something wins today. I drive to the kickboxing gym. Sex on a stick, Alex, the trainer, is here. I'm extremely ready for my trainer round. I'm going full force on him today. He'll be shocked from my power.

"Hey Lauryn, you ready for this?"

"I was born ready."

"Ok, let's do this," he placed his hands in fighter stance and motions for me to get ready. "Jab! Jab! Jab! Cross! Jab! Cross! Cross! Hook! Hook! Uppercut! Uppercut! Roundhouse! Jab! Jab!"

"Yeah!" I scream out.

"Again! Jab! Jab! Jab!" he yells.

I missed the jab and landed a cross instead. I'm required to do a burpee as punishment. I won't mix the combinations again. I absolutely hate burpees. Someone deranged created them to torture people. I want to be mad at Alex, but he's just doing what he's paid to do. My brain differentiates the difference, but my body hates the hell out of him right now. This thirty-minutes of non-stop action is like several hours of complete torture. Why did I ask for this today? Alex smirks at me like he's enjoying himself. Now, he's giving me a reason to be mad at him since he's enjoying my pain. Finally, I'm at round nine and I'm in a better space. I've finished. I have a complete sense of satisfaction from a workout well done. I remove my gloves and undo the wraps on my wrist. I'm ready to ring the bell and amble out the door as someone lightly touches me on the shoulder.

"Great job out there today!" Alex states with a smile.

"Thanks, I guess. I'm not sure if I should love or hate you right now."

"Well, it's definitely love," he declares winking at me.

"The way you tortured me today? Not likely, sir."

"Aww, I'll never do anything to hurt you. I would never force you to do anything past your capabilities."

"I'll keep all this in mind and thanks for today. See you tomorrow."

"Sure thing."

I venture towards the door, and I suddenly stopped when I run right into Tony, my ex-work hubby, coming into the gym. Well, he'll probably always be my "work hubby."

"Hey, buddy," I smile (my first genuine one this week), "I didn't know you worked out here."

"Well, I'm trying it. You spoke a good game about it, and I thought, 'why not?' What are you doing now?"

"Nothing much. I'm out of work," I chuckle.

"Not funny. You want to grab a coffee? I'll reschedule my workout."

"Nope, you're not rescheduling. I'll stretch while you work out, and we'll get coffee after."

"Deal."

Alex comes to greet Tony and get him started.

"You haven't gotten enough of this place, yet?" he teases me.

"Tony's a friend of mine. Since I recommended the gym, it's my duty to be here for him if it turns out to be a bad idea."

"Good friend," Alex comments.

"She's the best," Tony remarks.

"I'll be here doing some stretches while you get tortured."

"Hey, this sounds like a bad idea now."

"She's kidding. We don't torture anyone. Not on purpose anyway."

He leads Tony to start the process for his free trial. Tony's about 5'10 and he's a man's man. He probably weighs 225 pounds. He would also mention that he wanted to lose a few pounds. He complained that his girl wanted him to be no more than 200 pounds. I think they have a love and hate relationship. She nags him and he relents to give her whatever she wants. They're content for a couple of weeks and then the cycle starts again. She's not overly friendly, and it's not like she has to be. It's just something about her that makes me think she's shady. She definitely wants to keep with everything hot right now. She saw my Chanel bag and she subtly hinted to Tony that she wanted one. He's a softy, and he bought it. He will give that girl the moon if he could. I think he deserves better, but who am I to judge his relationship when mine just went down the drain? Tony finishes up, and he doesn't seem to have had the time of his life.

"You still want coffee," I ask?

"Certainly. I have to catch up with my work wife. It's been a minute."

"Mos def," I respond.

"Lauryn," Alex calls, "You coming tomorrow?" he asks.

"Of course."

Tony and I leave and go to the coffee shop in the shopping complex and catch up for a few hours. It's nice to chill and not worry about the state of my life. Tony's sensitive to my emotions and doesn't mention anything too heavy. Running into Tony is exactly what I needed today. He doesn't judge or give me any shit.

"You're sure you want coffee?" I ask.

"What are you thinking?"

"How about a cocktail? It's five o' clock somewhere."

"Well, you twisted my arm, girl."

"I didn't twist it hard at all."

"Well, STU is a shitshow, so cocktails all around."

"You ain't said nothing but a word, my friend. Let's go."

Tony and I trek to a great bar where the happy hour starts at 2:00 PM to hangout and catch up on all things STU. He shares the tea on the mad rush of people exiting. He also shares how he's scared they're going to fire him before he finds something else. I extend my support with anything he needs to help in his search. I think I've been blessed losing that job. It sounded like a curse when it happened, but now I beginning the think it's one of the best things that's happened to me.

CHAPTER 6
Stranger

His goal may have seemed complicated. He had to make sure Lauryn never allowed her d-bag ex-boyfriend back in her life. He couldn't believe what he saw as he took his daily stroll to get a glimpse of the lovely Lauryn. He didn't realize at the time what he saw would be the demise of Lauryn and Jackson's relationship. He learned Jackson cheated on Lauryn with her best friend.

He wanted to understand how a guy like Jackson scored a lady like Lauryn. With that fortune, he discarded her like leftovers. He studied him whenever Jackson didn't surround himself with people. He also studied him with his guy friends to understand his appeal. He understood and respected Jackson intrigued most women, but outside of his marginal good looks, he didn't get it. What did this guy have that made landing someone like Lauryn appear to be child's play? Jackson didn't deserve a woman like her.

He didn't anticipate learning anything extra special about Jackson until one day he saw him with Asia at a coffee shop. The meeting seemed innocent enough. Jackson had his laptop with him, but something didn't sit right about it. He figured he would be there for her when she discovered Jackson wasn't worthy of her. When they were hanging out, he didn't get a vibe like Jackson and Asia were close. He didn't observe any chemistry or sparks between them sitting in the cafe. So, the news of them getting together shocked him.

He should be happy about this news, but not at the expense of Lauryn's shattered heart. He hated she loved that degenerate, but she did. He knew he would never betray her. Jackson hadn't been worthy of her love. She represented a goddess, and Jackson hadn't been nothing more than a mere peasant. He didn't deserve to breathe the same air as her.

He wanted to express his joy with Lauryn's relationship status being single, but he lacked confidence since she may want to remain single for an undetermined amount of time. He wanted to cherish her body and soul. Jackson never worshiped her like she deserved. He could be the man for her. He would wait until the faithful day he could approach her and mend her broken heart. She'll always be adored and cared for if he was around. He wanted to go to Lauryn and comfort her now. He craved her in his arms until she felt safe and loved once again. He knew he'd been put on this earth to make things happen for her. She'd been on his mind so much.

He wondered by on her street only hoping to get a glimpse of her, but nothing could've prepared him for her losing it in public.

"Jackson, why did you hurt me?" Lauryn yelled. "What did I do to deserve this? I loved you!!!"

"Sweetheart," an older woman remarked as she tried to console Lauryn, "I'm not sure what this Jackson did to you, but it'll be okay. My grandson will make sure you make it home."

"No, No!!" Lauryn yelled, "I'm living in my own personal hell."

The scene of Lauryn's breakdown saddened him. He didn't care for Jackson and what he did to her, but this scene caused him to genuinely hate the man. Jackson never deserved her, and he wanted to console her. He desired to remove all her pain. He followed them to her building. He didn't trust this grandson to get her home without copping a feel. He didn't care if granny trusted him or not. He wouldn't leave anything to chance with her.

He hated she lost her job, even though he didn't prefer how much it kept her on the road. She loved working at STU. It demonstrated her power and drive, plus he thought she'd been damn sexy. Lauryn was good at her job. He'd been glad she received the coveted award, senior project manager of the year. He still remembered how her dress hugged every curve on her body.

Jackson casted himself as the man of the hour at the event. He sat there kissing and hugging her all night. He regarded her like she'd been the only woman on earth. This made him extremely upset. Now, he assumed it had to be all a ruse to avoid any suspicions about Jackson and Asia. He hated Lauryn kept having some shitty days. He only wanted to hold her in his arms. He contemplated deeply and didn't hear Melanie enter the room. Here she comes again with her opinion. She made it impossible for him to do anything without her putting in her two cents.

"Are you happy your precious Lauryn lost her job?"

"No, why would I be happy she's hurt?"

"You will get to visit her anytime you want now."

"I hate that she's in pain."

"You're not losing any sleep now. She found out about Jackson and Asia."

"Why should I? He never deserved her. He was fucking her best friend."

"And you deserve her?"

"I'll love her like she deserves to be loved. I'll worship her like my queen every day."

"If you say so, my love. I hope you get what you want."

"Don't ever call me your love again!"

"You are my love! Why do you fight me so hard over this?"

"You confuse sympathy for love. I keep you around because mom would've wanted that. I owe this to her. If it wasn't for her, I would've made you leave a long time ago."

"Don't get it twisted, my boy. I'm your first and last love. I'm your destiny. I'll let you live out this fantasy thing with her. You'll be back, baby."

"Don't hold your breath, Melanie. You're not my future."

"I'm the only future you're ever have."

"You're delusional."

"No, baby. You are. The sooner you face your reality the better you'll be. I'm your destiny."

"If you're my destiny, I hope to be struck down now."

"You would rather die than be with me!" She cried out.

"Yea, kind of. Being with you would be like a slow death."

"Wow! You're cruel and ungrateful. I've done nothing but love you."

"A love I never asked for. Why can't you just leave me alone?!"

"Gladly. You'll be back. You can't survive without me."

"I certainly want to try."

Melanie glanced at him with evil intent and ambled away slowly. He felt such a relief as she finally left the room. He began to wonder if his debt should be paid in full. She won't let go of the past. Melanie's delusion of what they were to another made her fantasize for something more. She didn't have the capacity to understand the depth of his emotions for Lauryn. He'd do anything for her. He yearned to be with her now.

He imagined himself consoling her by holding her in his arms. He knew she was facing unbelievable pain losing her job like she did and finding her boyfriend having sex with her best friend. He wondered if she'll be the same person having all of this dumped on her. Will some of her fiery essence disappear like her job? As much as Lauryn should be armed with the truth about her boyfriend, a small part of him wished she never found out. Her pain was more than he could bare. To drown out the nagging thoughts from Melanie's words, he zoned out by listening to "Earned it" by The Weeknd. The lyrics resonated with him. He pondered and closed his eyes letting the words reach his soul.

He naively hoped turning up the volume would make her irritating voice disappear. If only things with Melanie were that easy. She lived to torture him wide awake as well as in his dreams. He only wanted to take a few minutes to forget his reality and enjoy some music. He wanted to dream a little about what the woman who ruled his emotions and will ultimately be his wife. His imagination went wild. He fantasized what a night with Lauryn would be like. Would she be shy or ready to go at the end of their date? He wanted to kiss her lips and taste her tongue as he sucked on it. Would she taste like strawberries or peaches? She could taste like mango. He knew her essence would be filled with at least one of the fruits of passion. He would taste his passion one day.

His mind wandered about what the rest of her body would taste and feel like, and his wet dream didn't disappoint him. His hands wandered to his manhood to relieve the tension building there as he thought about Lauryn. He palmed and clutched himself. At first, the rhythm of his hand moved very slowly. He lost control and stroked himself faster and faster. His breath became labored as he pictured the beautiful Lauryn and her bountiful breasts. He imagined they were perky and would stand at attention once she bared all for him.

"You want me, lover?" she whispered.

"Of course. I've always wanted you."

"Show me how much you want me."

"How can I show you more than I am right now?"

"Move your hands faster, faster. Like you're caressing my body. Does this feel good, baby?"

"Better than good. Where have you been my entire life?"

"I've been right here. Waiting on you to come to me. I'll make you feel so good, baby."

"You're already making me feel good. I'm seriously about to lose my shit, baby. Damn, I want you more than life itself."

"Baby, cum for me."

"I'm cumming, baby!!!"

"Don't hold back, baby!! Let go!!"

"Agghhh!!!" he yelled out.

"That's right, baby cum for me."

"Agghhh!!" he continues to yell out.

"It feels good to let go!! Let it all out!!"

"I want to touch you."

"You will, baby."

"Why do you feel so far away?"

"I'm always with you, love."

"I need you, baby."

"And you have me."

"No, come here. Let me hold you."

"You know I can't do that. Why can't you be satisfied with just our talking? You know, I'm your dream. Your imagination. I'm really not here. I don't know you yet. I should go now."

"No! Fuck, I'm sorry for crossing the line. We're good. I won't ever feel good about being an asshole towards you. I won't push for the day you're truly mine."

"Close your eyes and concentrate on why you want me here. Think about how you want to stroke yourself one last time while imagining my naked body underneath you. Is that what you want, baby? Do you want me naked so you can do any and everything to me?"

"I want that so much."

"Well, tread carefully now."

Suddenly, there'd been an explosive reaction from below. He panted and shook from his act of masturbation. It surprised him. He trekked to the bathroom to clean himself. He believed in having a very clean and sterile area. After he saw his cum on his hand, he nearly freaked out. He scrubbed his hand like a maniac to ensure he'd removed every drop of the residue. He grabbed a black light to inspect his hand to confirm all the semen was completely gone. This fantasy felt real like she'd been here commanding his every move. He instantly knew he would do anything to please her in every way.

He would go and check in on her from afar the next day. He wanted to verify for himself if she was doing okay. He figured she'd be miserable. She didn't deserve the hand she'd been dealt. If he could do something to make her happy, he would. He had no idea how to make all this stuff fade to black. He wanted her to be radiant again. Her brightening the world shouldn't be suppressed.

Her kind of beauty shouldn't be contained. He dreamed about her face glowing for him. He had to be the one to make her happy. He knew she would be sad for a while. The life she knew was no longer. He wanted to do something even if it was a small gesture to make a difference for her. He would do the perfect thing. He hoped she loved red. Red would be a nice color for her. He wanted her to comprehend the depth of his love for her. His phone rang, and this annoyed him. The office couldn't operate without him. He wanted to avoid the call and continue fantasizing about Lauryn, visualizing her nude. Her beckoning him to come and claim his prize. He wanted so much more, but his damn phone wouldn't stop ringing.

He hit the answer button and barked, "What?"

"What? Is this the way you answer the phone these days?"

"My apologies, Mr. Gentry. I thought you were someone else."

"Well, I would hate to be who you thought I was. Anyway, tell me what you got for the STU case."

"It's all preliminary. I don't have much," he says.

"What's the plan? This case will net the firm three million easily if handled correctly."

"The plan is to do what I do best, Mr. Gentry. You've always trusted me to handle the business interest of the firm. I'll conduct this case like I did with Macliomillion. You had no complaints about how the case was settled." **(Macliomillion was a huge case riddled with allegations of misconduct. It netted the firm five million all from representation.)**

"No, son. I don't. I'll let you handle things. I get nervous if big money is on the line. We have to nail this. We need to make sure the client is happy with us."

"We'll nail it. The client is happy with the direction of the case. Finally, trust me to get this done."

"I need you to come in and update me on the progress. Cecily will schedule something with you preferably early next week. Hang on."

"Sir —"

Mr. Gentry didn't wait for him to finish his statement before transferring the call to Cecily. He didn't want to interact with her. They had a history, one he preferred not to revisit. Cecily wanted more than he could give her. She wanted marriage way too soon. He learned the hard way not to shit where you eat. Most of the time, he avoided Cecily at all costs.

"Well, Mr. Gentry has an opening on next Tuesday at 10:00 AM. Will this work for you?" Cecily asks without any formalities like, "how are you?"

He didn't care if she avoided him. They tend to have confrontational battles whenever he'd been forced to communicate with her. He would rather not speak with her since they have a sketchy past. He tried to get closure once, and he ended up on the losing end of the conversation.

"I'll need to check my calendar. Give me a moment."

"Take your time. It's not like I'm busy or anything," she replied with an edge.

"It won't take more than a few seconds for me to confirm," he stated in a reassuring tone.

"I don't have anything to do but schedule this appointment for your ass, so yea, do you."

He began to get annoyed with her tone. He didn't ask Mr. Gentry to patch him into her, and she acted like he purposely wasn't prepared for this interaction. She needed to learn how to separate personal and professional. If she couldn't, he'd have a discussion with Mr. Gentry regarding her behavior. He didn't go around making trouble for co-workers, but she was trying his patience.

"10:00 AM Tuesday will work."

"Great, goodbye," she replied hastily while disconnecting the call and not waiting on a response.

CHAPTER 7
Lauryn

I awake suddenly. I don't grasp what's real or what's a dream. I guess the more appropriate term would be a nightmare. I reach over to touch Jackson to reinforce I only had a terrible nightmare, but the other side of the bed is cold and empty. Everything comes back hard and fast. The betrayal. Losing my job. All of it.

I have to keep my mind occupied, and it's difficult considering I'm unemployed now. If only I still worked at STU, I would be able to drown myself knee-deep on a project in bumfuck America. This is the only time I miss going to a little town in Wisconsin or somewhere else where the biggest highlight is the cheese or the Walmart. I would work between 12 and 16 hours a day. I never had time to sit around. Most of the time I would pass out at the end of the day. I'd love to have some distractions right now.

The days are running together mostly with me in a rut about everything. Most of the time I spend hating Jackson for what he did. Other times, I hate to admit I still love him. Love like ours doesn't go away by simply willing it to be over. I could tell myself I don't love him anymore, but that's a lie. As much as I want to breeze past this period of pain and despair, it seems impossible now.

As I march past the bathroom mirror, I try to avoid looking at my reflection. My appearance probably resembles death. I haven't put too much effort in my overall presence lately. My hair is all tangled. Boy, it's going to hurt detangling it. I'm dreading doing the wash process. I'm tender-headed, and my hair is super tangly. I don't have the energy to deal with my hair today. Maybe, tomorrow I can tackle this mangy mess.

Today is a new day. I'm determined to do more than I did the last few days. I'm washing my hair today. It resembles a hot mess, and I need to get over myself. I could be a member of the *Walking Dead* after being bit. This is not a good look. I need to put forth more effort for myself. When I stare at the mirror, the image reflecting back should resemble a human. I'll make an effort with my wardrobe today, too. Not wearing a t-shirt and gym shorts. I love dresses, and I'm doing this for me. It's a shame I don't have anywhere I want to go. I'll apply a little mascara and lip-gloss just to rid myself of this ghastly appearance I've been sporting.

There's a knock at my door, and I'm surprised. I'm not expecting anyone. It's even more shocking opening the door to find Jackson peering back at me. I hoped he would respect my wishes and never grace my door again. I'm fairly certain how he got in. It was probably the old "hold the door for me" trick. People probably are unaware of his resident status. He's saying some garbage about wanting me back. He has some nerve coming here.

His annoyingly handsome face irks me. I want to slam the door right in it. In fact, I attempt to close it, but he's much faster than me. He catches the door and pushes his way into the great room. I'm uncertain if this could be considered breaking and entering because he isn't invited. I guess it could fall under this description if I bothered to call the cops. I wouldn't call them. No matter how angry I am with him, I don't want him hurt or dead. Calling the cops could potentially end his life. He's lucky I still love him and involving the cops is a non-starter. I couldn't live with myself if he got hurt unnecessarily. I may love him, but I also hate him.

He's pronouncing all sorts of proclamations I don't believe or want to hear. He claims he loves me. He'll always love me. He kisses me and for a moment I forget everything, and I melt into the kiss… into his arms. For a perfect moment in time, we were us again. I love him without a shred of doubt, and he adores me and only me. He's the man I believe in so much. He's the man I want to spend the rest of my life loving. This moment is perfect, and it eclipses everything I've felt in the last few days.

Regrettably, this moment crashes to a shocking end. Reality of what he did sets in quickly. The shocking image of him with Asia can't be unseen. No matter how much I want not to, I can't. I wonder if he ever fantasized about her in my presence. While we kissed? While we were intimate? No, I won't live my life second-guessing myself. The reality of Jackson and me has come to brutal and decisive end.

My reaction to everything is swift. My emotions are all over the place. He has to go, and he has to go now. What a jerk showing up and making me feel things! Why couldn't he leave me alone? Why did I let him in today? He tried to say all the right things, but I don't trust him. I won't ever again. No amount of seducing me will change what he did.

It doesn't matter what he would do to make things right. How in the hell can he do this to me? Did he think I would ever forget him being with Asia? Seriously, is he high or something? Did he really mention going to counseling with me? We aren't married so why do it? There's nothing we can do to make this work between us. I don't even want to try. Lack of trust isn't repairable, and I won't backtrack with him. I hope he doesn't come back again. He's finally leaving, and I can tell by the expression on his face he won't be coming back.

It's been a few weeks since Jackson came over. I'm so tired of being in this funk. It's time for me to put on my big girl pants and move on with my life. Yea, it hurts like hell, but I can't keep dwelling on it. There are things I need to do with my life, starting today. Luckily, there won't be any time for me to sit around pitying myself. My stomach is growling violently like a bear who wants to be fed. I haven't been eating properly. Cooking is out of the question even though the pantry and cabinets are stocked with food. I don't want to be around people either, but I must eat. Take out it is. I order a bowl of Shrimp Pad Thai, the perfect comfort food.

On the way to the elevator, there's Keith, my fine ass neighbor who lives on my floor in unit 1236. Keith is handsome, and did I mention he's fine? Like triple take fine. Keith is about 6'2, and he is chiseled in all the right places. I bet he doesn't have an ounce of body fat. The ripples representing his chest show through his polo shirt. I bet his chest and stomach muscles are perfectly packed.

His skin is a caramel brown, and I swear he looks sun kissed. He's strong and muscular, but he isn't bulky. He probably played football at some point. His physique is more like a wide receiver than a running back. His eyes are a light brown, and I'm certain his laser vision is able to dissect my soul. He could uncover my deepest secrets and desires. His hair is cut low, and he has a strong jawline. He could be on a magazine cover. He's confident, and I'm nearly 100 percent certain that the bedroom is his training grounds. I could learn a thing or two from him. I've seen him work out from behind and his ass is extremely firm.

"Hi Lauryn," Keith says in his ultra-sexy voice. "How are you?"

"Hi Keith, I'm good. How are you?" I reply.

"You're rather casual today. I don't ever remember seeing dress like this. I like it."

"Well, Keith I can relax and dress casually sometimes. It's not always business with me."

"Not always business. Interesting. Good to know. Hi, my name is Keith. Nice to meet you, Casual Lauryn." **(Is he flirting with me?)**

"It's nice to meet you, too, I guess. It's funny you've put me in a box labeled all business. I could say the same about you, sir." I'm smiling.

"I never uttered anything about you being in a box. You're much too intriguing. Nah, I'm always relaxed. YOLO is what I say."

"Great motto to live by."

"Yep, I'm a firm believer," he penetrates my eyes directly and winks. **(Is he flirting with me again? Why can't I test the waters? No one said I have to go in the deep end.)**

He scans his phone, and I stare at his chest imagining him with his shirt off. I exhale out loud. He turns to wink at me. I should be embarrassed, but I'm not. The elevator arrives and the door opens for us to enter. He motions with his hand I should enter the elevator before he does. I push the button for the garage for him and the first floor for me.

"How do you figure I'm going to the garage, Lauryn?"

"Well, you appear to be going out, so I figured you'd be driving. Am I wrong?"

"You're not wrong. I'm giving you a hard time. So, you're staying in I guess?"

"Yea, it's been a long day. I ordered some takeout."

"Did you order enough for two?"

I gasp embarrassed and uncertain how to answer, "I umm —"

"I'm only kidding. You didn't know you would see me today," he chuckles as the elevator arrives at the first floor. He grins at me and says, "Until next time, stranger."

I beam back at him as I exit the elevator, "Maybe, we don't have to be strangers," I flirt.

He presses the button and replies, "Glad to hear it."

As the elevator doors close, I approach the reception area to retrieve my takeout. On the way back to my condo, I'm smiling at the progress I've made. I did something out of character which makes me proud. It felt nice to mindlessly flirt with someone. I'm excited to discover myself again. It's been a long time since I've been single. It's time to figure out who Lauryn really is.

As I settle in for the night, I flip through my streaming services and land on *Big Little Lies*. I'm eating as I begin the first episode then the next one. Each episode is riveting, and I can't wait to see what happens next. I'm invested, and I have to know how this season will end. I finally notice my phone is vibrating non-stop. There are several text messages from friends I don't want to speak with right now. So, I ignore those messages. One text from Tonya has piqued my interest.

Tonya: Hey girl, what do you have up Friday night?

Me: Nothin' girl. Laundry maybe.

Tonya: Girl, do you want to go clubbing?

Me: Girl, no. I can't go clubbing with you.

Tonya: Why not? Aren't you and Jackson done?

Me: We are, and we don't speak his name.

Tonya: Yea, for sure girl. Get your cute butt back out there.

Me: Let me get back to you.

I used to love going to the club. So, why not? I'm not attached anymore. Tonya's right. What am I doing Friday night? Laundry is not enough incentive for me to stay home. I'm in my happy place dancing. I haven't danced in a club in such a long time. I used to hit the clubs a lot in college, but a lot has changed since then.

I worked so much and didn't have time to go out. The thrill to go out every weekend sort of diminished for me. My Fridays have been filled with traveling back home if I was lucky and crashing as soon as I could. My life had become depressing. No wonder he strayed. Nope, not blaming myself for that. Plus, if I stayed home, my mind would wonder back to Jackson. What if he snuck in the building again? He could kiss me again. We could do more. Would I get weak and drop my panties? Could I end up having angry sex with him? No, I won't let it happen.

A night of drinking and dancing may be what the doctor ordered to help with this funk. I realize dancing won't help me get over a relationship of more than three years, but so isn't sitting home crying. I have to get out. I inform Tonya I'm down and would meet her there. I'm excited about doing something different for the first time in a long time.

If I have enough fun, maybe I'll go out on Saturday night, too. I need to get out there to show everyone Lauryn isn't down for the count. I'm not some trash Jackson could throw away without a second thought. I'm a beautiful and vibrant woman who deserves to be treasured. I'm not searching for love right now. I may not ever want that again. What I want is a good time. It's been a long time, and I want to be with someone other than myself for a little while. Friday night will be my night to shine.

I finally psych myself into going out clubbing on Friday. This was never a problem pre-Jackson, but now I'm not feeling going to a club where randos may start grinding on me. It's not like people adhere to the personal space memo. I want to yell, "Back-up! Be at least three feet away from me unless you're invited into my space." I'm not looking forward to any unwanted individuals entering my personal space. I'm close to backing out when my phone vibrates.

I'm pretty sure it's Tonya. She has a sixth sense or something. She'd figure I'm changing my mind about going out, and she'll most definitely try to change it back. It's not her, but I don't recognize the number. I don't answer those calls. It's probably some telemarketer or something. They're calling cell phone numbers now. They left a message. I normally wouldn't listen to it, but something compels me to find out what the voice mail says.

"My love, oh my love," the caller says in a calm voice, but the voice sounds automated. "Where art thou, my love? I deeply desire to hear your voice, talk to you, but alas you're not answering my call. Should I be concerned, baby? Should I take this as a sign you no longer desire my love?" There is a pause, and the caller voice changes. "What am I supposed to do, my love? You're not answering me. Do you want to do this? I can't control what type of reaction you'll get from me if you continue to ignore me. I won't be ignored. Do you hear me? You'll pick up next time, my love." He no longer sounds calm. His voice is becoming frightening, and the call is disconnected.

The voice freaks me out, and I have no idea who it is. What if this is a joke? Could someone be playing a prank on me? It's not April Fool's Day, yet. I guess some people start early. Even though this is a juvenile prank, I'm pretty sure it's only a prank. They went all out, and had their voice simulated so I couldn't recognize them. Kudos for the effort. I guess the call could've been a wrong number. The caller only called me or whoever their "love." I love those fully committed to their prank. Oddly enough, this prank call has invigorated me to go out on Friday. There's no reason I should stay home and cry another night. It's time for me to get out there and show I'm single and ready to mingle. Well, not quite, but it sounded good, right? I'm single and working on being ready to mingle.

CHAPTER 8
Keith

I want to forget all about my day. Alice, the partner at work, assumes I'm her personal plaything. She cornered me near the copier, but she's not someone I would ever exchange bodily fluids with. I wouldn't go near her even if I was blackout drunk. She's extremely handsy, and people have said that's the way she is. Do I have to deal with the fact she likes to have her hands sail around my ass? It would probably be considered a punk move for me to turn her into HR for all her harassment, but I'm running out of options. I'm leaving work a little later than I normally would. Someone's calling my name.

"Keith," Alice calls out, "may I have a word?"

"Alice, can this wait until tomorrow?" I ask hoping to avoid a late night with this woman.

"No, it cannot. Are you a partner?" I glance at her with an annoyed expression without answering. "No! Get in here!"

I grudgingly dredge into her office hoping we aren't the only ones here. I have no idea how this lady made it as a partner. All she seems to do these days is troll around for sex, specifically from men in their twenties.

"How can I help you, Alice?" I want to end this as soon as possible.

"In the copy room, we were interrupted. I didn't get a chance to make you a proposal."

"What type of proposal?"

"I have a very high-profile client who wants to expand his real estate options in Austin, TX, and you would be perfect for my team. You want to be a partner, right? This could be your ticket."

"It sounds interesting. Why me? I thought Alec would be a shoo-in. Isn't he your go to guy?"

"Someone's done their homework. Alec is nearly washed up. I need fresh meat."

This woman is out of her mind. I glance at my watch to gage the time before answering, "Alice, I'm flattered. I'm working with Jacob on a huge proposition. It'll be his decision if I have the bandwidth or not. Can I get back to you?"

"Don't take too long." I turn to leave, and she says, "I can't wait to get my hands on your sexy ass. I hope your girlfriend doesn't mind sharing."

I attempt to leave in a hurry like I didn't hear what she said.

"Oh, and Keith," she breathes out huskily. "I don't care if she does mind sharing you one little bit. So, don't take too long making the right decision for your career here."

I barely escape her clutches muttering something about me having to be somewhere. This woman is a predator. I'm certain I'm not the only person having issues with her. She'll probably escalate her behavior. If this wasn't work, and if she was attractive, I would find her attitude (going for what she wants) a turn-on. She's the woman on *Botched* whose had too many plastic surgeries, and you don't recognize the "before" anymore. Yea, I watched the show with one of my "friends," and I liked it surprisingly. She's rail thin, and meat should be her best friend. She reminds me of a malnourished Jennifer Aniston, but definitely not as attractive. She's 40 something but looks like she's 60 on a good day. I thought she was near retirement during our first encounter. She's had one too many Botox treatments and too much face work, too.

She's been emboldened with her brand of sexual harassment. A brush here, a little too close, a rub there was how things started. I thought it was innocent at first until she grabbed my ass one day. I don't believe I'm alone, but who is going to snitch about this? Would HR even take this seriously? There aren't many women in leadership here. I won't be surprised if they let this slide for her.

This is something I have to deal with on my own. I'll need proof of what she's doing prior to making moves against her. It can't be my word against hers. She's been exceptionally bold lately, so it shouldn't be hard for me to get some video or at the least audio evidence. I bet she's into voyeurism. She may make getting evidence easy. I have to get out of here and get this out of my head.

My mind wanders to the other day with Lauryn, my neighbor. The elevator banter with her has surprisingly taken my mind off my work issues. She's fine. I haven't seen him around much lately. Not since the day he followed me into the building. Maybe there's a story there.

Lauryn completely glows when she smiles. I love her dimples. I'm immensely attracted to her. She isn't married yet. If I'm keeping it 💯, I hope she doesn't get married anytime soon. I would like to get to know her better, but she lives in the same complex.

I brush off thoughts about Lauryn and focus on what's going on at work. It wasn't all bad. Besides my unfortunate encounters with Alice, some interesting things happened to me. Jeff, one of the coolest brothers at work, came into my office to discuss an opportunity for me to raise my profile within the firm. Jeff is the only brother who is a partner at the firm, and he's making moves within the executive leadership team. Jeff would like to increase the number of African American partners at the firm. He realizes I have potential, and he wants to make sure I network with the right people and work on high visibility cases. He's in a position to grow talent, and it's great for me since I'm on his radar. Unlike Alice, Jeff has my best interest at heart.

I've worked at this firm for nine years including my interning years during law school. I put a lot of effort ensuring I'm managing my billable hours effectively to get the biggest bang for the buck. The next step is to cultivate and expand my network. My talent is on point, but I need to make sure I connect with the right people who can make the difference in my career. Luckily, Jeff is a key player in this process. He travels in the right circles, and he's trusted at the firm. Tomorrow is a significant day for me. I have a huge client I need to impress to gain their business.

I'm currently working on a particularly high visibility case with Jacob, and this could be the break I need to show my value. If the firm is serious about being equitable by having a more diverse and inclusive leadership team, I should have my shot within the next year to become a partner. Being a partner will be demanding, but I have what it takes. I don't have anything holding me back. I'm single, and my time is my own. I'll have to travel more with the increased responsibilities. I want to be more of a face for the organization and close some deals.

My professional life is coming together. Well, it's almost coming together with only one nagging problem…Alice. She's a problem I need to figure out how to handle. I wouldn't be surprised if her scrawny ass tried to lock me in her office for some hide-n-seek. I don't want to be on the losing end of the game. She has to be dealt with and soon. I'm meeting my boys for drinks tonight. My phone vibrates with a text from Sabrina.

Sabrina: Hey sexy, wyd tonight

Me: Getting drinks with my boys

Sabrina: Do you want a night cap? Stop by later.

Me: Always. I'll hit u when I'm omw

Sabrina: Bye baby, C u later

Me: Can't wait

I certainly don't plan on being in a relationship anytime soon. The thing with Sabrina is perfect. We meet for no-strings sex a few times a month and it works. I had to stop going out with Jennifer, who was an on and off "situation-ship" because she got too clingy. She wanted a commitment even though I told her at the beginning I don't want anything serious. It would never work with Jennifer. She doesn't challenge me at all intellectually, and this is a deal breaker for me. I must be able to have a conversation if I'm serious with someone. Reality TV doesn't constitute intellectually stimulating conversations.

It's Hump Day! The night I meet my boys (Jason and Sam) at the bar for drinks. We meet every Wednesday like clockwork. We've all been friends since we were undergrads in Memphis. Jason and I played football for the university. I was a wide receiver, and Jason was a corner. Sam didn't play football, but he did play basketball. He was my roommate, and we've had many adventures over the years. Jason and Sam are my lifelong friends, and some of the best friends a brother could ask to have.

After college and the end of my football career, my plan B became law school. Well, the NFL really was an unlikely probability. Sam and I attended Vanhogen Law School together, and Jason went to Vanhogen for his MBA. We all found great jobs in the metropolitan Nashville area following graduation. Sam works as an assistant district attorney in the DA's office. Jason is an entrepreneur who inherited his dad's string of dry-cleaning businesses.

It's basketball's regular season, and March Madness is happening soon. I love sports. Not a surprise there since I played college football. March Madness is the pinnacle of the championships for college basketball. The South Regionals are taking place in Louisville, Kentucky. Jason, Sam, and I are planning to go to the regional games. We've been traveling to the games for years now. As I stroll into the pub to meet them, I'm ready to start trash talking about the tournament. Every year, we play the brackets, and a majority of the years, I win. This year will be a dub like the previous years.

Sam comes back at me before I order my drink. He has a different strategy for his bracket and brags this is his year. I'm skeptical. He doesn't pick the right teams ever. He's likely to pick chalk. That's his MO. It hurts him as a team like Duke loses early. It's funny he'll pick the number one seeds in all the divisions to make the quarter finals.

Jason is pretty quiet, but I'm secretly worried about him because he doesn't brag. It's always the quiet ones who sneak in and win it all. I'm especially competitive and love to win. Jason takes a call, and we both give him a hard time. We could tell it's Jasmine from the way he lowers his voice. Out all of us, Jason is the only one in a committed relationship. I actually like Jason's girl, but that isn't a road I want to travel right now. I'm good with these casual friendships where there aren't any expectations.

"Hey Jay," Sam jokes, "Did your mama say you should come home?"

"Ha-ha," Jason comments, "Only if it's your mama who's waiting on me. I've always had a crush on her."

"Whoa," I declare, "Don't go too far. I don't want to referee any fights tonight. Your mama is fine though, Sam."

"Too far," Sam laughs, "Don't talk about my mama, man. All kidding aside, how is Jasmine doing?"

"She's good. We're moving in together," Jason announces.

"Oh, real?" I'm surprised, "Congrats!"

"Wow!" Sam exclaims. "Your life is no longer your own."

"Sam," Jason responds, "Don't give me shit about this. She's it for me. I thought you liked her."

"I do," I declare. "She's perfect for you. Don't worry about Sam. He's secretly jealous. He wants his own Jasmine."

"Real," Sam notes sarcastically, "You think I'm jealous of Jason being locked down. No, sir."

"Okay," I state, "if you say so."

We chat and joke over beers for a few more hours. We discuss our upcoming trip to Louisville for the regional tournament.

"You know you losers should just give up now and declare 'Hail to the King' of March Madness," I brag confidently.

"I will never in any circumstances grovel to you. I don't care how many March Madness years you win!" Sam huffs.

"Haters gone hate," I proclaim.

"Winners without grace gonna brag," Sam counters.

"Well, you said one thing right about winning. Thanks, my man."

"Will you guys quit it?" Jason asks exasperatedly. "Keith, we're fully aware of your prowess and gaming knowledge to all things sports. So there's no need to continually rub it in your noses. Sam, we're also fully aware of how you like to poke the bear to get this one on his high horse. So, let's call it a truce, since we're all aware of where everyone stands."

"Well, bruh. I guess I couldn't have said it better," I acknowledge.

"Yeah, man. Sorry. I do tend to invite this trash talking. What can I say? I do love to poke that bear," Sam agrees.

"I'm gonna chill with my predictions."

"I can't promise I won't poke the bear, but I'll try," Sam says with an innocent choir boy expression.

We talk a little more about sports and work. It's getting a little late , so I decide this rounds out the evening for me. It's time to call it a night. My phone vibrates with a text from Sabrina checking in to determine if I'm still coming by tonight. I'm definitely coming tonight. I need to relieve some stress.

"Yea, fellas," I declare, "It's been good. Until next week."

Sam responds, "It's still early. The Louisville versus Memphis game is coming on next. Don't you want to stay and watch it?"

I come back with, "I have to head home. Early day tomorrow."

"Work. Okay," Jason teases. "What's her name?"

"Damn, Jay," I laugh, "I expected this from him. I gotta get some rest. I have a lot going on at work tomorrow."

"Okay," Sam said. "If you say so. We'll see you next week."

I leave on this note and head to Sabrina's. She's what I need tonight. I knock on her door to find her dressed in practically nothing, and this makes me grin like a schoolboy.

"Hello," she says as she tugs me into the door and gives me a kiss.

"Hello to you, lovely lady."

"Do you want something to eat or drink?" she asks.

"No, I'm good."

"You're way to overdressed. Let's remedy this problem, shall we?"

"I like the way you think."

"Well, I'm a girl who always has a plan."

"A plan I can definitely get behind."

I follow her into the bedroom taking off my clothing along the way. We don't waste any time getting to the main course. Even though this isn't a committed relationship, it's important to me to please her and ensure she's fully satisfied. I always want to make sure a woman gets hers before I do. She convulses like she's having a seizure, so I'm fairly certain she isn't faking it.

It's too bad we can't have something more than purely physical. She's laid back, and I love this characteristic in a woman, but she can be a little shallow at times. This is a turn-off. She had a chip on her shoulder when we started kickin' it. Her ex did a real number on her. She wanted sex and not a lot of conversation. Things have changed somewhat. She's shared a little more, but I still don't know her like I should. She seems content with the status quo at her job, and her lack of ambition doesn't bode well with me. She has said on more than one occasion she believes her man should take care of her 100%, and she shouldn't have to work. She plans on being a stay-at-home mom. If my future wife and I decided together she would stay home, I'm good. I don't want someone coming into the relationship wanting to stay home. It's sexy if a woman is driven and has a career of her own.

Gaining our composure, we're all grins. We're not perfect for each other, but we work in bed.

"You were amazing," she murmurs huskily.

"You were too, doll."

"Keith, you never disappoint me. It's too bad we aren't emotionally compatible. You could be a good boyfriend."

"I guess so," I reply.

"You don't mean it."

"Well, it's too bad like you said. We want different things, and we're good."

"You're right. My last boyfriend made me want to take a break. I'm about having fun now. I'm definitely all about our situation-ship."

"We're good, Sabrina."

"I'll sleep like a baby tonight. Thanks for the nightcap."

"No, thank you, sweetheart. I'll sleep well tonight, also."

I shouldn't "hit and run," but tomorrow's going to be huge. I kiss her and get dressed. I drive home, shower, and get ready for the day ahead. I'm tired, but I can't sleep. My mind wanders to my sexy neighbor. She's intriguing and can be dangerous if she was on the market. I guess it's for the best that she has a boyfriend. I've never been the type to hit on a woman with a man, but like the saying goes, either you're single or you're married. Her boyfriend better not be caught slipping. She wore some itty-bitty shorts and my imagination is going wild.

"So, Keith, it was good crossing paths with you today. I want to show you I'm not uptight," she says as the right-side strap of her tank slips, and I witness her side boob. I desperately want more. "Do you like something here?" she smirks as she presses her breast in my face.

"Yep, I do, and I want more of it."

"Well, what makes you figure you deserve more?"

"You dropped into my dream. This is supposed to go the way I want it to go."

"Says who?"

"Says me," I welp as I grab her and show her who's dream this is. "What were you saying?"

"Do you like this?"

"I do, and I would like more. May I?"

"Since you asked so nicely, you may," she states and removes her tank top to provide me with a full view of the perfect set of 34C's I've ever witnessed. "Does this meet your expectations?"

"Nope," I say and she frowns. "It far exceeds my expectations." She beams at me.

I waste no time in kissing her while stroking her breast before taking them one-by-one in my mouth and not getting enough. It's thrilling conceptualizing she'll be mine in this elevator where we occasionally run into each other. She wants to be claimed as much as I want to claim her. She beckons me to continue. She wants all I have to offer. There's an incessant ringing in my ear. It won't stop. Why won't it stop? I need it to stop.

I wake in a cold sweat. For a moment, I'm confused about my surroundings. I'm not in the elevator with her. I'm in my bed, and it's 6:30 in the morning. Damn, it's time for me to go. I have a lot to do today, and I better get Jackson's girlfriend out of my head. It's not only dangerous, but reckless to want a woman I can't possibly have. I'm tripping anyway. If I had her, what would I want? A situation-ship? Nah, she's not the type. I can tell. This is probably a one-off. She should be easy enough to forget about once I'm buried in my work.

CHAPTER 9
Lauryn

I'm not sure I want to go out tonight. I'm having second thoughts about going to the club with Tonya. Tonya is my "take no prisoners" friend. She realizes Jackson and I aren't together anymore, so I'm pretty sure she wants to get my mind off it. I've been drinking a lot lately, and I doubt tonight will be any different. Getting drunk and dancing shouldn't be my remedy, but I don't care anymore. I want to let my body groove out a sense of abandonment. Plus, a little libation has never hurt anyone. I want to be numb. I don't want to experience this pain anymore.

If I'm going out, I want to be lowkey. Clubbing isn't what comes to mind as I envision lowkey fun. Tonya says, "I shouldn't mind getting some attention." I guess she has a point. I'm wearing my little black cocktail dress. It shows just enough skin to be dangerous. This dress perfectly accentuates my assets. My jewelry is simple, and I have on the perfect pair of stilettos to make my legs look amazing.

I'm not considered tall or short, so everything helps a little in the height department. I generally wear my makeup naturally, and tonight is no different. My sex appeal is on point, and I'm ready to go. I'm not driving. You already know I'm drinking tonight. I order an Uber, and it'll be here in three minutes. As I head to the lobby, I'm more like myself. More confident.

Prior to the elevator closing, Keith's voice yells out, "Hold the door, please!"

"Certainly," I utter in a barely audible voice, but I hold the door for him anyway. I could tell he's jogging to catch the elevator. His expression displays relief as he enters.

"Thanks for holding the door for me."

"No problem. What floor?"

"Garage."

"I didn't want to make any assumptions."

"Right." He glances at every angle of my body then comments. "You look really good. Are you going out solo tonight? No Jackson?"

"Thank you and no Jackson. Actually, we're not a couple anymore."

"Hmm, I guess one man's loss can be another man's treasure."

I blush, unsure of how to respond, "If you say so."

"Oh, I definitely say so. Where are you headed?"

"Blowing off some steam. It's been a while since I've been single. So, I'm hanging out with one of my sorors tonight." I could tell Keith wants to continue our conversation, but the elevator has arrived at my floor preventing us.

"Well, Lauryn, have a great night."

"You, too, Keith."

I cheese as I exit the elevator. I turn around to completely check him out as the doors close. He's fine and being in such close proximity to him makes my skin tingle. **(Objectifying is not a crime. It could be considered ill-mannered or wrong. Now, touching could be a crime and all the while be satisfying.)** I shake my head. I'm fresh off a breakup. I can't have another man on the brain, even if he is sexy as hell. When I arrive to the club, I text Tonya, "I'm here." She texts back I should meet her at the bar. This should be no surprise, but I want some liquid courage, like, right now. At the bar, this attractive man asks me if he could buy me a drink. He most definitely can. Lauryn is back in the saddle.

"What would you like to drink?" he asks.

"Vodka and cranberry please."

"I'm Hector. What's your name?"

"I'm Lauryn."

"A lovely name for a lovely lady," he winks at me. The drinks arrive, and we're vibing, so I don't ditch him.

"Thank you for the drink."

"The pleasure is all mine. Do you want to get a table or dance?"

"Table would be —"

"Hey, mama. It's so good you came. Who's your friend?" Tonya interrupts.

"Tonya, this is Hector. Hector…Tonya."

"Nice to meet you, Tonya. Can I get you a drink?"

"Likewise, Hector. Sure, I would love a Moscow mule," she winks as Hector shifts towards the bar to buy her drink. "Tonight, will be about forgetting a guy name Jackson. Hector may be a start for you, Lauryn."

"Actually, you shouldn't have mentioned his name."

"Asking about what happened is out of the question?"

"Yea, we're done, and we're not speaking about it."

"Cool. Enough said. Tonight, may you end up in someone's arms who will make you forget the name of the one I'm forbidden to mention."

"I'm not going home with anyone, Tonya."

"Yea, it couldn't hurt to suggest you live on the wild side."

Hector hands Tonya her drink, and we all chat for a little bit until Tonya finds someone who piques her interest.

"So, Lauryn what do you do?"

"I work in consulting." I didn't want to tell this perfect stranger I was in between jobs. It's not like it's his business. "What about you?"

"Really? Your work sounds so interesting. I've always been intrigued by consulting. I work at an architecture firm."

"Yours, too. What area of architecture do you work? Do you design?"

"I am. I work in landscape architecture. I work for a firm, and we do a lot of work for the city."

"Nice. I'm not knowledgeable about government work. I'm intrigued to learn more."

"Well, maybe we can discuss my career and stuff at another time. I don't want to bore you. What about you? Consulting seems like it's an exciting and powerful career from what I've seen on TV. Is your work like the show, *House of Lies?*"

"Believe me, it's definitely not. I never once had an exciting day like anyone from that show. I have worked in so many small towns where the most excitement for my week is coming home."

"Hmm, I thought it would be more interesting."

"Nah, it can be, but most of the time it's not interesting." The DJ starts playing some hype music, and I start bouncing to the beat.

"Hey, you want to dance?"

"Let's do it!"

Hector leads me to the dance floor. He's a mediocre dancer, but I don't let his lackluster dancing damper my mood. This club is playing all my favorite songs, and I sway my body to the rhythm of the music. I'm into the beats as I groove my hips from left to right. I didn't realize Hector doesn't want to dance anymore until he yells out he needs to rest and waves goodbye. I'm still in the mood to dance, so I don't mind him leaving. I dance solo for a little longer. Someone comes behind me, and I don't bother trying to figure out who it is. I dance with this stranger without uttering a word. I'm completely immersed into the music and having a great time when something suddenly changes my mood.

I turn around and Jackson is staring right at me. My great mood sours immediately. I continue to dance. I refuse to allow him to ruin another thing for me. I turn away from him and continue to groove to the music. I want to use this person's body standing less than six inches from me. I didn't see his face. My back faced him while we dance. He's turning out to be a perfect shield. He's not stumbling behind me, so I assume he's a decent dancer.

There were a few great music selections. Suddenly, the DJ decides to change the tempo of the music to a slow jam. I don't mind booty poppin' with this stranger, but I don't want to be close and slow dance with him. So, I say "adios" to my dance partner. After leaving the dance floor and recognizing Jackson, I need another drink. I hope he doesn't approach me. I don't want a repeat performance of our last encounter. I'm not in the mood. I gulp a double vodka cranberry like its water. I'm on to the next one as Tonya approaches me.

"Girl, I thought I saw Jackson."

"Yea, I saw him, too."

"No, girl, I thought so, but it's not him. He has a doppelgänger, girl."

"No way. What was he wearing?"

"I'm sure he had on a red shirt and some dark jeans."

"Yea, I think so, too. You aren't kidding. It's not him?"

"No, I went to confront him and once I got close to him, this guy wasn't Jackson. Up close and personal, you can tell the difference."

"Good. Now, back to my good time."

Someone tapped my shoulder, and I thought with dread it could be Jackson. Tonya could've been wrong about him. He could be here. If it's him, he's getting cursed out tonight. I turn around in a huff, but to my surprise it's Keith. My scowl turns into a sunny expression instantly.

"Hey Lauryn, I didn't realize we were headed to the same place."

"Hey, Keith," I breathe a sigh of relief.

Tonya whispers in my ear, "Who's he? He's fiiinnnee, girl."

"Keith, this is my sorority sister and friend, Tonya. Tonya, this is Keith. He lives on my floor."

"Nice to meet you, Keith. Are you single?" Tonya asks. Keith didn't seem interested in her, but I could tell he didn't want to be rude to Tonya. Why did jealousy over come me?

"I'm single, but I'm hoping we can finish our conversation from earlier, Lauryn."

"Sure, we can," I state.

"What are y'all drinking?"

"Vodka cranberry," I say.

"Moscow mule," Tonya replies.

I shouldn't have another drink, but this is the first time I have felt this chill since the breakup. This isn't like the drunken ice cream escapade I tell myself. Keith comes back with drinks for both Tonya and me. He asks me to dance, and we head to the dance floor. I'm starting to get mellow. They're playing my song. I want to sing out loud, but I'm not that drunk yet. I'm starting to feel really good.

We dance so well together, almost as good as I did with Jackson. Nope, not going to let him ruin this. In fact, this could be better than it was with Jackson. I take the opportunity to grind my ass against his crotch. I'm playing with fire, but I don't care. I'm more reckless than I've ever felt. If I want to twerk against a fine ass man, I will. Those drinks are really starting to hit me. We've been dancing for a while, and I need a break. He guides me to a table for a seat. My head is spinning, and I may be stumbling little bit. I have to pull this off. I will not be the drunk girl out and losing control.

"Are you okay, Lauryn?"

"I'm afraid I may have had too much to drink, Keith. It's been a bad month. No excuses, but, fuck, I lost my job and my boyfriend on the same day. Do you feel the room spinning, too?" **(Dammit! I'm saying too much. I'm losing control.)**

"No, I don't. It's not spinning for me. I'm so sorry about the job. I can't say I'm sorry about the boyfriend, though. You don't have to get into it if you don't want to."

"Fucking Jackson was cheating on me with my best friend. I found the asshole in my bed with her. My damn bed. Can you believe it? I lost my damn job, too. I hate the world, right now!!!!" **(Why in the hell am a victim of word vomit?)**

"Damn, that's fucked up."

"Right, isn't it?" I'm so upset. "I'm sorry. I shouldn't be complaining to you."

"No, whatever you need."

My head begins to get extremely heavy, and I'm swaying in my chair. "Whoa!" I exclaim. **(I'm not losing this battle. I've completely lost it.)**

He grabs me to ensure I don't fall. "I got you. Did you drive here?"

"No, I took an Uber. I should probably call one so I can make it back… uh…uh. Where am I going? Oh, yea home."

"No, sweetheart, I can't let you take a Uber. We live at the same place. I'll take you home."

"No, no you. I mean I'm not responsible for you. No, wrong. You're not responsi— ble for me. You maaayy wanttt to stayy." **(What am I saying to him? Am I that far gone?)**

"No, I'm cool. I can go. Let me take care of you."

"Damn, not only are you fine, but you are so, so umm, such a gentleman. Could I ride you tonight?" **(These are inside thoughts, Lauryn.)**

We stare into each other's eyes. They're mesmerizing. He stares at me like I'm the only one in his orbit. I lean in to kiss him. He doesn't withdraw. For a moment, we're both so into the kiss. He thrust his tongue into my mouth and swirl around my tongue. He's swallowing me up, and I'm letting him. We're playing tug of tongues, and it's so hot. He drags himself away as I want more. **(Well, maybe there isn't anything wrong with letting the inside out. Hmm, give me some more of those lips.)**

"I don't want to take advantage of you. You're in a vulnerable state. Plus, you've been drinking."

"I told you. You are a gentle mannn. You could have all of this, but you loook king out for me."

"Yea, I don't want our first time to go down like this."

"Our first time? What makes you sooo sure there will beeee a first tiiiime?"

"There will be. Just not now. You're not in a good place."

Tonya comes over to flirt with Keith some more, and my head is bobbing to what I don't have a clue. She gives me a look full of concern.

"Keith, how is my girl?"

"She's had too much to drink. I'm going to take her home since she's my neighbor."

"Thank you for looking out. Call me tomorrow, girl."

"OOO KKKKAAAYYY, I will." **(All conscious thoughts are gone to sleep it off I suppose. There is no reasoning with myself now. Just kill me already.)**

Keith assists me, and my head is suddenly extremely heavy. It's like it weighs a ton. I lean against him as he leads me out to his car. I stare at his package and wonder how he'll work it. If I were bolder, I would go after what I want. I've had enough liquid courage to go for it. What can it hurt?

"Keith," I bat my eyes at him unaware he won't be able to pay attention since he's driving.

"Yes, sweetheart?"

"Are you ah ah ah attracted to me?"

"We probably don't need to have this conversation while you're drunk."

"Draunkkk? Who's draunk?

"Well, sweetheart. I hate to break it to you, but you're drunk."

"I'm not sdrun druns. I mean drunnnnkkkkk." **(I'm one with the vodka now. Reasoninnng makes...me want to... what was I saying...Shit, I'm super drunk. Talking to myself and stuff.)**

"Ok, if you say so."

"U u u u don't believe me? Why, I'm not drunnnkkk? Am I drunk?"

"Sweetheart, you're drunk. Yes, I'm attracted to you."

"Well, I'm at at attracted to you, also."

"Are you?"

"Hell yea. What's not to be attracted to? You're fiinnnne as hellllll, handdddsome, and sexxxxyyy to boot. I'd be crazy not to be attracted to you. Plus, if I were as drunk as you claim that I am, would I admit any of this to you."

"Well, I wouldn't want you to be crazy," he smirks. "I guess that's the question of the hour. Would you admit any of this if you were sober?"

"Why notttt? I told you everything I found re- ree redeeming about you. You need me to repeat it for ya?"

"No, I think I got it."

"Oh, no," I start to sense my face is turning green, "Can you pull over? I may have an —," I cover my mouth, and he does it immediately. I push the door open fast and lose my stomach's contents like it's nobody's business. He reaches over to hold my hair back while I'm upchucking.

The next thing I know, my head is throbbing, and I'm waking in a strange bed. I regret drinking so much last night. I don't remember much past hitting on Keith at the club. How did I get home? Wait, am I still alive? Did I leave with a stranger? I'm afraid of what happened last night. I turn and find out who I'd gone to bed with. I'm in bed with Keith. He's still asleep. I glance at my clothes, and I'm surprised to find I'm wearing a t-shirt and it's not mine. Mortified, I'm planning to sneak out of here right now.

I can't figure out what happened between us. I suddenly remember how I threw myself at him last night, and it wasn't pretty. I practically told him to come and get it. Thirsty much. Did we have sex? I won't be able to face him if I did. I got to get out of here. I'm so embarrassed. I hope I can make it to my place without disturbing him. The next time I encounter him in the hallway I can pretend like this hadn't happened. I try to sneak out of the bed. Before I could, Keith grabs my arm.

"Morning, are you feeling better?"

"Umm, yeah. Thank you for the ride?" I say unsure if I should be thanking him for something else.

"Don't worry. You're not taking a walk of shame this morning. I had to change you out of your dress. You got sick again after we got here."

"Sick again? What do you mean by sick?"

"You were calling Earl."

"Oh, I'm so sorry." I'm so embarrassed.

"No worries. I was being a good neighbor."

"So, to be clear. We didn't, um, have sex, did we?"

He laughs, "No, we didn't. When we do have sex, you won't ask me if it happened."

"What makes you so sure we'll be having sex?"

"Yea. I'm pretty sure we will."

"You sound pretty confident."

"I am, but one can only hope, can't I?

"I guess. Thanks for everything."

"Anytime, you don't have to go."

"I'm gross right now. I definitely need to go."

"Well, don't be a stranger. I liked seeing a different side of you."

"Are you insinuating I'm not fun?"

"Never, mon amie."

"Well, good 'cause I would have words for you. Thanks again. Laters."

"I washed your clothes, so you don't have to worry about it."

"You're so sweet. Thank you."

He gets up to retrieve my dress from the dryer and hands it to me. I'm feeling rather yucky and don't want to wear my freshly laundered dress home. This t-shirt will have to do. Luckily, the t-shirt hung below my knees. I'm ashamed for getting sloppy drunk, and my fine neighbor witnessing it. Not a great early impression at all. I couldn't get back to my place fast enough. Jesse texts to inform me I have a delivery. I'm not expecting anything, and I'm curious about it. I can't get it until I shower. Assuming it's probably an Amazon order arriving early, there is no rush to get the package.

I go downstairs, and I'm pleasantly surprised. The delivery is two dozen red roses. I can't figure out who sent the roses since the card is anonymous. At first, I suspect Jackson could have sent them as his way to get back in with me, but the card didn't sound like him. The card read, "My darling, you'll shine again, and I'll await to see your brightness sparkle. As your lips join mine, I'll be the happiest man on earth." This doesn't sound like an apology to me. So, it's not Jackson. He sent me flowers plenty of times, but he never spoke like my parents. I'm displaying these beautiful roses. They didn't do anything to hurt me.

CHAPTER 10
Stranger

He's happy Lauryn's no longer wallowing in her home crying over a man who never deserved her. He hoped she loved the roses he sent. Every day will be a lot brighter with the beautiful roses for her to admire. She wore a little black dress to the club. It did things to him. He wanted to approach her the moment he spotted her, but some other guy beat him to it.

He hated she could laugh and chat with him, but he knew if he was patient she would land in his orbit. It took a little time, but his moment came as the guy, who happened to be a mediocre dancer, left her on the dance floor. This was his opportunity to seize the moment. She was dancing alone in her own world. The perfect song played as he joined her on the dance floor. He loved reggae, especially, "Murder She Wrote" by Chaka Demus & Pliers. This jam helped set the mood in the right direction. The staccato beats made her alert, and she began to wine like nobody's business. He was there for it, too. The off beats made him ecstatic. Watching her from afar, his body had a mind of its own. He moved towards her and matched her movements.

The way she rolled her hips turned him on, and he couldn't believe how close he was to his obsession, the one he loved. He drew her to him, and they rolled together in synchronicity. She grooved with him for the entire song, and he never wanted the moment to end. He'd been blessed with several more dances where he'd gyrated his hips and connected with hers. She wasn't facing him, so he couldn't gaze into her beautiful eyes. The music changed from the upbeat grooves to something slower, and this disappointed him. Something told him she loved her movements wild and uninhibited.

Even though he loved H.E.R.'s "Free," he figured she wouldn't want to face him and be close in each other's arms dancing to this song. The music came through and for a moment he could only hear the lyrics. He imagined her in his arms as he pulled her close while his hand roamed down to clutch her bountiful ass. He would caress it as he grinded against her. He stared into her eyes and began kissing her. The way her tongue felt against his made him want to suck more than her tongue. He had to snap out of it because he wanted to feel her in his arms for real.

He wanted to ask her to dance. Even though, his gut said she would decline the offer, he settled on asking her to sit with him, so they could get acquainted with each other. He didn't get a chance. She thanked him for the dance and left to join her friend. He definitely lost his opportunity to take things to the next level with her, but nothing could make him stop smiling from remembering how she felt as she grinded on him. He relived the dance with her on a continuous loop. This was by far the best memory he had with Lauryn to date.

He was elated if only for a moment. He searched around the club, but no one could come close to his Lauryn, and no one did what she did for him. Her beauty transcended every woman he had ever seen. She was brilliant, compassionate, kind, beautiful, and sexy as hell. What else could he want in the woman he desired? He suddenly had to unload his bladder and went to the bathroom. It wasn't deserted in there, and this was something he wasn't comfortable with normally. He didn't want his compulsive obsessive behavior about bathrooms to stop him from enjoying this night. Plodding towards the stall, he told himself to act normal. The guy in the next stall did something he considered unacceptable.

"What's up, man?" the stall guy asked the stranger as he began to unzip his pants to handle his business.

"Yea, what's good?" he responded keeping his face forward. He could feel the guy staring at him. He wasn't homophobic or anything, but wasn't this considered rude? There was still a code about bathroom etiquette, wasn't there? He gawked at the stall guy with an annoyed expression.

"Did you think I was hitting on you?" the stall guy asked with a laugh. "Paranoid much, man? Nah, I was about to mention you have tissue on your shoe. Wouldn't want you to embarrass yourself rolling back into the club. I have standards regarding who I hit on, and it's never in the bathroom."

"Sorry, man. I have this thing about bathrooms. No disrespect intended."

"None taken, but you should really take care of the tissue," the stall guy smirked at him while pointing at his shoe.

He couldn't be certain how to judge the exchange. He removed the tissue since the stall guy wasn't lying. His mind went back to Lauryn and their hypnotic dance. His goofy grin returned to his face as he left the bathroom. Lauryn could be his one day. He immediately saw Melanie and his mood changed drastically.

"Hey there, baby. You're here. What a surprise!" Melanie exclaimed.

"I'm not your baby, and why do you keep insisting on this?"

"You will always be my baby (in my Mariah Carey voice). Don't forget it! You can never forget your first love, baby, and I'm yours." He was so annoyed with her, but he didn't want to continue this conversation. Only he knew how dangerous Melanie could be if she was provoked. He didn't want her interfering with him and Lauryn.

"What do you want, Melanie?"

"To congratulate you. You seem to have gotten closer to your girl tonight."

"I'm surprised you would be happy."

"Why wouldn't I be happy?" she smirked at him.

"'Cause you never are."

"I'll always be your first and only love so it doesn't matter to me if you play around a little. I'm the only one you'll ever have this type of connection with. No, this little infatuation of yours doesn't bother me at all. You'll come back to mama."

"Love? Is this what you call what happened between us?"

"Of course, my love. You're everything to me, but I'm not worried about this little distraction of yours. You'll always be mine."

"I'm not yours. I never was, and I'll never be with you. You mistake what happened as love, but I don't. We won't ever mean anything to each other."

"Well," she glanced out in the club. "Your victory didn't last long. Your girl is leaving with someone else."

He didn't believe Melanie. She tended to lie. He watched as Lauryn followed a guy out of the club. He couldn't get to her in time to stop it. It hurt him to imagine her with someone else. How could she be leaving with anyone other than him? Couldn't she understand how he felt about her?

"So, your point, Melanie?" He didn't want her to figure out this bothered him.

"You're not what she wants, baby boy. You need to up your game if you want a woman like Lauryn Davidson to get with you."

He was extremely jealous, and he started to see red. As much as Melanie's words rang true, he couldn't admit it to her. She's this bad memory who never went away. Lauryn would acknowledge him, she would grow to love him, and he would be the happiest man alive. He could make her happy, and respect her like she deserved. He was consumed with thoughts of her, and he couldn't understand why she would leave with some guy who seemed like he had a different woman for breakfast, lunch, and dinner.

She wouldn't have to worry about him cheating or disrespecting her. He understood her need to succeed in her career, and he wanted everything for her. He would even pull a few strings for her work achievements, but he had a gumption she wouldn't appreciate his interference. He could tell she wanted to earn all her accolades.

He didn't like the way the guy was holding Lauryn as he led her out of the club. The way she ogled the guy unnerved him, too. How could he show her he was the one for her? How could he demonstrate this guy would never make her happy? He would persevere and be the man she not only wanted but needed and desired.

He hasn't waited patiently for nothing. He'll approach her and declare his love for her. He'll get out of the shadows and show her he was the man she needed. He wanted the meeting to be perfect. She needed to come face-to-face with him and fall in love immediately. He fell in love with her at first sight. Her angelic aura did so many things to him, and he wanted a taste for himself.

"I loved dancing with you tonight," he imagined Lauryn admitting to him.

"I'm glad you turned around. We belong together, right?"

"Of course, we do. Don't be silly."

"I'm glad you understand."

"What do you mean?"

"I've liked you for some time. I've been hoping for my chance."

"You always had a chance with me. You only needed to break out of your shell. I hoped you were interested in me. You never made a move, so I wasn't certain."

"Why don't I make one now?"

"Why don't you?"

He gently moved her closer to him and raised her chin so he could have the best access to kissing her. He didn't want to be interrupted as he finally kissed her for the first time. She melted in his mouth, and she tasted like his favorite food, mango. He wanted to take things to the next level, but they were in a public place. Plus, he didn't want to rush things with her. He would have a lifetime to make love to her endlessly.

"Mmm, I love kissing you," she moaned.

"I want to show you so much more. Let's get out of here."

"I'll go anywhere with you."

"I'm glad to hear it. I want to take you home and make love to you."

"Well, you're in luck because that's what I want, too."

"Let's get out of here."

"Lead the way."

He ushers her out to take her somewhere private for what he wanted to do to her. He didn't want to claim her completely until he expressed just how deeply he felt about her. She had to know she wasn't some fleeting affair for him. She meant everything to him, and tonight she would know just how much.

"I love you," he said.

"Don't you think it's too soon?"

"I loved you at first sight. So, no, it's not too soon. I want a life with you." *He lowered to the ground on bended knee and began speaking, "I realize we haven't been together long, but I don't want to waste another second. I want you to be my wife. I want you to mother my children. I want to spend every day worshipping you and making you forget the bad times you've had."*

"What are you doing?"

"I'm asking you to marry me. What does it seem like?"

"I didn't realize you would want that yet. We don't know each other well enough. This is rash, spontaneous —"

"And absolutely crazy. Yes, it is, but nothing will change between us next week, next month, next year...forever."

"You've changed my life. I thought it was too soon to have such strong emotions about you. Of course, I'll marry you, and I love you, too."

She jumped into his arms, and they kissed like they were being suctioned. He placed the diamond solitaire on her ring finger and beamed enthusiastically. She's gonna be his wife. He would have everything he's always wanted. He would have love, happiness, and money. He owed it all to Lauryn. She completed him and made him the happiest man on earth.

Stuck in his daydream, he didn't notice someone nearly knocked him off his feet until they accidently bumped into him. At least, he thought it had been an accident. It was the bathroom stall guy who spoke to him previously, but currently scowled at him. Maybe he stepped on his foot earlier or something. He started to brush it off as an accident and apologize just in case, so he could be on his way. This club had lost its appeal for him anyway.

"Sorry, man," he said, "I didn't see you there."

"Hmm," he glared at him with a curious expression. "Now, this is what I call hitting on you," he winked at the stranger.

"What? I'm confused. What's going on, man?"

"I wouldn't ever hit on a man in an intimate place such as a bathroom. You were vulnerable there. I thought you were cute, but, hey, I'm not a pervert. So, I waited until the right moment."

"Well, I'm not interested. I'm sorry. I'm not gay."

"Something tells me you could be."

"You're mistaken. The object of my affection is no longer here, so I'm leaving," he started to leave, but he wanted to get why this guy thought he could be gay. "What makes you wonder if I could be gay?"

"Ha, ha. I knew I would get you with that. My gaydar rarely lies. Maybe, you're in denial."

"No, I'm not homophobic. I'm not interested in the same sex."

"Ok, I could be wrong. Maybe, it's wishful thinking." The stall guy zeroed in on him like he hadn't faced his reality and wanted to remain in denial about what he wanted.

"Sorry. If this is any consolation for you, if men were my preference you wouldn't be a bad choice. Um, sorry, what's your name?"

"Ricky, glad to make your acquaintance," he says formerly as he does a little strange bow. "And you are?"

CHAPTER 11
Lauryn

STU kept their word and paid me for my last weeks of work plus my full severance package within two weeks of my departure if you even want to call it a departure. I didn't have to make any rash decisions regarding employment. Several months ago, I found a job at Food Will unexpectantly. I didn't need the money, but I desperately needed to figure out what to do with my days. Moping around would only lead to a deep depression if I'm not careful.

I'm a process improvement manager. I manage a whopping three people, but it's rewarding work. I've tried hard to get my life back on track following the blows I took. I'm developing the organizational processes for Food Will. I don't think this will be long-term at all. My severance is giving me some breathing room to figure out what comes next in my career. Not only am I working, but I'm also able to volunteer.

The renovation is nearly complete. I'm still waiting on a few items to arrive. I'm doing this project in phases. It's taken longer than I initially wanted, but I've been dealing with a whole lot. The reno didn't require any structural changes. It only needed cosmetic ones. I want the place to be just about me and flush out the past. Now, I'm happy to say I love my home. I sold my bedroom furniture to a great guy, Scott, whose getting married soon. The furniture is only a year old. Scott and his fiancée gain a virtually new great bedroom set. I'm happy they'll have quality furniture for a fraction of the cost.

A funny thing happened as I placed the furniture on the Neighborhood app for sale. I received two competing yet serious offers, and two others were nonsense. One of the offers screamed suspicious and piqued as a red flag. The interested party wanted to pay for my furniture with a check. Online. Who goes online to buy anything with a check? I refused his payment method and tried to kill the transaction. He reacted by calling me a bitch. He'd been extremely hostile. This was another warning sign showing this dude wanted to do me some harm. He requested we meet at night for the transaction. This was absolutely a scam. I'm glad I didn't meet this potential Craig's List killer.

I guess he thought he found a sucker in me. Who wrote checks these days anyway? I never heard of anyone going online expecting someone to accept a check. This reminded me of the Nigerian check con. Nothing about this made sense. I decided to do a pseudo internet search of the guy's name to find out what I could about him. I found three people with his name in Nashville. One appeared super suspicious, and my Spidey senses went wild with mistrust. I'm glad I trusted my instincts to reject the deal. How dare the Nigerian con artist call me out my name? He doesn't know me. I guess my life hasn't been exciting since the breakup. The highlights here and there sustain me.

On a positive note, I'm working. The Food Will opportunity came out of nowhere. I happened to be there volunteering one day. It's my belief one should be of service, and volunteering has always been a way for me to fulfill my purpose. During my struggles, it helped to have a reason to get out of bed. I find myself reminiscing on how all this started, and it brings a half smile to my face. Arriving at the Food Will, a man named Jim met me in the lobby area. Jim showed me around to begin my volunteer journey there. Jim's an older white man who didn't play.

"Hello, my name is Jim. We need sorters today," he states eyeing me suspiciously, "Do you think you can handle it?"

"Yes, I'll be happy to serve in any capacity you need."

"Ok, great. We've had a lot of young people come here for college credit. They tend not to do much. They want us to sign their acknowledgment form stating they worked for the day. I hope you'll be different than other kids your age."

Flattered, I responded, "Jim, don't worry. I'm here to help. I graduated from college years ago."

"Oh, really?" he displayed a very shocked expression, "I could swear you were a freshman in college or something."

"No, I'm not. Thank you for the compliment."

"No, thank you for your willingness to help out," he mentions while pointing to an aisle not far away from us as he continued to speak, "Go to aisle K, and they will instruct you on what they need today. How long can you stay?"

"I can stay as long as I'm needed."

"Great," he smiled, "we can use your help all day."

Spending the day organizing and sorting can goods really allows me to put my consulting skills to use. I suggested an inventory management improvement system to help aid staff as they gathered food to provide to those in need. At first, I didn't want to jump in right away with my suggestions. People tend not to accept suggestions right off the bat. This is something I learned in my years consulting.

Kathy, the lady I'm helping, mentions Food Will needs someone like me. I didn't initially want to consider working at Food Will. It didn't hurt to learn more about the opportunity. They're searching for someone to streamline their operations, and this falls directly in my wheelhouse. I may apply for the job without any expectations of getting it. I'm eerily excited with the possibility of what may come. I never imagined I would work at a nonprofit. The interview process happens pretty quickly. I'm surprised at how fast they're moving to fill this position. I'm happy to reveal I accepted their offer. I'm now fulfilled with the work, and I'm making a difference. I know for sure I made the right choice.

It's been a long day, but I'm content with what I've accomplished. I'm calling it quits and heading home. As soon as I come through my door, my phone vibrates. It's a text from Jesse alerting me I have a delivery downstairs. I head to pick my order from Amazon. I've been waiting on for days. This is a very special delivery. Yes, I love Amazon. Today I'm waiting on some stuff for the house as well as something to relieve my sexual tension since I've been working Idris Vy too hard. My vibrator has had a long journey, and now it's time for a new one. I'm also expecting some knick-knacks for the house from a furniture outlet store order, too. I bought a few new pieces for the change in the house. I go to speak with Jesse.

"Hey Jesse, what do you have for me today?"

"Lauryn, hello. You actually have quite a bit. You have flowers again and an order from Amazon and another package. Let me get someone to help you get it upstairs."

"Ok, thank you, Jesse."

I'm followed upstairs closely by an employee I don't recognize. He must be a new hire. He places the boxes neatly by the door. He gazes at me to indicate he isn't shy about admiring me. I'm not comfortable with the way his gaze roams my body. I want him to get out fast. I'm fairly certain nothing will happen to me. I'm not comfortable being molested by his stare. I hurry to find some tip money in my purse to get rid of this guy quickly. I doubt this guy will risk his job by doing something to me. I don't like the way he's staring at me.

He accepts the tip money, smiles, and thanks me. He doesn't appear to be in a hurry to leave. I have to create an excuse to get him out of my house. I almost forgot about the roses adorning my table after I success-fully got rid of the unwanted guest.

This time, I have three dozen pink roses and they're beautiful. Now, I'm wondering about who could be sending me roses. I can't believe I've been receiving them for months now. If it's Jackson, I would've heard from him by now. He isn't one to sit around and not act. He would've found a way to insinuate himself into my life again. It's probably not him, but who could have sent them? I'm in the dark. The only message I have is in the card, and it reads, "Beautiful roses to make you smile." I wonder if it could be Keith.

I haven't shared the fact I lost my job or the reason why Jackson and I aren't together with anyone other than Keith. I don't know why I told him. I guess there's something about him. He makes me want to bare my soul. I have to shake this off. It's not like I'm wanting some deep and meaningful relationship with anyone right now.

I haven't told my parents anything at all. I've been avoiding their calls, especially from my mom. She could figure out if anything is wrong with me in an instant. I couldn't bear it if I shamed or embarrassed her. I've let her down. As much as I wanted to put off the conversation with her, I can't avoid her any longer. My text messages stating I'm in a meeting aren't working. She has started calling me at off times like right now. I have no choice but to answer the call. I'm dreading this conversation. I don't know how to break the bad news to them. My mom is FaceTiming me. There's absolutely no way to avoid her now.

"Hello, Mama."

"Hey, baby girl. It's been a long time. Are you ok?"

"I'm doing ok, Mama. How are you? How's Dad?"

"We're good. You've been avoiding us. You don't sound or look like you're ok. Tell me what's wrong, baby girl." **(This is what I mean. This is exactly why I've been avoiding this call.)**

"Can't fool you and your mother's intuition," I groan.

"Baby, what's wrong?" Mama asks sincerely.

"I dreaded telling you and Daddy my news fearing you would be disappointed in me."

"Why would you ever think Dad and I would be disappointed?"

"Well…I was laid-off from the firm."

"What? How could this be? You were one of the best there. Didn't they feature you as the "it" consultant/project manager in the newsletter? Didn't you win consultant of the year last year?"

"I know. Apparently, the firm is having some financial issues, but not with any of my accounts. They're eliminating all the senior project manager positions, and they assumed I wouldn't accept a demotion. They were right; I wouldn't."

"It's simply poor management."

"You're right. They've wasted more money than I can count since I joined the firm."

"You'll land something soon, baby girl."

"I have, Mama. I'm working for Food Will as a PI manager."

"Great, baby. Is this long-term?"

"Probably not. There aren't any systems in place, and I can help them implement the right ones for sustainability. I'm happy with what I'll accomplish."

"Look at my baby doing what you do best."

"Thanks, Mama. I need your confidence right about now."

Mama, known by most as Carolyn Rose Stanley Davidson, is the chief financial officer at a top hedge fund in Atlanta. She is a no-nonsense executive whose business acumen rivals anyone in the industry. Living up to Carolyn has always been my goal. She's a trailblazer, and someone who I aim to emulate every chance I get. Carolyn would never let anyone lay her off. She would've predicted this coming and left the company two years prior fully understanding the firm didn't appreciate her contributions. I always aspired to be like her in the corporate world. Now, I'm only a disappointment.

One of the reasons I've been extremely driven to succeed is my mother. She broke so many barriers and glass ceilings to succeed in her own career. I want to be just as accomplished. My parents are one of the "Who's Who" in Atlanta. I didn't want people to assume my career is a handout I didn't deserve. I created a path for myself in Nashville, TN. After graduating from Nashville Tennessee University (better known as NTU), I considered moving back to Atlanta, but the opportunity at STU turned out to be what I needed. I could go out and prove I'm just as driven as Carolyn and charismatic as Marcus while maintaining who I truly am.

Marcus Andre Davidson is my father, and there isn't a person alive he can't charm. Mama couldn't stay mad at Daddy. He would charm her to forget all about her anger. Well, Daddy is best at finessing others with it. He could charm a lifeless lump back to life. He's a partner at a top prestigious law firm where his specialty is sports management. He serves as an agent for several pro basketball, football, and baseball players. He even represents some hockey players and women, too, in a variety of sports. Imagine that.

Early on, I became a huge fan of football, basketball, and baseball. Dad and I would go to all the home games in Atlanta. I missed catching games with him in person. With my past work schedule, I would Face-Time Dad simultaneously as a huge play took place to ask if he saw it. Of course, my dad saw the play. My parents served as huge examples of what winning looked like. I wanted to have some time to sulk before admitting my failure. Well, I guess it's been a few months, and I've dodged them enough.

Carolyn grew up in Atlanta, GA, and Marcus grew up in Chattanooga, TN. Both of my parents are proud NTU graduates. NTU is a historical black college and university (HBCU). My family has attended the university since its founding in 1912. One of the reasons I chose NTU, outside of its rich legacy, is the fact that NTU means a lot to our family. Each year, we make sure to attend the homecoming game and donate generously. My parents would come to town and make sure they were a part of the festivities with their friends, sorority, and fraternity members.

Of course, I pledged the same illustrious sorority as my mom and grandmother. I'm what's considered a "legacy," and I'm proud of it. My mom graduated with an accounting degree, and my father received his degree in business administration. My mom went on to get her MBA from a prestigious graduate school in Atlanta. My father in turn studied law at the same prestigious law school. My mom and dad fell completely in love with each other during their sophomore year at NTU, and they've been together since college. The example of love I saw daily is the ideal I want in my life. It's hard to believe I wasted nearly three good years on the absolute wrong person. I guess everything in life is a lesson on what not to do.

My dad is a sports agent first and lawyer second. When you learn about players landing those phenomenal contracts, my dad negotiates to make those types of deals every day. I've been lucky enough to observe him in action, and he helped me learn the power of true negotiation. Dad has a true finesse about the way he caters and coddles his players, but he portrays a lion in its den dealing with the owners and management in the franchise.

Dad began his law career working in an entirely different field. He tried a stint as a defense attorney and soon learned it didn't fit what he wanted in a career. He had no desire to keep the guilty out of prison. He didn't imagine he would eventually work in sports, something he loved for as long as he could remember. He's best at what he loves acting as a player's council and agent. This career has served him well. It's great to witness him be so fulfilled in his chosen path. I wish I had the same luck, but I must crawl before I can walk.

On top of my love life being in shambles, I can't help feeling like I'm a failure. My parents were married at my age. Mom achieved MVP type honors in her career. After receiving her MBA and becoming a certified accountant, she started her career with a small firm which didn't offer much growth and career advancement. Mom didn't let obstacles get in her way. Her drive and ambition paved her career from analyst to principal accountant for an investment group. She advanced into the senior vice president role at a major retailer. For the last decade, she has served as the chief financial officer for different corporations. She hoped to retire last year, and she gave it a try for a short time. Early retirement isn't an option for her. Plus, she's way too young to retire. She found retirement too boring within a few months. She wanted to work at a somewhat slower pace. So, she took a job with a hedge fund company. She stated this is the closest she'll probably ever get to retirement.

My mom made moves from companies at the right time. I wish I possessed a tiny bit of her intuition. As a child, I didn't understand at the time, but I witnessed my mom leaving an organization she loved completely without any hesitation. We learned later her former organization was completely engulfed in the Sarbanes-Oxley scandal. Since my mom worked in the accounting division of the company, she'd noticed something fishy with the cash flow and revenue. She questioned some of those in leadership, and they tried to give her some BS run-around. Mama didn't accept their excuses. She researched behind the scenes since things around the firm were becoming too suspicious. America learned two years later how her former company defrauded the American people. My mom didn't get caught in their misdeeds. I secretly believe she blew the whistle and is a true hero. I remember mama always making the right career decisions, and I've always admired her. Then, my mom mentions something to me about Jackson. Goodness, I don't want to speak his name. Since my mom has no idea what happened, I brave through it. Plus, Mama has always been super supportive of me. She won't judge me at all about him I'm certain.

"Hmm? Mama, I missed it. Can you repeat what you said?" I ask distractedly.

"Has Jackson been lifting your mood?" This is the only other subject I don't want to broach.

"This is difficult to talk about for me. Jackson and I ended our relationship."

"What? Really? When did you end things? What happened?"

"It's been a few months," I reply slowly, "we don't want the same things anymore."

"Baby girl, maybe you can work it out. I'm sure all the traveling placed a toll on both of you."

"Mama, we've simply grown apart. Can we drop this for now?"

"Of course, baby girl. I don't want to upset you."

"You're not. I have a lot going on right now."

I feel bad for not telling my mom the whole truth. What good would it do to discuss Jackson? One day, I'll probably confide in her. Of course, she'll be on my side. Mama always has my back.

"What's going on with you guys these days? I would rather not focus on me anymore please."

"Same ole same. You know, we're both working a lot. We've been trying to do more relaxing these days. I started golfing with your dad. It's bringing us closer. We've begun taking dance classes, too."

"How did you get Dad to agree to dance classes?"

"I'm golfing now. He has to give me something."

"Clever, Mama. How's it going?"

"Good. We're doing the Argentine Tango now. What a romantic dance!"

"Do I want to hear any more about this, Mama?"

"It's sexy, baby girl."

"Yea, no TMI, Mama! TMI!"

"Why, baby girl? It's only about learning a super sexy dance with your father I can use to my advantage during our alone time if you know what I mean," she winks.

"In case you didn't quite understand this, Mama, taking advantage of your alone time 'wink' is TMI. I don't want to imagine what you and Daddy do in alone time, Mother."

"What's the tone about, baby girl? You know your dad and I are sexual beings, young lady."

"This is exactly what I mean, too much information, Mom. I can't with you and eww. You, Daddy, and sex, no!!!"

"Well, I'm not sharing any of it with you. Somethings are better kept private, my dear. I have to keep things hot."

"Oh, dear. What am I going to do with you, Mama?"

"I'm keeping you on your toes, my dear."

"Ok, you've succeeded."

"Why don't you come home? We miss you. It's been too long since you were last here."

"I'll come home soon, but I need to get some stuff done here. I miss you and Daddy so much. I love you."

"I love you too, baby girl. I understand you need some time to deal with things. You've always been this independent, young woman. I hope you know Daddy and I will support you. This is a horrible time for you. It's gonna be okay, baby girl. Stay positive, and I'll touch base with you in a few days."

Speaking to my mom has made me perk up somewhat. She always has a way of making things better. She isn't slick. She mentioned the inuendo about her sex life to make me not dwell on my troubles. I'm close to my parents, and I miss them so much. I never knew how much a good conversation with my mom would do for my psyche until I spoke with her. I'm making a mental note to never avoid my parents during difficult times again. They're never judgmental, and they're the most supportive people in my life. They always have been, and I have no doubt they always will be.

It took some time to get into a rhythm at work. As you can imagine, working at Food Will is a whole lot slower environment than working in consulting. I didn't realize nonprofits had so many challenges. This is probably one of the most challenging things I've had to face in my professional career. As a consultant, we demanded results. It's not unheard of for STU to strongly suggest people getting fired if they didn't meet the expectations the firm set. Companies had to enforce what we strongly recommended, or the company would fail. STU pretty much had the license to do what they wanted.

Working at an organization where I'm a contributing member is refreshing. I have a vested interest in the success of this organization. It isn't about my former company, STU, making too much money, and then moving onto the next project to start the whole cycle again. Learning how to adjust to this paradigm has been one of my biggest challenges I've faced working in this new environment. I appreciate the growth and valuable lessons I've learned from this experience. The foundational items I learned at STU will allow me to be successful here. The soft skills and diplomacy I'm gaining here will last a lifetime. Now, things are in sync with the job. I know what is expected, and I certainly deliver beyond those expectations.

My job at Food Will has been more of an accidental opportunity. The rat race of consulting no longer worked for me. Food Will had many immediate needs including a better logistic and supply management system. The leadership didn't have a clue how to achieve this insurmountable obstacle. Lucky for them, I knew what they needed, and I know how to get them across the finish line. Convincing them to take a chance on me came with its own challenges. They were convinced I couldn't have the right solutions since I could only be a kid straight out of college with lofty dreams. In order to convince them I'm the right fit, I offered a crazy option. I told them I would work for a one month on a trial basis unpaid to prove my value. If things didn't work out, we could go our separate ways. Well, things certainly worked out since I still work there.

Now it's time to visit my parents. I've been away too long. I actually miss them a whole lot. Being aware they're not going to pity me or be disappointed in me has helped me make this journey now. I have an overwhelming sense of guilt since I've been putting off speaking to them and not visiting. I've been letting my unfounded fear about my career failure cloud how my parents would perceive me. I should've known my parents wouldn't be anything other than supportive. They supported me through everything in my life, and this blip is no different.

If I'm being honest with myself, I would admit my reluctance to speak to my parents had nothing to do with them and how they would react. It had to do with the shame I felt about losing my job and my boyfriend. I put a lot of effort into both, and it didn't workout. Knowing I only transferred my own reactions onto my parent's hypothetical reaction has made me come to grips with things. I'm being too hard on myself, and it's time I try a different approach.

As I drive to my parent's home in Atlanta, I acknowledge this is just what I need. My mom and I will go to a spa for the day to relax. Dad and I will go to a Hawks game, and we will also play a round of golf. As much as I hate to admit this, my life is a whole lot better in Atlanta. At least, it's right now. I will only focus on how relaxed I'll be following my two-hour massage. Yea, no guilt here, I'm getting a two-hour massage. My parents are full of life, and it's going to be great going home. I hope they won't try to cram too much into this visit.

I'm relaxed and feeling 100 percent better following my relaxing day at the spa. I didn't realize my stress extended so deep into every muscle connected to my head. Tension like that can't be any good for you. I'm in a trance just as I realize a blast from the past is calling my name. I turn my head abruptly to catch a glimpse of someone who'd been a friend and sister. It's Isaac's sister, Isabella or Bella as most people called her. Even though Isaac and I didn't start dating until we were in college, I knew him forever. Considering his sister is my frenemy, I'm surprised we dated at all in college. His sister and I were best friends from middle school through high school. It would've been okay if we simply drifted apart like a lot of friends do as they got older.

Bella pretended to be my friend while trash talking about me to girls and guys alike. She tried to give me a reputation for sleeping around, which couldn't be further from the truth since my hymen hadn't been detached. It turned out I didn't grasp she betrayed me before I shared all of my secrets with her. She tried to arrange for me to be drugged and raped. Luckily, she didn't succeed with the evil plot. I don't know why she hates me. I refuse to engage with her now. It's bad enough I endured her back in the day with Isaac. I don't have any patience for her ignorant ass. I won't tolerate her anymore since Isaac and I are history.

"Lauryn," she annunciates my name dragging out the letter "n." "How are you, girl? How long has it been? Too long."

"Bella," I reply as I nod my head towards her.

"There is no need to be salty, Lauryn. Those unfortunate incidents happened and are done. You keep bringing up old stuff. Can't you just let it go?"

"What do you want, Bella?" Since I didn't bring up anything, she must feel guilty like the rat she is. I hope she moves on. I have absolutely no tolerance for her today.

"Have you spoken with Isaac lately?" she smirks. She's overjoyed we aren't together.

"Nope, I haven't in years. Is he doing, okay?"

"Ha, years. He's great. Everyone in my family is doing great."

"Good. It's been nice running into you, Bella." I attempt to walk away.

"No, no. Not until we get a picture together first," she tugs me in a bear hug for a selfie.

I'm shocked and my face shows it, but the picture could have been worse. I smile at her and dislodge her arm from my upper body. I turn to leave without giving her a second glance as I hoped to have dodged a bullet. I guess I should've known she'd post our picture on social media with the note stating, "Look at what the cat drug out." Yea, I still strongly dislike Bella, and I hope I don't bump into her anymore. Following high school, she stayed in Atlanta to go to school, and we didn't cross paths until Isaac and I started dating. I couldn't avoid her and date her brother. He often thought I was being ridiculous. I could be holding onto high school stuff against his sister. Well, he never witnessed how evil she could be. I wouldn't be surprised if she put the bug in his ear to end things with me. His sister is the devil.

Sometimes, I wonder if she'd been the catalyst to him declaring we didn't work anymore. He adored her, and she could do no wrong. He would act as if I were paranoid and mistook Bella's intentions. It's only so much of this woman I can stomach. Plus, Bella and I were close once. You know, wear the same clothes, and get the same hairstyle close. She's the perfect shade of dark chocolate, and her beauty couldn't be denied. I still don't know what happened. She betrayed my trust, and I'll never trust her again to be in my inner circle.

Did I forgive her? Yes, I certainly did. Not for her sake. I did it for mine. It took some time and maturity to get there, but I did. She's still the same insecure girl who lives to shame others in order to be important. At least, in her own mind, and it's extremely sad. She hasn't matured any since high school. Going to the high school reunion in two years will be fun. Not! I'm probably going to skip it. It's not like I'm still cool with anyone from high school, and I don't want to pretend to care about how the likes of Bella and Stacy (Bella's new sidekick once we were no longer friends) are doing these days. I hadn't gotten far enough away from Bella's presence, and I dread turning back to the shrill of her voice.

"Lauryn, you shouldn't be such a stranger. I know you and my brother aren't together anymore. I remember how close we were."

"Say what?" I ask bewildered, "We drifted apart prior to Isaac and I becoming a couple."

"You're not still upset about the pettiness in high school. It's kid stuff. Any who, don't be a stranger. Something will come out about our high school reunion in a few months. It's gonna be lit," she waves at me like a pageant contestant before strolling away. Our ten-year reunion is two years from now. What's the rush?

CHAPTER 12
Lauryn

In my collection of mail, the invitation from Bella for the high school reunion prominently stands out. I didn't get a chance to go through everything yesterday. Well, let's be honest I didn't want to sift through piles of junk mail trying to sale me on new windows and stuff. I hadn't noticed the invitation until now. Who sends out cardstock invites anymore? I guess she's unaware of Evite. Aren't we trying to save the environment? No, we're talking about Bella. She probably doesn't even know what climate change is. I guess the impression I'm painting is she lacks intellectual competence. She's not the sharpest tool in the shed.

Instead of throwing the save the date straight into the garbage, I regrettably open it. I'm not surprised how beautiful and well-designed it is. Bella is a good hostess. I'll give her credit. They're having this thing Memorial Day weekend two years away. She's so dramatic. It's not like this is the save the date for her wedding. She's asking for a commitment with the save the date. She also includes if things change with our plans, we'll need to contact her within six months prior to the event to avoid additional charges. What the what?! Why am I not surprised she'll incorporate a cancellation fee along with making the registration fee non-refundable?

I'm fairly confident I'll be skipping it. Anyone I've wanted to have a relationship with from high school, I have one with. Plus, I can't deal with Bella and all of her bullshit. She's fake as those popular reality stars' asses. You know as well as I do white girls don't naturally have badonkadonk. I have to get out of here to work out. I generally do it early in the morning. It helps to center me for the day.

Since the upheaval of my life, exercising and eating right have become my only constants. I don't want to get too far off track from my normal routine. I rush back home to shower. I change into a simple A-line dress and some espadrilles for work. I apply some light makeup to my face and fix my hair. I grab a smoothie for breakfast and my phone rings. It's Kim, my old friend from STU, calling to check-in on me.

"Hi Lauryn, how are you doing?" she asks.

"Hello, Kim. I'm doing ok considering everything."

"Girl, I know. I can't believe STU got rid of you. It doesn't make any sense."

"Yea, some things happen for a reason. Maybe this is for the best."

"Yea, it's completely batshit here now. They're laying off people left and right. Anyway, I called to invite you to lunch today. There is too much to discuss, and I would rather not do it over the phone."

"Sure. Where would you like to meet for lunch?"

"What about the Italian place near STU?"

"Sounds good. Let's meet about noon."

"Sure."

As much as I would like to lunch with Kim, I don't want to get sucked into STU's gossip. There have been numerous scandals through the years, and I can't simply enjoy anyone's misfortune at all…not even STU's. I want to forget my time there. Should I tell Kim I'm super busy? I like Kim, and I do wonder how she's doing. My job is flexible and taking a long lunch isn't unreasonable. I never do, but it doesn't mean I can't.

No, avoiding Kim wouldn't be right. Kim has been a great friend, and I need to support her through all of this. The time has flown by this morning. I've been extremely busy processing improvement requests, and I didn't realize how late it had gotten. I glance at my watch and decide I should get going to meet Kim. As I head out of the office, my phone vibrates.

"Kim better not be cancelling lunch," I whisper. I reach for my phone out of my purse, and I'm surprised Kennedy's calling. We haven't chatted in a minute.

"Hey there," I answer.

"Hey, girl. How are you?" Kennedy asks.

"I'm doing well. How are you?"

"I'm good, girl. I ran into Asia, and she told me y'all had a fight."

"Is that right? Did she mention why we had a falling out?"

"I don't know the details. I figured you'd work it out."

(I knew Asia wouldn't admit to her sexual relationship with Jackson.)

"Well, we won't be working things out this time," I declare emphatically.

"Y'all have been friends for too long. You both need to get in a room and hash it out. Would you be willing to meet this week to resolve your issues?"

"Why would I want to meet with Asia?"

"Shouldn't y'all clear the air and work things out?"

"Nope, there aren't any more words."

"Lauryn, she'd like to rectify things with you."

"I don't care."

"You'll care once you understand completely what's going on with her."

"I'm on my way to meet a co-worker for lunch. Let me hit you back later."

"Ok, will do."

I'm perplexed by Kennedy's insistence on me forgiving Asia. What do we need to discuss? What more could Asia have to disclose? Why should I care about anything coming out of her mouth? I'm guessing Kennedy doesn't know why Jackson and I aren't together since she's lobbying for me to meet with Asia. I don't know what Asia told Kennedy about the situation, but I'm certain it's not the truth. There's genuine sympathy in Kennedy's voice, and it gives me the impression she's on Asia's side.

Maybe, I'm being paranoid. I glance at the clock, and I'm nearly late for lunch. I have to get moving to meet Kim. I rush into the restaurant, and I spot her immediately. Well, she couldn't be missed if she tried. She's extremely light skinned with natural fiery, red, and curly hair. She's petite with a curvy body. She tends to joke about how she's a small and hippy package. Sometimes, she gets mistaken as a red-headed white woman. Kim has no shame about using people's confusion to her advantage, especially at work. She detects my presence and waves. She jumps out of her seat as I approach her, and we hug as we greet one another.

"Girl, it's been too long since we have hung out," Kim remarks.

"Kim, it's been forever. I'm glad you reached out."

"I've been working with a lot of jackasses since you left the company. STU is making a vast amount of dumb decisions. You know a VC owns the firm now?"

"Really? I guess those financial issues were real. The firm is only getting worse. Hedge funds don't care about loyalty at all."

A waitress approaches our table. Kim asks for the drink menu. I give her a quizzical expression since she's working.

"No need for that look. STU laid me off today."

"What? They're getting rid of all the black people. This is suspect. I'm extremely sorry you lost your job."

"Thanks, girl. It's not your fault. Everybody is jumping ship or at least considering it. The people in charge are morons."

"What are you going to do Kim?

"I'm meeting with a headhunter tomorrow to start the hunt. What about you?"

"I've been working at Food Will for a couple of months. It's a chance for me to figure out what I want to do next. The work has been worthwhile and purposeful."

"Good. I would love to have the opportunity to do something chill. The money wouldn't work for me. I got some major student loan payments."

"That's understandable. Are you getting a decent severance?"

"I have about six months coming. I definitely don't want to run out of ends. I have to solidify something else soon."

"You're great at consulting. You'll be able to find something else soon. I'm certain."

"Thanks, Lauryn. I'm not sure if I want to continue consulting. It's too volatile of a place to work. If things are good, everyone at the company is on top of the moon. If things are bad, you get laid off. Yea, anyway, I wanted to tell you about some other shit going on at STU."

"Like what?"

The waitress returns with the drink menu. Kim orders a pinot noir. I decline the wine and settle for a sweet tea. I'm working, so drinking is out for me.

"Girl, there were several sexual harassment allegations filed against Thomason and Stanton. You remember Kaley Anderson?" she asks excitedly in a barely audible voice.

I squint to try and picture Kaley Anderson. She's probably the young blonde right out of college. It appears she's already had a boob job and some other work done.

"Is she the blonde with the blue eyes who's had a serious boob job recently going from a B to DD cup? I believe she works with Thomason."

"Yep, you got it. As for her work, it's subjective. Well, anyway, last year she started dating Thomason, and he had her sign a non-disclosure."

"Ok, since she signed the NDA, why is the firm paying for his sexual misconduct?"

"She never told anyone. The janitor caught them having sex in Thomason's office one Friday night. According to the janitor, neither one of them saw him when they were doing the dirty. He made a video of them, too. He decided to hold onto it as evidence in case he needed ammunition for anything. He didn't utter a word at first. They made a habit of this every Friday night. He saw them every time, like clockwork, and he made several videos."

"Did she give her consent?"

"Oh, yes, she did, and she isn't suing the firm or him. The janitor filed a complaint against the firm stating Thomason and Kaley's sexual acts have made him uncomfortable, and he threatened to bring a lawsuit for indecent exposure and sexual misconduct. Thomason's wife learned he'd been unfaithful. She's filing for divorce."

"In the meantime, Thomason and Kaley have gotten engaged. There's an unconfirmed rumor Kaley's pregnant, and she'll be leaving STU when she has the baby. Just as their engagement announcement came out, Melinda Harrison claimed she and Thomason had a sexual history. Melinda indicated she felt obligated to perform sexual acts to advance her career. She became the shunned whistleblower. Many people believed her about the sex."

"It didn't appear to be a stretch after learning about his involvement with Kaley. Melinda recounted they had sex for about three years. She claims Thomason abruptly ended the affair in February. She assumed he began things with Kaley then."

"Things between him and Kaley went from zero to 100. Within a few months, he purchased her a condo near you and a Benz. I heard he'd spend most nights and weekends with her before the split from his wife anyway. He now lives there permanently since his wife threw him out."

The waitress approaches the table interrupting Kim. She places Kim's wine and my tea on the table.

"Your meals will be out shortly," the waitress mentions. Kim appears annoyed with the interruption. She waves it off realizing the waitress is only doing her job. Kim immediately jumps back into the story as soon as she leaves.

"Melinda suggested there are others to corroborate her story, but no one has come forward yet. She claims Thomason required sex on a weekly basis to guarantee her career would advance. She couldn't contain how pissed she'd become when you were promoted. She grew bitter from giving Thomason the goods and getting nothing in return. No one believed you were having office sex with those gross white men. Don't worry about it," Kim continues.

"Whew! The last thing I need is people assuming I used my body to get ahead."

"Everyone knows you truly deserved everything you got there. The clients pushed for your advancement. Everyone knew you delivered," explains Kim as the waitress returns to the table with our meals without muttering a word.

"What's the deal with Stanton?" I ask in between bites. "I'm not surprised about Thomason. He's always appeared shady to me."

"Stanton has a male complaint of sexual harassment filed against him. It's alleged Stanton has complimented a male employee's ass multiple times. This is the quote allegedly from Stanton, 'he could make the guy feel good.'"

"Who's the guy?" I'm shocked and curious. "Is Stanton gay?"

"Girl, I don't know about either. To date, there haven't been any other allegations against Stanton. He's completely denied everything as false. This complaint is considered to be a 'he said/he said situation.'"

"Wow, I can't believe all of this! I'm glad they laid me off now. I wouldn't want to work in that shit-show."

"Girl, no one does. It's confirmed. Michael quit today. Tony's searching like a madman for something. He doesn't want to be let go."

"I know you would have preferred to leave STU on your own terms, but STU isn't the right place for any of us anymore. It's going to be a PR nightmare if Thomason has been having sex with all the white women in the office. Has he heard of 'Me Too'? Has Thomason admitted anything?"

"No, he claimed to have fallen for Kaley hard. He tried to deny his deep attraction to her until he couldn't any longer. He admitted they shouldn't have had an affair, but he's madly in love with her. He also claimed his marriage had been done for quite some time. They were staying together for the sake of the kids. My question about Melinda's situation is why didn't he have her sign a NDA? Clearly that's the way Thomason operates. At least with Kaley. Thomason also claims he only asked Kaley to sign to prevent people from using their relationship to hurt her. He only wanted to protect Kaley from cruel treatment."

Thomason's explanation made me think about Jackson, and how he claimed things happened with Asia. Could our relationship been like Thomason and his wife? We didn't have kids. We only had our dog, Chewy, a Cavalier King Charles Spaniel. Still, Chewy couldn't have been a reason for him to stay with me and hurt me like he did. He certainly could've left after Chewy died since we weren't married. No harm no foul. I don't want to wonder about what if anymore. It makes the pain become front and center for me. I'll only focus on Thomason's widespread allegations of sexual misconduct against him. If he's using his power in the firm to control women with sexual favors, that's unacceptable.

"Yea, Kim. I guess Thomason could be telling the truth, but on the other hand, Melinda has a strong point, too. If Melinda doesn't get those other women to support her, this will be a dead issue. The janitor has an unquestionably strong case for sure."

"Yea, you're right. The janitor settled out of court, and he got paid! He won't have to clean up office buildings anymore unless he wants to do it."

"Wow, I guess something good did happen out of all of this! I'm glad Michael is gone. I couldn't ask for a better boss, and I wouldn't mind working with him again. I'm concerned about you and Tony. I hope you both find something else soon."

"You're a good friend. Always worrying about everyone else. With your positive vibes levied our way, Tony and I will land something soon. I'm certain. Everything does happen for a reason."

"This time working at Food Will has given me a chance to consider different options for my future. I always considered going back to school. I may even want to get my PhD."

"Really? School? Nah, son, school's not for me. It's good enough for me to have my bachelor's degree. What would you get your PhD in?"

"I like economics. I know call me a nerd. I'll probably get something in the field of economics, strategic management, or operations management."

"Yea, you'd probably do well in those areas. You're always digging deeper than most people would to solve problems."

"Well, I may go back to school. I may also go back to consulting or do something entirely different. I'm grateful I have this chance to figure all this out. Don't get me wrong, when they let me go, my impressions were quite different. STU pissed me off, but they also did me a favor."

"How did they do you a favor?"

"If they didn't lay me off, I would still be working all the time. Life is more than work. Thank you, STU." We both laugh, and Kim agrees with my positive outlook.

"Now, we've exhausted everything there is to know about STU, what's going on with you?

"Other than getting my shit together to find a job?"

"Yea, other than that."

"Things are going great with my boo, Caleb. I called him right away in tears. He has my back. He told me, 'I got you, baby. Don't worry about a thing.' He wants me to live with him in Murfreesboro. He told me to only focus on trying to find something else."

"That's love right there. A real man will do this for the woman he loves. He'll be there for you in good and bad times. He's a keeper, girl."

"Don't I know it. Well, I'm grateful to have him. He's definitely a keeper. Girl, I don't want to live all the way out there."

"Good for you. I'm happy for you. It's not too far, girl. If you don't have to burn your severance don't do it. Save your coins as you're job hunting. When is your lease up?"

"The timing is great. I've been living month-to-month for a minute. I've been planning to move somewhere better. Somewhere better is with Caleb." She's smiling like a woman in love. This makes me a tiniest bit envious. I remember the affection I once had for Jackson.

"What about you? How are things with Jackson?"

"We didn't work out."

"Aww, that's too bad. It seemed like you two were headed to the alter."

"Not always. It's good, lady. I'm living my best life, and I don't need a man to be happy."

"You're right, girl. I want you to be happy."

"Oh, I am. Don't you worry." I don't want to get into what happened with Jackson. I'm happy she doesn't press things.

"I got a save the date for my high school reunion for two years from now."

"Wow! Planning ahead must be their thing. It should be fun. We're having ours in October."

"I probably won't go to mine."

"Why not, girl? I can't wait to show those bitches how good I look now. They treated me like a red-headed stepchild in high school. Eyes will be poppin' out now. I'm killin' the game."

"You're definitely the it girl now. You have a point. I should probably go to mine, too. I'm not feeling going to this thing single."

"Single or not, you're going to be the hottest thing there. Those chicks you love to hate from high school better make sure their boyfriends are locked-tight to their asses. Cause somebody gonna get some numbers!!!"

"You're crazy, girl. I guess I should show them what I'm working with now."

"Most definitely. That's what I'm going to do. I plan to shine, baby."

"I have no doubts you will."

For the rest of the lunch, we're casually chatting about various topics ranging from TV shows to politics. Prior to leaving, we promise to get together soon. As I go to my car, my phone rings with a call from Kennedy. I'm slightly annoyed. I told her earlier I would call her back.

"Hello, Kennedy."

"Hi, Lauryn. I waited for you to call me back."

"Kennedy, I'm leaving my lunch. I didn't have a chance to call you back. I'm walking out the restaurant's door as we speak."

"Ok, ok. Is it possible for you to meet with Asia?"

"I would rather not."

"Lauryn, you guys have been best friends for years. You owe it to yourself to have closure. Asia's been trying to reach you."

"No, I don't, Kennedy. What's the point in meeting her?"

"You should reconsider meeting her."

Now, I'm wondering what this could be about other than Asia's guilt. Could she have a sexually transmitted disease like herpes? A condom wouldn't work. I don't even know if they used condoms. I hope whatever it is she needs to discuss won't impact me. Jackson and I stopped using condoms about a year and a half ago and this worries me. Pregnancy didn't cause an alarm for me since I've been taking the Depo Provera for a few years. Damn him if this is a sexually transmitted disease. I won't let either of them forget this if I'm burned. I'm pondering what could this meeting be about, and Kennedy's asking me a question.

"Lauryn, are you still here?"

"No, I'm sorry. I must have been somewhere else. Can you repeat it?"

"Meeting with us won't be longer than 30 minutes. You won't regret meeting with Asia."

I don't want to meet with Asia at all. Kennedy's been like a dog with a bone with this. I'm not going to make this great for them. If they want to press me to meet with them, we'll meet immediately. I don't have the time or patience to deal with Asia right now.

"Let's meet at 4:30 today," I state urgently.

"Now, that's kind of fast. What about this weekend?"

"No, it's today or never."

I insist on today knowing full well I have the upper hand. As much as Kennedy will fuss about the timing, she knows me well enough to know I won't back down.

"Ok, let me contact Asia and get back to you."

Once the call ends, I ruminate why Asia wants to meet with me. I'm confused about what Kennedy knows. Asia would be too embarrassed to admit her role in my breakup, wouldn't she? I guess she could be proud she took my man. I don't know her anymore. I'm back at my desk pondering about what Asia could want.

I'm doing my best to avoid having thoughts of bashing in her head. Doesn't she realize she's taking a huge risk asking me to meet her anywhere after what I saw. She's lucky I don't roll like that. Carolyn and Marcus raised me not to go all full-fledged *WrestleMania* on her. I could dropkick Jackson in the nuts, though. They still make me sick, but I'm not whining over this shit anymore.

I have plenty of work to do. I can't concentrate being unsure about what Asia is plotting. Well, she's going to learn today. I don't care about anything involving her anymore. Jackson doesn't matter to me either. Kennedy calls to inform me 4:30 is a go, and we'll meet at the coffee house in Franklin. I'm not thrilled to go to this meeting with Asia, and every shred of friendship we had will end today. I guarantee it.

CHAPTER 13
Lauryn

Kennedy and I have been friends since freshman year. We all met around the same time (Asia, Kennedy, Tonya, and me). Even though Asia and I became best friends, Kennedy is considered one of my closet friends. She is originally from Nashville, and she majored in mechanical engineering, too. She works as a process engineer for a local car manufacturer. She has had an amazing career in manufacturing. She's on the fast track to be the general manager at her plant. I'm proud of what she has been able to accomplish in engineering. It's a tough field especially for black women. Kennedy is a true example of "black girls rock."

Kennedy got married two years ago to her college boyfriend, Eric. This didn't surprise anyone. They were just that couple. I'm surprised they didn't get married the day Kennedy and I graduated. Eric graduated two years ahead of us. They had a small break and dated other people for a short time. It's a known fact they were meant for each other.

Kennedy and Eric had what I would consider "relationship goals." They fit together. They make each other better in every way. Eric also happens to be Jackson's best friend. I'm not sure how the breakup will impact our friendships. I hope it's not like a divorce where one person is awarded the friendships, and the other one loses out. So far, I haven't lost any friends, but I haven't been hanging out with friends since the relationship ended either.

I'm still pondering why Kennedy has a strong desire for me to meet Asia. There's no way Kennedy knows the details of what happened between Asia and Jackson. If she did, she would never insist on this meeting. Kennedy is one to call you out on your bullshit. She has zero patience for what she considers "nonsense." She's a "take no prisoners" type of friend. She's deeply loyal. If you do something wrong, she will let you know you're wrong.

If she knew what they did, she wouldn't be on Asia's bandwagon. Once in college, Sherita, a friend from one of our classes, had a flirtatious moment with Eric, and Kennedy almost broke that girl's neck (not figuratively). She would've beat her down if cooler heads hadn't prevailed. Sherita offended Kennedy by not respecting the "girl code." Absolutely nothing happened between Sherita and Eric. From Kennedy's perspective, it didn't matter. Kennedy ended the friendship with Sherita, and to this day, she refuses to have anything to do with her.

As I arrive at the coffee house, good memories start coming back from time spent here. My grad school team would meet here all the time to study and complete assignments. The place is acutely comfortable. I would just relax and hang out for hours. Meeting here will dampen the happy aura I've always had when I come here. I won't let Asia steal another thing from me. I should've met them somewhere that doesn't hold special memories.

The coffee shop hasn't changed one bit. It's still calm and relaxing. The hair on the back of my neck prickles as I zero in on my old friend turned enemy sitting at the table. I agreed to this meeting, but I still don't know what to anticipate. Nothing could replace the last image I have of her in bed with Jackson. My expression is stoic as I approach the table. I refuse to allow Asia to witness how much she hurt me with her betrayal. Asia tries to display she's remorseful by nearly bursting into tears. I don't believe her tears are sincere.

"Hello," I announce as I adjust the chair to sit.

They both reply hello in unison.

"What is this about?" I ask impatiently.

Asia starts, "Lauryn, the last thing I wanted to do was hurt you."

"If this is what you asked me to meet you about, I'm not interested in discussing it. I'll leave right now."

"No, I guess it doesn't matter. Your friendship has meant the world to me."

"Hmmph, I find it hard to believe I meant anything to you. How do you treat people you hate?"

"I deserve your venom. I would do anything for your forgiveness."

"There isn't anything you can do. I don't even know why you would be this selfish and try to force a conversation today. Kennedy, why would you be involved with this? Do you know about her and Jackson?"

"I'm not sure what you mean," Kennedy replies.

"Do you want to tell her or shall I, Asia?"

"Kennedy, I'm sorry I misled you about the reason we're here. I didn't tell you what I did to hurt Lauryn."

"How did you mislead me, Asia?" Kennedy asks.

Asia goes from remorse to defeat in a matter of seconds. She appears to be too ashamed to admit what she's done. She isn't going to tell Kennedy the truth. Asia will not walk out of here like she's innocent. Like she didn't do anything to hurt me. No ma'am, I'm not that nice. She called me here for some crazy reason, and now all her dirt will come to light.

"I'm bored with this, Asia. Since you won't tell the truth, I will. I found Asia and Jackson together naked in my bed. It's obvious what they were doing. Kennedy, she has some nerve to ask me for forgiveness now." I wait a second for a response. I'm becoming completely irritated. "This conversation is finished. I don't care how you need to absolve your sins, Asia. This friendship is done if I haven't been clear." I stood with every intention of leaving.

"Wait, Lauryn, Asia hasn't told you the entire truth."

"What truth? I don't need an explanation about you and Jackson. This friendship died the moment you betrayed me. You put the fork in it."

"Kennedy, don't worry about it. Lauryn wouldn't want to know. She wants nothing to do with me," Asia utters as if I'm the one at fault and being unreasonable.

Kennedy ignores her, "Asia may have breast cancer. She discovered a lump, and you know cancer has hit her family hard. She's pretty scared. I don't condone any of the stuff with Jackson. I don't appreciate her using me under false pretenses either, but you should know the real reason she asked to meet you."

I pause for a moment. I'm shocked by this news. I'm not prepared for it at all. I gaze directly at her with a sympathetic expression and state, "I'm truly sorry if you have breast cancer, and I understand how scared you are. My prayers and sympathies are with you. I don't know what else I can do for you."

Asia let out a sob. "I don't know what happened, but I didn't mean to hurt you. I know you're not ready to forgive me. My emotions are all hyperextended now. I'm sorry I tried to rush you. I'm sorry this happened, and our friendship was ruined. I hope one day you'll be willing to forgive me. I know it's unlikely we'll ever be the same again."

"Asia, forgiveness may not be granted simply because it's requested. You betrayed me. If I decide to forgive you, it will be in my own time. Please don't ever reach out to me again. Kennedy, please respect my decision and don't intercede for Asia again."

"Lauryn, if I had known the truth, we wouldn't be here," Kennedy comments to me prior to directing her attention towards Asia. "Asia, I don't appreciate being a pawn here. You omitted everything about you and Jackson being involved. You lied to get me here. I don't blame Lauryn. I wouldn't forgive you either."

"I'm sorry I misled you, Kennedy. I figured Lauryn wouldn't come without you." Asia is crying hysterically.

"Asia, you haven't been making wise choices lately. This is between you and Lauryn. I can forgive your manipulation. Lauryn is entitled to her feelings. You did something that is extremely hard to forgive and forget. You have to live with the choices you've made."

I leave assured Asia has lost her mind.

(Don't lie in bed, girl, if you aren't willing or able to deal with the consequences.)

Since I don't have any plans for the evening, I head to the kickboxing gym to burn off some energy and built-up aggression. Alex is here today. He has on a tank, and his biceps are popping. His workout pants display the outline of his muscular thighs to a tee. Not just his thighs. He's working with an impressive package. I should get my head of out the gutter.

I need to relieve some of this tension. Inspecting the goods has never hurt anyone. He's the perfect eye candy, and a much-needed distraction for me right now. I'm staring at his lower region being fully aware I shouldn't. I wonder what Alex would be like in the bedroom. It's been too long since I've had some. I should turn away and focus on working out. Isn't that why I'm here today? To burn some calories. **(An ample amount of calories can be burned in the horizontal or even vertical way depending on what you're into.)** Shit, I have to get my mind out of the gutter.

"What's up, Killa?" Alex asks confidently with a sexy smile as soon as he notices me. Killa is my kickboxing name. It's a moniker I use since I've been known to kill the bag.

"Hey, Alex, I need to relieve all this aggression from today. I hope you got me."

"I always do. Why are you aggressive today? I think I like it."

"Something happened only the bag will cure."

"I got you in more ways than one."

"I bet you do, Alex. I'll be ready to go in five."

(Is Alex wondering about things with me, too? Ooh lala!)

I glance at the mirror ball and catch Alex checking me out. He isn't even hiding it. He's staring directly at my ass. He's ogling me like he's interested in more than a trainer/trainee relationship. What am I going to do about this? I guess I can flirt with him. In the least, I will burn a whole lot of calories by working out with him. Alex is someone I can appreciate how he takes care of his face and body. It has to end there. I can't touch him.

Following the workout, I'm physically rejuvenated and exhausted at the same time. Alex didn't disappoint me at all with his laser focused training style. He's pushing me beyond my limits in this workout. I'm completely wiped out. This workout has made me put some things into perspective. I'm no longer angry. I'm drenched with sweat and aching for some one-on-one time with my shower. It would have to wait for minute. I need to stretch.

I turn my head to find Alex working with some other clients. I don't want to interrupt him. I finish stretching, and I plan to leave discreetly. Something has changed between us, and I don't want to address it now. I need to remember the past. He would only mention how great I worked out. He made me feel like I did more than the average human. I grab my stuff to finally leave and make a fast getaway. I'm not fast enough, and I have to tie my shoes. Alex approaches me from behind me as I bend to tie them.

"Damn, girl, I don't think I can take this view without wanting to grab a little somethin'. You make me want things I shouldn't," he whispers near my ear.

"Alex, maybe it's not bad to want something forbidden," I flirt with him knowing I shouldn't.

"I like forbidden. It makes me happy."

"Happy, really?"

"Yea, I'm hoping this isn't just me. There's something between us. How about you give me your number? We can go out sometime."

"Is there a policy against fraternizing with clients here?"

"Well...no one has to know," he flirts by smiling and winking at me. "Can I get your number?"

"Ok, give me your phone."

He hands me his phone, and I key in my number under "Killa." Who says I can't have fun? He peeks at the phone and changes the name to "Sexy Killa." He texts me his number with the message, "Anxiously waiting."

"Good job today, Killa. Ring the bell on the way out if you were satis-fied with your workout."

I smile as I ring the bell five times to demonstrate how satisfied I am with the workout. I'm playing with fire. I probably need to leave this danger behind. I stroll out to my car to head home for a shower and to change. I have a few texts inviting me to happy hour. As good as the workout is for stress relief, I won't mind having a few drinks and chill with some homies. The happy hour is exactly what I need tonight. I take a quick shower, change into a cute outfit, and head over for some drinks at a bar near my condo. It's nothing like having a few watered-down drinks for two bucks a pop to get my mood right.

Lately, I've been in the mood to socialize more. Kennedy and I cleared the air and made plans to hangout more. We discussed Asia's deception and decided to leave it behind us. Kennedy had no idea she'd been played, and I won't hold it against her. I miss her since we haven't chilled in forever. Life's been unusually busy for us since we've been forced to begin "adulting."

Both Kennedy and Tonya are trying to encourage me to become more active with the sorority's local chapter, and I'm considering it. Now is a better time for me since I no longer work for STU. I like the work the sorority does for the community. Giving back is one of the cornerstones of my life. I'll visit the chapter and make my decision on whether to join.

Being in town more allows me to spend more time with these ladies, and we're getting much closer. They agreed to never mention Asia and Jackson to me. I wouldn't ever ask them to end their friendships with either of them. No one should expect me to be cool with them though. Not going to happen! Negative! I can't ever imagine a day where I'll want to be around them.

Kennedy and Tonya are big on brunch. When I say this, I mean there isn't a brunch place in town they haven't frequented. At first, I joined them to get out for something to do. Now, I'm a regular on Saturdays and some Sundays. It's not only their thing anymore; it's our thing. If I'm being honest, I love going to brunch. It's the highlight of my week. Is this kind of sad? Don't judge me! I'm kind of a foodie.

On the drive to meet Tonya and Kennedy for brunch, I can't stop myself from smiling. I'm kind of feeling myself. I look good in my cute sundress and espadrilles. Tonya prances into the restaurant as I park my car. Within minutes, I'm joining both Kennedy and Tonya at the table. Both of them notice my mood has improved lately.

"Lauryn, I'm glad you're happier these days," Tonya comments.

"I'm good, actually."

"What's bringing you joy these days? Is it someone I know like Keith, your fine ass neighbor?"

"No, Keith and I are only friends."

"I could've sworn there had been more between you two at the club."

"Oh, don't remind me. You witnessed me not being my best self. I'm embarrassed about how drunk I got."

"Girl, what? If I had his fine ass carry me out, I wouldn't be embarrassed. If I were you, I would've gone scavenger hunting on his body. The way he gazed at you proves he wants some of you, too. If you two were alone, he would've eaten you up whole."

"Girl, you're too much," I chuckle, wishing this conversation topic would change.

"If it's not a guy, which it doesn't have to be Tonya, what's making you smile these days?" Kennedy asks.

"It's been a rough time. Not only because of Jackson and Asia, STU laid me off a few months ago. You won't believe this. The layoff at work happened the same day I found Jackson and Asia together. I started working at this non-profit, Food Will, a few months ago. The work has been immensely meaningful, and I'm helping people who need it. I also started volunteering quite a bit. Overall, these life changes have helped me gain a different perspective."

"What the fuck?!" Tonya exclaims. "I can't believe you caught them the same day."

"Why would I lie about this?"

"Damn, girl. I didn't know," states Tonya.

"Yea, for sure. Working would have at least allowed you to have an outlet," Kennedy comments.

"I used the time to start volunteering at Food Will, and they needed someone with my skills. They offered me a job, and I took it. It's definitely not long-term, but it's something worthwhile for now."

"Good, girl. I'm glad you have something to fill your time even if it's temporary. I know you're like me and not working is a no-no," Kennedy remarks.

"You're right. I didn't work at first, and it started driving me crazy," I add.

"Have you started dating anyone?" Tonya asks.

"Dating? Are you serious? You do understand my long-term boyfriend cheated on me with my best friend. I probably won't trust anyone for a long time."

"No one mentioned anything about you getting a boyfriend, girl. Have you considered a 'homie love a friend' situation, or are you committed to your vibrator?" Tonya is never shy about asking anyone anything whether it's her business or not. "You should try Tender. It works."

"Whoa, Nellie. Personal."

"Tonya," Kennedy laughs, "you're overreaching into the TMI zone."

"You should venture out there. Don't get serious. You would only date casually. If you want to have sex, have sex. You won't have to worry about if he's faithful or not when it's only sex."

"Tonya, you do ascertain I'm not the type let him hit, and we're just cool the next day."

"YOLO, baby."

"Yea, let me think about it," I comment desperately wanting to change the subject to something else. "So, what's going on with you guys?"

"Well," Kennedy begins, "I have news I want to share with you guys." We both give Kennedy our complete attention.

"'I'm pregnant!!" Kennedy exclaims.

"That's great news!" I voice excitedly.

"Ooh!" Tonya shouts a little too loudly, "I'm going to be an auntie."

"We weren't trying, and I've been nervous. You know miscarriages are an issue for many women early in their pregnancies. We've passed the three-month milestone. I'm about four-months pregnant. It's safe to tell people now. We're super excited. Now you guys know why I never get a mimosa or have coffee anymore. We're planning to have a gender reveal party in a couple of weeks. I'll send you guys an invitation for the occasion."

"Do you need any help with the party?" I ask.

"Girl, no! Kassidy is going overboard," Kennedy laughs.

Kassidy is Kennedy's older sister, and they're tight. Kassidy is only two years older than us, and she's a resident at Vanhogen University Hospital.

Tonya speculates, "I'm hoping for a girl, a future soror."

Kennedy confirms, "I'm hoping for a healthy baby. I've had the worst heartburn this week."

I glance at my watch. "I have to go. I have a few things to do this afternoon. We're going to the game tonight."

"You're going to the Titans game tonight? With whom?" Tonya asks trying to be nosy.

"My dad's coming in town, and you know we love football."

"Eric is going to the game, too." Kennedy states, "Maybe you guys will see each other tonight, and no, before you ask, Jackson won't be with him."

"Kennedy, I'm truly happy about the pregnancy. I want to help. If you need anything, let me know," I state as I rise to leave.

"Sure thing. Have a great time at the game!"

I hug them goodbye and leave the restaurant on a mission. I finish up a few errands hurriedly. I want to be home when my dad gets here. He has business here this week, and I'm happy to hang out with him. Dad and I will grab an early dinner then go to the game. We speak on FaceTime quite often. It's nothing like hanging out. I love having my dad with me. Dad is coming alone because Mom's swamped at work. It would've been great if both of them could've come.

Dad comes right into the house. I'm busy cleaning. I stop to wash my hands. My parents bought the condo for me during my sophomore year in college. Apparently, this gives them carte blanche to walk in like they own the place. I guess technically it does, but the deed is in my name. I'm lucky this condo isn't in Atlanta, or I may have uninvited guests all the time. I amble towards dad with a huge smile on my face.

"Daddy, you made it here early. I'm extremely happy you're here."

"Baby girl. I'm happy I'm here, too."

"We should get something to eat then head to the game. Are you hungry?"

"I'm starving, and I knew you'd have the right game plan, baby girl. Let's go."

We go to a hip new Jamaican restaurant on the way to the stadium and enjoy some of their specialties. Dad is the same charming man as always, but I can tell he misses my mom. I'm sad mom couldn't come, too. The food met our expectations. We leave and head for the stadium.

As we're approaching our seats, Dad and I are busy chatting unaware of our surroundings. I don't recognize someone is trying to get my attention. I suddenly hear my name being shouted. I look in the direction of the voice, and it's Eric calling me. He's with my neighbor, Keith. How do they know each other? I led Dad their way to introduce him. I haven't encountered Keith since my embarrassing drunken escapade, and I'm nervous he'll make some comment about it since I don't know him well.

"Nice to meet you," they respond.

"Nice to meet you, too," Dad says.

"Hello, everyone. This is my dad, Marcus Davidson. Dad, this is Eric, Keith, and James," I announce pointing them out. "I didn't realize you two knew each other." I point from Eric to Keith.

"How do you guys know each other?" Eric asks in return.

"We're neighbors. How about you?" I ask.

"My firm works with Eric occasionally. We got cool a few years ago," he stares and smirks with a sexy smile like I'm the only one in the room.

"Keith," my dad begins, "You look familiar. Did you play any sports?"

"Yes, sir," Keith answers, "I played college football."

"Hmm, I believe you were a receiver for Memphis, right?"

"Yes, sir. I played for Memphis. You recognize me?"

"I'm good with faces. It's a shame about your injury. You definitely would've gone pro."

"Yes," Keith answers, "I recall pundits speculating I could."

"Wow, there you go, Dad. You never forget a face."

"Not when it comes to sports. You know that's what I do, baby girl."

"Where are you guys sitting?" Keith asks.

I glance at the tickets, and I notice we're sitting one row above them. I point in the direction of our seats. "We're right above you," I respond.

We make our way to our seats. Since both Dad and I are diehard sports fans who get extremely animated during games, we're extremely vocal. I convinced Dad to become a secondary Titans fan as well. We interact with Eric, James, and Keith through the game. Keith is surprised with my football knowledge. Eric informs him I'm not your average Jill dealing with anything sports related.

The Titans win the game against the Chargers 27 - 10. After the game, the guys invite us to hang out with them. They're getting drinks and something to eat. I'm game for drinks if Dad wants to go with them. He's game, and we head out with the fellas. It's fun hanging out with my dad and the guys. They give us a hard time since we're Falcons fans, and we give it right back to them. Before it gets too late, I remind Dad he has to call Mom, and we head out. Things are genuine and natural between

Keith and me. I'm happy considering I want to get past "the club incident."

Keith gazes at me in a way that reaches the depths of my soul. I try to brush it off or ignore there is any meaning behind it. This haunts me. I turn away and try to pretend like nothing has changed, and he didn't mean anything by any of it. As much as I want to pretend like things are only chill between us, I'm only fooling myself and not very well actually. Still, I need to act like this doesn't matter. I'm still healing from my past.

The next week, Dad and I spend a lot of quality time together at sporting events, going out to dinner, and hanging out. I'm thankful Dad has business in Nashville. I miss him a lot, and I want to hang out with him. I'm a daddy's girl getting to spend time with my favorite guy. I'm in heaven. Dad's into keeping fit, too, and we go jogging each morning.

Following the week with Dad, I finally shed no more tears for my failed relationship. Jackson is on my mind less and less these days. I can't say my dreams aren't haunted with the image of them in my bed. That's something I can't unsee. I know one day my dreams will be of something else. I'm patiently waiting until the day comes when there's no more pain in my heart.

At least I haven't encountered Jackson which helps. I don't want to be forced into having uncomfortable conversations or space invasions with Asia. I'm not ready to witness them being blissfully happy. It would hurt too much. I don't make scenes, and I can't fathom I would make one if I saw them. I'm not the girl who yells and hits people in public. Instead, I could beat their asses in private.

One day my heart will be healed completely, and this hole where my heart formally resided will be whole again. I'm pretty sure once this suffering is done, and I'll be ready to love again. Love again? Let's not take it too far subconscious. No pain is my desire. Today isn't that day. The throbbing pain in my heart will recede hopefully. I must believe one day all of this will be a distant memory that will teach me to pay close attention to people's character and their intent. I failed with Asia and Jackson. I won't fail again.

CHAPTER 14
Lauryn

My friends are having their gender reveal party today. Honestly, I didn't know what exactly to bring as a gift. How is this different from a baby shower? It's probably not. I'll treat it like a baby shower. I opt to give them diapers. What new parents won't need diapers? My mom advised me not to buy newborn diapers. Babies tend to grow out of those incredibly fast. I listened to her advice and buy a huge box of size one diapers along with a high-tech baby monitor. I can't go wrong with this purchase. Once I know the gender, I can get the baby something else that'll be dope.

As I'm coming in, I immediately spot several of my sorority sisters and other friends from NTU. It's good chatting with them. It's been a minute since we've crossed paths. The party atmosphere is turning into a good time. For a gender reveal party, the alcohol is flowing, and I didn't expect this. We chat for a bit, and I turn around suddenly where I nearly smash right into Keith. **(What's he doing here? Don't embarrass yourself.)**

"Hey, Lauryn," he grabs my arm to prevent me from falling, "You, okay?"

"Yea, I didn't notice you there. I should be more aware of my surroundings. Well, at least, this isn't like the drunken night at the club."

"Hey, I would've pretended I forgot about it. If I had known you would be here, I would've suggested we carpool."

"I guess if you want to conserve fuel."

"Exactly that's my mission. Conserving fuel. We all have to do our part for the environment, right?"

"Right," I face him to determine if he's serious, and he clearly isn't.

"Do you want to grab a table?" Keith is easy to have a conversation with, and I enjoy his company.

"Sure, why not?" I spot Jackson on the other side of the room. He's with a date, and she isn't Asia.

(Boy, does he go on to the next one fast! Stop judging! Well, it's been a minute, and it's none of my business.)

I won't let Jackson ruin my good time. It's good he's moving on, I guess. Why does his date look familiar? It doesn't matter. It's none of my business. I glance at the other side of the room where I spot Asia, and she appears to be alone. She's chatting with some of our sorority sisters. I shouldn't be happy about this development, but I am. I guess I'm petty. **(Guess she should've chosen our friendship.)** Keith notices my unease. He steers me in a different direction to sit at a table on the other side of the room. I'm appreciative of this. I don't want to be near either one of them.

"I guess this could be sort of awkward with him being here."

"I knew he would be here. Asia is here, too. I didn't realize they weren't together. I guess the grass isn't greener for either of them," I chuckle.

"Jackson's a fool."

"No argument there. They're not ruining my fun today."

"Cool. Well, maybe we can get to know each other better."

"We could. I'm fairly certain I already know something about you now."

"What are you fairly certain you know about me?"

"You're a ladies' man."

"Ouch. I never pretended to be someone's faithful boyfriend."

"Touché. Are you denying you're a ladies' man?"

"I wouldn't say I'm a ladies' man. I date (I won't deny it), but I haven't been ready for a committed relationship. Maybe, I haven't met or dated anyone I want to get serious with lately."

"Oh, I get it. I know all about being in a long-term relationship with a horrible ending. I'm basically chillin' and doing me."

"Lauryn, does this mean you want to date me?"

"You're funny. I'm not ready to date yet."

"If you were ready to date, would I be someone you would be interested in dating?"

"I could be persuaded."

"How could you be persuaded?"

"Are you prepared for the challenge? I recall you mentioning you aren't necessarily wanting a commitment with anyone."

"I also stated I may not have dated anyone I want to make a commitment to, also, if you were listening."

"Guilty. I guess I chose to omit a small insignificant part."

I'm enjoying flirting with Keith. The more time I spend in his company I've come to recognize I'm happy. I don't want to get too carried away.

Keith is indeed a player, and I have to guard myself from his charming ass. I could get into some serious trouble with this guy. We grab some food, drinks, and continue to enjoy each other's company. I'm doing my best to avoid both Jackson and Asia. I'm not surprised they're here. As far as I know, they're still friends with Kennedy and Eric. This is their day, and I won't do anything to interrupt it. If I cross paths with either Jackson or Asia, I'll go in the opposite direction. I appreciate Keith's assistance in helping me to avoid them. I'm relieved it appears I'll avoid both of them all together.

Kassidy gets on the mic, "Before we jump to the reason all of us are here, I would like to invite you all to the dance floor. This is a party people!!!"

The music suddenly gets hype and the energy level spikes. My foot involuntarily starts tapping to the iconic music stylings from Memphis. Most of the people here were either from Memphis originally or somewhere thereabouts and made their way to Nashville.

"Would you like to dance?" Keith asks me.

"Sure, I would love to dance with you. Sober this time."

"You know I had an ulterior motive for asking you to dance, don't you?"

"I do now."

We go out to the dance floor to groove a little bit and get this party started in Kassidy's words. Both Keith and I appear to be on the same page. I didn't notice anyone in the room, and the intensity we share staring at one another is electrifying. There are definitely jolting sparks between us. I turn around and back my ass against him. This moment in time is just right. There's no shame in my game. We dance like this for at least 15 more minutes, and Kassidy is back on the mic.

"Is everyone having a good time?" she yells, "Be patient everyone! We're going to get to the reveal. I want to voice my praise and admiration for the couple of the hour. Kennedy or Kendy as I like to call her is the best little sister ever. She's loyal, caring, devoted, honest to a fault, and a great sister and friend. When she told our parents and me about the pregnancy, I told her God knew best by blessing these two amazing humans to grow their family. Kendy is going to make the best mom. All her nurturing with family and friends throughout the years has prepared her for motherhood. It's impossible to be prepared for every one of life's upheavals, but she'll have the best start with a husband like Eric. You happen to be the best brother. If Kendy screws the pooch, you'll still be my brother."

"Girl, please!" Kennedy yells back.

"Back to my important and timely speech prior to the interruption... Eric, you're the best thing to happen to my sister and our family. I know you're going to be the best dad ever. I love you guys. Can everyone give it up for Eric, Kennedy, and the soon-to-be." We all drank to them.

"Now, enough of my speeches. Are y'all, ready for the spectacular reveal of the day?"

The crowd yells, "Yes!!"

Kennedy and Eric chose to have the cake cut to reveal the gender of their child. Kassidy is the only person who knows the gender. Kassidy asks everyone to start a drum roll. Keith and I enjoy the buildup and excitement stemming around the gender announcement. Kassidy crosses her arms in the air to signal for all of us to stop. She grabs the knife and cuts into the cake. The cake reveals a blue and a pink piece. Everyone is puzzled and confused for a second.

"You're having a boy and a girl!!" Kassidy yells.

Kennedy and Eric are shocked and appear to be two seconds from passing out. They have a higher likelihood of having twins since Eric is an identical twin. Eric's twin, Derrick, is at the party, too. Plus, Kennedy's and Kassidy's mom is a fraternal twin.

The crowd yells, "Whoo Hoo!!!"

Everyone is excited for them. I have a sudden urge to go to the ladies' room. I excuse myself from Keith indicating with my hands I'll be back in a moment. I plan to congratulate Kennedy and Eric following the potty break. As soon as I leave the bathroom, I nearly crash right into Jackson and his date. Talk about an awkward situation. Crossing paths with Jackson isn't my idea of a great party activity. He appears to be happy with his new girlfriend. I guess he's moved on with his life. That's good, I think. He won't be popping up in here to beg for me to forgive him hopefully. I guess it's interesting his date isn't Asia. I don't want to gloat. This shit is hilarious. Talk about crash and burn. Paradise didn't last long. I'm not surprised the light isn't as alluring as the dark. Sneaking around had to be the appeal.

"Hello, Angel! Sorry. Shit! I guess old habits are hard to break. I shouldn't call you that anymore."

"No, Jackson you shouldn't. Hello, how are you?"

"I'm doing pretty good. How are you, Lauryn?"

"I'm doing okay." I glance at his date waiting for an introduction. I'm uncertain if he'll introduce us.

"Lauryn, this is Londyn. Londyn this is Lauryn."

"Nice to meet you," I stare at her intently.

"It's nice to meet you as well. How do you and Jackson know each other?" Londyn asks.

"We went to college together," Jackson blurts out.

Apparently, he doesn't want his date to know about our past. Hmm, interesting. How should I play this?

"College only, Jackson?" I ask coyly.

"Is there something I should know?" she asks.

"No, not at all. I'm sure he'll reveal all at some point won't you, Jackson?" I'm deliberate with my response.

Jackson tries to act as if I didn't make things awkward with his date. He wants to waltz away from this. In a way, I don't blame him. I don't know how involved he is with this girl, but she'd be crazy not to be curious about our history. If he cares about her, he'll be honest about what we meant to each other once. Good luck to him explaining this. It would be interesting to be a fly on the wall as he admits I'm his ex-girlfriend, and she's cognizant of how much we resemble each other. I know I wouldn't want to be a replacement for someone else. It's like the football player who married a woman who resembles his famous ex to a tee.

It's annoying. Jackson is dating a girl who could be my replacement. She's wearing her long hair straight. Her skin tone and body shape are the same as mine. Her eye color is hazel. I guess Jackson does have a type. It's weird what you discern about someone by paying attention to them. I could be gazing in a mirror. I'm scrutinizing her face to determine what the differences are between us. If I didn't know better, she could be related to me. I don't know my birth family. I guess somewhere in this warped universe it's possible we could be related. Talk about weird. It would be extremely weird if we're related. If this whole thing didn't seem awkward, I could ask her some questions about her family. Well, enough about Jackson and his new "me." It's time for me to get back to the party.

"It's good seeing you, Lauryn. I hope you're happy with Keith." I stop in my tracks.

"What? I'm not with Keith, Jackson. You're the only one who's moved on apparently."

I couldn't help myself. I told myself I wouldn't be that woman if we crossed paths. He brought this on himself by insinuating something about me. Then again, I don't want to give the impression I'm the jealous ex. I guess I should've walked away when I had the chance.

"Lauryn, I'm not trying to be messy. You were hurt, and I have regrets. I genuinely want you to be happy."

"Ok, Jackson. I wish you well, too. Nice meeting you, Londyn."

As I walk away, I overhear Londyn asking Jackson who I am. I'm glad we didn't get into a drag out fight at this party. That wouldn't be a good look. This is a win for me. I still want to punch him in the face. I stroll in the opposite direction, and I'm face-to-face with Vincent Thomas. I didn't realize he knew Kennedy or Eric. This is a small world. It's been a long time since I've seen him. We went out a few times in the past. He played in the NFL, and we weren't serious. He only casually dated then. Things didn't go far with us.

"Vincent Thomas. I can't believe it's you. How long has it been?"

"Lauryn Davidson. Wow, baby girl! It's nice to see you," he exclaims as he bear hugs me.

"What are you doing here? I didn't realize we had mutual friends," I say.

Keith and Asia approach as we're chatting. I have no idea why Asia is standing here appearing uncomfortable since I'm not acknowledging her presence.

"Umm —"

"Asia, as I told you, there isn't anything for us to discuss."

"Lauryn, I didn't come here to speak to you. Vincent is my date."

"Vincent Thomas. Long time, man," Keith interrupts.

"Keith Alexander. How are you, man?"

"I'm good. Sorry about the Re —"

"Alexander don't even speak those words," Vincent interrupts. "You know what it's like. Well, maybe not exactly since you never got a chance to play in the NFL. I'm actually happier than I ever imagined. I love being a high school football coach. What are the odds you would be here? We haven't crossed paths in years?" Vincent asks.

(His girlfriend, omg. How did they even meet? I guess Asia upgraded.)

"Yea, I didn't get to experience any of the NFL. I do know disappointment from a dream getting cut short. I'm also satisfied with my career choice. I didn't realize you stayed in Nashville after your stint with the Titans. I guessed you would've gone back to the west coast," Keith comments.

"I grew to love Nashville, but the west coast will always have my heart. This party is hella dope. I wanted to tell yo girl no when she invited me. Gender reveal party sounded hella whack."

"You and Vincent are a couple?" I inquire since I want to be nosy.

"Yes, we're a couple." Vincent says,

"How long have you been dating?" I ask.

"Not too long. We work at the same school. I'm guessing you go way back. It didn't even come to my mind to ask if you knew Lauryn when I found out you were sorority sisters."

"Asia and I know each other very well in fact. We —"

"Lauryn, don't you and Keith have other people you want to chat with here?" Asia asks trying to prevent me from telling her sordid background with Jackson.

(This isn't my business. Vincent may deserve someone better than Asia. He should figure this out on his own.)

Before I could leave, both Asia and I grab our stomachs. We scream out in agony. I can make out a loud noise from across the room, too. I don't know what's happening. There's an uneasiness in my stomach that tells me I could shart at any moment. If you don't know what a shart is, let me educate you. A shart is the marriage of a shit and a fart. The spillage of the shit and the noise of a fart. I can't allow it to happen in the middle of this ballroom. The pain in my stomach is intense. I don't understand what's happening to me. I have to get to the bathroom fast to prevent something extremely embarrassing from happening.

"Are you guys, ok?" Keith asks sincerely. Vincent stands next to Keith, and he seems worried about us, too.

"I have to go to the bathroom," I yell and start running back towards it.

"Me, too," Asia yells as she follows me.

While dashing towards the bathroom, I see Jackson head the same way as well. Asia's right on my tail. I don't have time to process what is happening to me. I need to hit the toilet right away. I'm completely drained, and all of my guts have spilled out. I spend several minutes in the bathroom, and I'm hoping whatever happened is done. I rush out of the bathroom stall to witness my face in the mirror. I resemble death warmed over. I'm suddenly nauseous. I couldn't even gather myself. I speed back to the toilet to upchuck. I don't know what's wrong with me. I have foreign agents coming out of both ends. I'm completely gross. I need to get out of here and back home quickly. I can't stay here in this condition.

I'm still confused about what's happening to me. Do I have a stomach bug that hit me like gangbusters? Is the explosion of fluids finished? Do I need to stay near the toilet to be on the safe side? The bathroom smells very gross since both Asia and I lost our guts in here. If I stay in this bathroom any longer, I may have several more rounds of disgusting fluids expel from my body. I can't stay in this infestation of puke and bowel movement all around me. Asia is struggling to get herself together, too.

"Are you okay?" I ask her.

"No, it's like a demon possessed my internal organs, and he wants my life."

"Same here. I have to try to make it to my car. I have to get home."

"Yea, I can't stay any longer either. I don't know if the urge to go will come back."

"Good luck on making it back without an accident."

"You, too."

I rinse out my mouth and find the energy to leave the bathroom. People are asking if I'm ok, and I nod as I continue to get dizzier. I'm falling, and I can't stop myself. I have to brace myself for the impact. People are engrossed in conversations around me. I can't shift a muscle. My vision has gone dark. Am I blind? I felt fine 30 minutes ago, and then all of a sudden, it's like my life could be ending. I try to show those around me something. I want to reveal how I'm doing. Everything's moving in slow motion. I try lifting my head, but it hurts too much. I want to shout, "I'm ok." I'm not sure I am. I can't be good if I'm suddenly nauseous and dizzy. Why am I not able to speak? Why do I appear to be blind? What is happening to me? I try hand gestures. I fall flat. I can't do anything. I brace myself for what would come next. Would anyone help me? Would anyone know how to help me? Before I come to a realization of what's happening, everything around me goes black.

CHAPTER 15
Keith

I proceed into Lauryn's hospital room once the doctor leaves. She's small and fragile laying there in the bed. Something in my heart tugs witnessing her in pain. I don't want to disturb her if she's asleep. I'll observe her if only for a moment. Not like a stalker. I want to make sure she's okay. As soon as I enter the room, she stirs as if she could tell I entered. She stares directly at me.

"Hey there," she greets me weakly.

"How are you, beautiful? You worried me."

"I have food poisoning. I guess mercury poisoning to be exact. I'm not sure if Asia or Jackson have the same thing or not."

"Wow. I wonder how you have mercury poisoning. You must have eaten something different than the rest of us. The hospital is asking everyone to get tested since we were at the same location as you all who got sick."

"I hope you don't get this. You're too nice to go through this hell."

"That's nice of you, but you don't deserve it either."

"Thanks."

She's extremely vulnerable in this moment. My heart is pounding, and I know I want her. I want something real with her. She's been through a lot. She may not want to try something long-term with me. I'll go at her pace. I won't put any pressure on her to try with me.

"Are you up for company? I can certainly let you rest. I wanted to make sure you're okay."

"I'm glad you're here. Please, have a seat. I guess you know Vincent from your football days."

"Yea, we actually played in some summer leagues together in high school. We were always cool. How do you know him?"

"We went out a few times years ago. We weren't serious."

"Good to know."

"Why?"

"You know why. You're not ready to admit it yet."

"Am I —" She stops speaking suddenly and grabs her head. She's trying desperately to mask her extreme pain.

"Are you okay? Let me call a nurse for you."

I press the call button to get help for her immediately. The nurse comes right in. I don't know what exactly to tell her. I'm not sure what's wrong with Lauryn. Luckily, she's able to speak for herself.

"I have a bad migraine. I'm a sufferer. Is it possible for me to take Rizatriptan with the medication you've given me for the mercury poisoning?"

"Let me check with your doctor. I'll be back soon with an answer."

As the nurse leaves, I feel helpless. I don't know what I can do to help her. She's in a lot of pain.

"Is there any way I can help you?"

"You can turn off the lights for me, please."

I turn off the lights, and she slowly massages her temples. I can help her immediately by taking on the job. I gently remove her hands and replace them with mine. I ease into the massage gently then apply more firm pressure in an attempt to alleviate the pain she has. She moans and it validates I'm doing a good job.

"This helps. Thanks, Keith."

"How long have you had migraines?"

"Since high school. They're awful."

"My sister has them. I sympathize with you."

"Thank you. This is good. You have good hands."

"You're welcome. I certainly can't let you suffer in silence. That's not the Alexander way."

"Good to know," she smiles weakly.

"When you're better, we can go out."

"I'm not ready to date yet, Keith."

"I don't recall asking you on a date. You eat, don't you?"

"Of course. I have to eat."

"Well, we can eat together. If we go somewhere that we mutually enjoy as friends, it won't be considered a date, ma'am."

"I guess you have a point. I'm in too much pain to argue."

"There isn't a need for us to argue about this ever."

"Okay, you may have a point. I like you and hanging out with you should be fun."

"I guarantee it will be sweetheart."

"I'm glad you're confident about our non-date."

"Yea, confidence has never been a problem for me."

"Somehow, this doesn't surprise me at all."

She's trying her best not to show me how much pain she's experiencing. This makes me want to remove all her pain, and the reality hits me; I can't. This realization saddens me. Her pain causes me to have a much stronger emotion than sympathy or even empathy in my chest. I'll ignore this irrational feeling. It's probably only heartburn anyway. It's not like this means anything, right? She doesn't even want anything to happen between us. She doesn't want to figure out if we could be a thing. Not yet anyway. Should I let it bother me? Her body gives it away. She may want more. The body doesn't lie. She's too scared to try. I don't want to push her. She's gone through a lot. I'll exhaust her with my charms.

The nurse arrives to notify Lauryn it's ok for her to have the medication. There shouldn't be any adverse effects with the medication she's currently taking.

"Can you hand me my purse?" Lauryn asks me.

"Sure," I answer as I reach for her purse and hand it to her.

I fill a glass of water for her. She throws her head back swiftly to ingest the medication. The strained façade presented starts to disappear within moments. The medication is beginning to work for her. I didn't plan on staying long. I want to make sure she's safely asleep. I won't feel good leaving her alone and in pain. I'm drawn to her, and it's keeping me here. I can't make myself shift an inch to drag myself away from her.

I gaze at her awe-striking face as she falls asleep, and she appears ethereal and angelic. She drifts off to sleep, and I kiss her on her forehead then her cheek. I could stay here catching a glimpse of her in this peaceful state all night. I need to get some things done today. As I turn to leave, I linger to glance at her for a moment.

Damn, this woman is going to be the death of me. I know there's something between us. More than I can explain. It's more than a friendly neighborly kind of thing. It's something about her. Going against all my normal safeguards I place with women, I have to get to know her better. I have dated my share of gorgeous women, but her beauty is transcending. It's hard for me to put it into words. Her wit, intelligence, and charm are what makes me want to come back for more. I know the timing isn't right.

My phone buzzes as I stroll towards my car. I glance at a text from Sabrina. Normally, I would welcome a text from her. Now, I don't want to be bothered. I don't want to burn any bridges. I simply tell her I'm not available tonight. The thing I like about Sabrina is she doesn't get offended if I can't make it. The same goes for me if she can't make it. My phone buzzes again. This is a phone call I can't ignore. It's Mama calling, and she'll hunt me down if I don't answer.

"Mama, how are you?"

"How do you know it's me?" Mama asks incredulously.

"Well, Mama, there is a thing called caller ID where you can tell who's calling you," I try to explain as diplomatically as possible.

"Don't get smart with me, Keith Michael!" Mama states sharply.

"I'm not. I simply wanted to explain how the phone works."

"I know what caller ID is, boy. If you think you'll be talking smart to me because you have a fancy law degree, you're mistaken."

"I would never, Mama. Let's forget about it. What can I do for you?"

"Well, I'm hoping you'll get back together with Courtney. She's the perfect woman for you. Plus, you aren't getting any younger, and I want grandkids sooner than later."

"Mama, I haven't gotten back with Courtney, nor do I plan on getting back with her. Do you want me to be happy?"

"Of course, I want you happy."

"Well, why would you want me to marry someone who isn't meant for me?"

"Courtney is perfect for you."

"I beg to differ, Mama. Trust me on this. Let it go. Courtney and I are done without the possibility of resuscitation. You should consider what we had as DOA."

"Keith Michael, you're being unreasonable."

"No, I'm not, Mama. I would prefer not to talk about Courtney."

CHAPTER 16
Stranger

The stranger arrived at the gender reveal party without being recognized by anyone. He had an uncanny ability to blend into different surroundings. He looked forward to this event. He caught a vision of her, his beautiful doll, Lauryn. Being this close to his love (even if not within touching distance) made him smile. He could view her beauty from his vantage point. She wore a very pretty dress which accentuated her curves but allowed her to appear lady-like without being too revealing. He liked she respected herself and always dressed appropriately. She wore her hair with those curly tendrils framing her face. He liked that her makeup appeared natural and fresh-faced.

She didn't need any of it. She's naturally gorgeous. She's average height about 5'5. Her height and body stature perfectly meshed with his. A small smile appeared on his face as he gazed at her. She had the same effect on him every time he crossed paths with her. It amazed him how he never grew tired of her face. He couldn't imagine he ever would. She fascinated him, and he desired to learn everything about her. He could stare at her all day and never get bored. She had an exotic face like a model or an actress, but she would never be in the limelight. Not that she couldn't do this, but decision-making and problem-solving roles suited her better.

He knew the first time he laid eyes on her. Not only would he love her for her beauty, he knew he would also love the way her brain worked. He witnessed her making snap decisions at work only those confident in their abilities could ever make. She managed crisis and took charge each time. She remained calm, collected, and poised. She made decisions driven by data. She didn't allow her emotions to cloud her judgment. She did all of this by keeping the best interests of her team and the clients in mind. She projected herself as a no-nonsense and empathetic leader who commanded results.

He glanced over at her, and she sat with some guy. He didn't like it, but what could he do? She sat much too far away from him, and he didn't want to bring any attention to himself. His name didn't appear on the invitation list for this event. He had to blend in to avoid being discovered. He probably appeared like a lovesick teenager staring at her. She brought out the best in him, and he wanted to confide in her. One day, she would learn what she means to him but not today. He would have to settle with staring at her from a distance. He would imagine what everything would be like if he could replace the guy sitting with her. The guy should be him. If he could swap places with the infiltrator, he would without a doubt.

He would settle for staring at her as he daydreamed about wanting something more. He loved the way her neck appeared inviting as she craned her head to gaze out at a distance. How should he approach her? It wouldn't be cool to hit on a woman at a baby shower anyway. Would he seem like scum if he went up to her to spit, "Hey shawty, you lookin' good today. What's your phone number, baby?" Hearing the words in his head, he knew she'd walk away and leave him standing alone in the middle of the floor. He couldn't think about approaching her. Her friend's gender reveal party created joy for the parents and friends alike. The day should be about her and her babies, apparently. They just made the announcement. He didn't quite comprehend the purpose of a gender reveal party. When did people start having those? What's the significance? He just didn't get it. Did the parents get two gifts at this reveal and the baby shower?

He reveled at how people weren't bothered by the whole idea of the gender reveal party. He wondered who invented this new method to exploit friends and family. This reminded him of other made-up days where huge corporations made fortunes like "Sweetest Day." What the hell is Sweetest Day but a second-rate Valentine's Day? Don't get him started on the holidays where fortunes were made for big brother. He could go on about them longer than anyone cared to hear. What a scam! He would tip his hat off towards the inventor of this newfound way to make people spend money because it happened to be pure genius. He should have created this. He would've been richer a lot sooner. He would have to remember this event when he and Lauryn were expecting their first child. These guests would certainly be the type of people who would like to "pay it forward."

He hoped he could get close enough to caress her. If only he could brush her arm, he would go home satisfied. She drew him in like a moth to a flame. He wanted to move closer, but he feared being detected. Just as he started to venture her way, he nearly ran into someone who could potentially recognize him. He shifted left to go in a different direction because he didn't need this. He had to stay the course by blending into the background. Avoiding them only placed Melanie on his radar. He didn't accept Melanie's meddling, nor why she continued to follow him everywhere. Her jealousy of Lauryn made her erratic. He hoped she wouldn't be a problem for him. He had no clue how she knew where to search for him. He wanted to get rid of her, but he couldn't cause a scene.

"Melanie," he hissed, "what are you doing here?"

"I'm here because you're here. I have to make sure you don't do anything stupid."

"What could I do that's stupid, Melanie?"

She laughed, "there are many ways for you to embarrass yourself or me, but I don't want to give you any ideas."

"Embarrass you? How is this even possible?"

"You could state your undying love for her here for one."

"Why would it be wrong? I have strong feelings for her."

"Tsk. That's irrelevant."

"I love her more than anything."

"No, baby boy, you don't. My undying love for you doesn't matter, I guess. I won't lose you to your obsession with Lauryn. You're only allowed to be obsessed with me."

"I've told you too many times. I don't love you. I'm not in love with you. We don't exist. There will be no us in the future. I'm not obsessed with Lauryn. I just love her, but you wouldn't appreciate something like this. You're incapable of loving anyone. You certainly never loved me."

"You're mistaken. There will always be an us. We're forever connected. You have my love on a regular basis whether you want it or not."

"Do you seriously believe this is love?"

"Of course. There are different ways to love someone. I'm completely committed to you. If you weren't obsessed with the 'chick' of the month, you would realize how much I love you."

"There you go again. Confusing my genuine emotions of love as an obsession."

"What makes you think you aren't obsessed with her?"

"I'm not. I want to be near her, to smell her scent, stare at her eyes, kiss her lips and neck…"

"Please spare me with what you long to do to her."

"Melanie, you have no idea what it means to love someone. You're making it your life's mission to make me as unhappy as you are."

"You have enough. You don't appreciate what you have. I'm yours anytime. You just stare out in space at a woman who will never give you the time of day."

"I don't want you, Melanie."

"Since when?"

"Since I fell in love with Lauryn. Well, I've never wanted you actually."

"You don't love her. You love the idea of her. Tell me some facts about her."

"I don't have to tell you anything. Who cares how you feel? Everything important about her is in my heart, and one day she'll appreciate I love her as much as I do. She'll return my love."

"I hate you! How dare you tell me you love another woman? I will make sure nothing ever happens between you and Lauryn. She will never love you! You're pathetic!"

Before he could respond, Melanie stormed away. "You have no idea whose pathetic here," he mumbles.

He considered following her to ensure she didn't cause any problems, but later decided her leaving would be for the best. He didn't follow her. Melanie continued to be a thorn in his side, but he didn't want her to ruin this day. She'd become a problem he wished would disappear permanently. How could he shake her? Why did she always pop up at the most inconvenient times? He yearned to search for Lauryn, but he didn't get a chance. He nearly crashed into a beautiful woman, who turned his head, but he wouldn't be distracted from Lauryn. He's not blind. He recognized this lovely creature, but he could only admire her beauty. She blushed and fluttered her eyes at him. He stared at her for longer than he should have. He shouldn't allow himself to get distracted. It didn't matter how striking this woman happened to be. He noticed a slight twinkle in her eyes as she stared at him. He found it very difficult to turn away even when he knew he should.

"You look familiar," she recalls holding his gaze.

"I probably have one of those faces. If we ever met, I would definitely remember you."

"You're one of those guys."

"What do you mean one of those guys?"

"Yea, the flirt and flatterer type of guy."

"I'm flirting, huh? I'm only stating facts."

"Facts, huh?"

"Facts on facts on facts. You're gorgeous. This shouldn't come as a surprise to you either."

"Now, I'm gorgeous and cocky since I boast about being gorgeous. I like your method to attempt to get a girl's number."

"No, I'm sorry. I'm flattered, but there's someone else. I'm not the type of guy to cheat."

"That's good to hear. Well, your loss," she winks and laughs at him. "Well, I have to get back to my friends."

"Meeting someone pretty with a great personality is never a loss."

"It shouldn't matter if I'm pretty since you're not interested."

"I may be involved, but I'm not blind."

"Well, duly noted virtuous one who isn't blind."

"Nice to meet you."

"I would say the same, but we never exchanged names. Oh, well. I'm sure that's for the best. See you around, stranger."

"The pleasure will be all mine."

"Of course it will." She turned to leave him befuddled.

He glanced over at the other woman he recently interacted with, and who for reasons he didn't understand placed a small hold on his heart. He couldn't be seriously having a strong connection with her. Could he? It had to be as simple as acknowledging she's attractive. His heart could only belong to Lauryn. He wouldn't allow himself to be distracted by someone he couldn't have the future he dreamed about with Lauryn. It didn't matter how attractive and sexy this distraction happened to be. He had to focus on Lauryn once again. He turned to find her, and he noticed suddenly the agony and pain reflected in Lauryn's face. He feared something could be seriously wrong with her, but he had to help in some capacity. He hated having to hide in the shadows. She practically sprinted to the bathroom.

When Lauryn exited the bathroom, she appeared to be somewhat recovered, but she also seemed pale like she would faint at any second. He tried to advance closer along with many others. He got within 20 feet of her. She fainted and hit the floor hard. He hoped she didn't get hurt worse with her fall. She fell before anyone could catch her. He wished he could do something to help. He could only yell for a doctor. Luckily, Kassidy and Derrick were present. Both of them were residents at Van Hogen University Hospital. He didn't know their specialization, but any doctor would be better than no doctor at this time. Lauryn didn't appear to be the only one afflicted by this illness. Both Asia and Jackson had the same reaction as Lauryn, and he had to figure out what happened to them and why.

A petty part of him felt Jackson was getting what he deserved, but he let that go. He didn't have a spiteful bone in his body. He wanted to focus on Lauryn, and he hoped she would be on the mend soon. As the ambulance left with Lauryn, he chose to follow behind to discover for himself if she recovered. Who could he trust to give him a status update? He bowed for a quick prayer for his beloved. He couldn't bare it if she suffered at all. He vowed to sacrifice anything if it meant Lauryn would be okay. He refused to be selfish, but she remained to be his focus.

He will send her a nice bouquet of flowers. He's confident she'll make a full recovery but having her recover in a dreadful hospital pained him. He would give his left arm to be in her room right now. Some guy he didn't recognize filled this role. He couldn't quite place him. It came back. He remembered this guy from the club the night he danced with Lauryn. Something told him this guy will be a problem. He didn't like it.

Why was this guy even here? Did he crash this party, too, or did he have a relationship with the couple expecting the baby? There were too many unknowns swirling in his head. Most of his thoughts were focused on his newest competition for Lauryn's heart. This guy probably could have any woman he wanted, so why did he have to want his girl? He could tell the guy wanted Lauryn even if he pretended otherwise. Sweat formed on his brow. This happened when he was concerned.

CHAPTER 17
Interloper

He leered around the room with a sense of satisfaction. Soon, his enemies would get theirs, and he would be there to see every minute of it. He could barely contain his joy. He found himself lucky when he stumbled upon this gig with the caterer, Cuisine for You. It happened to be the same company who'd been hired to cater Kennedy and Eric's gender reveal (whatever the hell a gender reveal was). It sounded like some "old bougie shit" folks would use to fleece others to him, but all of that didn't really matter. This gender reveal would serve a dual purpose, one where he would get his deeply desired revenge. He chuckled in a way most would consider sinister.

He shouldn't have been this caught up imagining the ruins of others. He could taste the victory, and it tasted sweet. He didn't really smile much normally, but the edges of his lips curled into a small grimacing grin. He'd been in too deep imagining how he would embarrass those three that he didn't notice something he should have. He found himself face-to-face with someone from the past. He could envision the wheels turning in her head. Did she recognize him? She appeared puzzled. He needed to get away from her understanding fully if he stood there any longer, she would put two and two together.

"Excuse me. Can you get me more pinot noir, please?" she asked not indicating she recognized him at all.

Annoyed by her request, he responded, "You should go to the bar to get another drink, ma'am."

"I'm aware I can get a drink at the bar. Aren't you the wait staff?"

"Yes, I'm here to serve the guests their meals and any supplemental items for the meal."

"In case you weren't aware, wine compliments my meal. I'd appreciate it if you did your job. I would hate you to lose out on the rest of your pay because you didn't do your job properly."

"Sure, I'll get your wine right away," he hurried away mumbling to himself. "That bitch. She treats people like she's better than everyone else. She'll get hers one day."

He hurried away and returned with her pinot noir. This super extra woman should be happy he didn't have time to add something special to her drink. He wished he had five more minutes, and he would've given her bathroom time. He considered revising his current hit list to include her. She should be taught several lessons about how to treat people. It didn't matter if they were the working class or not. This heifer had to learn to humble herself. He could certainly be the one to teach her this lesson. The revenge he has planned for the gang of three won't compare to what he'll need to do this woman. He planned to make her life a living hell by ruining all her self-confidence and uppity behavior she has now.

This probably made him sound like a monster, but he'd be doing a service to mankind. This translated to the equivalent of an embryo miscarrying where the life isn't viable. He provided a valuable service to those around him. Even though most people may not agree with his methods. He found they agreed with the end results. His diligence should be respected and admired quite frankly. If he didn't ensure people paid for their sins, who would? Weren't there vigilantes out there making sure people who wronged others paid for their crime?

"Charla," he hears her friend call out to her. "Stop harassing the wait staff."

"Why shouldn't I? He needs to earn his pay, wouldn't you say?" Charla answers her friend before she directs her attention to the interloper. "Thanks for getting this so quickly. Here take this for your time and effort." She hands him a $20 tip and looks at him like he should be grateful.

"Thanks, ma'am," he murmurs, "enjoy the rest of your evening." He walks away and pockets the twenty. He doesn't go too far. He wants to hear the rest of their conversation.

"Look at all of the men up in here," her companion states. "There's no way we're going home solo tonight. I'm looking forward to the after party."

"Speak for yourself, lady. Remember, I came here with a date. We're both friends with the couple."

"Oh yea, your boytoy from work."

"He's not my boytoy!"

"You still letting him hit at work?"

"Why do you sound like a dude?"

"You didn't answer the question."

"Well, work sex happens to be the best sex ever! Why would I give it up?"

"Well, you could get caught and get fired for one."

"Well, it's not like my boss is going to find out. He has his head so far up his ass."

"Well, I hope to do more than live through you vicariously. I'm going to shoot my shot with someone tonight."

"Well, good luck with that, lady. Finding someone perfect for you may not be as easy as you would like. You're so picky."

"I am not. That waiter you were giving such a hard time is a cutie. It's too bad he's poor. You know, I don't date guys that don't have ends."

He had enough of their conversation and walked away. He lingered towards the corner to observe Lauryn, Jackson, and Asia eat their meals with vigor. He wanted to squeal with complete joy and euphoria. His plan would indeed work. It would just be a matter of time before things exploded, and he meant literally. He couldn't wait until the fireworks happened. He didn't have patience. He wanted the suffering to begin. Someone tapped him on his shoulder, and he turned suddenly to face her.

"Hi," the woman with Charla earlier purrs to him, "I'm Mystique. What's your name, handsome?"

"Is that your stripper name?" he asks jokingly.

"Wow! I'm a stripper now. My mom liked mysteries. I won't hold it against you. You have a sense of humor, so what's your name?"

"Oh, just some poor starving waiter," he responded in a snarky tone.

"Oh, about that. My friend Charla is so…how do I explain it. I can't be real with her. I don't care that you're a waiter. I don't really. She's uppity though. She would not stop talking about it if I dated someone who waited tables."

"So, we're dating now? Since when?"

"Come on. I think you're cute. Let's start over. I'm Mystique."

"Why should I start over with you, Mystique? I don't even know if I want to know this side of you. I definitely don't want to know the other one that has to impress her friend."

"What can I do to make it up to you? I just want to show you how sorry I am. Can you take a break with me? I'll show you just how I can redeem myself," she licks her lips.

He has been frustrated, and he could use a little stress reliever. He takes a quick break with Mystique to relieve some of his anxiety. Surely, she could be good for that. They disappear for more than 10 minutes and come back into the venue separately. Mystique wipes her mouth, takes a swig of mouth wash, and refreshens her lipstick before returning.

He wanders back to join the other wait staff to avoid any suspicion. He noticed some of the wait staff eyeing him and assured them everything had been okay prior to him taking a short break. He had to get back on track and focus on his main reason for being here. He searched out his enemies and knew things would pop off any minute. When he found them, he knew things were about to go his way. He snickered when he realized his plan worked flawlessly. Asia, Lauryn, and Jackson screamed out loudly shocking the room. All of a sudden they all stampeded towards the bathroom. He gawked in a barely audible tone when he witnessed them began to lose it. He wanted to laugh, but he knew this would cause him to have unwanted attention. He forced himself to keep his joy internal hoping nothing would translate to his face. His poker face never wavered in the past, but today would reveal whether he truly masked his emotions.

He glanced around, and some of the same wait staff members stared at him again. He had to tamper down any suspicion they may have. He couldn't have these dipshits ruining his plan. He heard one of the guys whisper he needed the pay for the day because his family depended on the money. He couldn't afford to work for free. He no longer worried about being discovered. He felt bad for the guy. He had to reassure him the company would pay him what they owed him even if its under-the-table. At least, he assumed they would. Cuisine for You depended on good reviews and a reputation of treating its employees well.

His enemies were in the bathroom for quite a while though. Admittedly, their appearance switched between green and grayed out. He hoped the damage wouldn't last beyond today. It worried him when they all passed out, and someone called 911 because they weren't responsive. The ambulance transported them to the hospital. He followed them to the hospital to learn more about the status of the patients. He had to figure out his next move. Since he hadn't planned this contingency, he didn't have the right uniform with him to be inconspicuous. He had to change into something else since he didn't blend in at all. People would jump to the conclusion that he worked in hospitability with one glance of his outfit. He would be noticed pretty quickly roaming the halls. He couldn't allow this outcome. He had to blend into the surroundings.

He removed the wait staff jacket in the car. He wore only a white t-shirt with black slacks now. Removing the jacket made him nondescript, and he blended in much more. He could roam around without being detected. He needed to make sure he didn't stay too long. He wouldn't be recognized. He strolled the halls of the hospital like an invisible person with caution. He had to check on the patient's condition to understand if there would be any permanent damage.

He didn't learn anything valuable, and he couldn't get into the area where the patients were being housed. He would need some sort of credentials he supposed. He didn't like being out of control. He had to know the measure of the damage done to his enemies. He desperately needed to know if there should be a contingency in place. He had to keep his eyes and ears open to discover what's going on with the patients. He wondered if they've been diagnosed with anything. He couldn't just hangout waiting for the information as a sitting duck. Someone may recognize him.

He realized the last place he didn't to be was here, but his curiosity caused him to investigate what went wrong. He had to know. He had to mitigate any potential issues. How would he be able to do that if he hadn't come to the hospital to investigate. He constantly had to deal with the nagging in his head wondering if he made the right choices...the right decisions. Nothing about what he did or didn't do was easy. His life had been built on complicated choices. Like everyone, he chose to believe he also made the right choice that suited him and his family. No one else mattered. He didn't have time for entanglements, arrangements, or relationships. Keeping himself neutral had been paramount.

He stumbled backwards when he discovered someone who could identify him if they were paying attention. This couldn't happen. Not now... not yet. He needed more time. He had to figure out how to get out of this predicament. The mercury couldn't be linked to him. Logically he knew it couldn't. He did all the right things, but his emotional side came up with theories and predicaments that would get him caught. He couldn't get let his emotional side win. He had too many lives to destroy.

CHAPTER 18
Lauryn

’m very excited to be leaving this hospital. Time has been at a standstill. I've been in this hospital for a week, but it feels like a month. Originally, the doctors thought I had simple food poisoning, but I have a case of mercury poisoning. My treatment includes chelation therapy. Hopefully, this therapy is only temporary. I'm better today, but there are some lingering aftereffects from the poisoning. I still don't have a clue how I ingested mercury. That's not your run-of-the-mill seasoning used to cook food.

Keith is such a great guy. He delivered my car home for me. Now, he's here to drive me home from the hospital. He's making it hard for me to maintain my stance of not dating him. This doesn't mean we shouldn't be friends, though. I want him in my life but only as a friend. That's all I'm capable of having right now. Plus, Keith is a player, so I can't go there with him.

I'm attracted to him and flirting with him is ill-advised. I don't want to end up in bed with him, and it only means we're casual. Is it possible for me to be in the friendzone with this sexy man? Am I being delusional? I'm going to try to be friends even though the failure rate is pretty high. How many times have I imagined what's under those clothes? Even now, he's dressed casually in a t-shirt and shorts, and my mind is wandering. The definition in his chest is poppin', and it's making me hot. Now, I'm wondering if he has a smooth or hairy chest. I wouldn't mind running my hands all over it. I couldn't possibly stop there, could I?

(Calm down, bad girl. These fantasies won't help with this friendzone idea I'm imagining.)

My mind and body want to venture into a dangerous place picturing Keith au naturelle. I have to shake these crazy good and bad thoughts. Otherwise, a friendship between us will be virtually impossible. I didn't realize Keith entered the room while I had this conversation with myself. His mouth is moving, but I have no idea what he's communicating. I guess that's what I get for fantasizing about him being naked.

"I'm sorry, what?" I ask absentmindedly.

"How are you doing today?"

"Much better than yesterday, but I'm not 💯. Thank you for coming by all this time I've been stuck in here."

"No problem. I want you to have brunch with me, but are you up to eating anything?"

"Something light maybe, but I'm not sure about going out on a date with you."

"Who said anything about a date? A bunch of my friends will be there. Technically, it won't be a date."

"Ok. Sorry I assumed."

"Would it be wrong if this is a date?"

"Well, with my recent dating history…it's not you —"

"Don't you dare say, 'it's not you, it's me,'" he laughs.

"Well, it is," I laugh, too.

"Are you ready to break out of this joint?"

"Is it possible for you to swing me by my place for a shower and to change?"

"Of course, sweetheart, great idea. I have your keys from when I returned your car for you."

He reaches into his pants pocket to retrieve my keys and hands them to me. A nurse comes into the room to discharge me. She glances at Keith like he's a lollipop she wants to lick. Technically, I don't have a right to be mad at her, but a part of me is. He's way too sexy, and it should be a crime. The nurse begins to flirt, which is kind of rude, right? She has no idea if he's my man or not. This chick doesn't care about relationship status. I'm being extra since we're not in a relationship, but she doesn't have that intel. She's not concerned with me at all. It's funny how thirsty she's being right now.

I'm uncertain if he's interested in her or not. The possibility of him being with her makes me want to chuck my lunch. Why am I having such a huge negative reaction to the idea of Keith with this nurse? I'm not jealous. Am I? Keith is certainly entitled to date whomever he wants. In fact, since Keith has a healthy dating life, he may want her. He's rarely alone. I don't want him with her or anyone else. Did I really just admit this to myself? What does this say about me and this whole friendzone concept?

"Hi, I'm Stacia. What's your name?" The nurse smiles at Keith like a lovesick puppy.

"Hi, Stacia. I'm Keith. Thank you for taking such great care of Lauryn. I'm extremely happy she had the best nurses available."

"You're welcome," she responds.

"Ms. Davidson are you ready to be released. I have your papers here. Once you sign them, I'll wheel you out to Keith's car. Keith, you want to drive around to the pick-up in five minutes."

Once Keith leaves, Stacia practically shoved me into the chair. I don't want to ride in the wheelchair at all, especially not with "Nurse Hatchet." I want to argue against this, but it's hospital policy to prevent me from suing them probably. I'm a good girl, so I get in the wheelchair for my ride to the exit. Keith jumps out of the car to usher me into the passenger seat. He put on a big show and kisses me seductively. Stacia lingers like she wants to say something to Keith. We settle in and drive away.

"Stacia seemed interested in you."

"You think so?"

"Yea, definitely."

"She's not my type."

"Really? She's cute."

"I guess. She's not my type, though."

"What's your type?"

(Damnit, why did I ask him this? Conversations are very easy with him. Everything just flows.)

"Do you really want me to share my type, sweetheart?"

"Sure, why not? Stacia is pretty, and you're not interested. What exactly is your type?"

"Being pretty isn't everything, but I'm really attracted to a woman who's about 5'5 or 5'6, light-skinned, with long, curly hair, and a body that won't quit."

(I'm blushing hard and regretting I asked him this particular question.)

"Hmm. That's pretty specific."

"That's my type right now."

"It's best we discuss something else."

"Your wish is my command, sweetheart."

"You'll give me anything I want?"

"Within reason, yes."

Why is this man driving me completely insane? How will I ever be able to resist all this charm, sexiness, and intellect? Tonya would suggest

I give Keith a test drive, but I want more than sex from him. A test drive isn't something for me. Nope. I better keep this in the friendzone. We don't utter a word on the rest of the drive home. Being his friend is really going to suck. Being around him will be dangerous for my emotional and physical health. Damn, what a predicament! I gaze at his entire body in a sly way hoping he doesn't realize what I'm doing. If we don't take this to the next level, I'll let my imagination run wild. Checking him out won't hurt. I'll stare at his assets until my heart's content. We make it back to our floor, but I need to get myself together before we go back out.

"Keith, I'll need about 30 minutes to get ready."

"You're a woman after my own heart. You'll be ready to go in 30 minutes?"

"Yea, I don't play. I'm serious about not wasting time."

"Ok, see you in 30."

I mean what I say. I don't waste time. Time is a valuable commodity you can't get back. I rush into my place to shower right away. I really wish I had told him 20 minutes only because I'm starving. I'm extremely hungry, and I could literally eat a cow. The hospital food makes me want to gag. It's terrible. I'm nervous about eating though. What if something doesn't agree with my condition? That could be embarrassing. I won't worry about it now. I finish my shower and wash my face in 10 minutes flat.

I dress in a cute A-line yellow sundress and wedges. I place my hair into a high ponytail and put on a very light application of makeup. I usually receive a lot of compliments in this dress. Not like I'm trying to impress anyone. **(Well, just because we're only friends, it doesn't mean I shouldn't care about my appearance in his presence.)** With five minutes to spare, I grab my purse and go over to Keith's place.

"Wow," Keith remarks with a huge smile on his face as he gazes at my angles and the definition of my body. "You look very nice. You weren't kidding about it not taking you long to get ready."

"Thank you. I never lie."

"That you don't," he comments by not hiding the fact he's staring at my assets. "You ready to go?"

"Sure, it should be fun."

On the drive to brunch, we're listening to some random jams on a livestreaming radio station. He likes to listen to Old School R&B and Old School Radio. This gives me another reason to like this guy, damnit. His taste in music is in sync with mine. Suddenly, "Real Love" by Mary J.

Blige comes blaring through the speakers, and I want to sing all of a sudden. I'll wait until the chorus. I'm not really a singer, but I can blend like nobody's business. This will not be like my Beyoncé experience either. I stupidly tried to go a cappella that night. Not wise. I realize my strength is background and blending but not performing solo. Keith smiles and joins me singing this song. We smile all goofy at each other while bobbing our heads like someone who grew up on this. In fact, I did. My parents loved some Mary J. When the song ends, we burst into laughter.

"I like it when you let go," Keith mentions.

"I love this song."

"Is it just the song, or could it be you're really searching for a real love?"

My cheeks suddenly are heating up and turning into an unbecoming shade of red. Did I just walk into this one? "I'm not sure real love exists," I reveal with a sad expression.

"Maybe, you just haven't had real love yet."

"I guess. You could be right. Well, I guess I'll have to state I'm undeclared about love."

"Well, even if things didn't work out with your ex, didn't you love him or are you stating you've never been in love?"

"I guess it's not right to minimize what we shared. I loved both of my ex-boyfriends. We weren't meant to spend our lives together."

"It rarely is. It's good you found out love is only one component to make a relationship work."

"Thank you, wise Buddha. I could easily become the bitter old cat lady who closes her heart to the idea of love in the future."

"Hmm, okay. I guess you really do want real love."

"Not really what I'm trying to convey," I burst out trying to conceal the fact I'm blushing.

CHAPTER 19
Interloper

The interloper parked his car in the emergency room parking lot of Vanhogen University Hospital. He sauntered out of the car and studied the façade of the building. He spotted a group of employees standing by a bench next to the designated smoking sign. He casually glided past them and stood two feet on the other side. Leaning against the rail, he pantomimed like he needed a lighter. An Asian nurse in pink scrubs offered him a light. He proceeded to start smoking the cigarette. He nodded appreciatively and gave her a slight smile. He took a drag of the cigarette and wondered how the hospital could condone having a designated area for smoking. He shook his head at the hypocrisy. He stood there not really a smoker although he has smoked a blunt or two.

He noticed the group of employees were breaking up, and he started to follow them into the building. They crossed the street. Noticing most of the group had disbanded, he put out his cigarette gingerly and casually strolled behind them. He maintained a distance close enough to be part of the group, but not close enough for the group to be suspicious of him. The employee in front scanned his ID to let the group into the employee only entrance. They held the door for each other until the interloper approached behind them with an ID in hand. He wore scrubs and a white coat. He made sure to hold the ID at an angle where the employees couldn't distinguish his ID from any others. They let him into the building.

He followed them inside the back of the emergency room. One of the nurses peeled off from the group and went to the nurses' station in the emergency room. The group stated, "Until next break, Brittney." The nurse called Brittney glanced back, smiled, and held both of her thumbs up. "Later guys!" she cheerfully stated to the group. He followed the other three nurses in the hall to the elevator, and they all waited for the next one to arrive. When it came, they all boarded. One of the nurses pressed two of the floors. They asked the interloper for his floor number, and he took a glimpse at the floors that were chosen before responding. The group of nurses were going to the third and fourth floor. "The fifth floor please," he stated. The elevator door closed. They arrived on the third floor, and one person got off. When they arrived on the fourth floor, the two other nurses exited. The interloper left the elevator on the fifth floor.

He strolled to the nurses' station, and he glanced at a single black nurse posted there. She answered the phone as he walked up. She appeared to be extremely busy and showed a touch of impatience as he asked for help to find a patient. She asked him to wait a minute since she would be off the call soon. He waited patiently for her to finish. She completed the call and appeared flustered because the shift would end soon. Her backup wouldn't be on time. She asked him how she could help him. The interloper assumed a fake Nigerian accent to ask if Jerry Jones could be found on the fifth floor. The nurse searched for the information on the computer stated he wasn't located on the floor. The interloper acted like the information couldn't be correct. He'd been informed Jerry Jones would be admitted to this floor.

He banked on the nurse becoming impatient at this point, and his "Jerry Jones" act worked like a charm. She told him to go to the third floor to find the patient in CCU. He picked up a pen and a scrap of paper from the desk. He wrote the information on a piece of paper. Before placing the pen back on the counter, he grabbed a USB flash drive with the name Vanhogen University Hospital on it from his coat pocket. He returned the pen and placed the USB flash drive next to the pen on the counter. He thanked the nurse for all her help. The phone rang at the nurses' station, and she waved him away to answer the phone. The interloper repeated this same action, pretending to search for different patients like Tom Jones, Jerry Smith, and Tom Smith on other floors in the hospital. Each time he repeated the same action. He left a USB flash drive at the nurses' station. He held a huge sense of satisfaction knowing his plan had a 95% chance of working. He slipped out of the building and left to drive home.

Once he arrived home, he removed his white coat, retrieved a beer from the fridge, and turned on his computer. As his computer booted, he turned on the television to have something to do as he waited. He began watching the Atlanta Braves play the Cincinnati Reds. The game lacked any fanfare, and it didn't hold his attention. He considered changing the channel to something else when he noticed his computer screen bleeped. The bleep indicated the payload had been installed onto the hospital's computer systems with backdoor access open to him. He logged onto the computer to view the hospital's credentials of his chosen victim, Becky Turnstall. Her username and password were retrieved from the backdoor. He took them to access the VPN of Vanhogen University Hospital. He wanted to obtain the medical records of specific patients. The outcome yielded the results he hoped to gain from this venture.

He found the patients in the system rather quickly. He concentrated on Lauryn Davidson's name. He needed to confirm her diagnosis and be aware of her prognosis. No such luck for him. The nurse, Becky, probably didn't have as much access as he needed, but the access she had allowed him to proceed with the plan. He made sure to copy pertinent information like Lauryn's medical information for future use. It'll be good to have any additional information on hand. He became slightly perturbed he couldn't find everything he wanted with one clean sweep. He would have to make another trip to the hospital. He hated making multiple trips to locations. He believed in getting things done in one fell swoop. The risk of getting caught increased. He never desired to be detected.

With the needed access to the system, he began to make an official badge. This would allow him to come and go in the hospital without anyone being suspicious. He had to make sure his appearance would be nondescript, so he could blend into the background. He didn't want to be noticed visiting the hospital. If someone pesky tried to undermine his plan because of carelessness, there would be hell to pay. He wanted to find out more regarding Lauryn's case, and he wondered if there would be any long-term ramifications from the poisoning. Donning an official badge, he headed to the hospital the next day. He eased into the employee entrance without a second glance. He decided to go to the hospital during shift change. There weren't a lot of people at the nurses' station at this time. He cruised the halls without anyone being skeptical of him being there. The hospital constantly had different interns and residents. The likelihood of the nurses recognizing every intern or resident seemed less likely.

The nurses' station on Lauryn's floor appeared empty as he approached it. This happened to be his lucky day. The entire floor seemed like a ghost town. He knew he had to hurry because Lauryn would more than likely be released from the hospital very soon. He needed information about her case. He smirked contemplating how hospitals need to be much more secure than they were. Maybe, as soon as all of this is over, he could provide a high-level security technology to hospitals. He didn't have time to think things through now. He had lives and relationships to ruin while seeking his much sought after revenge.

He heard some shoes clicking on the floor as he headed to Lauryn's room to view her chart. He noticed others there visiting their loved ones. He smiled at them as they passed. They murmured "Hello" and "Have a good day" to him. He loved how friendly people were in Nashville. They were much different than the residents of New York where he once resided. New Yorkers wouldn't give him a second glance let alone bid him "Hello" and "Have a good day." Moving south brought a sunnier disposition to his days. Too bad he encountered people like Lauryn Davidson to bring in rain clouds. Taking advantage of the vacant floor, he sought out the nurses' station to retrieve the information.

He took his time roaming the halls to get what he needed but was careful not to be discovered by others who could potentially recognize him as someone who did not belong. The nurses on the floor were conducting rounds, and this made him happy. He went to great lengths to understand the ins and outs of how this hospital operated. He didn't like leaving anything to chance, and he would blow a gasket if anything foiled his plan. He may have lacked authority and power in this institution, but incompetence wouldn't be accepted or celebrated. A sound in the hall caused him to quickly scan the perimeter because technically he shouldn't be snooping around at the nurse's station. His eyes roamed the floor only to learn two nurses were approaching him. She started working at the hospital recently, and she didn't quite have everything down pat yet. The training nurse displayed some annoyance with the other nurse…and they barely noticed him.

He picked through patients charts until he retrieved Lauryn's. Since he'd made sure to be appropriately dressed, presumably no one would be wary of him reviewing the chart. He could discern more about the case. He learned her prognosis and release date. He repeated the process with the other two patients' charts without anyone being suspicious. He put the chart where he found it. He ventured towards the nursing station where the new nurse appeared flustered and at a loss. The training nurse stepped away leaving the new nurse alone. If he had more time, he would get acquainted with the cute new nurse. He wouldn't mind taking her to the on-call room. He would have a boatload of sex as soon as this scheme is done. Did he really find the nurse attractive, or could he hit on about anyone now? Something lured him towards her, but he wanted to ignore it. He didn't have time to socialize or get engrossed in anything.

"Doctor, are you ok? Do you need any help?" The new nursed asked him.

"Shit," he mumbled to himself, "No, I'm just turned around. I'm new here," he stated with an air of confusion.

"Join the club, I'm Erin," she declared holding her hand out to him.

"Erin, very nice to meet you," he glanced at his phone like it vibrated. He jerked the phone to his ear. "Dr. Jackson, I'm on the 4th floor. You need me on the 6th floor. I'm sorry. I'll be there right away." He put the phone back in his pocket and gave Erin an exasperated expression. "Duty calls. I hope to run into you again," he yelled out as he jogged in the direction of the stairs.

"Wait! What's your name?" Erin asked.

"If I told you, I'd have to kill you," he announced with a smirk.

"You're crazy!" she laughed.

The phone at the nurses' station starts ringing off the hook.

"Sorry, I got to get this," she apologizes. "Third floor, Nurse Anderson speaking."

"Gotta go. Bye now!"

"Hold one moment. Hey, what's your name?"

He pretended to not hear her but gave her a wave as he opened the door to the stairs. He grew disgusted with his behavior. He could get caught by a piece of ass he hadn't claimed yet. He wouldn't be deterred by his momentary lapse in judgment. He moved at a pace to avoid attracting any attention as he left the hospital in the same inconspicuous way as he entered it. He rushed out to the parking lot to become a distant memory for anyone in the building. He didn't make it far. He suddenly heard someone screaming in his direction.

"Doctor, doctor. Over here. We need help!" A woman yelled.

"Oh shit!" he muttered, "I may have to play doctor for real."

A frantic woman waved him over to her. He ran over to the pair in need. A man, who appeared to be in distress, laid on the ground. These people needed real help, and he felt some kind of way about it. This may seem strange considering he normally didn't dispense empathy. He shouldn't be considered a monster no matter what some people thought of him. He couldn't be discovered as a fraud. He would improvise to help this couple out. He nearly panicked. He watched enough medical dramas to speak the medical jargon to get this guy the help he needed.

"What seems to be the problem?" he asked the woman.

"Adam, my husband here, passed out. We were on our way to visit my sister and her new baby."

"Okay, let me get a look at him."

He checks for a pulse, and he's happy to hear a strong one. He may not be a doctor, but he is well-versed in CPR. He wanted to get this man to the ER doors ASAP.

"We need to get him to the ER."

"Please call someone to help."

"No time. I need your help lifting him," he snaps.

He didn't have the time or the energy to explain to her why she needed to help him get her husband to the doors of the ER. They struggled getting Adam upright but moving him went surprisingly well. They jerked opened the doors of the ER, and the interloper yelled out.

"I need someone to help him fast. I found him out in the parking lot passed out suddenly according to his wife. He hasn't been drinking, and his pulse is steady."

"Thanks, doctor. We'll take care of this."

The nurse gets some help, and they drag a gurney around to retrieve Adam. Adam's wife turned to thank him, but he disappeared. She didn't have a clue when he vanished. She looked around for a moment before she realized her complete focus needed to be on Adam and whatever was wrong with him. She'd been grateful the young doctor helped her, but she had to put all of her effort and energy into making sure Adam is healthy and okay.

He slipped back out to the parking lot avoiding anyone who could inconvenience him any longer. He did something good today. Adam may survive because of him. He smiled for a brief moment feeling a sense of accomplishment for doing his part as a doctor today. As great as this felt, he had to head back focus on his mission. People had to pay, and he had to make it happen. He slinked away in his car to parts unknown as easily as he arrived to the hospital.

CHAPTER 20
Lauryn (Next Year 2017)

Luckily, the side effects from the mercury poison are non-existent now with several months of treatment. I'm back to my old self. I'm surprisingly still happy working at Food Will, but the pay sucks. I do enjoy giving back but Food Will isn't a long-term option for me. As long as the work is challenging, I'll be at Food Will making a difference.

I guess my priorities have changed a lot. I need to figure out what's most important to me. This will drive me to figure out my next steps. I'm fortunate to have this chance to do this. I have enough savings to get through this with very low impact. I'm also blessed to have a home without a mortgage. That's something I don't take lightly.

Keith has been on my mind lately, but it's best to stop thinking about him. He's what wet dreams are made of, and I need to shut off the image of us in an intimate setting. He's creeping into my subconscious more than I would like. The only acceptable way for me to be in close proximity with him is to have other people around.

Mostly, I'm not in a hurry to hang out with him again. I speak fast and keep it moving. I've only spent time with him a few times since brunch. My mind is playing several tricks on me. I have imagined sex with him. It would be earth shattering. I would be a weak pawn and easy prey in this man's hands. That's why I should avoid him like the plague. I could fall hard and fast for this man.

Contrary to Tonya's suggestion, I'm not mentally prepared to have sex with someone like Keith. I guess if I could break down and have a one and done, it would have to be with someone like Alex. Keith, on the other hand, is someone I could fall in love with. He checks all the boxes, but he's a bigtime player.

Over the last few years, I've seen Keith with a few different women. He's not the person I want to help me get over Jackson. I guess he could be if I'm only interested in one night, but something tells me Keith could be addictive. I may want more than one night. I have a strong feeling he'll leave me very satisfied with a five-gold star rating. Could Keith be my one and done? It may be impossible to forget about him. Plus, he lives on my floor. This could be resident suicide. I have sex on the brain right now, and I need Keith out of my mind.

I guess running into him in the hall shirtless has my brain going overboard. I'm probably just horny because it's been a really long time. The damn vibrator isn't doing it for me anymore. I need some skin-to-skin action. I haven't had a drought like this since Isaac and I ended. I should focus on something else. I'm going to the kickboxing gym to work out and distract myself. Alex is my trainer today, and we're alone.

"Hey, Lauryn. We haven't really had the opportunity to spend time together. I want to change that."

"Wouldn't going out with me compromise your job?"

"I'm attracted to you. This is not a career for me. We should just go out and get to know each other." As he speaks, he scanned my entire body. I should be offended, but I'm not.

"No, there isn't anything wrong with that."

"We both have to eat right? How about one night this week?"

"Dinner has never hurt anyone. When would work best for you?"

"You tell me what works for you, and I'll make it work."

"I'm free tomorrow night."

"Tomorrow night it is."

"Ok, it's time for me to workout, sir."

I work out extra hard this morning, and Alex isn't going easy on me at all. I like Alex, but I don't want things to go south between us. He's a great trainer. I guess hanging out with him shouldn't hurt. Plus, Alex is very nice on the eyes. He's six feet tall with low-cut, curly hair. His skin is somewhere between a caramel color and a brown paper bag. His eyes are dark brown, and his mouth is delectable with dimples. He has full, sexy lips that probably could swallow me whole. Imagining his lips on me excites me in more ways than one.

I'm such a horny chick. I'm imagining all sorts of dirty things his mouth could do to me prior to me chastising myself for having these dirty thoughts. Is celibacy really a choice? Am I making this choice freely now? What am I doing? I have never thrown caution to the wind and just had sex with a guy. Plus, if things go bad, I may have to find a new kickboxing gym.

Would one night of passion be worth leaving this gym? Now, this is a tough one, and I have a lot to consider. Sex or gym. Sex or gym. The gym would win hands-down every time. Now, if something does pop off between us, we must agree we'll remain cool no matter how this turns out. From my perspective, he would only be a one-and-done for me. I absolutely love him as my trainer.

I'm in an Uber on my way to meet Alex at the restaurant. He greets me with a hug and a kiss on my cheek. The date with Alex is really a lot of fun. We're laughing and joking the whole meal. I haven't had this much fun in a while. I didn't realize how late it's getting. As much as I would like to stay, I have to get back home for a decent night's sleep.

He strolls towards me and kisses me. His lips are magic. Everything I imagined about his mouth doesn't compare to the reality. His hand lingers to cup my ass, and I jump suddenly. I don't know if it's because I like this too much or if my hormones are going overboard. Either way, I have to get this under control. He senses my hesitancy.

"It's okay if you want to go slower. I just like the way we connected tonight."

"I agree. We have. I like you, but I haven't dated in a while."

"Taking this slow isn't a problem. Is it okay if I kiss you again?"

"Sure, I'd like it if you would."

He reaches down to cup my face and kisses me tenderly. I nearly reconsider my resistance for this whole one-and-done. The way his tongue feels makes me want to reconsider everything I've been programmed to believe. He gazes at me deeply before we break away from one another. His face indicates he's hungry for more.

"Alex, I really had a great time. I should head home. I have to get to work early. I need to call a Uber, too."

"You don't have to call an Uber. I'll drive you home. I had a great time, too. I would like to do this again."

"I'd like it, too."

"How about Friday night?"

"As in three nights from tonight?"

"Yea. Too soon?"

"No, I'm free on Friday."

"Let's get you home."

I'm getting ready for another date with Alex. He's been flirting with me a lot at the gym, but luckily, I've been there during slow times with not many clients. He's a master trainer and mostly trains by himself, especially at non-peak hours. I don't like crowds, and I tend to go during those times for some personalized attention.

We're going to the movies, and I'm wearing something casual. I rock a pair of skinny jeans, an off-the-shoulder sweater, and stilettos. I grab my jacket just in case it gets a lot colder tonight. I'm channeling my favorite superhero, Wonder Woman, as I meet Alex in the lobby. He greets me with a kiss as he hugs me close.

"You're beautiful," he voices as his gaze shines.

"In this old thing?" I joke.

"Well, it may be old to you, but I love this outfit on you."

"Thank you. You're such a charmer."

He leads me out to his car, and we head to the movies that serves dinner with the show. I'm a big fan of dual-purpose theaters such as this one. We both like scary films and decide to check out the latest *Purge*. I freak out during one of the scenes and jump into Alex's arms.

He chuckles, but he likes that I'm in his arms (if his tender caress along my arm is an indication). As the film ends, I have a lot of energy. It's Friday night, and I don't want to go home just yet. Home has been pretty lonely since Jackson and I split. I have to admit I really enjoy spending time with Alex. He makes me laugh, and I haven't done that in quite some time. Not a real hearty laugh anyway.

"I don't want the night to end yet. Do you want to go get drinks and learn more about each other?"

"I'm having a great time with you Alex, and it's still early. I would love to get drinks."

"Perfect. Let's go."

He places his arm around my waist to lead me to his car. We drive to a lounge to have dessert and drinks. With a few drinks in, I'm beginning to feel very mellow.

"You wanna do some Molly?"

"I'm not sure."

"I'll take care of you."

"Okay. Why not?"

We're laughing and suddenly we're kissing. Alex suggests we go to his apartment since things are getting heated. I should decline, but my body wants this. In the end, my body wins.

I have no dissolutions about what will happen tonight, and a big part of me is excited about what's to come. He escorts me into his apartment and draws me near him immediately. We're kissing and stroking each other. Before long, I'm falling back on his bed and tugging his shirt off. In between kisses and body caresses, we both start undressing each other.

We're hungry for one another, and everything is simply amazing. We're breathing heavily as we concentrate on removing every drop of clothing to get to the main course.

He only broke away from me for a minute to get a condom, which is a relief because I don't want to stop the momentum to insist he grabs a rubber. Alex's foreplay game is much better than the finale. He slams into me, and his rhythm is way off from mine. We aren't connecting at all. There isn't any synergy. He's pulling while I'm pushing. He's simply not in sync with me.

He doesn't realize I'm not enjoying myself. I didn't peg him for a selfish lover, especially with the way he performs magic with his tongue. I guess that's why his oral game is on point. His actual game is leaving a lot for the imagination. Hey, I did want a one-and-done. His performance is guaranteeing there won't be a repeat act. He comes, and I smile at him awkwardly. I clean myself pretty fast. It's time for me to leave.

"You were incredible, babe. You wanna stay with me tonight?"

(Shit! I can't utter hell no! I don't want a repeat!!)

"Alex, as much as I would love to stay here, I have such an early day tomorrow, and I need to go home. I won't get much rest with you lying next to me," I wink and lie my ass off.

"Give me a minute then I'll drive you home."

"Don't worry about it. I'll call an Uber."

"Lauryn don't be ridiculous! You're my date, and I'm responsible for getting you home safely."

I hurry to the bathroom to get freshened and dressed to go home. He's ready to go as soon as I exit the bathroom. He must have used another bathroom because I used his primary. At least, I hope he used another bathroom. On the drive, we're pretty quiet, and I yawn to indicate how tired I am. We don't need to chit chat. He catches on fast and doesn't try to force a conversation. He parks in front of my building, and he smiles at me. I want to jump right out, but I still need to walk a fine line to make sure he remains my trainer.

"I want to get together again, Lauryn. I hope we will soon."

"Yea, ok. We'll see."

As I'm leaving, he gently grabs me to kiss me passionately. I really have to find a way to inform him this isn't happening. This is certainly a one-and-done. Maybe, Tonya is right about having sex with someone to forget someone else. My mind hasn't wandered on my ex at all tonight.

Well, I guess I messed up with mentioning him. Even that's not quite true. I may have reminisced briefly during Alex's interlude of wham and bam. Jackson is a great lover, and this less than spectacular experience made him come to mind. Damn him! I wave goodbye to Alex and proceed to head to my place. I jump in the shower and hop in the bed. I fall asleep surprisingly fast.

Following our time, he called me to go out again, but I pretended to be busy. I have to face the music. It sucks to be misled. I must woman-up and be honest.

Avoiding him is getting me nowhere. The problem is I like him as a friend and a trainer. I never should've crossed this line with him. Something tells me Alex will be okay with us not doing the dirty tango anymore. He liked me, I suppose, but he'll move on to another woman once I tell him we should just be friends.

It's been a couple of months since my date with Alex. I hope it doesn't get ugly because we crossed a line we shouldn't have. I guess I'll find out following work if Alex will remain my trainer at the gym. I avoided his schedule, but I miss how he trains me. I must deal with this now. It has been slightly awkward, and I don't want to lose my favorite trainer. Working out is one of my favorite past times. It probably sounds crazy but, I tend to run in the morning and kickbox in the afternoons.

I hope the new terms will be okay with Alex, since we definitely won't be a thing. I could be way off base. Alex may just want to be friends, too. He may not want this to ruin our trainer/client relationship. I'm heading into work, but I better "woman-up" with this Alex situation. I have to make it clear about what's going to happen with us moving forward. Resolving the issue with Alex will help ease the tension I've imagined will happen between us the next time we cross paths. It'll probably be today.

I feel anxiety as I slowly stroll into the gym. It's now or never. I refuse to lose Alex as my trainer, but am I being selfish? What if he wants more than I'm willing to give? Alex and I stare at each other, and he beams at me. The gym is deserted. Now is the time to have this conversation.

"Hey, stranger," he flirts, "How have you been?"

"I've been good. How about you?"

"No complaints. Do you have a second to chat?"

"Yea, I've been wanting us to clear the air between us."

"Yea, me, too. I hope you're okay, but I think we should only be friends."

I smile, "Yea, I happened to be thinking the same thing."

"Great, I didn't know how this would go. I'm glad we're on the same page."

"Me too, friend," I smile at him, and we shake hands.

We chat for some time longer, and Alex takes everything surprisingly well. He understands I'm not in the place for relationship or casual dating either. He still wants to hangout as friends. We hug in a strictly platonic way. He's very cool and things aren't awkward at all.

The workout burned my legs and thighs, and it turned out to be grueling. I wondered if he meant it when he said we should be friends. He's punishing me like a girl he loves to hate. He had a humungous grin on his face when the workout finished. He's a sadist, or I'm a masochist because nothing about that workout should make either of us smile.

I'm happy with our situation now. We go out every so often, but it's strictly platonic. Ladies, it's possible for men and women to be friends. I didn't even have to speak with him about our night together. It's like it never happened.

It's a really cold February morning. I've been running a lot more lately, and today of all days I decided it's a good day to go. What in the hell am I thinking? It's cold as crap out here. I haven't been sleeping well, and I've been waking at 4:30 AM naturally every morning. It sounded like a good idea to get out and run since I couldn't sleep. Well, until I got out of the bed and into the cold.

I open the door to my patio to check out the weather conditions. The wind hits my face and reminds me I don't like cold weather. Well, I'm not one to complain too much, but it's cold out here. I have to get hype to go out there now. I'm whispering some nonsense about "Once I start running, I won't feel the wind. It won't bother me." I'm awake now, and I got to get this run in. Going back to sleep now is futile.

Exercising always puts me in the right frame of mind. I quickly put on my gym clothes and stretch. In the hall, I run right into Keith. Great. Just great. I'm not sure about what his perception of me is right now. I've been distant and avoiding him since the brunch. He's going for a run, too. Again, just my luck. I'm surprised he's pleasant towards me. In fact, he didn't seem to notice or care I've been acting dodgy.

"Hi, Lauryn. I'm surprised you're here this early. Are you going for a run?"

"Yea, I've been running for a while now. I just don't usually go this early."

"If I'd been the paranoid type, I would assume you've been avoiding me."

"Me! Avoiding you! Of course not," I utter nervously.

"Ah, okay. Since we're both here, would you like to run together?"

"Sure, just try to keep up with me," I joke.

"I'm sure I can," he comments while checking me out.

I turn away suddenly. I'm getting nervous with the way he's gazing at me with his smoky, light brown eyes. I'm like a schoolgirl with her first crush staring at him. Damn, why am I doing this? I should be avoiding him, but no, I'm running with him. Why? I have to remember Keith could be my kryptonite. Shaking off these feelings, I stretch to prepare for the run.

We're pretty quiet while we run. He listens to his music, and I listen to mine. He occasionally asks me a question, but overall, it's like a normal day of running for me. We finish faster than I would've running alone. As we board the elevator together, he asks me to join him for a recovery drink. I have some time, and against my better judgment I agree to join him. I glance around his place, and it's decorated very well. He has great taste in décor. This is a bachelor's pad, but it's neat and very well configured. Could he have designed this place himself? If so, color me impressed.

"Nice place. Did you decorate yourself?" I ask.

"Thanks. I did actually. I love putting my stamp on a place."

"Wow, I'm impressed. You amaze me with the more I learn about you."

"Thanks. Would you like to learn more? Is it too soon to ask you out?"

"I guess it depends on what your expectations are."

"My expectations?"

"Yea, your expectations. Do you want to hang out and get better acquainted?"

"Yea, you've met all the expectations I have right now."

"I'll offer you friendship without benefits."

"Hmm. Without. I see."

"Yea, I just want to keep it 💯 with you."

"Yea, that's cool. I've wanted to spend some quality time with you for some time, but the timing has never been right."

"You sound confident like it is now."

"Not really. Why wait? Other than my reservations about you and dating someone in the building, I understand how that could be problematic."

"Not sure if we'll be dating."

"I misspoke," he declares with a smirk, "I have my misgivings, too. I'm not sure if hanging out with a woman in the building is considered dating or something I want to do."

"You misspoke, counselor?" I smirk, "I guess it should be ok to hang out with you."

"How's tonight? We could get dinner and/or drinks."

"I'm actually free tonight. Where do you want to go?"

"We could go to one of my favorite bars, but it's not close."

"Why don't we stick around here and go to the neighborhood bar across the street? We're in striking distance in case we drink too much."

"Hmm, you think you'll have too much to drink?"

"I just like to plan ahead."

"Maybe we should discuss why you're avoiding me."

(Shit, shit. I didn't dodge this question very well.)

"It's not fair to assume I'm avoiding you. We just haven't run into each other too much lately. With work and other priorities, my schedule has changed a lot."

"You're protesting a lot for someone who isn't avoiding me."

"Well, I'm not avoiding you."

(I'm avoiding him every chance I get.)

"Ok, I guess we'll just have to see about this, won't we?"

"Whatever, Keith. What do you mean by this?"

"Well, it's quite simple, Lauryn. I raised a concern about you avoiding me, and you denied it. I guess, I'll be running into you a lot more now since you're not avoiding me."

"I guess you will. I should really get going. I need to get to work."

(Damn, he trapped me with his logic.)

I head to the door. We aren't dating. It's mind boggling as to why I'm acting super strange around him. I'll hang out with him tonight and learn more about him. No harm no foul. I'm strangely excited about going out with Keith tonight. Should I be excited? Probably not. I have to stick with the whole friendship without benefits I mentioned to him. Why am I making more out of this? We're just hanging out. I didn't notice his question since I'm busy walking through scenarios in my head.

He follows me to the door and asks, "…You…okay?"

"Hmm," I respond absently.

"Well, until tonight," he states with a smile.

"Until tonight."

I'm scared about Keith because I want more with him. Yep, I admit it. This is extremely dangerous. I want to kiss him again. The drunken kiss shouldn't count, but it had me panting and wanting more. I've also had too many wet dreams about this man. I have to start making sense of this. I'm jumping the gun way too much. I need to stop tripping and just have fun tonight. I just need to keep it casual and just be friends. I need to keep things in the right perspective where he's concerned. Only time will tell, but I hope to be strong.

As I get ready for work, I think about Keith. Why are my mind and body in conflict? Wanting anything other than friendship is a recipe for disaster. I've pictured his body completely naked. Sometimes when I run into him, I zero in on how defined and toned his incredible body is. My fantasies have led to performing some sexual aerobics with him. I tried something out of the norm with Alex, and it failed miserably.

Jesse calls to inform me I have another package downstairs. It's still a mystery as to who's sending me flowers every two weeks. At first, it shocked me to receive the roses, but now they come like clockwork. Don't get me wrong, I'm appreciative someone thinks I deserve to be sent such beautiful flowers. As soon as the roses die, replacements are sent. There is a different sweet and enduring note each time.

The person must be someone I'm at least familiar with because I get the flowers at home. So far, no one has admitted to sending them. This is driving me crazy. My secret admirer's identity needs to be revealed. The person covered their tracks, and I'm unable to find out who it is from tracking. Why is this person being this secretive? It bothers me not having a clue whose sending the flowers. No one has tried to reach me in any other way. I guess one day my secret admirer will be revealed.

This is making me be more aware of my surroundings than I would be normally. I'm glancing around at people when I'm at various places like coffee shops, grocery stores, and places I frequent to determine if someone is looking at me in an admiring way. Who could this admirer be? Is it someone I've helped while volunteering? How did they retrieve my home address? It's scary to think some random person may have access to this information. I hope the person doesn't have any maleficent intent. I hope this person only wants to make me smile. Something tells me this person is rooting for me. He wants me to be happy again. Is this being naïve or gullible? Probably both since I don't have a clue about who sent them. I hope my gut is right about him.

I'm careful going out because this person could be crazy, too. Since I don't have his identity, it's hard for me to acknowledge what his true intent and motivation is. He's only made nice comments on the cards like, "You're beautiful," "keep showing me your dazzling smile," "love the woman you are," or "you make the world a lot better," etc. You get the hang of it. He's very complementary, but there's no mention of what he wants from me. He doesn't mention he'll make a move and introduce himself. I'm at a loss, and I'll continue to hope he's my own personal Genie. What more could a girl ask for? He flatters me, and his messages uplift me.

Following a leisurely coffee break, I head back to work. I have a busy day ahead since we need to prepare for the giving season. The department in charge of sending out promotional material isn't as efficient as it should be. I have a meeting with the department manager, Charla. We don't see things the same way. I hope this meeting is fruitful. Charla is one of those types of managers who's territorial over her work, and she takes everything personally. We graduated from NTU together, but we weren't friends. I think she'd been friends with Kennedy and Tonya. She also wants to tell my team what we should be doing. I side-eye her every chance I get. One, we don't report to her, and two she has no clue how my team should be assisting her. She's been advised to stay in her lane. I stroll into the conference room just in time for the meeting with my notepad ready to go.

"It's great you could make this meeting, Lauryn. For a minute there, I just knew this meeting would have to be rescheduled. Well, time is money. Not here since we're a nonprofit. You guys get what I'm saying, though," she laughs and states this in an authoritarian tone.

"It's 10:30, and I'm right on time. Why would we need to reschedule this meeting?" I respond and glance at my watch for dramatic purposes. "Let's get started," I state as I sit. "Please tell me exactly about the problem you're having."

"Well, Lauryn, we're trying to get these promotions out, and we need more temps to get them out there faster with the mail and everything."

"Ok, Charla. Let me provide you with some clarity. I don't need you to tell me what the solution is. I need you to simply tell me what your problem is."

"Forget it, Lauryn, if you don't want to help. We'll get some temps hired."

"Charla, I'm trying to help you, but I need you to simply state the problem you need solved."

"We aren't getting the promotional materials out in time."

"Ok, thanks. The next steps are to setup an 'As-Is' process flow session."

"Why can't we do it now?"

"I need to setup the brown paper to properly document the process. Today, we'll work through everything that'll occur during the session. You and your team will be prepared for the discussion."

"I'm still uncertain why you can't just tell management I need additional staff."

"I won't tell them you need additional staff."

"Why? Because it's me, and you don't like me?"

"Charla, you're being ridiculous. This isn't personal. I don't have anything against you. This is my professional character I'm protecting. Why would I tell management you need additional staff without me conducting analysis of your current state? My opinions are respected, and I want them to remain this way."

"No one is trying to ruin your professional character. You're being ridiculous! This meeting is over!" She leaves in a huff and rushes out of the room. She slams the door as she leaves.

The door slam could be heard all over the floor. After a few minutes, Jonah, my team member comes rushing into the conference room. I'm still sitting in the same spot shaking my head at her unprofessional behavior.

"Hey Lauryn," he whispers, "are you okay?"

"I'm fine. You should probably be checking on Charla since she's clearly upset."

"She's always like this. I'm surprised she's still working here."

"I've had a few run-ins with her, but this is by far the worst."

"What did she want from us?"

"What she really wants is for us to get her more employees without doing any of the work to justify it. What we'll do is the current state process flow. She didn't ask for our support. The president asked me to help with the problem she's having with her marketing. I'd simply giving her the benefit of the doubt and an opportunity to be the voice of her department, but she wants to do this the hard way. I can do it the hard way just fine."

"Yep, boss, that's why I love working for you."

"Come on. Let's go back and create a schedule for this project."

We leave, and Charla is coming our way with a scowl on her face. Her scowl becomes devilish, and I swear if looks could kill, I might just die from her stare. Well, I'm pretty glad and fortunate her expressions won't come near killing me. Later in the day, I thought about clearing the air with Charla because we're both women, and we should support one another. It's very cliché that women can be another woman's worst enemy in the workplace. I want to change this and figure out how Charla and I could find a common ground for us to work together. We're the same age after all, and we're both minorities. It's important we aren't enemies. I want to have a positive working relationship with her.

Now is a good time to stroll by her office for a chat. As I round the corner, I notice her door is shut. I should go the other way. I turn to leave and hear a moan come from her office. It's like two in the afternoon. (**"Is she really getting an afternoon delight?"**) I'm not a hater but come on. She'll probably get away with this, too. I don't want to be viewed as a creeper, and I attempt to leave quietly. I don't get far before a man comes out of the office zipping his pants. (**"Ooh, he couldn't zip his pants prior to leaving her office."**) He turns back to her and whispers, "See you tonight, baby. I'll return the favor." I hear her giggle, and I've had enough eavesdropping for one day. I don't want to be judgmental. People are free to get theirs true enough, but this chick here acts like her shit don't stink. She acts like she is God's gift to Food Will. I don't trust this woman. I'll definitely continue to watch my back around her. I recognize the guy who came out of her office. He's on her team. I guess she loves being the boss in more ways than one. He may be her significant other, too. I hope she'll act more professionally now since she's gotten some. She acts like she has a stick in her ass.

CHAPTER 21
Stranger

He strolled into the kickboxing gym with a purpose. It didn't surprise him to find Lauryn there. He'd been following her for some time. He didn't like the way the kickboxing trainer "examined" her. Didn't this place have some sort of rule about fraternizing with the clients? He didn't have any problems reporting his behavior to the owners. She shouldn't be subjected to some trainer flirting with her while he should be working. He hated watching the pretty boy try to make Lauryn his prey. He didn't trust the guy, and he would make sure Lauryn steered clear of him one way or the other.

The pretty boy would lay it on thick to make her feel like she's the one for him. Would Lauryn fall for his simple game and end up in his bed? He wanted to believe she wouldn't, but her decision making has been questionable. Her vulnerability worried him. The trainer ogled her like he wanted to have her as a meal, and he didn't like it one bit.

He could imagine the lines he plied on her. "You're beautiful girl. A woman like you can't be single. If you're single, you won't be for long. I can help you ease some of your tension. Let me love this body of yours." The more he pondered the cheesy lines, the more he wanted to punch something. Being in this kickboxing gym provided the perfect outlet for him. His frustration would be channeled very soon with a bag rather than a person. He had to sign up for a trial to avoid any suspicion of his being there. He stared aimlessly in Lauryn's direction trying not to appear like a stalker. The trainer with Lauryn suddenly appeared next to him.

"Welcome, my friend. Would you like to have a free workout today? Try it out, and you'll want to join this amazing club. Would you like to have a trial? I can certainly help you."

"Does now work?"

"Definitely, let's get some info from you prior to a tour of the gym."

The trainer grabbed a tablet and handed it to him to provide some basic information to receive the free workout. He would never provide any accurate information. He would give this location a fake name as well as the number of the burner phone he used sometimes. He didn't trust the security in this place, and he wouldn't be providing his real identity. He hoped to finish the paperwork and catch Lauryn. He had absolutely no interest in this gym, but she made this trip worth it. He glanced over at her, and she sweated profusely. She didn't seem to mind, though. She put in every effort to perfect her form, and he could tell she concentrated as she worked out. No surprise her body resembled a temple. She ate good food and exercised often to maintain her perfectly defined body.

Why did he find her more attractive with sweat glistening on her face and her flexed muscles displayed each time she hit or kicked the punching bag? Her dedication and drive to stay physically fit as she maintained the demands of a career impressed him. He continued to stare in awe. He had no doubts she committed the amount of time required to stay in shape. He stared in Lauryn's direction hoping for a glance, and the trainer came back over to check-in with him. This annoyed him and interrupted his "gawk fest" of her. The trainer showed him around the gym. He hadn't begun his workout as someone tapped him on his shoulder. He hoped Lauryn would somehow be the one tapping him. It wasn't her. There stood Melanie, yet again, ready to spoil his "wishful" thoughts.

"What made you come here?" he hissed.

"To join the gym, silly. Why would I be here?"

"Your being here will ruin things for me. Your constant jealously doesn't bode well for you. Adorable...not. Why this gym instead of another gym?"

"Because of you, lover. What brings you here? Her, right?" she asked pointing at Lauryn.

"Of course, I'm here because of her."

"Well, lover, don't slip away from me. I won't lose you! Not to her! Not to anyone!"

He scanned the site to observe Lauryn leave, and this irritated him. "See what you've done, Melanie. You've made me miss her."

"I haven't done anything. I'm not wanted here. I'll go. Good day."

He scowled as she turned away and left the building. The trainer approached him. "You ready?" the trainer asked.

"I got a call from work. I need to reschedule."

He left the building not waiting for the trainer's response. He had no idea where Lauryn went. He pondered where she would go. Probably not straight home. He chucked it up as a "win." He smiled noticing how translucent her skin glowed as she worked out. She smiled during her entire workout. Could his tiny gestures be helping her? He could be the reason for her happiness. He observed a certain lift in her spirits, and he would love to witness her reaction each time new roses arrived. He remembered the first time she received the roses. She smelled them, and her face illuminated with pure joy. He trudged away with a lift in his step. Someone bumped into him, and he nearly tripped on the sidewalk. This pissed him off. The person didn't mutter an apology for knocking him off his feet.

"Hey, man. Do you have a limited vernacular? 'Excuse me' must be a foreign concept," he stated angrily.

"It would be if I'm at fault," the man answered.

"Wait, what? You tripped me without an apology. What's up, man?"

"Sorry. I have a lot on my mind."

"Don't we all."

"Look, jerk. I apologized. What do you want me from me?"

"Sincerity would be nice."

"Yea, yea. You're right. I wasn't raised in a barn. Something my mom would say," he choked out as he teared up. "I'm sorry I bumped into you. You weren't hurt, were you?"

"Nah, man. I'm good. Are you okay?"

"It's been the worst day ever."

"It's not any of my business, but are you okay?"

"Not really. My mom died today."

"Aww, man. I'm sorry. I lost my mom last year. I can relate. Don't worry about earlier."

The guy appeared to be lost, and he considered leaving. Something compelled him to ensure this guy would be ok. When he lost his mom, it devastated him. The pain he endured with her loss remained with him. He remembered how his mom would smile at him as she woke him for school. The memory caused him to smile.

"Hey, man," the guy began, "how did you get past it?"

"Huh? Get past what?"

"Your mom's death?"

"I haven't gotten over it. I doubt I ever will."

"Will this consistent pain always linger?"

"No, it changes, but if your mom meant to you what my mom meant to me, you'll forever have a tiny piece of you missing. Hey, man I got to check this message." His phone buzzed with a text from someone not identified in his contacts. He didn't want to leave this guy in this state of despair, but he had to check this message. "Sorry, man. I have to go, but Godspeed and condolences for your loss."

"Thanks, bruh."

Unknown: Call me ASAP

Stranger: Call whom?

Unknown: Why don't you save numbers? This is Andrea Johnson.

Stranger: Give me 5 min

Andrea worked with him, and she tended to freak out about various issues with clients. He didn't need five minutes, but he would get back to her on his time. He didn't jump through hoops like a lackey. He would make her wait and give her a call when he desired. He took a leisure stroll to his car and warmed it up before connecting his phone to Bluetooth to make the call. The phone rang twice before Andrea answered.

"This is Andrea Johnson speaking."

"Andrea, I'm calling as you have requested."

"Thank you. I've been freaking out here. I really need your help with the client, STU. They're not very agreeable. It's imperative you address the Stanton and Thomason issue. They've been calling non-stop, and I don't have a clue what to tell them."

"Andrea, I need you to calm down. This case is like any other one where the scumbags we represent want some sort of miracle to save them. Did Stanton admit anything yet?"

"No, he's still claiming he's innocent."

"What about Thomason?"

"Same."

"Well, the answer I gave them last week still stands. They need to settle if they don't want this blown up in their faces."

"They're insisting on speaking with you in person. They refuse to speak with anyone other than you. I understand you didn't plan to work today. Do you mind coming in to handle this? I'll owe you big time."

"Andrea, we're colleagues who help each other. You don't owe me anything for doing my job."

"Please still consider accepting a payment for the trouble."

"Thanks. Talk to you soon."

CHAPTER 22
Lauryn

'm completely refreshed and excited about meeting Keith for happy hour. I have no idea what I should wear. This isn't a date, but rather a non-date with a guy I'm having serious erotic thoughts about. I mean constantly. **(Relax, girl. You're about to give off some thirsty vibes.)** I'm standing in my closet trying to figure out what mood I want to project tonight. I pick out several outfits. One is a brown suede skirt paired with a cream cami, distressed jean jacket, and brown riding boots. Another is a burgundy sweater dress paired with black ankle boots, distressed jeans. Then there's the navy V-neck sweater, black leather jacket, and navy knee-high boots, and a jean miniskirt. Or I could do the burnt orange scoop-neck shirt, black jacket, leggings, and black thigh-high boots.

The suede outfit isn't chill enough. I may be giving off, "I want to date you, vibe." The burgundy dress screams, "first date vibe." The distressed jeans outfit is laidback and hella chill. This outfit definitely projects, "I'm the chill girl who will watch the game with you." The miniskirt outfit screams, "we're dating and having sex vibe." Feminist don't get your panties in a knot. I believe a woman should be able to express herself anyway she wants. I wouldn't own all these outfits if I didn't believe this. I'm having an internal struggle not with my clothes, but how I'm going to keep my emotions on lock with this guy.

I choose to dress casually in distressed jeans, V-neck sweater, leather jacket, and knee-high boots. I place my long, curly hair into a ponytail. I apply some powder, mascara, and lip gloss. I choose a simple thin silver necklace, tennis bracelet, Apple watch, and silver hoop earrings to complete my ensemble. I examine myself in my full-length mirror and decide to give myself a thumbs up for this outing for drinks with a friend. I head out to tread my way to the bar since it's not too dark yet. I meet Keith in the hallway on the way to the elevator.

"We have to stop meeting like this," I joke with him.

"Yea, the neighbors are going to wonder if something's going on with us," he replies.

The elevator dings to alert us of its arrival. We enter the elevator, and Keith presses the button for the first floor. He escorts me to the bar around the corner from us. Keith's dressed casually, but very nice. He's wearing a dark blue cashmere sweater and some dark-rinsed jeans. His shoes are Cole Haan's men's casual wear, but they fit perfectly with his outfit. He wears an Apple watch to complete the ensemble. We continue to amble to the bar. We get there in time to get great seats and beat the happy hour rush. We find a table in the back where we could view the TVs, but it isn't as loud. It's early in the evening, and there are several regular season NBA games tonight, plus a slew of college basketball games. It's a basketball fan's mecca tonight.

"It's good there are back-to-back games tonight. I love basketball season," I comment.

"Me, too. Yea, I love a good game. I'm excited for March Madness next month."

"I love to go to basketball games in person. The crowd and the energy are just an indescribable feeling I love."

"I get it. There's energy you can't replicate through the TV."

"I try to catch as many games in person as possible."

"I've dated women who pretended to love the sport because I did."

"Really? I don't get the point. If you don't like something, don't fake it."

"You wouldn't be pretending to love sports, would you?"

"Never! What kind of women are you dating? Do you remember me at the Titans game back in the fall? Did you catch the cross over the kid from Michigan maneuvered prior to his assist in the alley-oop? Impressive and on an NBA level." We were both observing the screen at the time.

"Alright. You're proving to be a sports aficionado. I'll never question you again. Your crossover knowledge is exceptional. Color me impressed."

"It doesn't take much to impress you," I smile at him.

"Not at all. I'm not difficult."

"Is that right?"

"Certainly. I've given you another reason to reconsider your stance on us dating."

"Dang, I guess I walked right into that, didn't I?"

"Yea. You kind of did," he winks at me.

Even though the bar isn't crowded yet, it's still taking the waitress a long time to get our order. I don't mind because we're having a great conversation. She finally arrives, and we order some drinks. Keith orders a bourbon neat, and I order a mojito. We share some potato skins and spinach dip. The waitress leaves, and things start to get a little serious between us.

"Is it okay if I ask you a personal question?"

"Sure, shoot!"

"Is there any chance for you and Jackson to get back together? I'm just asking for a friend."

"No, not at all. He hurt me worse than anyone ever has. I trusted him with my love, and he destroyed me."

"I feel you. He's a fool. I wouldn't do that."

"Well, everyone claims they won't hurt the other person by cheating, but as a lawyer, you should be aware of high percentage rates of divorces caused by infidelity. I'm sure at the alter the bride and groom swore they would be faithful. Life happens and people change."

"How did we jump to marriage? I just want to date you."

"Date me exclusively?"

"Definitely. I don't like to share if I'm into someone. Never did. Not even as a child. My report card would have great marks, but the comments read I need to work on sharing with others."

"Wait a minute. You don't like commitments. That's what you told me, Craig." Will he catch it's from the movie, *Friday*? If he does, another check in the "I should date Keith" column.

"Well, Smokey, I haven't dated anyone I wanted to be committed with. This doesn't apply to you since we're not dating."

He got the reference. It's over. I'm falling. This guy is trouble. Not only is his sex appeal on one hundred, but I really like him. He has great taste in movies. "Pardon moi, I'm wrong. I make mistakes."

"Why don't we discuss what's next for you and me? I'm very interested in you."

I'm very uncomfortable. I guess it's because I'm interested in him, too, but it'll probably end with me and my broken heart. The promises I made are close to going right out the window. **(I want him. Mayday, I'm in trouble. What am I going to do now that I've admitted this to myself? I hope the anxiety I'm feeling isn't showing on my face.)**

"I told you I lost my job at the club," I begin with my unconvincing attempt to discuss something else. I'm not sure why I'm this nervous, but he's staring at me in a way I might like too much.

"I like how you changed the conversation, Lauryn."

"No, I just want us to get better acquainted with each other."

"Okay, I'll bite. What exactly happened with your job? I'm sincerely interested."

"I prepared to give a kick ass presentation, which happened to be a formality. The real prize dangled in front of me for years included the promotion I worked very hard to achieve. Imagine my surprise as I read an email laying me off. They told me even though my accounts have been making money for the firm, they would be eliminating my position. They didn't believe I would accept a demotion."

"That's bull. Were there others laid-off?"

"I'm uncertain about all the layoffs, but everyone with my position either got the axe or demoted. Sad but true. I happened to be the only black person and woman in my previous role."

"I'm very sorry. I assumed you found something else since you mentioned going to work earlier."

"I'm working at a non-profit, Food Will," I announced. "I enjoy it, and it's perfect for now."

"Your new op sounds interesting. Would you like another drink?"

"Yes, I'd like another." He flags the waitress.

She comes over to retrieve our drink orders and apologizes for the wait time. We continue our conversation about Food Will, and what I plan to accomplish there. He's impressed I chose to work at a non-profit when I could've easily gone to work for a profit driven organization. He really gets me, and he understands not everything is about making money and making the big corporations richer. I had to learn the hard way how much I value a home life.

We're having an intriguing conversation as the waitress comes over to bring our drinks and asks if we're ready to place our order. I order a turkey burger with fries, and Keith orders a cheeseburger with fries. I really want to change the conversation since I no longer want to discuss STU or Jackson. I also must be mindful about how things could slide down a slippery slope to mindless flirting between us. I chose to forget how I completely embarrassed myself at the club by drinking way too much. This time is different because I've only had two drinks. My cutoff. I probably had at least six drinks at the club. Not a great decision on my part.

I want to learn more about him other than he played football in college. I still can't believe my dad recognized him at the game. I learned he's from Memphis, Tennessee. He graduated undergrad from a school in Memphis, and he went to law school at Vanhogan University. He injured himself while playing college football. He could've possibly had a career in the NFL. He tore his meniscus and ALC during his senior year. Because all of this happened at the time of his final eligibility year he missed out. The recovery time for this type of injury ranged from 12 to 18 months, so his draft opportunity didn't appear favorable. It's sort of obvious his injury remained to be somewhat of a disappointment. He only appeared to be slightly sad to have missed out on playing professionally. He appears to genuinely mean it when he discusses ending his football career helped him figure out what he wanted to do with the rest of his life. He doesn't have any regrets because he loves what he does.

My dad believes he would've been a first-round draft pick. I wouldn't blame him if he did feel a little salty since he lost his one in a million chance to play in the NFL. It's not my business. I don't want to over-step and mention what it could have been for him. His career's trajectory changed after football couldn't be relied on any longer. He didn't wallow around in a funk. He created a plan B and followed through with it. This makes him even more irresistible to me. **(Shit! I'm in deep.)**

He began working at Jefferson & Jones Law Firm (J&J Law Firm). He's on the partner track with them. Lawyers work a lot of hours, es-pecially those on the partner track because it's all about those billable hours. It reminds me of the consulting life. He chose a specialty which has afforded him to have a work life balance. Keith spent most of these last few years having a very good time. I respect the fact he didn't try to gloss over his playboy days. He clarifies he isn't a playboy. He's just a guy who has a few friends.

(Whatever that means. If he says, he's a guy "with friends," the "with friends" is the definition of playboy. Why do I care so much? Do I want him to be mine? Stop it now! I'm not in the frame of mind to be his or anyone else's at all. Look at what happened with Alex. Do I want another cluster fuck? No, I don't.)

He mentioned he's ready for a change. He wants to spend his time with someone he shares something more meaningful with. Someone he could share his life. He has a great father, and he wants to be like him one day. This is a different side from the player I pegged him to be. The player is easy to dismiss. This guy who wants a meaningful relationship with someone is not. Is he seriously ready to be in a committed relationship with someone? His dangerous magnetism has me focused on his bedroom moves. I'm having a hard time sitting still wondering how dangerous and tempting he'll be after this. He handed me the final blow by showing me his romantic and serious sides. Keith has a cunning ability to charm my pants off, and my heart can't survive the lethal punch it most certainly will receive. I inhale deeply and tell myself to slow this crazy train down. **(He never clarified whether he wants any of this with me or not. He just mentioned he's ready for something real.)** Discovering he wants more than a casual fling makes something flutter in my chest. The thing is…I don't want him to have this with anyone else.

While learning about him, I'm more intrigued with every word he utters. He tells me about his close-knit family. He has two siblings, RJ and Sheila, and he's the youngest. They all live in Memphis, and he makes monthly trips home to visit. Learning about his family piques my interest regarding his childhood.

"So, what were you like as a kid?"

"Well, curious and very active. I didn't give my parents any trouble. Curiosity didn't kill the cat. It fed my psyche to pursue a law career."

"That's cool. We have curiosity in common. I love problem solving, which helped me to determine I would like to become a mechanical engineer."

"Hmm. You don't really fit the engineering mold."

"I'm fascinated. What mold is stereotypical for engineers?"

"Sometimes engineers come off as rigid and inflexible. I don't get that vibe from you."

"That's a common misnomer about engineers. Well, some engineers aren't rigid, but some are just like you described. It's probably why I'm not a hard-core designer, and I pursued consulting instead. I'm a people person, but I love data."

"Would it be rude to call you a nerd right now?"

"I could be offended, but I'm not."

"If it helps, you're a really cute nerd."

"It doesn't hurt at all. What's your favorite past time?"

"It has to be watching sports.In person or on TV, it doesn't matter. You're a master at changing the direction of the conversation. You sure you weren't a lawyer in a past life?"

"At one time, I considered it, but I soon realized it's not all about court room drama. I guessed before I knew you were a receiver in college, by the way."

"How did you guess? Are you an expert like your dad?"

"Not an expert, but I have eyes. Your body is perfectly sculpted, and your hands are solid. Your height and size scream football. Definitely wide receiver. I'm pretty sure you didn't drop many balls."

"I could go so many places with your entire statement, especially the piece about balls."

"As long as it's not, 'that's what she said.'"

He laughs, "Nope, I like to be more creative. I guess your analysis background makes you an expert. You seem to have special knowledge about my body."

"I'm not blind. It's not a secret you have a very nice body."

He laughs, "I could ask you to further elaborate on my perfectly sculpted body and my hands being 'solid.' I'd love to hear more of your feedback, but I don't want to make this awkward."

Trying not to be too embarrassed, I change the subject. My face begins to heat as it starts to turn bright red. All I need right now is to start blushing like a schoolgirl.

"So, did you do play anything other than football in high school?"

"Yep, I was a triple threat. I played basketball and ran track, too. What did you do you in high school?"

"I was on the debate team, the track team, and the dance team."

"What events did you run?"

"100 and 200 meters. I also ran the relays."

"We have a lot in common."

"You want to race someday?"

"Nah, you might win," he jokes.

"Afraid to lose. Hmm, I see you." I do the universal sign for watching you.

"Not really," he laughs, "I just don't sprint anymore these days."

"Aww. Your injury? I forgot. My bad."

"Don't worry about it. It's cool."

"Did you do anything else in high school? You seem like one of the popular kids."

"Yea, I suppose. I was Homecoming king and in a whole lot of clubs. You know typically high school stuff."

"I'm not surprised you were Homecoming king."

"Why?"

"Well, you're just the type. You probably had all the girls in high school. I bet if your yearbook were available, it would show you won, 'Most Handsome,' too."

"I'm not sure if I should confirm or deny your allegations, but enough about whether I won the title, 'Most Handsome,' or not. Tell me more. How was it being Homecoming queen?"

"I wasn't Homecoming queen. I didn't meet the criteria. I could've been considered basic in high school. I participated in some clubs like you, but that's about it."

"Basic and you are not likely. I won't believe it. You brought the boys to the yard."

I blush as I state, "Well, you would be wrong. No boys came to my yard for sure. I happened to be super skinny with braces. Not ideal for a beauty queen."

"Well, some things have certainly changed," he flirts with me.

My face is growing even hotter. He could sense me getting very uncomfortable, so he doesn't press the issue further.

"Can I ask you a random question?" I ask.

"Sure. Shoot."

"When is your birthday?"

"It's actually soon. In a few weeks on March 6th. When is yours?"

"My birthday is next month, too. It's the 22nd."

"You're not supposed to ask a woman this, and my mother would kill me if she heard me ask you. How old will you be on your birthday?"

"No worries. I won't tell her you asked. I'll be 27. How old will you be?"

"I'll be turning 29."

"Ooh. One more year before 'Dirty Thirty.'"

"I feel good about it. A lot in my life will change by then."

"Yea. Like what?"

"A man can't tell all of his secrets."

"Ah. Okay. I totally get it."

"On another note, I knew there had to be something beyond the obvious for me to like you," he states. "We're both March babies."

"So," I tease, "you like me, huh?"

"Of course," he mentions as he winks at me. "I like you. I like you, a lot."

I'm in a lot of trouble, but I really like the way I feel. Things with us are going in a direction I'm not prepared to face. Not yet at least. I pivot the conversation yet again to his work. He practices real estate law, which is a very fascinating topic to me. He generally deals with commercial property deals. Occasionally, he goes to court, but mostly his work doesn't require court appearances. His enthusiasm and excitement increase as he mentions real estate acquisitions, and it's refreshing. He makes property acquisition sound so stimulating, and the heat is growing between us. Most of the time, he's been able to have a balanced work life compared to other fields of law. This is a plus in my book since he's able to have a social life.

"So, what's your dating situation? Is there anyone special?"

"Not yet, but I'm open for the possibility," he smiles at me.

I'm suddenly hot again, and I hope I'm not still blushing. Why do I keep putting myself in awkward situations with this man? I'm having a really good time with him. He listens as I chat about figuring out my career, especially about my uncertainty with consultant life. I explain to him how much I love volunteering, and I want to continue doing it if I get an entirely different role. He listens to me intently and provides some good feedback to my questions. I just enjoy being with him, and we're uncovering we have some of the same interests. To my chagrin, we have a lot in common. We share a mutual interest in sports, dancing, poetry slams, movies, theater, and travel. It seems our mutual interests are endless.

We talk for a few hours before finally realizing its late, and we decide to call it a night. We head back, and I'm elated. I want him in my life if only as a new friend. It could potentially lead to something else in the future, but for now it's good having him as a friend. My neck is really bothering me. A good night sleep will be the remedy. I try rolling and stretching my neck in the elevator. I suddenly have a terrible strain. I reach my neck to gently massage the ache forming. Keith notices my discomfort. He doesn't utter a word. He only zeroes into my pain point. When we arrive at my place, he holds me by the shoulders.

"Why don't I come in for a minute and give you a neck rub? You're uncomfortable. I don't mean to brag, but I give an amazing massage as you know very well. I've had a great time, and I don't want the night to end yet. We could catch the game, and I can massage your neck."

"I'm having a great time, too, but a massage might be too intimate. You did have me at catch the game, though."

"Intimacy with me extends beyond your neck and shoulders. I'm offering a strictly professional neck rub. I hate you're struggling to get the knot out. Just let me in, and I'll make your neck pain free."

I couldn't argue with his logic at all. My neck hurts a lot. "You're right. Come in. Would you like anything to drink?"

"Nah, I'm good."

He didn't lie about his magic fingers either. I could fall into Lalaland quickly with the rhythm of his touch. I lower the volume of the game, so we could chat. We're immersed in conversation for hours. We have a tremendous amount of chemistry, and we're really clicking. I can't deny this fact. I finally glance at my watch because I didn't realize how late it's gotten. It's after 1:00 AM. It's a Friday night, but it's still kind of late for hanging out with my sexy neighbor. We're not running out of things to discuss. I could do this all night, but it would be wise to bid him goodnight. We could easily go from friendly to "friend-ly" faster than a car can go 100 mph from zero to 60 seconds.

"I hate to end this night, but it's really late. I had a great time." I smile sheepishly.

"Lauryn, thanks for going out with me. I enjoyed spending time with you tonight. I hope we'll do it again sometime."

"I would love to hangout again."

"How about sometime next week? We can catch a movie, preferably an action flick."

"Sounds good." I accompany him to the door.

"Goodnight Lauryn," he whispers, "By the way, you're really cute when you blush."

I'm slightly mortified, but I don't want to give him the pleasure to rub it in. I'm very embarrassed.

He teases, "Why do you look like you're naked in a room full of strangers? Don't be embarrassed. It's only me, and you're so cute right now."

"I guess cute will work to describe me. It kind of sounds like I'm your kid sister."

"I'm trying to keep this above board, okay? You're beautiful and sexy. I want to stop imagining what's under all those clothes you're wearing and see for myself."

"Oh shit! I guess I should have just let you call me cute."

"Once we're beyond the PG stage, and you want me to keep it real with you, I will, sweetheart."

"What's wrong with being PG? We're friends, right?"

"Sure. We're friends." He peers at me sneakily.

"Yes, we're friends."

"Not for long, but I'll wait until you want something else."

"You're very confident this will change. What if you're wrong?"

"I'm not wrong. Your face and body tell me a different story than your tongue. I get it. Jackson did you dirty and trust is hard for you. I'm willing to work for it. I'm willing to show you we could be good together."

"Okay. I guess I'll be pleasantly surprised by all of your hard work and effort."

"Aight. No doubt. I really should get out of here."

He reaches out to hug me, and I basically fall into his chest. I'm still very embarrassed, but his body is too much of a temptation. He kisses me on the jaw and walks out of the door. Part of me wants a real kiss, but I'm certain things between us wouldn't end with just a kiss. He could take me to places I'm not sure I'm ready to go.

"Until next time, sweetheart."

He turns to stride away. I gaze at him as he wanders back to his place for longer than I probably should've, but this man is just as yummy strolling away as he is approaching me. What am I going to do? I close the door, and I head upstairs to my bedroom. I jump in the shower to cool off some of the heat radiating from my skin. Yep, it's going to be a cold shower. I can't stop smiling or remembering every moment about tonight. I can't remember the last time I had this much fun. I'm glad I decided to hang out with Keith. He's a smooth operator. My face is glowing red as he pops into my mind. I'm very embarrassed. I resemble a teenager with a crush.

I could've been with Keith tonight if I could handle something casual. I can't do casual with him. **(I know what you're thinking. I did exactly what I'm describing with Alex and look how things turned out.)** Keith is a whole different story. I can tell he would rock my world. It's an assumption, but he seems skilled in the art of pleasing a woman. Every inch of him would excel or even provide a masterclass. It won't be wham, bam, thank you ma'am at all. Attempting something casual with him would be suicidal. My failed attempts to recover would be considered shameless. I'll have to settle with Idris Vy and some more wet dreams. My future looks bleak. I'm a coward. Keith got me wet with only gazing at me. How does he do it? I mean my panties are soaking again, and he hasn't even touched me yet. I better forget this because it's sure to end badly. I could never walk away from Keith if I have a night with him. What alternative do I have? I want to forget about it.

What if I did throw caution to the wind and give into my primal wants and needs? The way he gazed into my eyes tonight, I'm fairly certain he would be down. He probably wouldn't hesitate either. Could I possibly keep Keith three car lengths from my heart? Not possible. I already like everything about him. If we had sex, things would change. There's a strong possibility I'll have a broken heart after it's all said and done.

Am I tripping focusing on the what ifs? How can I spend so much time debating about this? In my heart of hearts, I can't have "no strings sex" with him. He already means something to me. Well, I just need to keep him in the friendzone. No matter how much I like him, and I do like him. Anything other than this isn't an option. He has potential pain written all over him. I can't play with fire. I'll most definitely get burned.

I've enjoyed his company a lot. The massage has my neck relieved and relaxed. What can't this man do? He has my body on fire simply from a great conversation and a neck rub. I can imagine what it will be like as he actually kisses me. I still feel his lips on my cheek. I wanted to turn my head to meet his lips. **(Down girl! Stop confusing yourself. Focus on something wrong with him.)** Why didn't I recognize a flaw? Shit, this guy can't be perfect, can he? No way.

It's taking everything in my resolve to keep this in the friendzone. Something is telling me to take Jay Z's advice and be a grown woman that goes after what she wants. If I'm being real with myself, I want him naked and in my bed. Yep, I finally admitted this to myself at least. I want him, but what am I going to do about it. I have to be real with myself. I probably shouldn't be wanting anyone right now, since I'm fresh off a breakup. I would probably mess up everything with him. I like him a lot. He's super chill. It will be best to be his friend. I can do this. I can be his friend. I can handle being around him.

Well, on the off chance I can't handle a friendship with him, I need guidance and prayer for the right direction. Mama would always tell me, "God can help you when no one else can." She's right. Only Jesus holds this honor. Thank you, Jesus, for your perfection. I probably need to get on my knees and pray for strength because I'm not going to make it. I sure hope this prayer helps to dampen any desire lurking in the shadows of my heart and soul. I'm weak to the flesh's desires, and my current desire is Keith Alexander in all his sexiness.

"**Lord, I need your strength and guidance. I'm trying to be a good girl here and taper my libido, but this is difficult. I'm positive you already know the situation but let me confide in you. I like Keith a lot. I mean A LOT. I would date him if there would be a chance for us to be in a committed relationship. I'm failing with the effort to be his friend. I've had unhealthy (well, kind of dirty) thoughts about him, and I'm probably going to lose all resolve pretty soon. Please don't be disappointed in me. I want to be honest about how I feel. I need you to guide me through these tested waters to make the best choice for me. Thanks for listening to me, Father. I'll close with the Lord's prayer. Our father, which art in heaven, hallowth be thy name. Thy kingdom come; thy will be done on earth as it is in Heaven. Give us this day our daily bread, and forgive us our trespasses, as we forgive those who trespass against us. Lead us not into temptation but deliver us from evil. For thine is the kingdom, the power, and the glory. Forever and ever. Amen. I would like you to bless my loved ones, family, and friends. Please help those in need. May you bless all mankind. Amen.**"

Hopefully, this prayer will cleanse my brain and give me some clarity. I'm really hoping I don't have wet dreams and fantasies about my sexy ass neighbors. I probably shouldn't say that right after my prayer. "Lord take the wheel. I'm a work in progress." Please allow sleep come to me easily. You know I need it.

CHAPTER 23
Lauryn

After happy hour, I stopped pretending Keith and I didn't have a strong connection. We just mesh very well, and we get along like two peas in a pod. Keith and I have been going out more as friends. I love being around him. His energy is very contagious. I'm uncertain how much longer I'll be able to maintain our PG relationship.

We "hang out" at least three times a week. He just texted to ask if I wanted to shoot pool tonight. I really want to go out with him, but I have to be honest. I'm really bad at shooting pool. People always brag about it being about the angles, and I should really get this being an engineer and all, but execution is something quite different than design.

I choose a cute, casual outfit for this evening. I'm wearing an off-the-shoulder sweater, skinny jeans, brown leather jacket, and ankle boots. I add some essential elements such as a bangle bracelet, my silver band for my Apple watch, and a pendant necklace. As always, my makeup application is light and natural. I'm just finishing with styling my hair, and the doorbell rings. I give myself one final inspection and head to the door.

I open the door to a casually dressed Keith in a brown leather jacket, a polo, and jeans. I greet him with a hug and a kiss on the cheek. I stay in his arms a little longer than I should have if I'm still considering us to be "just friends." It's really good to be held in his arms, and I have to nudge myself out of his grip. It's very necessary for me to break away from his embrace.

"You look nice tonight, Lauryn. Are you ready to go?"

"Yes. Thank you."

We go to a local billiard where we can shoot pool and have dinner. No surprise, Keith is very good at shooting pool. He serves as an excellent teacher, too. Keith teases me by joking he found the one activity where I completely suck. He's happy to help me become a pool shark. "Shark" would be quite a stretch for me. There are moments when I have to lean over the table to bank the shot in the hole. I'm not versed on this at all. I tried a few angles, but I'm beginning to look like a cross between a seagull and a swan. Not graceful at all. **(You shouldn't wonder if I sank a single shot because I didn't get that lucky.)**

I could sense his stare as I posed my body over the table. He would often come by me and reposition my body to properly shoot my shot. His proximity to mine as he positions me is exhilarating. My body shivers as he spreads my legs with his to position me for the corner pocket shot. I inhale his clean masculine scent. The fragrance is somewhere between a cool ocean spray and fresh laundry. I inhale deeply and almost lose myself in him. My strength is waning. I can only imagine what it would be like to be in his arms. To make love to him. Being this close may cause me to weaken my resolve sooner rather than later.

After few hours, we decide to call it a night. I can't let this go further. Not yet anyway. I'm strong when he hugs and kisses me on my cheek at my door. I breathe deeply and embrace him tightly, but I have to stop myself from lingering. Ending nights with him is getting to be one hard task. Cold shower tonight. Check. Use Idris Vy in OT. Check.

Why am I suddenly like a woman in heat? I keep remembering those intense and sexy moments between us tonight. Those are very dangerous for me. What if he were to bend me over the pool table, strip my clothes, and do me right there? **(This fantasy doesn't involve people at the bar, so you can get your dirty mind out of the gutter.)**

How can I keep forgetting how fine Keith is? I ponder this for a minute. Nope, I can't get it out of my head. Is it possible to develop an immunity to someone who causes you to wake with hot sweats? The heat generated from those vivid dreams is very real. In my dreams, he's doing all sorts of wicked things to me. Am I being remotely realistic trying to have a friendship with him? My body wants him to stroke every single part of me until I scream out his name repeatedly.

I'm out of control. I have to stop daydreaming about him like this. Reflecting back on my prayer has helped me remain grounded. I have a sense of peace and calm. I battle the weakness of my flesh daily, but I'm making the right decision keeping him in the friendzone. I wanted to keep my distance, and he's been a godsend since the poisoning. He definitely isn't a devious person. I doubt he would ever intentionally hurt me.

Fear is holding me back. Can I trust what my body wants? Keith assures me, he wants something very different. He wants someone he can "build a relationship with." **(Could he really mean me? Could I be his next boo-thang?)** This is probably wishful thinking on my part. He did flirt with me. I guess it could mean something. Past relationships have me doubting myself constantly. It's time to go to sleep and stop fantasizing about a man who'd definitely rock my world if given the chance.

I still have a few things I want to organize around my house. I go by the hardware store where I run right into Jeremy. He's being extremely friendly. He asks me to have a cup of coffee with him to chat. He's a cool guy, so I agree to have coffee. We decide to meet later in the week at a coffee house not far from where Jeremy works. When the day finally arrives, I enter the door and find him immediately. He appears to be way too eager. I brush this off quickly as paranoia. I'm hoping this meeting won't be awkward.

He floats different ideas for the best way to navigate his way through college and change the direction of his career. He wants to discuss his options. He doesn't plan to work at the hardware store forever unless he becomes the store manager. His dedication is inspiring, and it makes me want to help him. Part of my service is to help anyone further their career options if I can. It's my responsibility as a black educated woman to do this. This shocks Jeremy. He isn't used to people helping without wanting anything in return. I inform him my investment in him will yield success, and this is the return on my investment and time. It's worth it to give back and help others. He can one day pay it forward and help someone else.

Jeremy reveals he has a huge crush on me. This doesn't shock me somehow. He hasn't veiled his adulation very well. I only hoped he would never act on them. One can only hope sometimes. He mentions he looks forward to me coming into the store. I don't want to hurt him, but I don't feel him like this at all. To make things easier, I mention we can be friends since I just got out of a long-term relationship. I do my best to make him understand I'm not ready to date anyone. Hopefully, he'll be cool, and we can remain friends. Friendship is our only option since Jeremy isn't really my type. He is about 5'7, and average looking. He doesn't create a spark or a sizzle. There isn't anything wrong with him. I'm just not attracted to him. He's cool, and I only want a strictly platonic friendship. We can definitely be homies. I respect him a lot. I'm not the right woman for him.

I like the fact he decided to go back to school. He took a hiatus for several years. He's pursuing a bachelor's degree in management at NTU. I want to offer Jeremy advice to help him transition into the career he wants. He seems to acknowledge I'm not ready to date. As I'm leaving the coffee meeting with Jeremy, I feel light and anew. It's been too long since I've been able to support and mentor someone. All these little lessons I'm continuing to learn are leading to providing service. Everything really does happen for a reason.

It's hard to believe it's March now. Days are flying by, but I really love March. Not only because it's my birthday month, but spring begins. Spring is my absolute favorite season. I also really love birthdays. I especially love celebrating other people's birthdays even more than mine. Learning Keith's birthday is in March urges me to do something special for him. His birthday being near mine makes me smile. We're at lunch commemorating his birthday. I hand him a funny "friend" card and a

Titan's jersey. He seems to be touched by the sentiment. Because of specificity about "the friendzone," he kisses me on my forehead as he holds me close. The kiss isn't passionate at all, but the heat is still radiating between us creating a spark I can no longer deny. **(How am I turned on from a kiss on my forehead? It's probably the way my body is molded into his chest. Argh!! I can't be this close to him.)**

I try to push him away in a way to avoid any awkwardness. Needless to say, I'm not successful. All he does is smirk at me, and he releases me from his grip. The fact he let me go disappointed me more than it should've. It's been a few days since we saw each other at his birthday outing. Not running into him makes me sad. **(I'm all over the place. I want him. No, I have to stay away from him, and on and on…back and forth.)** We're in the hallway at the same time, and I don't want to keep playing ping pong about this. I approach Keith in the hallway between our homes. I'm suddenly happy to run into him. It's like every nerve ending in my body is on alert.

"Hello Keith, how are you?"

"Good. Someone has a birthday coming around soon, and I want to take you out. Does this work for you?"

"Sure. What do you have in mind?"

"How about dinner at 7:00?"

"Sounds good. I don't really have plans in the evening."

"Well, you do now."

Today is the 22nd, and my birthday. My phone is going off with birthday wishes. There are also a few cryptic ones from numbers I don't recognize. Nothing can dampen my day. The joy I'm experiencing today is the exact opposite of the pain I felt last year. I'm definitely turning a corner. I truly understand the necessity for me to overcome adversity and to be challenged more than ever now. Those unpleasant memories only prepared me for what I'll face next. As with any national holiday, I don't work on my birthday. Well, at least in my mind, it's a national holiday.

Today is full of fun, hassle-free events. I meet Kennedy and Tonya for lunch, and we have a very festive gab session. Next, I head to the spa for a massage, facial, and a mani/pedi. The massage is completely relaxing and puts me to sleep. I must have slept for some time because Corey, the massage therapist, reminds me not to rush getting up as he leaves the room. I'm completely relaxed and happy following a day of friendships and beauty. Now, it's time to get ready for my dinner non-date with Keith. I take a quick shower and choose to wear a purple A-line dress to compliment my skin tone along with a pair of Jimmy Choo stilettos. I wear very simple jewelry with my hair down to display my voluminous curls. There's a knock at my door, and I rush to answer it. I'm kind of excited.

"Hello, gorgeous. Happy Birthday, sweetheart."

"Thank you so much."

He lingers in the doorway, "Are you ready to go?"

"Yes. Let me grab my coat since it may get chilly."

We leave to go to a nice Thai restaurant, and it's an incredibly chilly night. We laugh and discuss our dreams and what not during dinner. At the end, he presents me with a small token for my birthday as he would like to call it. It's a Falcons pullover hoodie and women's cut V-neck t-shirt. It's so cute, and I'm not surprised since Keith has great taste.

"Aww, a man after my own heart. Thank you, this is such a sweet gift. I actually checked out a pairing similar to this, but I never got the chance to get it. These are much needed items for a true fangirl like me."

"You're welcome. I hoped you would like it."

We chat for a bit longer then head back to the complex. We trek to my place, and I'm unsure if I should ask him to come in or would it be super risky? I glance at him fully ready to thank him for the night. I'm not prepared as he places his arms around my waist and tugs me towards him. He leans in and kisses me not on the cheek. Not like this game we've been playing for months. He kisses me on the lips deeply with so much passion. He parts my lips with his tongue and devours me like I'm a steak. I'm not complaining. This kiss is everything, and I don't want it to stop. We don't stop kissing for a very long time. It's like we're both starving to kiss each other.

He kisses my neck, and I moan like I'm on fire. He comes back to claim my lips once again, and I don't stop him. I want his lips on mine once again. I want to taste his tongue playing water polo with mine. I'm caught up in this emotion. I don't want things to end between us. He releases me, and I hold my head on his chest for a beat. The reality of the kiss is rearing its ugly head. What am I going to do now? I'm certainly hoping things won't be awkward now that we've acted on our desire.

"Yea, sorry about this. Well, I'm not sorry I kissed you. You want to keep this between us in the friendzone, but it's getting difficult for me. I like you, and I won't be able to keep pretending I don't want more much longer."

"Keith, I understand. I just need some time."

"I'm not asking you for a commitment. I want to determine if there's more between us worth pursuing. If there is, we owe it to ourselves to give it a shot."

"Okay, just give me a little time, please."

"Okay, I can. Good night."

"Thank you for everything. I really had a great time tonight."

"I'm glad because I had a great time, too. See you soon."

He leaves, and I'm not sure if we're at a turning point for something more or nothing at all. I like Keith a lot. Should I allow my past to control me? Is my heart too fragile to try? I have to figure this out. Sighing, I head into my place. I need another shower and one that's particularly a cold. His kiss surpassed any in my imagination. My wet dreams will most definitely be worse now that I've tasted and felt his lips and tongue. Why, oh, why is this happening now? I'm not in a good place for this. Maybe, I won't ever be in a good place. **(What's the alternative? Being single and alone, maybe with a dog. I really loved Chewy. Another dog maybe what I need. I'll look forward to becoming the dog lady. I don't like cats, so don't think about it.)**

I try to convince myself into giving things with Keith a shot. In the end, I'm a coward. I start to avoid him. I have to prevent things from going too far. **(Yea, I know I should "woman up and be about it." In my work life, I take challenges by the horn and crush them. In my personal life, I'm passive now. Somehow, I'm allowing my fragile heart to rule me.)** What if I do something stupid like fall in love with him? I really could. If you saw him, you would understand why. I'm not ready to give my heart to anyone else. He must remain in the friendzone.

Since I've been avoiding Keith at all costs, I chose to spend the bulk of my time with Alex. We're like brother and sister, and there's absolutely no chance for us to repeat the bad sex. Occasionally, I chat with Jeremy, but we haven't gotten around to hanging out again. He happens to be calling now.

"Hey, Lauryn. How are you?"

"Good. How are you, Jeremy?"

"Really good. Can we get together for drinks or coffee this week?"

The last time I saw Jeremy he admitted he had a crush on me. **(Talk about an awkward moment.)** I hope he doesn't mention this because he's not what I want. He's not it for me. I hope to just hang out without it being weird.

"I can't this week, Jeremy. What about next Tuesday or Wednesday night?" I inquire.

"Wednesday is good."

I'm really busy this week with work and plans with friends, and I'm unsure what Jeremy wants to discuss. The last time we met things started off cool. He made things awkward by mentioning his crush. I'm meeting Jeremy next Wednesday at 5:00 PM. I just hope it's not weird.

It's Wednesday and work is done. I'm driving home to change prior to meeting Jeremy at a bar downtown for happy hour. I'm wearing jeans, a simple sling top, and some wedges. My jewelry and makeup are natural and simple. I want to be more relaxed than my work gear. I reach the bar, go inside, and Jeremy stands to greet me. I join him and order a Moscow mule from the waitress at the table taking our orders. I also order some happy hour food. Jeremy is distracted. He must have something on his mind.

"Jeremy, are you okay?" I ask.

"Lauryn, I told you I had a crush on you last time we met for coffee. It's more than a crush. I really want to have a chance with you. I want to be more than friends."

Hmm, still awkward. This is exactly what I wanted to avoid. I definitely can't hang out with him anymore. I have to shut this down. He'll probably assume it won't take long, and I'll give in. I have to figure out how to get him to believe we will only be platonic and friends. I didn't lead him on or allow him to believe he had a shot with me. I provided clear and direct communication about my lack of desire to have a relationship at all. I understand now how being nice and trying to avoid hurting him didn't work. Only the truth may work with him. I'm not remotely interested in him in a romantic way. How do I tell him this? There's a long pause. I need to formulate the words to clearly convey I don't want to be with him. I hate for things to remain awkward between us.

"Jeremy, I'm really sorry. Weren't we meeting to discuss how you'll transition from an hourly worker to the corporate America setting? In case you don't remember, I recently broke-up with my boyfriend and we were in a long-term relationship. I'm not remotely interested in anything more than friendship. Will this be a problem for you?"

"Lauryn, I really don't want to make you uncomfortable. I'm generally persistent, and I go after what I want. I believe you'll never get it if you don't put in the effort to get what you want."

"I truly appreciate your confidence, Jeremy. I'm just not in the right headspace for relationships, and I would rather we remain friends."

"I'm okay with being friends. I'm glad you're willing to help me with my career. I guess I wanted the world. I had to take my shot."

"It's great to be confident, Jeremy. You really have to remember to use this same confidence and energy as you're trying to advance your career."

I hope this does the trick by steering the conversation to something strictly professional. About an hour later, I provide a legitimate excuse to leave. He's disappointed, but this won't sway me. As I'm leaving and staring at my phone, and I run right into someone. This someone has a very hard chest. My eyes lift slowly to view my sexy neighbor who I've been avoiding since "kiss gate." Why is he here? I shouldn't be around him. My body will simply betray all the hard work and effort my mind has worked to maintain. The boundaries where bounds aren't defined. This is a losing battle. I just don't trust myself around Keith now. I need an excuse to escape him. I didn't realize my hand rested on his chest. We hold each other's eyes for a beat.

"I'm very sorry, Keith. I'm all over the place and not paying attention."

"Hmm, I noticed. Are you leaving?"

"I am. I have to get home, and, umm, do laundry." I answer really quickly.

"Laundry. Huh?" he questions raising his eyebrows.

"Laundry is serious business, sir. It relaxes me to wash loads and loads of laundry."

"So, you wouldn't have time to grab a drink with me?"

"Yea, the laundry…I missed last week, and things are getting out of control."

"I had a great time, Lauryn. I can't wait to see you again," Jeremy utters as he creeps behind me unexpectantly.

"Okay, I'll catch you later, Jeremy," I comment nervously, and I don't know why I'm nervous.

Jeremy plods away to leave but glances back at us just has he exits the restaurant. Why am I feeling some kind of way for hanging out with Jeremy? It's not like Keith and I are dating.

"So, wait. You used laundry as an excuse to end your date with ole boy?" Keith asks amused.

"No date. Only drinks with a friend. I really have laundry to do. Why would I lie?"

"Sure, okay."

"I'm pretty OCD about laundry and everything being in its place."

"Hmm, interesting, but you missed it last week."

"What? Yea, that's why things are getting out of control."

"This is getting better by the minute. Well, one drink and I promise you'll be free to do your laundry," he gazes at me in a way that pierces my soul.

"One drink," I give in to him.

I simply can't refuse him when he gazes at me like he's doing now. He's not going to make this easy for me. I really should leave to get the laundry done. I shouldn't follow him to the table to have one drink because that one drink always becomes more. I shouldn't stare into his beautiful eyes and hope we kiss again. I shouldn't wonder about what his naked glory would do to me. I haven't stopped visualizing him nude. I shouldn't do a lot of things, but I ignore what I shouldn't do and follow him to a table to have one drink.

"What will you have?"

"I'll have a bourbon on the rocks," I declare. I need some liquid courage to keep my nerves steady.

"Rough day?"

"You don't know the half of it."

"Well, it looks like your day just got better," he smirks at me.

"You think so?"

"Oh, I know so."

"Well, I'm gonna make you earn it."

"I earn everything I do, baby."

"Do you now?

"I'll get your drink and show you how actions speak louder than words."

He strolls towards the bar with so much swagger that I almost lose my resolve. This may turn into more than one drink.

CHAPTER 24
Lauryn

It's late May, and I have successfully dodged Keith in the building since running into him at the bar. He has reached out with texts and calls, and I've made up so many excuses about being busy. I realize I'm not being fair. I shouldn't let my fear of being with him stop me. Keith's track record as a player makes me nervous. I guess he's never lied to me about his lifestyle. I can't develop real affections for him. No, I shouldn't. Feelings for him could be a recipe for a disaster in the making.

It's lunch time, and I need to go downtown to buy a dress at a shop I love for an event I'm attending this week. At the shop, there are a few other adorable outfits that I must purchase. **(Okay, I admit that I may have a little problem with shopping, but I never spend more than my allotted amount per month.)** Since I spent my lunch shopping, I'm grabbing a sub sandwich and salad at the shop next door, and I'll eat at my desk. While crossing the street to get in my car, someone calls my name.

On instinct, I turn around quickly to find out who it is. I'm shocked it's my ex, Isaac. It's hard to believe he's here. Isaac happened to be my first real love, and my first everything. We dated at NTU from my sophomore year until the fall after he graduated. I lost my virginity to him. Everyone figured we would be together forever, but nope, we didn't last with his move to New York. We didn't exactly end on the best note. It's been about six years since we've come face-to-face. I hold no grudges towards him. We weren't meant to be.

Falling in love with him in college happened relatively easy. I've known him forever. I grew up around Isaac and his family. I probably loved him all along. Admitting my love for him proved to be a difficult task. It scared me to be vulnerable with him. Isaac happened to be very patient with me allowing our love to grow. He never pushed my buttons regarding us having sex. Following the breakup, I regretted being with him. I also hated him for a really long time. Everything changed with Jackson. I guess one day I won't hate Jackson anymore either if history repeats itself. I don't regret having loved Isaac now or anything we shared.

He treated me with so much respect, and he cherished me. He treated my virginity like a gift. He never rushed me, but my anxiety and nerves figured he would get tired of waiting. He selflessly made sure my experience was as painless as possible. Don't get me wrong it was rough, but he handled me tenderly. His popularity around campus made me acutely aware if I didn't make him happy someone else would. He never pressured me, but I pressured myself. I probably started having sex with him out of insecurity. I hadn't been completely ready emotionally. Luckily, Isaac treated me as delicately as I felt. We may have met at the wrong time, but I don't believe we did. We were destined to be each other's first loves, but not the last one.

When he got his job and moved to New York, I, like other young girls in love, convinced myself we could make our long-distance relationship work, and we did for a short time. We couldn't make it work with the distance and being so young. I couldn't stop bawling for a long time. I can't believe I'm running into him now. Isaac is still fine and sexy. I'm over him, but I'm not blind. He's about 6'2, and his skin tone is a deep mocha color. His body is lean and fit like a basketball player. I have a perfect view of his chest. He still has perfect abs. I can spot the outline of his chest through his shirt. He definitely has an eight pack. **(It may be over, but I'm not immune to sexy abs.)** Isaac's hair is styled in his signature dreadlocks. He doesn't look any different than the last time I saw him. I'm certain he still has his signature charm. I wonder what he's doing in Nashville.

"Isaac, how are you?" I ask as he saunters over and embraces me.

"Mio amore, I'm good. I can't believe I'm running into you. Man, you're still beautiful. You're more beautiful now. How is it possible?"

In fact, it's weird hearing Isaac call me an old nickname. "Thanks, Isaac. What are you doing here?"

"I'm moving back here. Next month in fact. I'm glad I ran into you. I guess it's kismet."

"Kismet. Huh? How so?"

"Mio amore, I've been thinking about you lately about how we ended. I'm not proud of it. I'm ashamed of the foul way I behaved when we officially broke up."

"Isaac, its water under the bridge and so far in the past. You ending things happened to be the right choice for both of us. If we tried to stay together, things would've ended poorly. I would probably hate you right now."

"You don't now?" he asks tentatively.

"No, I don't. It hurt at the time. I got over it a long time ago."

"Are you single by the way?"

"Yes, I'm single."

"May I have your number?

"It hasn't changed,"

"You blocked me, I guess."

"Well, you dumped me." He grabs my phone and puts his number in my contacts.

"Okay...are you free tonight for dinner? I'll be here for a few days if tonight's not good."

"I'm free tonight for dinner."

"Do you still live in the condo?"

"Yes, I do."

"How about I scoop you up around 7:00 PM?"

"Okay, that'll work."

He hugs me again and gives me a kiss on my cheek prior to us going our separate ways. I can't believe Isaac is back in Nashville. If nothing else, it will be great catching up with him tonight. What are the odds of me running into Isaac today? He hasn't changed at all. He may be more sculpted now. He isn't bad on the eyes, either. He's fine. I can't go down memory lane. He hurt me. I may have forgiven him, but I haven't forgotten. I can be friends with my ex, right? Maybe not Jackson. It's way too soon. I can certainly be friends and cordial with Isaac. Tonight is about friendship and hanging out. We should be able to chill and enjoy each other's company. Before we dated, we were friends, and we used to hang out all the time. I'm excited about dinner.

I chose to wear something simple that screams "having dinner with my friend." He won't be coming home with me tonight. I'm wearing a wine-colored halter A-line dress, with silver Jimmy Choo shoes, a silver Chanel bag, and matching accessories. I wrap my hair into a bun. My appearance isn't considered sexy, so he shouldn't have any ideas. I put on some light powder, mascara, and lip gloss. I'm not sure what to expect, but I want to have a nice night out.

I'm at the elevator, and Keith wanders over as I wait. I hope this isn't going to be awkward. It easily could be since I've been avoiding him for a while. I peek at his lips, and it only reminds me of the kiss we shared on my birthday. I can't seem to forget the kiss no matter what I do. The strong kinetic pull I experience every time I'm near him is going off like a fire alarm right now. I'm trying my best to ignore it. I won't allow him to have a clue he makes my body go crazy. I have to stay calm and cool. It will only work this way. I need to have the upper hand here.

"Hi, Keith."

"Hello, Lauryn," he remarks coolly, "You look really nice."

"Thank you. You look really nice, too. Big date?" I joke.

"Thanks. Not really. I'm just going out with friends, but it looks like you might have a big date."

"No, just hanging out with an old friend."

"Oh, I see. Maybe we can get together again soon?"

"I would like to see you again," I admit.

"I'll hit you sometime soon."

"Okay. Until then."

The elevator opens, and the tension eases. Things shouldn't be this awkward with Keith. We aren't even officially dating. I probably made it weird since I started avoiding him. Why do I sense he's mad at me? He's cool, but there's something about the way he's staring at me.

"Keith, have a nice evening."

"You have a nice evening as well, Lauryn."

Leaving the elevator, my heart is beating very fast. Why is my heart pounding like I ran a marathon? I should constantly warn myself falling for Keith is dangerous. My imagination is running wild with images of Keith and me. I don't notice Isaac is in the lobby waiting.

"Lauryn, hey. I've been calling your name," he says as he treads over to embrace and kiss me on my cheek.

"Oh. Hi, Isaac."

"How do you feel about Thai?"

"I still love Thai."

"I figured you did."

"Lucky guess."

"Nah, I remember everything about you, mio amore."

"Do you?"

"I certainly do. Ready to go?"

"Yea, I'm ready."

"Somethings...I'll never forget," he winks at me.

We amble outside to his car, and he opens the door for me. I'm comfortably seated in the passenger seat as I turn to my left as Keith drives by. I swear he has a scowl on his face. Did I imagine it? Is Keith jealous? Why does he have a scowl on his face? I don't have any more time to ponder what it could mean because Isaac begins a conversation.

"Mio amore, I wonder how much you've changed."

"Well, I have definitely grown a lot since we were together. I'm no longer the silly girl who would eat ice cream for breakfast. How much have you changed?"

"Hmph, I liked her a lot. I changed some. I'm wiser, and I'm more direct about what I want."

"Are you now? You've never had a problem being direct. It's a stretch to call this your weakness."

He laughs, "You're probably right."

The drive to the Thai restaurant is less than 10 minutes. It seems like I blinked twice and he's driving into the parking lot. The wait staff is Johnny on the spot to get our order. This is one of my favorite restaurants, and it's great Isaac remembers. I order a glass of merlot, spring rolls, and pineapple fried rice with shrimp.

"Your favorite meal is the same. Maybe you haven't changed much."

"I'm surprised you remember."

"I remember a lot about you," he smiles at me. He orders the bottle of merlot since he wants wine, too. He orders panang curry and a spring roll.

"Mio amore, I've been reminiscing a lot about us lately."

"Us?" I ask confused.

"Yea, what we meant to each other."

"As in past tense, Isaac."

"I realize we are past tense. I miss you."

"Is this going to be an awkward dinner?"

"It doesn't have to be awkward. What would make it awkward? You're single, right?"

"Yea, and the fact I'm single is very recent. I dated my last boyfriend for a very long time, and I'm not interested in anything now."

"Oh, okay. Am I making you nervous by reminiscing about our past?"

"Not really. It's just…what we had…has been over for years. I didn't have any experience with love or anything. You taught me a lot about love. I couldn't have anticipated what I wanted or needed in a relationship. I don't doubt I loved you, Isaac."

"Have you gained the experience to understand what you need now?"

"I have an idea. Let's catch up."

"Sorry, I'm not trying to make you uncomfortable. What have you been doing since we last saw each other?"

"Well, I went back to work."

He chuckles, "You know what I mean."

"Well, it's been a crazy couple of years. I started a new job in the non-profit sector, and my ex cheated on me with Asia of all people."

"Not yo girl, Asia. Damn, I can't believe she would do you like this. Who's your ex if you don't mind me asking?"

"You had to ask me. Jackson Emerson. You remember him?"

"Yea, he graduated a year before me. Hmm, I didn't take him for the type to do you dirty."

"Well, I didn't either or I wouldn't have been with him for as long as I was. Well, the people closest to me did me the dirtiest. I can handle any enemy."

"I hear you. I get your reluctance with relationships, but I would never cheat on you."

"No, I suppose not. You would definitely dump me before cheating on me."

"That's right. I'm way too honorable," he jokes, and we both laugh.

"All kidding aside, what brings you back to Nashville?"

"Well, I got this great gig here, but the last few years have been kind of complicated. I'm divorced. My marriage lasted for two years, and I have a three-year-old daughter. We share custody, but we're trying to figure things out with my move here."

"Wow, I didn't anticipate you got married with a whole family and stuff."

"Yea, I probably didn't cross your mind at all."

I ignored his statement and asked, "Where are you working?"

"Santosh Software Development. I'll be their director in the networking division. I'm going to like being back here."

"That's cool. Have you found housing yet?"

"Not yet. I want to live downtown, but I have temporary housing with Santosh. They'll give me time to find something I really like."

"Your mom must be extremely happy about your move, and you'll be closer to Atlanta."

"Yea, that's another reason I'm moving back here. I want my daughter to spend more time with my family. She's super tight with my ex-wife's family, and I want the same with mine."

"What's your daughter's name?"

"Bella like —"

"Like your sister, Isabella. Your favorite girl," I mutter sarcastically.

"My daughter is actually Gabriella. I'm still uncertain about what happened between you and Bella. You were such good friends once. I figured you two patched things up after I saw a pic with you and her on the Gram."

"Not quite. I ran into her the last time I went home, and she's still the same ole Bella," I can't sugarcoat this for him anymore. His sister is an asshole. "Well, anyway. It's great to hear you talk about your daughter. Do you have a picture of her?"

"Of course. She's my baby girl. I didn't want to be the guy who has a million photos of their kid and bombard people with them. I guess I'm him. Let me show you a picture of my her." He grabs his phone and shows me a picture of Bella. She's beautiful. She's brown skinned and the color of milk chocolate with curly hair. She's as beautiful as a doll.

"She's beautiful, Isaac. You did well. Well, you and your wife did well."

"Ex-wife," he clarifies.

"Duly noted."

"How are Kennedy and Tonya?"

I notice he didn't waste any time changing the subject when I mentioned his wife/ex-wife. I wonder what's their story. They could only make it work for two years. Our relationship lasted longer than their marriage.

"They're good. Kennedy and Eric got married. Tonya is still Tonya. She hasn't changed at all."

"I guess she's still the life of the party?"

"Yep, she's exactly the same. They're my peeps, though."

"Yea. I didn't know Kennedy and Eric got married, but I'm not surprised they did. They were connected at the hip in college. It's too bad we're not all as lucky," he gazes at me regretfully.

"Things are as they should be. You have a beautiful daughter despite your marriage failing."

"You're right. Bella is the best person in my life. I wouldn't trade a thing for her."

"It's nice to see this side of you as a father."

We eat the rest of our meal and chat about how Nashville has changed since he lived here. He drops me off at home and kisses me platonically on the cheek. We plan to meet next month for dinner after he's settled in. I'm enjoying hanging out with Isaac and learning about his life in New York. It's hard to believe he got married and has a child. I'm surprised his mom didn't inform my mom about this. Our parents are still thick as thieves. Then again, mom could be aware, but she could've chosen not to tell me since the breakup with Isaac had been rough.

I'm not surprised about the flow and good time I've had with Isaac. We were never awkward around each other. Well, minus the post-break-up years, I suppose. I wouldn't call this time awkward since we stopped communicating. Like everything with time, wounds heal. We can be friends now. Our breakup proved to be inevitable. Our beautiful time together in college isn't diminished or ruined by us staying together longer than we should have. I understand this more than ever now that I'm older. A memory of our ending comes back like it's the present.

I'm very excited. I'm boarding the plane to visit Isaac. It's been a month, and I miss him so much. There've been too many cold showers. I remember a time sex talk made me nervous. I'm a woman now with womanly desires. I'm positive Isaac will help me fulfill my deepest desires this weekend. A smile is plastered on my face when Isaac meets me at the arrival gate. We greet each other with a simple kiss. I'm not into PDA, so we definitely won't get down and dirty. He seems off, but he's been working a lot. I hope we'll have the best weekend. Isaac lives in Manhattan in a small studio apartment. He's doing well financially, but the rent in New York is way more expensive than Nashville. His place is very nice. He uses his space well with a murphy bed camouflaging as a bookcase. We don't waste any time getting reacquainted with one another's body as the door closes. He makes love to me like it's our last time with so much vigor and passion. I had no clue about how our lives would change in a few days. I assumed he missed me like I missed him.

The weekend is filled with activities in and out of the bedroom. We didn't get much sleep, and I had no complaints about it. He took me to "A Midsummer Night's Dream," an off-Broadway show. We also went to Silvia's, Carmine's Italian Restaurant, the Met, and shopping of course.

With all the fanfare, I'm surprised I could give him the "good-good" without passing out. My second, third, fourth, and fifth wheel jumped in and didn't disappoint me or him. We christened every corner of his studio and the stairwell when it seemed damn near impossible for us to make it to his apartment before a sexual explosion would happen. His mood changed to a melancholy one on the train headed to the airport for my return trip to Nashville. It's hard to put my finger on why. He stops me and grasps my shoulders as he proceeds to kiss me with passion very slow and deliberately. I don't mind the PDA. He'll miss me like I'll miss him. Sometimes, we must do uncomfortable things for our loved ones. Suddenly, his demeanor becomes very serious. I don't understand why.

"Mio amore, I need to discuss something important with you."

"Sure," I respond. I have plenty of time. My flight doesn't leave for a while since he got me here hella early.

"I love you, and I probably always will —"

"I know you love me —"

"But this long-distance thing isn't working. Even if we weren't in a long-distance relationship, I would probably make the same decision."

"I don't understand. What are you trying to tell me?" I ask in a strained voice. I'm getting agitated.

"I love you more than anything —"

"You mentioned that."

"But we're not working anymore. I hate not seeing you for over a month. We're really too young to be this serious, too."

"Let me get this straight. Do you want to breakup because you don't get to see me enough or is it because we're too young to be this serious? I'm confused. Which one is it?"

"It's both. I don't want to be committed to you anymore. I want to see what else is out there before you know...well, I'm locked down."

"What? You consider me or rather us as being locked down?"

"No, it's not that you have me on lock. This is difficult. I don't want to hurt you."

"Well, you're not doing a great job with your goal." The tears are building up. I won't allow them to flow here. Don't cry in front of the guy whose breaking your heart.

"I'm sympathetic to this breakup hurting you, but I don't ever want to cheat on you. I wouldn't hurt you that way."

"Is there someone else, Isaac?"

"No, not really."

"Either there is or there isn't."

"I haven't cheated on you not physically or emotionally."

"Just tell me. Is there someone else?"

"I'm interested in dating, and I want to have fun. I don't want a commitment to you or anyone. I haven't been single in several years."

"And being with me is no longer fun?"

"You're not here."

"Why did you fly me out here if you wanted to breakup? I can't believe it. You wanted to have sex for the last time. Am I right?"

"No, not at all. I still love you, and I won't diminish what you mean to me. I didn't want something to happen from my end or your end, and we end by hating each other."

"Are you trying to circumvent some future possibility? Plus, how do you know I don't hate you, now?"

"I'm not interested in anyone else right now. I just don't want to miss something I could try if we weren't together. I want to see what else is out there."

"Ok, fine we're done!" I hiss angrily and turn to leave before my tears start flowing down my face. I'm flabbergasted how the greatest weekend I've had quickly turned into the worst. I cried until I had no more tears left. Isaac texted me several times, and I ignored him until he no longer tried to reach me.

It took me forever to get over him, but I did. I haven't looked back since. Being with Isaac taught me a lot. I gained resilience and strength from his disregard of my love. **(Can I picture us together again? Nope, not likely. I doubt he appreciates the woman he helped to create.)**

CHAPTER 25
Keith

At work today, things are interesting. Jeff comes into my office to inform me about a senior partner who'll be retiring soon, and how this will open opportunities for both of us. Jeff's been mentoring me for over a year, and I've met several key people who may be allies or support to help with the advancement of my career. Last year, Jeff mentioned I needed more visibility, especially with the upper brass. With his help, I've been working on more substantial cases that will lead to advancement. I've networked a lot to expand my professional circle. Jeff doesn't just give useless speeches about increasing the number of African Americans in key positions here. He's making it happen by "walking the walk." He's quite an impressive person who can help this firm in many positive ways. He's helping to bring more diversity and inclusion to the table. It helps the firm to have unique ideas and perspectives to drive better decisions.

I have a 60% probability of success with the connections I'm constantly making. I have to work hard and show I'll definitely deliver but just getting in front of the decision makers is critical in this process. Jeff is a driven person, and I hope he can be trusted.

It's Wednesday again. I'm meeting the fellas for "Hump Day Happy Hour." We need to figure out how we'll conduct the fantasy football draft this year. We've had some epic drafts in the past. As the reigning fantasy football Super Bowl champion, I'm invested in how things will be done. These guys are probably going to make my draft pick 10th place. They're trying to throw shade about me winning two years in a row. They're trying to cripple and handicap me. I'm not faded since "all I do is win." Their amateur attempts to try to compete with me are humorous.

Since things are at a standstill with Lauryn, I wonder if Sabrina is available tonight. Just like "Hump Day Happy Hour" is a constant so is "Wind Down Wednesday" with Sabrina. She either reaches out to me or vice versa. Either way, we both will scratch our itch without regrets. Well, it's always been a constant until recently. I can't pinpoint what's been frustrating me the last few Wednesday nights. I shoot Sabrina a quick text to ask if she wants some company tonight. She immediately replies with a thumbs up. She never disappoints me when I want to come through. Something is dampening my mood about seeing Sabrina tonight, and I don't understand what it could be. I'm not even sure if I want what lies ahead tonight. I'm lukewarm about meeting her, but I don't understand why. This is my idea. I try to shake it off. It isn't productive to second guess my decisions. Sabrina and I always have a good time. Tonight shouldn't be any different.

As soon as I enter the pub, I head over to Jason and Sam's table immediately. I'm ready to start trash talking. Sam beat me to it. I couldn't even sit and order my drink. He comes at me hard. He's been listening to some fantasy football podcast, and he claims he's ready to win this year. He doesn't care what he has to do to beat me. He'll make crazy trades. Stalk the waiver wire each week. It doesn't matter to him. "It's going down this year," he claims. Admittedly, we're pretty intense about the outcomes each week.

This year, Jason wants to open the draft and make it coed. He wants his girl, Jasmine, to play since she's wanted to play for years. Jason is planning to ask Jasmine to marry him soon. Sam has been somewhat chauvinistic with women playing fantasy football. He recently started dating Erica, and she doesn't appear to be very knowledgeable about sports. Now, Sam is pushing for the league to be coed this year, too. I don't have a problem with the league being coed. I'm certain I'll win anyway. It doesn't matter because I don't mind taking women's money. It spends just as good as any man's.

Jason asks, "Keith, do you know any women that you would like to invite to play fantasy football?"

"Jennifer may be interested in playing. I'll ask her. How many women do we need to fill?"

Lauryn may want in, but I don't mention her name since I'm not sure what's going on with us. If things were more defined, I would ask because she would bring some real competition to this league. I remember how she diagnosed the play at the football game. It's impressive and sexy as hell. I have to jump back into this conversation since I notice Sam's answering my question.

Sam comments, "It would be nice to have five. You know for balance, and I don't want the women to feel some kind of way."

I state, "I'll see what I can do."

We joke for nearly two hours. Since it's June, the NBA finals are in full swing, and there's a lot of smack-talk at this table. There's a game tonight, but I'll probably miss it. It comes on too late. All Sam can trash talk about is Sunday's game, and how Kevin Durant ran a clinic on Lebron. I'm a huge Lebron fan, and Sam's a pure hater. I'm not worried because LeBron's a beast. The series isn't over. He's heckling me for another 30 minutes. He's definitely on a roll. He probably won't stop, so it's time to bounce.

Sam asks, "Where you going, bruh? The game's starting."

"I have to head out. Big day at work."

"Sure, it's work," Jason teases.

"You know I grind. Of course, it's work," I laugh.

"We don't care if you're about to go hit, man." Sam accuses me.

"Are we meeting on Monday?" I changed the subject. "We can catch the game and finalize the draft party details."

"The game! Ha!" Sam shouts. "It's gonna be a sweep. There won't be a game Monday."

"We're not getting swept, man. We'll see on Monday."

Everyone agrees, and we're getting together Monday evening. I suggest we meet at a different location with an extended happy hour and more selections. At this point, Sam yells, "Strip club!" We all laugh. This isn't really new. Sam always wants to go the strip club. He swears the food, especially the wings, are the best. Somehow, I doubt he wants to go there for the food.

It's time to go to Sabrina's. I haven't hooked up with her much lately, and it's time to change this predicament. I changed a lot when I started hanging out with Lauryn, but I can't stop my life for someone who only wants to be a friend. Sabrina will help keep my mind off "my friend." At least, I hope she will. Why has Lauryn been on my mind lately?

I had sex with Sabrina tonight, and it wasn't that great. My head isn't in the game, and I'm not sure why. I guess I do, and her name is Lauryn. She's constantly on my mind. I'm very frustrated driving home. It's time for us to figure this out. I'm tired of playing cat and mouse. She wanted more following our kiss. Sometimes, all it takes is a little push. I have to deal with this tonight, damn it. I need to calm down a bit prior to contacting her.

Since I'm still extremely wound up, I turn on the TV to catch some of the game. It's half time, and the score is 67 – 61 with Golden State leading. I need to go to sleep. Tomorrow's going to be a really big day. I'm sure the Cavaliers will get this win tonight. I head back to my bedroom to call it a night. It'll be impossible for us to win the whole thing if we lose this one. We'll be 0-3. I'm calm enough now. It's time to text Lauryn.

Me: Lauryn, wyd

Lauryn: Nothing much

Me: Are you free tomorrow night? Bubbles appeared on my phone for a few minutes, and she finally answers.

Lauryn: Umm, yea. I'm free

Me: We need to figure out what's going on between us. Do you like French food?

Lauryn: Figure out?

Me: Yea, figure things out. French food?

Lauryn: Yea, I like French food

Me: See you tomorrow, sweetheart

Lauryn: GN Keith

Me: GN sweetheart

The next morning, I check my text messages. I'm secretly hoping there'll be a text from Lauryn, but I only have a message from Sam.

Sam: 3 – 0 Cavs going down

Me: ●●

I glance at the time and decide it's time to get out of here. I have a lot on my plate today. Arriving at work, I start developing the strategy for the Wilmington development. This is a huge commercial development in Murfreesboro, Tennessee. I have to prepare the schedule to review the title, surveys, and any third-party reports. I also need to prepare the draft, review, and negotiate documents that'll be necessary to complete any loan documents, purchase and sale agreements, leases, and any other ancillary documents. The work on this project will be time consuming, but I'm eager to figure out how this particular client will help solidify my position at the firm.

Lunch time comes fast. I have to grab something quick. I'm making such a big dent in drafting the loan documents to make it possible to finish everything today. I grab a sandwich from the café downstairs and eat while finishing my work. I'm relieved to be done. I peek at my phone for the first time since this morning. I have several text messages. Sam, "the hater", has answered my earlier message.

Sam: Jus keeping it 💯

Me: ● or do u want Michael Jordan tears?

Sam: Michael Jordan tears for damn sure

Me: ●

There's one from Jennifer and my mom. Jennifer wants to hang out tonight. I text, "I'm busy, maybe another time." I can't blow off my mom. I need to call her, but I don't have time to give her the attention she deserves. I'll take my chances and respond to her text. I'm in trouble because mom doesn't really text. She certain she's making sense, but no one understands her texts at all.

Mom: Hey, baby. When r u coming home?

Me: Soon. It has been busy at work lately.

Mom: Ok, mk it n nxt 2 weeks.

Me: Ok, Mom. I will.

Mom: Luv Luv

Me: Luv Luv, Mom

I laugh because my mom messes up texts with words only, she recognizes. I also have a text from Lauryn, which makes me smile. I head home to get ready for our date. Yes, it's a real date. I'm not playing anymore. Tonight, we'll figure out if this thing between us is worth pursuing. I'm really tired of her avoiding me, and I want out of this "friendzone," too. She's afraid, and I want to disassemble her walls and to crack her impenetrable shield. We could work if she's willing to give us a try.

I plan to push her in the right direction. I haven't exactly figured out what I want with her, but we don't have to rush things. We should just go with every desire we have. Lately, I find myself daydreaming about her, our kiss, and what could follow. A memory of all the times I held her in my arms flashes in my mind. The pressure from her taunt breast grazes my chest as we embrace. I have tried to be a gentleman, but I'm a man.

I want to discover everything about her, with and without clothes, preferably. There'll be no more fighting these emotions and desires. It's time for action. Things are changing tonight. For the better. I'll approach her with my A-game charm. She needs to believe I'll be good for her. We're going to get past her fear of the unknown. It's time for us to do this.

CHAPTER 26
Lauryn

I'm flustered from reading the text from Keith. He said we need to figure things out. I'm scared about what we need to figure out. I haven't been exactly fair to Keith. I guess I have sent him mixed messages. I'm being a fraud right now with all the talk about holding people accountable. I do this for a living, but when it comes to my love life, it sucks. I'm being a complete coward and running away like a scared little girl. Why don't I put my big girl pants on and face whatever this is between us? The infamous kiss is like wow! Shit, it did something to me. This scares me a lot. He isn't Jackson. Do I want a relationship with him? As much as I've been trying to say no, the answer is yes. **(Hell, I know the answer is yes. I want him. I want him to be my man.)**

As much as I love sleep, it's not imminent tonight. I'm the type of person who gets their daily recommended amount of sleep. Instead of "you are what you eat," "you are how you sleep" is my motto. Here, I'm tossing and turning all night. I won't stop myself from imagining where the kiss could lead. I keep imagining Keith naked. What would his touch be like? If the kiss is any indication of what's to come, I should be very afraid. Following another endless night of insomnia, I finally fall asleep at about 3:00 AM. It seems like I'm only asleep for about 15 minutes when my alarm buzzes. It's hard to believe it's time to rise. I hit the snooze and try to sleep for at least another 15 minutes. My phone is going off again, and it hasn't been 15 minutes yet. I closed my eyes refusing to wake from my slumber.

The buzzing is just enough of an annoyance to make me pay attention. It's Isaac texting, and I'm sure he's back in town. This is another complication I don't need right now. I should ignore the text and roll back over, but no such luck. Falling back to sleep is impossible now. Grudgingly, I decide to answer the text and face this day with lots and lots of coffee.

Isaac: Mio amore, I'm back. I would love to hook up.

Me: Hook up?

Isaac: Just get some dinner. Did u think I meant more?

Me: That's generally what hook up means.

Isaac: Nah, I don't need to rush u. When things are right b/t us it will fall into place.

Me: Yea, ok. When do you want to go out?

Isaac: How about tonight?

Me: Not tonight. I have plans. **(Anxious much)**

Isaac: What works for you?

Me: How about Saturday?

Isaac: It's going to be hard not seeing you tonight.

Me: Good grief Isaac. I told u.

Isaac: I know, I know. Jus' kidding. Later, Mio amore.

I'm beginning to wonder if hanging out with Isaac may not be a good idea. He's willing to allow me to set the pace and be my friend while I'm figuring things out. I don't quite trust this will work. He has slipped in one too many innuendos about us getting back what we once shared. I'll tread very lightly with him to make sure I'm clear about the status of our relationship or lack thereof, so he'll get I mean business.

This is some shit. I shouldn't have to ponder about my ex who broke my heart. He kind of lost this privilege by wanting to wander around for the next piece of ass. It's petty of me to keep finding ways to discuss the specifics of our demise, but, hey, it is what it is.

What an uneventful day at work! Now, I'm ready to get out of here. Well, there were a few eventful moments today. I nearly cracked my skull by nodding off during a conference call. I jerked up right before my face nearly went splat on the desk. My sleepy state changed real fast. I desperately needed coffee and sodas for the rest of the day. I learned my lesson. Going to sleep on time is a requirement for me. It's time to find out where we're going tonight. I'll shoot Keith a quick text.

Me: Keith, how are u?

Him: I'm good. Feeling good for a Thursday. How r u?

Me: What time should we meet?

Him: Why would we meet?

Me: U may have something up after

Him: I'll drive. Meeting doesn't make sense.

Me: Didn't want to assume. You could have plans later.

Him: No plans later. Why would I? That's rude. Plus, I told you we need to figure this out.

Me: I make no assumptions. What time should I be ready?

(I'm not addressing what we need to figure out.)

Him: How is 7:00?

Me: That works

Him: C u soon sweetheart

Me: C u bye

Finally, I'm leaving the building to head home. I hope the traffic is light. I don't need to be stuck in traffic being this tired. Luckily, I don't hit anyone, and I arrive home in record time. All I want to do is hit those sheets. I'm tired. As soon as I get out of my car, my phone vibrates with a text to sour my plans. I board the elevator and read a text from Alex. It's like grand central with people wanting to get at me today.

Alex: What it do?

Me: Nothing much, wyd?

Him: Hey, are u up to hangout this week?

Me: This week is busy. How about Monday night?

Him: Monday is good. We need to talk.

Me: Ok, c u

I'm curious about what Alex, and I need to discuss, but I'm too tired to dwell on it now. I have a dozen thoughts swirling in my head. There are three different men in my life. Well, honestly two are friends and one isn't my friend no matter what story I'm telling myself. According to Tonya, this isn't a bad problem to have. She's wrong though. This is a bad problem for me to have. If I didn't find Keith attractive, he could be my friend all day. I take a much-needed nap. I sleep for an hour, and now I'm refreshed. I consider cancelling the date with Keith tonight to get more sleep. Did I just call this a date? A major slip of the tongue. That's all it could be. Anyway, I shouldn't cancel because I'm tired. He'll have more ammo against me since I'm avoiding him if I pull a no-show tonight.

Right on time, there's a knock on the door. I open the door to find Keith with a bouquet of flowers. This is very much like a date. Why is he a damn walking sex symbol? Shit, this is going to be a tough night. He's wearing a suit, and it's tailored to fit him perfectly. **(Yes, I'm checking him out. Damn, is he wearing Armani? I love a man who knows how to dress. How am I going to survive tonight? Damn, what am I going to do?)**

"Wow, you're very beautiful."

"Thank you. You're very handsome."

He hands me the flowers, and I thank him. Keith could be the one sending me the flowers every other week. I admire the flowers and wonder if I'm overthinking the secret admirer thing. It's such a nice gesture for him to bring me flowers. Something tells me he isn't the secret admirer type. It doesn't appear like he's the one. The flowers I received the other day are still vibrant. I'm even more curious about whose sending them.

"I have to put these in water. Would you like something to drink?"

"No, I'm okay."

"These flowers are very beautiful and unexpected, Keith. Thank you, again. You really shouldn't have."

"You're welcome, and yes, I should have. It's just me being me, sweetheart."

(Damn, I may find out what he's working with tonight. He's starting this date off right.)

There's a full-length mirror in the entrance of the restaurant. I notice how we fit with one another. We're seated right away since Keith has a reservation for us. The waitress approaches us right away to ask if we want anything to drink or any appetizers. She basically eye fucks Keith and smiles like I'm not here with him. I sure hope it's not going to be the night the waitress wants to flirt with my date. We both order water as we peruse the drink menu. We decide to order a bottle of merlot since we mutually share a love of red wine.

Tonight, things with Keith are different. We're both sharing different sides of ourselves we haven't shared. Keith has plans for the future and his family. He exudes confidence and it makes him very attractive. There's nothing like a man going after what he wants. A flash of us together biblically shows me exactly what it would mean to me.

We chat about how it's clear more than ever that African American professionals need to have committed sponsors rather than mentors to help navigate our careers. The same could be said about women. This is necessary to achieve success in the corporate game. It's very refreshing to dive into these various issues within corporate America with a guy I respect.

Keith explains how he'd always been driven and motivated to succeed. He'd always been a natural athlete. He also had to keep his grades up. He not only graduated from high school with great achievements in sports, but he also captured the second ranking of the class. He's grins at me all cheesy like and admits, "I was the salutatorian of my class."

"I'm not sure what to make of your grin. You must have been the valedictorian," he mildly accuses me and grins, so I'm aware he's only joking.

"You got me! That's not why I smiled at you. I love it. You're super smart. It's very sexy."

"Sexy, huh? Maybe I'll conjugate some verbs for you later."

"Ooh, I can't wait."

He tells me more about his childhood, and why he loves life. I could listen to his voice for hours. I absolutely love learning more about him. It's great discovering what drives him, what he's passionate about, and how he's willing to be open. I'm nervous. I'm happy he's sharing himself with me. The conversation is about to take a turn to what I've been dreading. I could tell by the way he's gazing at me.

"We need to deal with what's going on between us, Lauryn."

"What exactly are you insinuating is going on with us?"

"Are we going to play like there is nothing between us?"

"No, I'm not trying to play games. I'm nervous about my feelings toward you."

"Yea, this is unchartered territory for me, too. I appreciate you have reservations because of your last relationship."

"I do, yes. I have other reservations about you, too, Keith."

"What are they? Let's talk about it."

"You are...hmm, how should I say this nicely?"

"Don't hold back. I'm a big boy. I'm capable of listening to constructive feedback."

"You're a playa, and I don't do playas. Not going down this road with you."

"I don't consider myself a playa. I haven't been committed to anyone in a very long time. It doesn't mean I'm incapable of commitment."

(I refuse to talk about this now. Shit, he's making me nervous.)

"Where did you go, Lauryn?"

(In my damn head, that's where.)

"I'm here. You're right. Maybe I've been stressing out about what this could mean between us. Why don't we let life happen? Let's not stress or label things."

"I'm capable of this. 'No stress Keith' is my middle name. Now tell me more about you. I'm pretty sure I've revealed everything about me earlier."

I chuckle, "What do you want to know?"

"Let's start with the basics."

"I told you I'm from Atlanta, and I have very successful parents. They adopted me as a baby. I couldn't be more like their biological child. My parents had a very difficult time conceiving because my mom had terrible fibroids and endometriosis. They even tried in vitro fertilization, and it wasn't successful. My parents decided they didn't have to have a biological child. They were meant to be my parents. Through the matching process, they were chosen by a lady who wanted to remain anonymous."

"Do you ever want to find out about your birth parents?"

"Not really. Nothing's missing for me. I've always known my parents adopted me."

"How do you feel about being adopted?"

"I don't have any negative feelings about being adopted. I'm Marcus and Carolyn Davidson's kid not through blood but through love. I'll treasure them always. I didn't miss anything. My parents are and have always been my rock and salvation in spite of me not being their biological child. I've been blessed to have the greatest support system. Whenever I refer to my parents or they refer to me, it's never about me being adopted. They've never once referred to me as their adopted child. Yes, I am adopted. They're my parents, and I'm their child. I usually don't tell anyone I'm adopted because it becomes a test about how different I am. People tend to assume their relationship with their parents are better because of biology. This is absurd quite frankly. How many times have you heard a story on the news about some biological parents treating their children like crap? It's about the individuals and the love they have. Love isn't only biological."

"I hope you understand my curiosity. I've always been interested in adopting."

"No, it's fine. It's great you would consider adopting. There are too many African American kids who deserve a great home yet most end up in foster homes until their 18. I'm lucky. I spent every day of my life with my parents. They were with me from my very first moment and have supported me through everything."

"It sounds like you had a great childhood. I would like to meet your mom someday."

"Well, I may have to make sure it happens," I announce as I wink at him.

"I'm going to hold you to it. Hopefully, she'll like me."

"Yea, I doubt there isn't a lady alive who doesn't like you."

"I guess, but I'm having a difficult time with one specifically." He stares at me with those smoldering eyes. There's no room for me to misinterpret what he means. "If the right woman shows up for me, no other woman will matter. Would you be willing to be this woman?" I'm out of breath for a second. How should I respond? He's killing me right now.

"What's wrong? I'm having a good time. Aren't you?"

"Nothing's wrong. I'm having a great time, too."

"Hmm, if you say so," he states as he winks at me.

(I'll be damned if he's making me wet by only staring at me. I'm in too much trouble.)

My face is frozen in a smile. I'm pretty sure I resemble an idiot. Plus, he has a way of making me blush like a schoolgirl. I won't deny my reaction to him anymore. I may be playing with fire, and I won't be surprised if I'm on the burning end of the stick. He's turning the tables on me now. At this moment, the waitress comes to ask if we're interested in dessert or anything else. She's still committed to shooting her shot and glances at Keith like she wants to be his dessert tonight. She doesn't pretend to care if I'm with him or not.

"Sir, would you like some of our delicious desserts tonight?" she asks. I'm very happy. Keith ignores her obvious attempts at flirting with him. He's staring directly at me.

Keith asks, "Do you want to share some of this brownie with ice cream?"

"Sure, why not?" It's not a norm for me. I'm feeling spontaneous tonight.

"Would you like the dessert with two spoons?" The waitress asks with a tone which indicates she's annoyed. I should've snapped back. Someone has to be the adult here. Keith responds to the waitress. "Sure, we're planning to share the dessert," he speaks in a very direct and respectful way. "Would you like something else, sweetheart?" he asks me to make things clear we're together.

"No, this dessert will be perfect."

The waitress stomps away abruptly to fill the order. I sure hope she doesn't sabotage the food. I'll inspect the dessert. I wouldn't put it past this chick to contaminate it, but she may not because we only ordered one. She clearly wouldn't mind spending some extracurricular time with Keith. I don't blame her. Extracurriculars are causing me to have brain fog right about now.

"Lauryn, we discussed not labeling what we are to each other. Who needs the stress? I would like to ask you something."

"Okay, ask away."

"Things became awkward following our kiss. You've been ghosting me. Why?"

"I haven't been ghosting you. I just —"

"You just what?"

I inhale a deep breath, "I didn't expect to want all I wanted."

"What do you want?"

"More. More than you can imagine."

"What's wrong with wanting more? I want more, too."

"You aren't in a vulnerable state."

"Everybody's in a vulnerable state."

"How will I be certain you won't hurt me?"

"I guess it's a possibility, but you can also hurt me."

"I wouldn't hurt you."

"You could, though. I'm enjoying getting to know you, Lauryn. This is scary based on everything you've experienced. Don't judge me based on what happened with him. I've been pretty honest with you, and I'll continue to be honest."

"I don't want to compare you to Jackson. I get it. Conceptually, you're not him. I'm navigating through the unknown. I want to allow myself to navigate it with you."

"Let's not get too deep right now. Tonight has been incredible. Better than I imagined."

"You imagined us?"

"Yes, I imagined going on a date with you."

The waitress returns with the dessert. I side-eye it. Keith chuckles at me.

"Could she have done something to the dessert because I ignored her? She could be upset because I don't know her, and I came in here on a date and refused to dump my date for her."

"Sure, it sounds ridiculous when it's verbalized, but she figured she had a shot. She didn't care if we're together. That chick's thirsty."

"She's kind of obvious. Besides it's her MO."

"Why is it her MO?"

He points to the waitress who's flashing her chest at a guy across from us at another table. This guy is dining solo, and she's full throttle with her flirting now.

"I guess you're right. She definitely jumped onto the next one."

"I could be hurt, but I'm not. Let's eat this brownie."

We eat the scrumptious brownie with ice cream. After a few bites in, Keith pressed his finger right next to my lip.

"Ah!" I sigh as he touches me closely.

"You must have missed this. You had something there on your lip," he proceeds to lick his finger. Something in my stomach turns as he shows me such intimacy. Maybe, it's only butterflies.

"You could have kissed it off," I exclaim boldly.

(Why did I suggest he kiss me?)

"Are you flirting with me?" he asks and stares at me seductively, "Would you like for me to kiss it off? There's some still lingering." I turn bright red, and he leans in to kiss the tip of my lip to remove the brownie and ice cream. "Hmm, it tastes good."

"Now, who's flirting with whom?"

"Well, you gave me the idea," he says innocently.

As on cue, the waitress returns and interrupts us. She wants to check if we needed anything else. Keith pays the check, and we proceed to leave the restaurant. There's a high amount of sexual tension between us as we drive home. It isn't a good time to discuss any of this now. On the entire drive back, I'm nervous. **(What do I want? The kiss was very good. The sensation of his lips on mine makes me want to moan. I want more. I want all of him. I want more tonight)**. I'm having an internal argument with myself. This sounds every bit of crazy. My body is craving more of his kisses. My mind is weary wondering about venturing into unchartered territories with this sexy ass man. **(Could it hurt to have just another taste of his luscious lips? Nah, it couldn't hurt at all).**

I'm going to be in a boatload of trouble tonight. My body is like an inferno sitting next to him. This isn't even a time when alcohol is a contributing factor. I only had a glass of wine, so, no this isn't why I'm flirting with danger. I've been fooling myself, and my body is in the driver's seat now. My body wants what it wants. There may be a war between my mind and body, and I'm positive my body will win tonight. Comprehending this doesn't freak me out either. Tonight, maybe it's what I need. It could be the beginning of something beautiful. It will be life changing, and it's time for me to change my life. As scared as I am to do something reckless tonight, I'm also scared to go home alone. The way Keith gazes at me tells me to trust him to bring me to the promised land. I have to wonder if he'll surpass all the fantasies, I've had about him. Something tells me I won't be disappointed with his performance. Not at all.

I can't keep pretending like I don't want things to go down this way. It's no point in lying to myself. I may not admit anything to anyone else, but I have to be honest with myself. The way my body is tingling and responding to Keith can't be ignored. Tonight, is the night things will cross over and change between us. I'm very nervous and excited at the same time. The back and forth between us at dinner piqued my sexual curiosity even more. Why does the Marvin Gaye song, "Sexual Healing" seem worthy for what's about to go down? The lyrics resonate with my mood.

I'm expecting more than an explosive night with him if a big gun like Marvin Gaye is poppin' in my head. As I ponder this, nothing about sex with Keith could be ordinary. I haven't even sampled him yet, and I know this shit is going to rock my world. That's why I've been so afraid. He may give me some lovin' I don't want to ever forget. How will I get over that shit if this only for one night? I can't even think like this. I want this with him. Let the chips fall where they may. I must live in the moment and treasure every second of tonight. All the while hoping, this will last for more than one night.

I'm anxious about what will happen next. I won't be running scared. My body is calling for him, and there's no denying what I really want. I hope it won't be a mistake. If it is, I hope it's the best mistake I'll ever make. My phone vibrates, and I ignore it at first since I'm still technically on a date. I need a distraction from these erotic images. I check my phone to uncover who's trying to reach me. I'm surprised it's Alex again. He must really need something.

Alex: Hey, Lauryn. Let's get together earlier on Monday? Like sometime around your workout?

Me: Yea, works for me.

Alex: C u. Goodnight.

Me: You, too. Later.

"Should I be worried? You're antsy over there," Keith asks.

"Me, antsy. Never! I'm only anticipating the rest of our night. The after-dinner fun."

"Oh really?"

"Yes, really."

"Well, I'm ready to go up. How about you?"

"Let's do it."

We approach the elevator to hurry this along. The sexual tension between us is thick enough to be cut with a knife. It's taking the elevator a minute, and this is unusual. It may be broken. I'm considering asking if he wants to take the stairs. As I contemplate this as a real option, the elevator finally dings indicating its arrival. It opens, and its completely empty. I'm unsure if I'm relieved or not. Too many things could happen in the closed confines of an elevator. **(You've seen those movies where the hot sex happens in the elevator. The people generally have the same built-up tension Keith and I share.)**

As the door closes, we stare at each other intently, and this staring game is taking forever. He suddenly waltzes over to cup my face with his hands before he grabs me into a close embrace. It's as if he's been waiting for this moment as long as I have. It's more than clear tonight the bubble will burst, and tension has to be eased. Will I be on the receiving or giving end? I'm excited about the possibilities. He holds onto me tightly. He leans in to kiss me. This kiss is slow and controlled at first. As much as I'm trying to fight what's happening with us, I want to kiss him again. I release my tongue into his mouth and our bodies become one. I could taste the chocolate cake and merlot on his tongue. I want so much more. He releases me and stares at me intently. We're lucky the elevator doesn't stop until it arrives at the 12th floor, our floor. My libido is going into overdrive. My desire won't be quenched with this one kiss.

CHAPTER 27
Stranger

He strolled into the French restaurant with the intent of spying on Lauryn and her date. He had a great view of them from his table. He didn't want to be obvious as he stared at them. As soon as the waitress saw him, she zeroed in on him like a moth to a flame.

"Hi there, handsome. Are you dining alone tonight?" she asked.

"I'm alone," he answered.

"What a shame! I'll make sure you have the best night."

"How are you certain?"

"Leave it to me, handsome. I'm making sure you're fully satisfied," she said as she winked at him. "I'm working, but I'll never resist a handsome man like you. What would you like to drink?"

"Thanks," he murmured, "I would like a glass of merlot and a salad with ranch dressing."

"Is house okay for the merlot?"

"House is fine."

"Are you ready to place your entire order?

"Why not? I'll have the boeuf bourguignon."

"Great choice, handsome. I'll put in your order right away."

She pressed her breast out for him to view quite a bit of cleavage, and she sauntered away. He smirked at her insinuation. This could be a way for her to get more tips. He glanced over in time to witness Lauryn's date kiss her seductively in the restaurant.

He nearly crushed the stem of his wine glass as he glared at them. He wanted his lips ravaging hers and not some neanderthal who didn't have the class to respect her and not suck down her throat in public. She's far above an attention seeker without self-respect. His blood began to boil as he stared out at them. Public kissing.

What would he do to her next? Get her in the bathroom and have his way with her? He wanted to stop this. She deserved better than to become his flavor of the week tonight. He's a regular at Baskin-Robbins and is no stranger to the multitude of varieties.

He didn't grasp why his meal hadn't been served yet. He put in the order over 30 minutes ago. This restaurant had been rated to have the best food without a long wait. Well, he hadn't begun eating, and Lauryn and her date were wrapping things up. He wanted to follow them and ruin the rest of their evening.

No such luck since this food is taking longer than it takes a bonsai tree to grow. What are they doing back there? Willing the food to be ready? His agitation showed on his face. He couldn't disguise or hold back his displeasure over the situation. He primed himself to go off as the waitress made her way back around to him.

"Excuse me, ma'am."

"Ma'am is my mom," the feisty waitress replied. "What would you like, handsome?"

"My order is taking an extremely long time to come out. When will I get my food?"

"My apologies. We're behind in the kitchen because we had a call-in. Let me go and check on your meal. I'll find a way to make this better for you. I aim to have happy customers."

"You don't have to do anything special. I'm hungry and ready to eat. I need my food out here in the next five minutes, and your tip won't be impacted."

"Thanks for giving me a chance to make this right."

"Don't make me regret it."

"No, sir, I won't."

She returned with his meal. He hoped to avoid this because he wanted to lay low. The waitress upped her game, and she continued to flirt with him. Did he misinterpret the waitress' intent?

He felt bad about giving her the attitude earlier. She really didn't do anything to warrant it. He would have to do something for her now. Lauryn and her date left, and he wouldn't have to suffer any longer with their bedroom stares at one another. The waitress came back over to check on him once again.

"Hey, handsome. Do you need anything else?"

"Not really. I want to apologize for the way I acted. I guess the hangry man in me acted an ass with you."

"Don't worry about it. You're good. Are you ready for your check?" He nods.

"Thanks for being so understanding."

She returned with his check, and he smiled as he read the contents of the receipt, "I'm thinking I would like something else."

She sighed, "You're sure it's not provided on the receipt?"

"I like what's being provided, and I would also like a piece of chocolate cake with ice cream on top."

"No problem, handsome."

She wrote her number and stated she would be off in an hour if he wanted dessert. He smiled at her. He settled the check and gave her a $500 tip for all her extra effort. She came by one more time to flirt with him. She glanced at the tip and literally whooped as she stared at the amount. He realized she didn't normally receive tips like this one. What a shame! She was pretty, but he thought she could be broke.

As he left, he texted her to meet him at a bar around the corner from her job. An hour later, she surprised him by coming into the bar dressed in a very sexy red dress. She held a bag which he assumed contained his chocolate cake. He couldn't believe she brought the cake. This made him pleasantly surprised. She turned him on a lot watching as she gyrated her hips as she walked in the sexy red dress. She'd be good enough for the night. Lauryn be damned.

He couldn't deny his horniness, and he had to do something about it. Lauryn could be doing the guy from dinner. This drove him crazy. He would forget about it all tonight. The waitress would make him concentrate on something else altogether. She strolled over to him with a purpose. He saw the way the other men in the bar stared at her, and this made him want to protect her. He quickly met and guided her to the bar to sit.

"I'm glad you came. I'm kind of shocked you're here," he told her.

"Oh, handsome. I have every intention of making you cum tonight. Just tell me you have condoms. Plus, I feel bad about your dinner. I really want to earn that generous tip."

"I do have condoms."

"Do you have a problem with my plan?"

"I don't."

"Let's go."

"Where?"

"If you have to ask, I picked the wrong guy."

She grabbed his hands and led him into the bathroom of the bar. She pushed him inside a stall and locked the door behind them. She pulled him in for a kiss aggressively, and she went for what she wanted from him. She tugged his pants, and he began to resist her.

"What's wrong, handsome?"

"I'm not into public places. They're dirty."

"Are you into me?"

"Well, yeah."

"I'll make you forget all about where we are. Plus, this place isn't so bad. It's actually pretty clean."

"Hmm, I'm not sure."

"Let me take your mind off the bathroom."

She pressed her chest against his, and her hands began roaming until she found what she'd been looking for, his member, all the while kissing him to make him forget about "the bathroom." She discretely removed his boxers and began pumping his dick right away. This stunned him. He hadn't been with anyone as confident in her sexuality as this woman.

She didn't mess around. She got right to the point and demanded what she wanted. He stopped concentrating on his environment and only focused on the here and now with her. She wanted him, and oddly enough he wanted her, too. He had to forget about Lauryn for now.

"I want you to fuck me now, handsome. Is this something you're up for?"

"Yes, I am."

He turned her around, lifted her dress, and jerked off her panties in one swoop. He reached in his pocket to grab the condom. He immediately put it on to get to work. He didn't waste time with foreplay and went straight for a full thrust. Bam! He thrusted into her without abandonment. Her thigh clapped upon impact, and "Bang! Bang! Bang!" could be heard coming from the small bathroom. Neither one of them cared.

He enjoyed this unattached fuck with a nameless woman. She took his mind off Lauryn. Unfortunately, she didn't stray far from his mind. He thrusted harder trying to forget her beautiful face. He wanted to focus on this chick whose body rotated in the right rhythm as he hit her sweet spot. His thoughts continually ventured back to Lauryn. The woman before him transformed into her. In his mind, he no longer fucked the waitress. He made sweet love to his lady love, Lauryn. He started caressing her hair and face as he plowed into her backside. He seductively kissed her on the neck and murmured sweet words into her hair.

"Oh, baby, so good. What will I do without you?"

"Shh, handsome. I don't need you to lie to me right now. Just don't stop what you're doing."

"Nothing would stop me, baby. You're everything I want."

They both climaxed at the same time. The waitress smiled at him following the explosive sex. He no longer saw the woman of his dreams. He saw the flirty waitress, and how he never got her name. If he did, he didn't remember. He probably should find out her name but decided against it. She'd assume he wanted something other than sex, and he couldn't have it.

"This was good playa, but my name isn't Lauryn."

"Sorry..."

"Sorry isn't necessary. I just want you to know who I'm not."

"No, I shouldn't have."

"Shh, it doesn't matter. I gotta go. We can do this again if you want."

"Cool. I guess."

"No pressure. See you."

She dressed quickly and kissed him on the cheek. He wouldn't be repeating this. He didn't believe for one minute she wanted "no strings sex" indefinitely. He couldn't stand the sight in the mirror for betraying Lauryn. He wouldn't allow himself to be sucked in again. He had to break away and be deserving of her. He wanted to curse at his weakness. He shouldn't give in to the flesh.

CHAPTER 28
Lauryn

He guides me to my place and holds me around my hips. I don't want the night to end, but I don't want to appear needy. He turns me in his direction and gazes deeply into my eyes. He swoops in to capture my mouth with intensity and want. After we release from the most intense kiss I've ever experienced, we breathe in each other heavily, essence for essence. He embraces me as I embrace him. What comes next? I'm very nervous about the possibilities. I don't want to rush anything. This isn't open to guarantees, but I'm savoring what we have. I'm excited and anxious at the same time. I'm not naïve enough to assume it will be another night of cold showers. Tonight, we'll go to brand new heights. I'm secretly thrilled about it. Everything's about to change for us. I hope the change will be for the better.

"Lauryn, should we stop?"

"No, I want you, and I don't want to stop," I murmur huskily.

He grabs me tighter, and his tongue slips deeper into my mouth. We're intoxicated with one another. We haven't made it out of the hallway. I'm very overwhelmed with desire. I try hard to focus in the now and not about changing my mind about a night of hot sex. I don't want to be the responsible one either.

"Your place or mine?" I ask surprising myself.

"Mine. I don't have any condoms on me."

"Yours it is."

He lifts me, and I wrap my legs around his torso. He leads me to his place, and he kisses me as we go. I'm impressed at how he maneuvers his key FOB to enter his home without missing a beat with kissing me. Every part of my being is on fire. We haven't even made it to his bedroom. There's no time to observe my surroundings. I'm lost in his mesmerizing lips and nothing else matters. He lowers me to the floor for a second to discover different parts of my body. We're in the kitchen, and his lips are on my mouth first then my neck. His hands are under my dress caressing my legs.

In between kisses, he says, "Lauryn, I want this very much. We may not make it to my bed."

"Hmm, you're probably right," I chuckle.

"I really want to make sure this is what you want. I don't want to take advantage of you at all."

"Shush, I want this. Let's go to your bed now."

He stops kissing me long enough to resume carrying me to his bedroom. He puts me down as he releases the tie on my dress, causing it to drop to the floor as I fall back onto the bed. I slip out of my shoes. I only have on my matching navy bra and panties. He takes in my entire body in a way that could make any woman insecure. It's the exact opposite for me. He reaffirms what I already knew. I'm a goddess. He doesn't rush things. It's like he's committing my entire body to his memory.

"Damn, woman…why are you this sexy? I imagined your beautiful body an infinite amount of times. Nothing could've prepared me for your reality."

"You're sexy, too," I purr at him.

He starts kissing me again, and his hands are rubbing my thighs. He slips his hands between my legs and inside of my panties to remove them in an instant. As he slid his finger inside me, I moan in pleasure. He gazes at me as his fingers navigate my body. He starts kissing me deeply, and his hands haven't stopped moving over every inch of me. I remove his suit jacket to expose the definition of his chest and biceps as my hands roam over his body.

"Sit up for me, baby," he commands huskily.

He unclasps my bra. He kisses me once again fully thrusting his tongue into my mouth. His tongue leaves my mouth, travels to my throat, and lands on my breasts. I'm getting very hot as his tongue swirls around the tip of my nipple. I begin to tug at his shirt. I pop a few of his buttons to reveal his chest.

"Aah!" I expel. "Sorry, I may have to get you a new one."

"No need. I have plenty."

I'm extremely hot right now. He stands to remove his clothing in one fell swoop. He stares at me for a second longer than necessary as he lays next to me. He starts kissing me again. His tongue explores my entire body as I explore his. Oh, fuck, I'm losing it. I recover fast and with the knowledge I would explode if he doesn't enter me soon. He glances at me with a piercing gaze. He perceives what I need, and his stare guarantees me he'll give me what I want. He grabs something from his nightstand. It's a condom, and he carefully places it on. He gives me one more chance to back out. There's no way in hell I would back out now. I'm horny as shit.

"Are you sure you want this?"

"Yes, I'm sure. I want you."

He's gentle as he slips on top of me. I need to adjust to him. It's tight at first. There is some tenderness and no pain. He puts me first with every fondle, squeeze, and thrust. He doesn't rush. He's sliding inside me and fitting like a glove, and it's remarkably natural. This is where we belong. He pumps faster, and it doesn't take long for me to lose control. I gyrate along with him with every pump.

"Damn, you feel so good. You're well worth the wait," he grunts as he thrusts into me.

"Keith, oh, Keith. So good. Don't stop!"

We conquer several positions without missing a beat, and I have multiple orgasms. The sex is indescribable. **(I'm in trouble.)** As quickly as this thought enters my brain, it leaves. I'm allowing myself to melt into complete euphoria. We both climax for the final time, and Keith holds me tightly. We lay in each other's arms for several minutes.

He goes to the bathroom to get something to clean up, and I use this opportunity to view his bedroom. It's nice. He smiles at me as he approaches to clean me as well. That's sweet.

I should be going back home. I'm in too deep under Keith's spell. He gets back into bed and holds me in his arms protectively. I'm elated he's holding me. This is a lot more than sex. **(What if it's not? What if it's more?)** "Negative Nelly" must get out of my head. I have no idea what's going to happen between us. Would he be holding me in his arms right now if this didn't mean anything? I have to get out of my head and enjoy this for what it is. I'm getting sleepy, and it's so comfortable in his arms. He turns to ask me a question.

"Are you staying with me tonight?"

"Staying is not a great idea. You may have buyer's remorse in the morning."

"Not likely. What will convince you to stay?"

"It's not like I don't want to stay. I really need to process what happened."

"No pressure. I really like you and would love for you to stay, but I'll accept your decision."

He pulls me close to him and holds me in his arms. He kisses me on my jaw trailing towards my neck. His hands start to roam, and I have to stop this. We'll be going for another round if I'm not careful. As tempted as I am, I'm not doing this again tonight. I should get home and get some sleep. He's irresistible and walking away will be extremely hard. I better leave now, or I never will. I yawn and this gives him ammunition to convince me to stay.

"You should stay, and your body agrees with me."

"As much as I hate to leave you Keith, I must."

"You don't have to leave me."

"I really have to go."

"I know. No pressure at all. You're invited to stay."

"I should go," I say as I kiss him.

My clothing and shoes are scattered all over the room. I slip out of the bed with the sheet covering me. Keith smirks.

"Why are you suddenly shy?"

"Since the lights are on and we're not all over each other anymore, I guess I'm a tad timid."

"You shouldn't be bashful, sweetheart. You're beautiful from your head to your toes."

I hurry to get dressed because if I linger any longer, I won't be leaving tonight. He jumps out of bed and puts on some clothes, too. I start towards the door, and he follows me. He tilts my chin and kisses me deeply and tenderly. His hand starts caressing my back and precedes to drift down to rub my butt. As much as I enjoy his mouth on mine, I tenderly push him away.

"If we start this again, I'm pretty sure I won't make it home tonight."

"Hmm, what's the problem?"

"I'm sorry. I wish I could stay, but I have an early day," I say as I withdraw from him even though I want to stay.

He's disappointed as he remarks, "I understand. Really, I do. I had to try, right?" he smiles.

"I'd be disappointed if you didn't," I counter approaching the door, and he closely follows me. "You don't have to deliver me to my door."

"Yes, I will make sure you make it home safely."

"It's down the hall."

"Even if it is, I'm escorting you home. What if something happened to you? It's very late."

He's being ridiculous, and I'm secretly pleased he's walking me home. Arriving at my door, he reaches towards me, grabs me in his arms, and kisses me deeply. I don't want him to stop. I really don't. I better stop him, or I'll end up in a Kamasutra position begging him not to stop. I let him hold me in his arms for a while longer before I release myself from his embrace.

I close the door and stand still for a moment remembering every aspect of the mind-blowing sex. This could never be one-and-done for me. A major part of me wants to run to him for an encore and something more in the morning. Why did I run away? I could wake in his arms. Is this me protecting myself from the inevitable? I don't need to dwell on it. I want to focus on the memory of the amazing night we shared. I'm unsure if I'll ever have a repeat. At least, I'll have tonight. Taking a shower and sleeping is the only thing I'm currently mastering.

It's the next day, and I have a lot of energy surprisingly. I stretch out and yawn. Keith and his magic moves had me sleeping like a baby. I slept really well considering my dreams were crazy and seductive. I guess those orgasms were all I needed to relax and get some sleep. Now, I need to get up and go for a run. Last night happened to be spectacular. Why am I unsure about what last night meant? I need to clear my head since I have all these confusing images and ideas swirling around about Keith. Running will help with it. I'll get a better grip on reality after some exercise.

I hope running into Keith won't be awkward now since we've done the deed. He says he wants to be with me, but he didn't mean it. Where do we go from here? It could've been only sex for him. Is having sex what we needed to figure out? The explosive chemistry between the two of us won't be denied. Nothing's really changed besides the physical nature of our relationship.

Now, I'm doomed because I couldn't walk away from this man if my life depended on it. The sex was everything. My imagination didn't quite compete with the reality. Reliving last night, my whole body begins to tingle. I definitely want to be with him again. Last night changed things for me. I've been lying to myself. Admittedly, I wanted much more for some time now. The kiss on my birthday only validated it.

Did I make a mistake last night with him being my neighbor? How will I act if he brings a date home? What do I want? Am I prepared to date without exclusivity? I'm not, and I won't settle for less than I deserve. I don't share. I'm an only child. If he isn't okay with this, we had a wonderful night. I'll remember it for the rest of my life as one of my best memories.

I finish running, and I check my phone eagerly hoping to have a message from Keith. There isn't one. It's still early. Why am I panicking? (**Because you did something out of character, and it makes you uncomfortable. Before you say anything, Alex isn't the same. We weren't ever going to be more.**)

What if our time together didn't resonate with Keith like it did with me? What if he didn't experience the same connection as I did? What if this was all he wanted? Shit, maybe I'll be mature about this if I'm a one-and-done for him. Nah, I'm not mature. I'm also not the clingy type who'll beg him for more. I really need to be cool about all of this.

Since I need to keep busy, I get dressed for work. I can do this! Focus on work! My body trembles again sensing his touch. The way his strong hands stroked my body. My body is betraying me. It wants more of him. I got to get him out of my thoughts. It doesn't matter how he puts it down if it's only sex. (**Who am I fooling? I won't forget the way Keith laid it down last night.**)

I need to try and psych myself up. "I'm awesome no matter how Keith thinks of me. Anyone would be happy for me to be with them. If he doesn't want this, others will." (**Why isn't this helping me to cheer up?**) I want him to want me as much as I want him. Like my man would. (**Shit, I got it bad. What am I going to do if he doesn't want a relationship and wants things to be "casual" between us?**)

My phone vibrates, and my heart leaps hoping it's Keith. Sadly, I'm disappointed because its only Kim. She wants to meet for lunch. Meeting with Kim will help to keep my mind occupied. It's been a minute since we've hung out. It'll be great to catch up. This will help me momentarily forget about last night.

Having lunch with Kim is the highlight of my day. We're gossiping about all things STU plus everything else she has going on in her life. Kim has started working for a local manufacturing firm, and she swears its set in the 1950s. The men call her darling or sweetie. She won't stay at this company long since there aren't any growth opportunities for women or people of color, and she's tired of being patronized.

Caleb asked her to marry him, and she wants me to be a bridesmaid. I'm extremely happy for her but not particularly about being a bridesmaid. How does that saying go? "Always a bridesmaid never a bride." I've been a bridesmaid more times than I care to admit. I'm really over it. Plus, the dresses suck. We both have to get back to work. We cut the lunch short, and we promise we'll catch up soon.

The rest of the day gets busier than expected. I didn't have time to breathe let alone worry about things with Keith. I check my phone as I'm leaving for the day, and there isn't a peep from him. No news is good news, right? I drive home very exhausted from work and kind of annoyed. I worked until freaking nightfall, and I didn't even realize it.

It's hard to reconcile the kind and charming Keith with the one who has ghosted me the morning after. I try telling myself things are casual between us. Damn, I don't believe it any more now than I did when I said it. This is exactly why I didn't want to go down this road with him.

Did last night mean anything to him? He has dated quite a bit, and this may have been only about hittin' it. I unsuccessfully try to convince myself that I only wanted to test drive him. **(Could this had been a mistake? What the hell is wrong with me? My big girl pants didn't prepare me to be rejected. You don't test drive a Bugatti just to go home empty-handed.)** How did I get home? It's very dangerous to go blank while driving. This hasn't happened before. I'll have to watch this crap.

I settle in on my couch, and I try to chill. I want to free my mind of all things negative. They're only counterproductive to any progress. My phone vibrates, and I'm excited hoping it's Keith. He's driving me crazy by not being available. I'm acting like a typical teenage girl whose crush isn't feeling her. I don't want to relive my teenage years, but my confidence is extremely low right now. It's Isaac texting me.

Him: Hello Mio amore. Looking forward to tomorrow night. Are we still on?

I start to respond, but I'm confused. Could Isaac be the distraction I need to get my mind off Keith? Isaac may want more, and I don't. Would I be doing him dirty or leading him on by going out with him? He said he could wait, and there isn't a rush for us to get back together. Too much has happened. It's been over between us. If he tried to rekindle things a year or two following our break, I definitely would've given him another chance. That ship has truly sailed.

Isaac's divorced with a child. I doubt he would truly be willing to have a platonic friendship with me. We were once friends, and it's very plausible for us to be friends again. Is it impossible to believe we could be friends now that we're older and wiser? I realize I should respond to his message.

Am I being too harsh with him? Isaac and I were good together, but we were in college. Isaac has plenty of positive attributes to consider in a boyfriend. Fine as hell. Check. Faithful. Check. Dependable. Check. Great in bed. Check. Wants a relationship. Check. Truly sorry. Check.

He makes great boyfriend material, but I won't get stuck in Lalaland. I remember what it was like when he wanted out of the relationship.

There are some cons I'd have to consider as well. Broke my heart. Check. Has an ex-wife that could be messy for his next boo? Check. Has a daughter. Check. His daughter isn't a negative, but baby mama drama could be. Check. Broke my heart. Double check. **(I realize I said it before, but it has to be remembered.)** Don't feel him like that anymore. Check. It won't work. I'm not sure if I'll ever get passed Isaac leaving me like he did. I don't trust he won't do it to me again.

I'll probably need someone to get my mind off Keith. Would I be using him? I don't want to hurt him. I'm really confused about what I should do. Why did Keith fuck with me like this? I wasn't ready for this. I'd been happily avoiding him for months. He pushed me at every opportunity acting like he wanted something real with me. I guess that's his move to get women in bed. He acts like the man who adores the woman and pretends to want something meaningful. Well, the joke's on me.

Me: Hi Isaac. It'll be great to see you tomorrow.

Him: Counting the hours, Mio amore.

His response doesn't sound like someone who would accept being my friend. I take a long bath to forget this day. I finish my bath and change into my pajamas to go to sleep. I check my phone again, and I'm disappointed as I prepare to go to sleep. Keith hasn't reached out today. I'm left to assume he got what he wanted, and I should stop wasting my thoughts and time on him.

I didn't realize how sleepy I am until I start to nod off. I don't fight it. I fall into a deep sleep. I'm trying my best not to dream about anything remotely related to Keith. I'm not successful. His sexy ass had me wet dreaming all over the place.

"Baby," Keith murmurs, "I want last night every night. Believe in us."

"Why are you ignoring me like I'm just another chick?"

"I'm not. I want you. Let me show you how much."

His perfect mouth encloses over mine, and the heat is almost too much to take. I can't resist him if I wanted to, and, no, I don't. The electric shock that's streaming through my veins is nearly paralyzing as I'm drawn closer to him. Any doubts I've had about us dissolve like Alka Seltzer in two ounces of water. I'm left feeling like the bubbles after they've lost their fizzle.

"Believe in us," he whispers as he kisses me again, "Believe in us."

"Why should I believe in anything?"

"I want this. I want you. Believe in us, please."

"Action speaks louder than words.

"Well, let me show you how much I want you."

He doesn't allow me to utter another word before he fully consumes me physically and emotionally. The heat envelopes me entirely from my belly to my limbs. This feeling scares me, but I'm also thrilled by it. I don't want this to end, but somehow I know it will.

My body jolts with the realization that I'm dreaming about us. How is he affecting me this way? I know I've gone out with him for a while, but we've "pretended to be friends" the entire time. Now what are we? Is my subconscious onto something or am I just fooling myself because I want this man? I wish I knew. I've never felt this insecure about anything before. But what if I'm wrong. I could be one of his casual flings. Didn't he use that term to refer to "his casual friendships"? I couldn't even say side chick since he's not committed to anyone. I could be a damn fool to throw caution to the wind like I did. Did Jackson's betrayal make me an idiot with judgment issues?

This is going to drive me completely mad if I keep pondering about what Keith wants. I have to move on and stop thinking about what occurred. It happened, and now it's time for me to keep it moving. Apparently like Keith has. I refuse to continue thinking about how foolish I've been by trusting him blindly. I have to be smarter than this. Why would I blindly trust a notorious player not to break my heart under two days? I have only myself to blame. It's time to go back to sleep and move on from the mistakes I've made. I only hope he doesn't consume my dreams anymore. I want to relax and sleep without wondering if he wants me or not. Time will only tell if he does. I need to practice a bit of patience. This is my last thought before sleep calls my name.

CHAPTER 29
Lauryn

I t's the next morning. I'm somewhat drowsy, but I'm still agitated. I check my phone, and there's a text from Keith. It must have come in after I fell asleep. It's a simple text, and it's more confusing than if he chosen not to text at all. At first, I considered not responding, but I'm clearly the adult here.

Him: Hi, I hope today was great and tomorrow's better.

Me: Hi, great things happened yesterday. Have a good one.

Him: "K, thanks you, too.

This text is shit. Did he think he was texting a coworker? This is a standard corporate text. I mentioned Saturday to see if he'll want to spend some time together. It's not a workday after all. I shouldn't be surprised he didn't take the bait. Did I imagine something between us the other night? Yeah, something hotter than a Bunsen burner used in chemistry class. It had to be more than a physical connection, and I've been resisting it for months. Denying it had been impossible.

What if the emotional connection is only one-sided, and I did more than I should've? I don't regret our hot, explosive encounter. If it's only sex for him, I have to protect myself and my heart. I'll have to figure out a way to coexist with him since we live on the same floor. This will be the absolute last time I get down with anyone who lives in this building.

Am I really an idiot to believe we could have something? He chased me relentlessly until I gave in and submitted to his will. Could I have been a chase, and now the thrill is gone? I hate to think our night together could've been nothing more than another notch on his belt. I didn't peep him as the type to collect the number of women he bedded. This isn't high school, and who gives a shit about collecting women as objects anyway? He never came across as that type of guy.

I want to believe he didn't use me for sex. If this is his end game, why did he exert the effort getting to know me and go as slow as he did to score? No, it has to be something else. For the life of me, I can't figure out what it is. Why would he be this vague in his texts? It's apparent if he wanted something other than casual, he would be clear and deliberate with his correspondence.

This is another example of me leaping to the wrong conclusion with a guy. He only wanted sex with me. I don't care what his mouth muttered.

His actions tell another story. It's my fault. I should've put my guidelines out there. If he only wanted sex, the terms of the agreement should've been established prior to the bases being fully loaded and action taking place.

I'll give Keith a few more days to reach out and give me some indication as to where we stand. He never said point blank, "I want to be in an exclusive relationship with me." Would it have made a difference prior to his advances? Maybe not. I wanted him last night. I still want him. It's extremely hard walking out the door without looking back.

Part of me grasps I shouldn't blame him for what happened. I'm a consenting adult, and I'm glad we had sex. My body is still shivering from everything I experienced. The physical embodiment of our time together is more than I could ever hope and imagine with a possible new partner. I want to discover what life has to offer us. I'm staying positive and believing Keith is different. Please don't prove me wrong. Hopefully, whatever happened with him isn't simply his lack of interest. He could be on to the next one. My imagination is running wild with images of Keith with another woman because he got what he wanted. I didn't imagine the gleam in his eye afterwards begging me to stay the night. I don't want to be wrong about us.

I won't play this game with Keith anymore. WTH? What does his text even mean? I guess he answered what the other night meant to him. Absolutely nothing. It's clearer to me now more than ever. He played the hell out of me. I avoided him over a year, but he initiated this with me. He wanted something special. His special only included getting in between my legs. This could've been a good thing, but it only boils down to being a freaking one-night stand. Why do I hate the J Cole "Work Out" song now? I could bump to this beat when the lyrics had nothing to do with me. I'm not trying to be that chick. Thinking about our night like a damn one-night stand is only depressing me. It felt beautiful and memorable. It didn't feel like a hit and run.

This freaking song, "Work Out," is playing in my head like a damn merry-go-round now. I never wanted to be his one-night stand, jump-off, or anything remotely resembling it. For some reason, I assumed we meant something to each other since we spent so much time together. Crazy me. **(Well, kick rocks, Keith. Baby girl is moving on. I don't want to see him though. Avoiding him will be an issue moving forward. I get upset every time I think about it. He used me.)**

Enough of the pity party. It happened. I'm not the first woman to get played by a smooth-talking, fine ass man, and I won't be the last. I'll control what happens next. It's time for me to get ready to volunteer this morning at the Adoption Family Center. I have a busy day to keep my mind off him. I'm having lunch with Kennedy, too. Volunteering always gets me in the right frame of mind. Working with those less fortunate than me helps for me to put things into perspective. I have a great life with a few bumps and challenges, but I'm not afraid someone will kill me or my children because I'd been in a domestic abuse situation. My heart bleeds for them.

The morning goes by too fast, and now it's time to leave to meet Kennedy. When I enter the restaurant, I have an eerie sense someone's watching me. Something's off. I turn around quickly, but I don't recognize anything out of the usual in the restaurant. I brush it off as simple paranoia. Why would anyone be watching me? I rush towards where Kennedy is seated since I'm running late. We greet each other with a sisterly hug. Kennedy is distracted like she has something on her mind, but I don't want to pry if she isn't ready to discuss it.

"I hope you haven't been here long," I say. "Time flew by, and I didn't realize how late it had gotten."

"No worries. I just got here."

"Kennedy, how have you been? Is something on your mind?"

"I'm doing good actually. I do have something on my mind. I'm not sure if I should share this yet, but you're one of my best friends."

"What girl? Is everything okay with you and Eric?"

"Eric and I are great, but there's something else on my mind."

"Girl, I would never judge you. I'm here to listen if you want to talk."

"I'm pregnant. How did I get pregnant again? Well, I'm positive on the how. The twins are barely six month's old."

"Congratulations, girl! Assuming from your reaction, you guys didn't plan it?"

"Girl, no. We have twins at home, but I guess postpartum sex is lethal. My tubes are getting tied during this baby's delivery."

I laugh, "Eric could always get a snip."

"Yea, he made an appointment. We got it covered."

"How are you guys dealing with having another baby?"

"It's a blessing. We're scared. We'll have three babies under two. Shit, we're worried about how we'll manage."

"Girl, I'll help you if you need a date night or something."

"I have yet to tell the nanny. I hope she doesn't quit. I have some time before it's an issue. Girl, catch me up. You're my mommy break. I need adult conversation."

"Aren't you the cutest little mommy?"

"Seriously, I love my kids so much, but between work and motherhood, I need a break."

The waitress arrives with our food, and we start eating. In between bites, I notice Kennedy seemed strange. Well, like she's kind of puzzled. I'm certain she wants to get in my business.

"Do you want to ask me something, Kennedy?"

"You're holding out. Have you and Keith been doing the damn thang since my reveal party?"

"We weren't. Not then, anyway. Ask your question?"

"Are you dating him now?"

"Well kind of," I say with uncertainty. I'm not sure how I want to explain what's happening between Keith and me. It's probably showing on my face.

"Wait, are you getting serious with him?"

"I'm really not sure. At first, we were hanging out. Just casual stuff. No pressure. The other night, we went on a date, I guess."

"What do you mean you guess?"

"We went to this really upscale French restaurant, and afterwards we had sex. Girl, he's sexy. I wanted to explore every inch of his anatomy. Don't judge me please."

"No judgments here. Eric speaks highly of him. He works with Keith's firm. They became friends a minute ago, and they hang out sometimes. Eric says he's mad cool, but I get the feeling he isn't the relationship type. You aren't into being 'friends with benefits.' Could you deal with it?"

"Honestly, probably not. The other night had to be damn near the best sex I've ever had. It'll be hard to say no. I'll catch some feelings. I definitely don't want to fall for a guy who only wants to be casual. This will end badly. I'll break it off now. We'll be at least civil."

"You're saying he gave it better than even Jackson. He had you under his damn sex spell."

"Why you bringing up old stuff, Kennedy? Yes, Jackson's a fantastic lover. It came near perfection. Definitely off the charts but I don't care to remember how we were at all since he slept with Asia. Everything related to our sex life has been wiped out. In my recent sexual history, Keith wins. I still have to end it. I don't want to have a broken heart. It's the only choice I have."

"Don't break it off yet. You need to find out what Keith wants. You have no idea what he wants, do you? He may want something real with you."

"You're right. I have no idea what he wants. I doubt he wants something real. He sent me some random text the day after, and it alluded to friendship. Maybe he's telling me what he wants. He wants to keep it casual. I'm extremely emotional because of things with Jackson. I should've stayed in my lane."

"I swear if Eric had messed me over like Jackson, he would be a dead man."

"Eric loves you way too much. He seemed miserable on your break. I don't remember the dude's name you dated after college."

"You don't know the half of it."

"Do tell. I really need to think about something other than me right now."

I'm eager to learn about this. I didn't realize there's a story about the infallible Kennedy and Eric's love affair. They fell in love at first sight. I don't imagine there's too much new to discover about them. Like anything else though, everyone has secrets. No one's relationship is perfect, and what's perfect anyway? What may appear perfect more than likely has cracks!

"I dated Ken (yea, I know, Ken and Kennedy). Couldn't I be more original? I wanted to test the waters. Could someone else make me feel like Eric? We weren't serious. I figured Eric and I were completely done. Ken and I were on a date. I liked Ken, but I still loved Eric. He's my first and only love, really. Don't waste tears for Eric. He dated someone, too, and he came into the same spot as Ken and me with his date, Felicia," she begins.

"Talk about being hot seeing him with her. I'm talking about I was literally hot. I couldn't stand seeing my man, who I love, with some other chick. I realized Eric and I were destined for one another, and I ended things with Ken on the spot. I confided in Ken, 'It wouldn't be fair to keep dating him with Eric owning my heart,'" she continues.

"I approached Eric's table and asked to speak with him. He tried to play me like he didn't have time for me, but Felicia had enough of him being consumed with me all night. She told him, 'You need to resolve this shit. You've been staring at her the whole night. I had to be delusional to attempt to come between you two.' She left the restaurant. She later hooked up with Ken, and they're married now. Ironic, right?" she states.

"At least, some good came out of those dates. Well, Eric didn't make it easy for me. He acted all mad for a minute because I ruined his date supposedly. I told him we needed to stop playing. I still loved him, and he admitted he still loved me. He took me home, and we've never been a part since that faithful day. We like to call it our true anniversary," she laughs.

"There's hope. It's a fact you found your perfect match in Eric," I reassure her.

"You're right. I couldn't be with anyone else. Will you hook up with Keith again?"

"I won't lie. I wouldn't mind, but my heart couldn't handle it. He'd break it. The other night happened because I didn't allow my conscious to interfere. Plus, spontaneity won. The whole night still plays on rotation in my head. We'll see though. You'll never guess who's back in town."

"Who, girl?"

"Isaac."

"Isaac. Your Isaac?"

"He's not my Isaac, but yea, THE Isaac I used to date."

"Wow, I didn't think you would ever get over him. Is he visiting or living here?"

"Well, I got over him. He's moving here. He's hinted that he wants us to get back together."

"Are you serious? Your life is getting interesting. Would you consider getting back with Isaac?"

"I know right. That's a hard pass on getting back together with him."

"I totally get it. He hurt you bad. How does he look now?"

"He's still fine. Don't get me wrong, but he has serious baggage. He's divorced, and he has a three-year-old daughter."

"What? Isaac's been living. How are you certain he wants you back?"

"He admitted it. He wants to pop back in like nothing's changed. He basically inferred we could get back what we had. He thinks I haven't changed. I'm only willing to be friends with him. Isaac and I have plans to go out tonight. I'm not in the right headspace for a relationship."

"Are you sure about this?"

"What do you mean?"

"What if Keith wants more?"

I smile, but I didn't answer right away. What if he does want more? Could I be down for a relationship with him? Is my reluctance only because of my two past failed relationships?

"Your smile tells me everything. You'd be down for a relationship with Keith. Don't you need to make things clear with Isaac since you definitely want Keith?"

"Tonight, with Isaac isn't a date, Kennedy. We're hanging out and catching up. He's back here. It shouldn't hurt to be friends."

"If you say so. You could be playing with fire."

"It'll be fine, girl."

Kennedy may have a point about Isaac, but I'm positive he'll be alright. Keith with this lame ass text is another story. My body is still reeling over what happened between us, but I won't trick myself with thoughts of more. I need to get out of this hole and keep my dignity intact. Since we've only had one night together, I'll forget about it, right? It's not like it matters to him anyway.

Why am I surprised though? I predicted this would just be about sex, didn't I? Now, I'm uncertain how to navigate this situation. Well, I'm not joining his rotation that's for sure. I should chalk this time as "post break-up to figure my shit out."

The only thing I'm extremely concerned about is him living this close to me. It's not like I'll be able to avoid him forever. I wish I hadn't committed the equivalency of "eating where you shit." Yea, it's not my job, but it might as well be. If I'm not working, I'm home. Why did I let my libido run my life? I could be dealing with a completely fucked up situation now.

I'm not going to stress over Keith's confusing text anymore. I need to relax before I go out with Isaac. A long soak will help me relax and free my mind of anything stressful. I'm having a nice glass of wine to help mellow me out. This won't impact my night since it's only one glass.

I'm very relaxed, and I catch myself falling asleep in the bath. I'm certain a night out with Isaac will help me not dwell on my confusing dating status. If Keith wants to ignore me or act like what happened between us meant nothing, I'm gonna do me. C'est la vie, baby!

I quickly glance at my phone and notice more time has passed than I realized. I jump up to get dressed. I'm wearing my yellow fitted bodice

A-line dress, a pair of tan espadrilles, a simple Tiffany necklace, bracelet, and a silver watch. I spray a splash of my favorite perfume, Chance by Chanel. I'm wearing my hair down in its naturally curly state. This has nothing to do with Isaac loving my hair this way either. I'm doing stuff for me.

Isaac may have genuine emotions for me, and I need to respect him by not giving him any false hope. I don't want him to assume there's any possibility of us getting back together. Now, I'm wondering if I should cancel this dinner with Isaac. Am I sending him the wrong message by going out with him? He did say he could be my friend, and he accepts I'm not interested in a relationship. I hope he meant what he said to me. We used to have a good time together. I hope we'll be able to be friends. It's great he's moving back to Nashville.

"I look good if I may say so myself. It's time to go downstairs to meet Isaac."

As soon as I arrive downstairs, Isaac is coming through the front door to greet me.

"Hello, mio amore," he kisses me on the cheek. "You look really nice."

"Hey, Isaac. Thanks, you don't look some bad yourself."

"Thanks, mio amore. You ready to go."

"Yea, let's go."

We chat some during the drive about what he misses about the east coast. He's excited about being back in Nashville, though. We arrive at the restaurant rather quickly and we're seated right away. I'm eager to order because I'm really hungry. The waitress comes over, and I order my entrée along with my drink choice. I want to be nosy about Isaac's marriage, but something catches my eye, and it causes me to pause.

Keith is with a very cute girl. Her skin is mocha colored, and she has long 3C curly hair. Her hairstyle is dope. I wonder who does her hair. **(Nah, I won't share a stylist and a man, unknowingly. I have to draw the line somewhere.)** I'm annoyed with him being with her, but I recognize style. Yea, I'm 100% certain I'm another chick off his list. I'm glad to understand this, so the rest of this night won't be complicated. I'll ignore his ass and keep it moving.

I'm determined more than ever to enjoy my night out. I won't let Keith and his date bother me at all. I don't care about what he's doing with her. He doesn't matter to me at all. He's one-and-done. I'll keep telling myself this. **(His damn text makes sense now. He's just doing him.)** I ignore Keith and his date and decide to concentrate on learning more about Isaac. The waitress comes back with our orders. This is great since I'm extremely hungry. '

"How are your parents, Isaac?"

"They're good. The fam is good. How are your parents?"

"Good. No complaints. My mom called herself retiring. You know how long that lasted."

"About all of 20 minutes if we're talking about your mom."

"You know my mom. What was she thinking she would do?"

"Housewife," he says unsure.

"Are you talking about my mom?"

"Not likely. I know she's a great cook, but your mom was always handling her business at work, too. I think home life would bore her to death."

"It would. She wasn't realistic. She's back grinding like old times."

"Is your dad still sealing all the deals?"

"You know he is."

"Yea, that's him for sure. How are you enjoying your new gig?"

"It's going to be a great fit. I have some flexibility with this role, and I'm able to work from home which will help if I want to visit my daughter sometimes."

"That's wonderful. It must be somewhat of a struggle juggling work and parenthood at a distance."

"Yea, my ex-wife and I don't get along, but we agree about Bella, and we get along for her sake.

"Well, that's good. Bella shouldn't have to suffer through this. It's bad enough you're divorced."

"Yea, I never planned to get a divorce, but Sadiya, my ex, and I weren't on the same page about money. She's a big spender, and she's aware of how much I love to save. The money issues were huge, but they weren't my only problems. She would always threaten to leave with Bella. I got tired of her threats. If she planned to leave, I wished she would do it."

"Wow, Isaac, I'm sorry about your marriage."

"We rushed into it without taking the time we needed to have mutual understanding and complete love for each other. We have a beautiful daughter. I don't regret we were married. I wished she'd been willing to compromise and not give up on us without a fight."

"You sound like you still love her."

The waitress comes over preventing him from responding. She asks if we're enjoying our meals, and if we need anything else. I use this chance to glance over at Keith. I shouldn't, but I can't stop myself. He's staring right back at me. This is surprising. I almost considered raising my glass to toast him and smile, but I'm not petty.

"I will always love her, but I'm not in love with her. She's the mother of my child, so for this alone, I'll always love her and want the best for her."

"Honestly, it sounds like more to me. Are you sure you didn't quit too soon?"

"I didn't quit, but it isn't simple. I'm fairly certain she cheated on me as well."

"Oh no, really? I'm sorry. Do you have any proof?"

"Yea, she messed around with this guy who worked with me. His life took a messy turn with too much drama. She wasn't aware he video-ed their times together and would get off on them at work. The asshole bragged to me about it when we were divorcing."

"Was this the grounds for your divorce?"

"Nah, I didn't want it to be public knowledge. I honestly only want to protect Bella, and I don't want her to have messed up emotions about her mom because we're divorced. We didn't divorce because of infidelity. We simply ended things due to irreconcilable differences."

"I'm in awe of you right now, Isaac. A lot of people would get infidel-ity on record."

"I know, right. Well, I haven't always made the best decisions, espe-cially with you, but I'm a pretty decent guy."

"You're a decent guy, and your daughter will appreciate that you have her best interest in mind."

After taking another bite, I glance at Keith, and he's staring directly at me again like he's annoyed. How dare him? What? Only he gets to go on freaking dates. Who in the hell does he think this is? Some deep-seated patriarchy, where men do what they want, and women have to grin and bear it? Nah, partner. Not today.

There's something about the way he's gazing at me. It unnerves me. I start to sweat quite a bit. I've been doing my best to ignore Keith for most of this dinner, but now it's getting very difficult. He's all in my face with another woman, and I don't like it. I realize I don't have a right to be jealous, but it doesn't matter.

"Mio amore, I'm having a great time with you. It's like old times."

"Not exactly old times."

My face is completely heated with jealously, but it probably appears as if I'm blushing. Isaac misinterprets my flush appearance, and he uses this opportunity to take his shot. He leans in and kisses me. This is a shock, and I'm flustered I don't push him away fast enough. I finally break the kiss, and he assumes it's because I don't like PDA. He smiles at me, and he's very happy about the turn of events. I excuse myself immediately because I need to pat my face dry and figure out how to get this situation under control.

I gain my composure and return to the table where the meals have been removed. I peer over at Keith, and he's peering right back at me, too. There's too much to unpack. What's really going on? Why does it bother him if I'm out with someone? He's been ghosting me anyway. With all of this going through my mind, I need to get out of here. Keith is staring at me hard and making me self-conscious. I had been having a great time with Isaac.

Well, before he decided to kiss me. Why did he have to kiss me? I shouldn't have ignored his obvious repressed emotions and suggest we be friends. He wants transparency, so it's only fair he accepts we aren't getting back together. Everything I felt for him died over the years. I care about him, but I don't love him anymore. What am I doing here with him? I'm too conflicted to be out with an ex who clearly wants us together, and I don't. Damn, I misread this whole situation.

First, catching Keith with someone this soon following our night together is enough to drive me ballistic. This is really screwing with me. I want to forget about him. I wanted to focus on having a great time with Isaac. Well, until he lost his mind and kissed me. We were discussing his marriage and child. How did it lead to his lips on mine? I don't get it.

I guess I'm being naïve assuming we could just be friends. He told me he wanted us to get back together, and I stupidly assumed he would accept my terms. How could he want us back together? He hasn't spent enough time with me as a full-grown adult. I'm still reeling over the impromptu kiss. I'm practically mute and barely sociable. I have to get out of here fast.

"Mio amore, you're very quiet. Are you okay? You look like you have a headache or something. Do you still have migraines? Are you suffering from one right now?

I didn't have a migraine, but this has turned into a great opportunity to leave. I begin to show deep distress on my face and do what any normal person would do in this situation. I lie to get out of here. Keith's stare is drilling deep into my soul. I sense he's angry with me but why? Isn't he here with someone?

From their body language, it's clear they're familiar with each other. Why am I guilty about Isaac kissing me? Why do I care if Keith is dining with a very beautiful woman? None if it should matter. We're both single and living our best lives. Now, I want to get out of here. I don't want to play Isaac, but there won't be an us. He kissed me, but I have to be clear. Too much time has passed, and I don't want what we had in college.

"Yea, Isaac. I'm getting ill. I would like to leave."

"Of course, mio amore. Let me get the check."

He gets the waitress's attention and pays for our dinner. He treats me tenderly and guides me out of the door. I want to stop this, but it could cause him to be suspicious. If I want him to assume I have a migraine, I'll have to go along with this. I'm trying my best not to bring any attention to myself. We don't rush as we exit the restaurant. As we're leaving, I notice Keith is still with his date. I need to get out of here and catch my breath. I really shouldn't let Keith run me away, but I'm not strong enough to deal with this precarious situation right now.

Isaac continues to be concerned about me on the drive home, and he's being very sweet. I do remember how he would care for me. Maybe I'm being too rash about the past? Maybe I should picture what Isaac and I could be to one another. He's the first guy I ever loved.

Am I really compensating because of Keith's lack of communication? I'm not one of those girls who has to have someone. Why am I considering something with Isaac? This isn't anything I would have considered if I didn't witness Keith with another woman. I refuse to let him control my destiny. I'm getting angry all over again. I want to forget about this night. I'll probably draw a bath and have a long relaxing soak. Isaac clears his throat, and I have no idea what he's saying. How long have I been ignoring him?

"I'm sorry. I didn't hear you. My head…"

"No problem. I asked if I need to park in the garage to carry you upstairs."

"No, you don't have to carry me upstairs. I'm okay to make it on my own. I'll crawl into bed."

"I'll give you a massage. I remember how it would help you in the past."

"I appreciate it, Isaac, but I want to get some sleep. I hope you don't mind."

"Of course, I don't mind. I want you to get better."

"I will. I need to rest."

"Ok, mio amore. I'll call you tomorrow to check on you. I'll always worry about you."

"I appreciate you worrying about me. I'll be okay. I'm going to bed and rest."

As he stops the car in front of my building, he says, "Good night, mio amore." He leans over and kisses me on the cheek.

"Good night, Isaac."

I could be an award-winning actress. I gingerly stroll to the door like I'm really struggling. I committed to this scheme. I have to keep up my act and not make Isaac suspicious. I don't remember the name of the new doorman, but he wants to assist me to the elevator. I glance to quickly check if Isaac has driven off yet, but he hasn't. I allow the new doorman to assist me to the elevators. I convince him I'll get there on my own, and luckily, he agrees. I rush home because I need to relax. A warm soak is calling my name. I pour a glass of wine and run my bath. I slip out of my clothes and hope to wash this whole day away. Unfortunately, the wine and bath doesn't help much. I even added candles, but they don't help either. Keith and the unknown woman keep interrupting my sense of Zen. He claims he's not really with anyone and only dating. My mind drifts to a place where it shouldn't.

"Keith," the mocha bombshell purrs, "let's get out of here. I need what only you can give me."

"Of course, sweetheart." (**Yes, I think he calls everyone sweetheart.**)

The scene flips to them in the car, and she grabs him by the shoulder to kiss him hard. She starts unzipping his pants, and he pauses her. (**Why does this make me happy?**)

"Wait! We're in the car. I'm not big on public sex anymore." (**My happiness doesn't last long.**)

"Well, why don't you just drive, and I'll take care of you."

"I guess I can't turn this down." (**Spoke too soon about any happiness.**)

It doesn't take a rocket scientist to know what she does on the drive to his place where they do the dirty. He takes her exactly where he took me the other night. It's HER moans and screams this time heard in his home. This building has really great insulation, so no one hears anything in the hall actually. She's probably in his bed right now. This shit is driving me bananas. I can't think about this anymore. I need to focus on something else.

(Why am I playing a game I won't win? I'm usually better at determining what's a wise bet. I don't know what part of me got me into this predicament. Well, I do. My crazy libido. Well, I have to face it. I'm 0 for 2 in the love game now. Just quit while I'm ahead. Focus on work, volunteering, and heading to becoming the dog lady.)

This water is getting cold anyway. I throw in the towel and change into one of my negligees. It doesn't matter if I'm not getting any tonight. Who says I can't be sexy for myself. I've chosen the wine-colored negligee since it pairs so well with my wine. Come to think of it. I could use another glass of wine. I trot downstairs and grab a bottle of merlot.

I'm in the middle of pouring a glass when there's a knock at my door. I have no idea who it could be. I'm not expecting anyone, and Isaac doesn't have access to come upstairs. I doubt it's him. I start to ignore the knock since I don't answer the door for anyone I'm not expecting. Whoever it is probably has no idea whether I'm home or not. There's another knock, and they're persistent. Who in the hell is this? They sound like the po-po at my door. I feel like giving them the business for disturbing me.

Well, I won't be rushing to let in this disturber of my peace. They can just wait until I've finish pouring my glass. A good glass of wine should never be rushed. It must be savored. I drain the glass of wine before waltzing to the door to answer it. I throw the door open completely forgetting I'm not appropriately dressed for company. This better be important. Whoever it is better beware because I'm not in the mood.

CHAPTER 30
Keith

In law school, I journaled. Now I do it when I have things on my mind. (October, 2016) I told myself I could deal with this. I'd been chasing Lauryn for months "as friends," but I really wanted more. Have I been fooling myself? Yea, hell yea, I'd been. Even as friends, I find myself not wanting to maintain my situation-ships like I used to pre-Lauryn. I treat women well, but I don't want to be committed to any of my "friends."

Don't get me wrong. The ladies I spend time with are great. There isn't anything special with them to make me want more than something casual. I'm not immune to relationships. I've had them in college and during law school. My last relationship didn't end well. I guess it made me really jaded. I chose to concentrate on my career.

Following the gender reveal party, things changed with Lauryn. I enjoyed hanging out with her, but I wanted her in more intimate ways. I've been patient, but, damn, it was taking a very long time. I should've been able to live my life as usual, right? Why didn't I want to be with anyone else? It's hard to believe I would be content to be with her alone. What's this woman doing to me? She's driving me absolutely insane.

I get Lauryn wanted to take things slowly. I've been having a good time with her even without having sex. One of the things I like most about her is she likes sports. We've been going out a lot, and things were different with her. I've enjoyed getting to know her better, too. I always knew there was something between us. There's definitely a strong gravitational pull if she's anywhere near me. I won't define us yet. The chemistry had been there for us to have sex, but I refuse to push her past her comfort zone. My feelings for Lauryn have sneakily crept into my heart. I never expected to want something substantial, but I do want it with her. She's been hesitant because of Jackson, I suppose. I really hate he ruined her. I'll be the one to heal her shattered heart.

(February, 2017) I want to be with her a lot these days. Like the time we went to a billiard's club to shoot pool. I'm really great, shameless brag, and I won't deny it. I'd been surprised how much Lauryn really sucked. She tried very hard because she's competitive, but it'd been a losing battle. I enjoyed her attempts to make a shot the absolute wrong way. She's definitely made the date more fun for me. I had a great vantage point that night of her desirable body without appearing to be a creep. I absolutely couldn't stop staring at her ass as she leaned over the table.

Damn, her ass resembled a perfect peach in that moment. Very round and perky. I'm patient, but I'm not dead.

My patience is running thin, and I want to hold her. I got an opportunity I didn't plan. She hadn't been holding her body correctly at all to bank any shots, but I didn't care since it gave me what I wanted. I got her in my arms. Correcting her had been more fun for me than it was for her, I'm sure. Soon things gotta change drastically for us. It's taking all my resolve and control not to seduce her. Having sex had to be her decision. She doesn't seem ready, and I don't want to rush her. Following all our "dates," I had my share of very cold showers. She is worth the wait, but I'm starting to get antsy.

It just happened. Out of the blue, my interest in other women had completely vanished. She assumes I'm still a "playa," but she's wrong. Words don't matter. She has to trust and believe I'm different. I have to prove I'm a man of integrity. I don't have an issue with it since I don't lie. I'm a hardcore truth teller. Sometimes, it gets me in trouble, but I'm true to myself and the truth. "To thine own self be true," is my motto. I haven't considered changing my lifestyle for anyone in a long time. She makes me want to be better.

(This "just friends" shit isn't working. The question is, "what is my next play?" What will I do to break down the barriers she's carefully crafted to protect herself from hurt, pain, and maybe even love? Did I say "love"? What am I talking about? I want to date her and get to know her better. It has nothing to do with love. It's incomprehensible to be considering being in love. Nah, this isn't that. This is just a strong mutual attraction where I'm hoping will lead to so much more.)

(March, 2017) It's been nice knowing her birthday is two weeks after mine. She'd been irresistible that day. She wore a different type of lipstick or something, but her lips were calling me towards her. I couldn't hold back any longer. It could have been a mistake, but something told me it hadn't been. I went in for a kiss. She responded completely to me. She wanted what I wanted. She didn't push me away like I half expected her to do. I figured she would pretend like she hadn't been into it. She surprised me with her mutual desire. She forgot all her inhibitions as we kissed like were the last two people on earth. Her expression changed drastically once we detangled from each other She'd been spooked.

I ran into her sparingly over the last few months. She avoided me quite effectively. She hasn't been as responsive as I would have like. She claimed to be very busy, and she didn't have time to go out. She mentioned something about work being hectic. She hasn't been around to go running at the same time of day anymore either. I didn't run into her in the halls. It was like she completely changed her schedule. Why couldn't I get her out of my mind? She'd been driving me crazy with her avoidance act.

I accidently ran into her at happy hour. I understood her reluctance about getting involved. Her ex did a number on her, but damn, I'm not him. He's an idiot who didn't appreciate platinum and settled for silver. I noticed she hadn't been too busy to meet some rando for drinks. I put her on the spot to force the issue. We had drinks, and she appeared uncomfortable. She struggled with what was happening between us. I'm not a jerk. I let her come to terms with it. After we had drinks, she continued the vanishing act. Why is she playing games?

(April, 2017) I caught a break when we shared an elevator ride. I remember how the slight brush of her hand against my chest created an electric shock. The current that flowed caused us to stop and look at each other intently. I couldn't see anyone around us. I wanted to draw her into my arms and kiss her again. I didn't get a chance with doors opening, and people began rushing in.

The guy at happy hour wanted to stake a claim, but it had been obvious by the way she acted they weren't together. Did he really assume he could intimidate me? All 5'7 of him couldn't intimidate a kid if he tried hard enough. It didn't faze me she had drinks with him. He didn't have a chance in hell with her. She created a laundry date to ditch him. Now, that's sad. That dude couldn't even compete with laundry. I guess I should have been happy. If a woman would rather do laundry than spend time with you, that would have to suck.

She probably didn't trust herself enough to get close to anyone. Not then anyway. Well, I was willing to show her she can trust me to take care of her. I gave her a call soon after about going on a date. The time had come for us to figure out what this thing was between us. I grew tired of playing cat and mouse. I had to show her I was a tiger going out for his hunt. Tigers rarely lost their prey. I ran into her about a month ago at a place around the corner getting some coffee. She appeared uncomfortable, nervous, and almost panicked. Her reaction had been borderline comic relief. She tried to fabricate something fast to avoid having to admit anything to me. She created some fictional excuse about having to clean her house or something. She didn't have anything better than laundry or housecleaning to avoid what I could give her. She's killing me. Is this shit worth it?

She'd been convinced I believed her fabrications. She had to work on it. She acted all jittery around me. I made her nervous, and it made me want to poke the bear even more. I tried to give her the time she needed to come to terms that we had something strong between us. I'd been drawn to her. The magnetism between us became damn near impossible to ignore. She'd been drawn to me, too. Her eyes didn't lie. I didn't expect to start running into her again since there have been weeks where I didn't catch a glimpse of her at all. Lately, we crossed paths a few times a week.

She's been avoiding me like the plague. This made me angry at her, too. She needs to figure out what she wants.

We're in the elevator again. She'd been willing to talk to me, but she had the nerve to ask me if something was wrong. How could I admit to her I'm jealous? Watching her with another guy drives me crazy. She should've been going out with me. She dressed very sexy. She was definitely going out, but she claimed it wasn't a date. Imagine my surprise when I saw her get in a car with a dude mimicking actions that closely resembled a date.

I would have been lying if I didn't admit how this slightly pissed me off. She'd been dressed to kill for this dude with locs. Friends my ass. Nothing about the way he undressed her with his eyes resembled friendship. This guy has her snowed if she believed he didn't want more with her.

(May, 2017) She probably considered him a friend, but he sure as hell didn't want to be friends with her. I don't usually get jealous of women with other men. Why did I then? She dressed sexy as hell for him. I wanted her dressing like that for me. She was delusional if she didn't comprehend this had been a date. She had to be the only one in the entire establishment who didn't believe they weren't on a date. I'm a guy. He didn't want to be her friend. He had a deep hunger unsatiated by the way he stared at her. He wanted her. The only friendship he wanted with Lauryn led to him taking off her clothes.

I should just say fuck it, but I care about her. When I drove by them, I wondered if this guy would be going home with her. This made me more upset than it should.

Am I tripping? I don't want to be her friend either. It's been cool getting to know her, but I want more. I'm not sure how to define what I want from her. She doesn't want anything casual. Funny thing, I don't want casual either. Being jealous as hell doesn't quite describe adequately how I feel. I want something permanent with her. I told her we need to get everything on the table the other day. I'm tired of playing this "friend" game. We need to figure out what we are to each other. It's probably more than both of us are even aware. Everything will change tonight on our date. I didn't mention it's a date because she gets like a rabbit in the face of a wolf if intimacy is on the table.

Tonight. I have no doubts about the date. She's tempting, and I want everything from her. She'd turned me on too much. I don't plan on waiting much longer. The choice will be entirely hers, but I don't plan on making it an easy one. I won't force anything, but there will be no promises I won't play dirty. She's been sly flirting with me all night. The quick preview of our lips meeting over dessert had all my senses going wild. The sparks between us are completely electric.

If she's wondering if we'll go our separate ways tonight, she's crazy. She's staying with me tonight at least for a little while. The electricity flying between us is completely magnetic. I get she's gone through a lot, but enough is enough. It's been awhile since her relationship with "Jackass" ended. I really don't care how it makes me sound. It's time for me to make her mine.

About last night. She couldn't even try to deny our bodies' deep connection. It was time for us to stop playing. We kissed with more passionate, and she didn't run this time. She wanted this. Her eyes didn't lie. The sex was explosive and very much worth the wait. My mind and body had been consumed with her. She matches every one of my moves.

Our bodies were synchronized to the beat of a perfect song. She sensed what made me happy and predicted what I wanted without me asking. She met every thrust openly urging me to go deeper with her body and her moans. She quenched every thirst and desire I've ever had. How could she do all of this with only one night together?

I wanted her to stay the night with me. I wouldn't have minded a repeat performance. Who needed sleep anyway? What if this happened to be only first-time luck? Could this magic be repeated? She declined to stay. I'd been slightly disappointed since I don't ask woman to stay the night. Is she playing my game?

She may have gone beyond her comfort zone tonight, and she needed time to compose herself. After last tonight, I'd give her anything she ever wanted. After making sure she made it home safely, I showered and fell into a deep comfortable sleep. Something I hadn't done in a very long time. I'm certain I owe this to her.

I wake up energized and full of life. I'm ready to face Friday with vengeance. Unfortunately, today is a crazy workday. I haven't had a chance to call or text Lauryn at all. I hope she's cool with everything, but I want to give her some space to process everything, too. I don't want to pressure her at all. It's a good thing I'm very busy at work. Remembering our night together makes me smile. I'm all about getting a second round with her very soon.

I grab some fast food and head home. I eat fast, shower, and finally sit for a bit to send a text to Lauryn. Keeping it simple is the best option. It's late, and she's probably asleep already. I want her to realize she's been on my mind all day. I wish I had a chance to get a break and check-in with her. It's been too busy lately. I barely had time for restroom breaks. I've been eating at my desk as I slaved away. Working this hard sometimes requires a lot of sacrifices.

I've been handed several acquisitions which have to be closed by Monday morning. This means I have to work on Saturday, too. Bad timing, I know. I rarely work until late in the night, but I'm not lucky tonight. I don't get out of the office until after midnight, and I'm starving. This isn't the norm for me to eat this late but waiting to the morning doesn't make sense.

Now, I'm certain I want something substantial with Lauryn. I need to close some loose ends. Sabrina texts me to get together this week. She implies it's important that we speak. The sooner the better for her. She didn't want to me to come by her house. She wanted to meet at a public place, and I'm okay with that. What we need to resolve can't be done in her bed. I'll finish everything for the acquisition by mid-afternoon today, so I agree to meet her tonight. I want to clear all of this up as soon as possible. Absolutely nothing will happen with Sabrina tonight or any night moving forward. We haven't hooked up in a long time, but I don't want to muddy the waters. It's a good idea for me to cut my ties with her, and I need to do it tonight.

Imagine my surprise as Lauryn comes into the restaurant with the same dude from last month. Her "friend." I stare at her with tense animosity. She ignores me for most of the meal and is fully absorbed in her conversation with him. My skin boils. As much as I want to finish this conversation with Sabrina, I'm drawn to Lauryn and what's happening with this guy.

I'm not misinterpreting what this guy means to her. Is he the reason why she's been ghosting me? She said she's friends with him, but I'm not getting a friend vibe from this guy. I could've been considered a friend until recently. What are we now? She's been very reluctant for us to take things to the next level. What should I believe?

I fully assess Lauryn's situation. Is she on a date? We make eye contact, and she's flustered. Is it because of me? All of a sudden, Lauryn's date kisses her, and I'm pissed. I'm gripping my water cup tightly. I could crush this cup if I don't calm down. Sabrina becomes exasperated with me. I'm consumed in my own imagination featuring Lauryn and this guy.

"Keith, we have to talk about what's been going on with us."

"Yea, you're right. There are some things we need to discuss."

"We need to stop this thing between us. No more situation-ship. No more sex. I started dating someone, and we have a deep connection. We've decided to be exclusive. No hard feelings?"

Wow. Guess something is going my way.

"None. This is great!" I smile.

"What? Huh? 'Great?' You're not disappointed?"

"Nah, I actually met someone, too. I'm glad you have someone worth it now."

"Yea, I'm glad, too. It's been great with you, Keith, but I do want more than what we have."

"You're completely right. I hope we'll still be friends."

"Let's just say we'll be cool at a distance. I'm pretty sure my boyfriend won't be good with me being friends with someone I have a past with."

"Yea, I completely get it. Well, at least we don't hate each other."

"Never, Keith. I'll always have a soft spot for you. I hope your girl-friend realizes how special you are. You always treated me with respect, and I always figured you would be a great boyfriend."

"I'm glad we're on the same page."

I'm glad Sabrina and I had this conversation. Now, I'm able to politely make my exit. Lauryn and her date left a while ago. Since Sabrina and I met at the restaurant, we wish each other well and part ways. I'm happy to have all of this settled. That door is completely closed, but I'm still unsure about what's going on with Lauryn and this guy.

I'll rush home hoping Lauryn is alone. I have to confront her right away. This is out of character for me, but I want answers. What do I mean to her? I'm livid trying to rationalize her being with him now. What would I do if he's there? I guess I'll find out. Why is it taking an extreme-ly long time to get home? Normally, 15 minutes would pass by without a blink of an eye. It's taking an eternity. Did the forces of nature combine to fuck with me today? Why today of all days? I have never wanted to be somewhere so badly.

Every light between the restaurant and home turns red. Some of the lights are still set for rush hour traffic. Will anything go my way tonight?

(Why is every damn light red and taking forever to change?) I'm considering running this light because no one is coming, but if I do this, I'll hear sirens going off. It'll be just my luck to get a ticket tonight.

I have to be patient for a little longer. Could this be a sign? Could the universe be telling me to leave things alone with Lauryn tonight? Fuck this, I need clarification. What's going on with us? I need answers tonight. I'm about to lose my damn mind if I don't get to the building soon.

Finally, I round the corner to enter the parking garage, and someone is having problems with the garage FOB. There is a line backing up to enter. Could everything be happening today? I consider getting out to help them to get in. What's the problem? It's a pretty simple mechanism. I guess this person must be new to the building holding up the line. The one time I'm in a rush, and I'm stuck behind the person whose challenged with technology. The guy finally figures it out and not soon enough if you ask me.

As soon as I get out of my vehicle, I'm accosted by one of the neighbors. Jerome or Jessie is his name. I don't kick it with him. I'm unsure what he wants. I don't have time for any of his BS! He tends to make off-colored comments he thinks are cool because he has "black friends." You know the type. He's followed by a petite woman and a child about three or four years old.

"Excuse me, playboy. Can I talk to you for a minute?" he asks.

"Okay, and you're —"

"Jerome, man. We have a mutual friend, Lauryn."

I don't like the way he says her name, "I guess we do."

"Well, while we're on the topic of Lauryn, I should warn you she's been under a lot of stress."

"I understand what's bothering her."

"I'm not sure you do. She hasn't been herself, and I don't mind asking you to leave her alone because she wants this."

He points to himself. Is he serious?

"You've been spending too much time ignoring what she needs."

Now, I'm getting irritated, "It's best if we end this conversation. I have somewhere I need to be tonight." He doesn't need to know I'm on my way to see Lauryn right now. It's none of his damn business. It looks like he needs to mind his own business.

"Jerome, we're here with you. Are you going to waste our time, me and YOUR kid, to get with some thot? You got all you need right here, baby."

I guess Jerome has a thing for black girls. You wouldn't guess it with his nerdy boy next door appearance. I have never met a white Jerome before. I guess it happens. This chick is attractive, but she's ghetto as shit. This a major turn-off for me.

"Who I'm with is none of your damn business."

"It's my business if they're going to be around my child."

"Do you ever get tired of hearing yourself speak? You're like a broken record. No one is going around your child. At least not today anyway."

"Look, Jerome. I'm not here to flirt with you. I'm looking out for our baby. I want him to be safe. Do you even love him anymore?"

"Of course, I love my son. If you weren't such a bitch, I might still love you. I'm sure things will go like they should. My son needs me, and I need him."

It's unclear what's going on here with this shitshow. I try to disengage and leave while they're arguing about their own crap.

"Where are you going, man? I haven't finished," Jerome hisses.

"No, you are. You have a lot you need to deal with right now. Why are you this concerned about a single woman? You need to be concerned with your woman and child. This woman here appears to want you. Why aren't you working on your own issues?"

"Want me?! Please! She used me, and she wouldn't recognize a good thing if it bit her in the ass."

"Mama!" the cute kid yells.

"Sweetie," the mom responds to the young boy, "What's wrong?"

"I want to play Minecraft, Mommy. This iPad's not working."

"Ok, we'll deal with it in a sec. Give Mommy a chance to chat with Daddy."

"Ok, Mommy."

"Jerome, we need to stop playing and get back to doing what we do best."

"Mommy, my iPad."

"Wait a minute, baby."

Hey, little man. Mommy and I need to talk about something important. I'll make sure your iPad is working."

"But, Daddy."

"No buts, little man. Your mommy and I need need to settle something. Don't we, Mommy?"

"Yes, baby, I need to talk to Daddy for a few minutes. Talk!" She turns to Jerome.

"You're playing a game you won't win, sweetheart."

"You're such a spoil sport. I want to get out of here and do something."

"Like what I'm thinking involving no clothes once baby boy goes down?"

She giggles and smiles at him. One minute he goes from being a shit to her to the next wanting to fuck her. What's up with this dude? He's coming at me like he's Lauryn's savior or something. I'm over these people wasting my time. I'm removing myself from this strange situation.

"I'm out. I'll tell Lauryn you asked about her the next time I see her," I proceed towards the elevator without looking back.

"We're not done here," Jerome snarls.

"Yea, I believe we are."

I make a mad dash to the elevator and jump in as it opens. I don't want to be caught waiting for the next one. I hit the close button right away to avoid Jerome boarding. I've had enough of him for one night. I'm in the elevator longer than I would've liked because it stops on every other floor. You have no idea how annoying it is to stop on all these floors, and nobody boards the elevator.

I finally make it to our floor. I make sure my composure is in place as I approach her door. I knock on the door with an urgent motion, hoping to interrupt anything going on in there. It probably sounds like the police is knocking at her door. I don't care about messing up anything for this guy if he's making a move. In fact, I hope I'm messing up his night. I don't want to appear like a lunatic, though. I want answers about us, and I'm not leaving until I get them.

CHAPTER 31
Lauryn

I wonder who's knocking on my door with such urgency. I consider not answering it for a minute. The knocking continues, and I decide it's best to answer. They don't seem to be leaving. I temporarily forget I'm wearing sexy nightwear without a robe and a glass of wine. I drink down the wine unsure how long this unwanted guest will take because I need my wine. My mind is crazy since I saw Keith with someone else. It has to be someone in the building. At least, I hope it is since I haven't received any notifications from downstairs that someone is here for me. I last saw Keith at the restaurant with a woman, so I figured it wouldn't be him. I guess it could be one of my neighbors, but I'm unsure of what the emergency could be.

Banging on my door like they're the police. I don't need this crap. I'm a black woman living in this nice building. I sling the door open, and I'm surprised Keith's standing there. I didn't get a chance to ask him what he's doing here. He doesn't hesitate to grab me into his arms. He starts kissing me passionately. I'm more confused now than ever. Even with my confusion, I don't want him to stop kissing me. Eventually, we stop kissing, and we cling to each other. He follows me in the house and shuts the door behind him. He slowly gazes at my body from head to toe like he's exploring me for the very first time.

"Are you alone?" he demands.

"Yes. Why?" I shout back. The nerve of him coming to my place like he owns it.

"Interesting little number you're wearing."

"I'll wear what I like. It's my house, and I'm alone."

"You're sure you're alone?" he peers at me like I'm hiding something.

"Don't you dare accuse me of anything. Who are you?"

"Look, I'm sorry. I'm tripping. I need to clear the air with you. Who's the guy?"

"Who's the girl?"

"Ok, I shouldn't have come here with my guns all blazing. You drove me crazy with him. Especially, after he kissed you. I lost all perspective."

"You're here because you're jealous?"

"I guess I am."

"What do you want from me? You're FOS with the text message you sent. Did the other night mean anything to you?"

"It meant everything to me. I —"

"What do you want from me?"

"Who's the guy?"

"Isaac, my ex-boyfriend from college."

"What is he to you now?"

"Nothing. He wants to get back together. It's way too late for us to be a couple again."

"Why did he assume he could kiss you?"

"I have no clue. I guess I gave him the wrong signal. You flustered me by being with someone else. Who is she by the way?"

"Her name is Sabrina."

"What is she to you?"

"Honestly?"

"Yes, you're asking me all these questions. You need to be able to spit your truth, too."

"Sabrina and I are only casual friends. You could call it a situa-tion-ship."

"Situation-ship?"

"A casual friendship."

"Do you mean your friend with benefits?"

"Kind of. Generally, it's classified differently. Friends with benefits is just about smashing. In our situation-ship, I truly respected Sabrina. She met my friends, but we weren't in a relationship. We both chose to end things."

"So, you were on a break-up date?"

"I guess. Yea, it could've been a break-up date. We agreed things between us were done. We're both dating other people now, and I want you."

I gawk at him shocked. This had been unexpected. He wants more than a sexual relationship with me. I didn't prepare for this scenario. I'm scared and excited about the prospects of us being together. Well, let me be honest. I'm more than a slightly excited. I'm still uncertain why he sent me an unbothered ass text. He hasn't acted like someone who wants to be with me since we did the dirty, and I have to have answers.

"You want me. You haven't contacted me since we were together. Not really. Your text message basically stated, 'thanks for the ride lady.'"

"I'm extremely sorry. I didn't mean to come off as ambiguous. I've been extremely busy at work. I didn't have time to breathe since we were together. I also didn't want anything hanging over our heads. I wanted a clean slate coming into a relationship with you. I didn't want any of my loose ends left dangling to interfere with us. Why did you have to be so damn sexy for him tonight? He kissed you…Did the other night mean something to you?"

"The other night meant everything to me. I'm afraid of how much it means to me."

"I'm afraid of how much it means to me, too."

"Why?"

"I haven't wanted anyone like I want you in a long time."

"How do you feel about me?"

"I like you a lot more than cake, and I love cake. Let me show you how much."

He pulls me to him and kisses me with vigor. I'm incapable of containing myself either. I wrap my arms around his back and deepen the kiss. He reaches beneath my negligee to graze in between my legs, and I don't stop him. I want and need this so much. I didn't realize how much I craved this until this exact moment. It's like a drug, and I don't mind the addiction. What is the aphrodisiac that's driving me crazy? Is it his pheromones?

"No underwear?"

"Why do I need underwear?"

"Hmm, I like it. I like it a lot."

I start kissing him on his neck, and I reach under his shirt to pull it off. He pulls the straps of my negligee down and begins sucking on my bare breast. I moan I want this so much. He stops to ensure I want this.

"Bedroom?" he asks.

"Upstairs," I command.

He picks me up and kisses me at the same time. I wrap my legs around his waist as he carries me into my bedroom. Tonight is more impressive since he carries me up the stairs. He places me gently on the bed.

He removes my negligee to reveal my unapologetic and unashamed naked body. He touches me, and he savors just how wet I am. I rise into a seated position to undress him. He doesn't let me do this task alone. He scrambles out of his clothes much faster than I'm able to fumble through undoing his buttons on his shirt. All in all, we achieve the goal of getting naked in record time.

He gently pushes me backwards and opens my legs. His tongue gently kisses me on my neck. He reaches my breasts and tantalizes my nipples with his delectable tongue. He roams over my entire body, and I repay the favor in full. I'm shivering with anticipation. I want him now. I'm certain he senses the desperation in my eyes. He reaches for a condom in his pants pocket and slips it on like a man in charge. He enters me without a second consideration. He begins in missionary only because we're semi-permanently lip locked. I have no doubts we'll be moving on from this basic position in due time. He wants me on top to ride him, so I can absorb his entire girth. Keith is a talker during sex, and I'm here for it. He's pretty demanding, and it's hot as hell. There's something about his tone that makes me want to surrender repeatedly. He brings out the temptress as well as the miniature-sized freak in me.

"Do you like this baby?"

"Yes, Keith. I like it!"

"You're mine. Tell me you're mine!"

"I'm yours, baby!"

"That's right. Say my name. Tell me what you want."

"Keith, baby. I want this. Please make me come."

"You'll come, baby. Who makes you feel like I do?"

"Nobody, baby. You're the best I've ever had."

"Damn right. Tell me again. Who's the best?"

"You, baby!!"

I'm unsure if it's the commanding words or the way he strokes every bit of me that's driving me insane. Then, it happens. The orgasm I'm experiencing right now is everything. There are stars shining brightly through my eyes. Like, literal stars. I'm not imagining it. I'm kind of dizzy from the exact precision of his motions. I climax on top, and he turns me over quickly for loving in doggy style. He doesn't miss a beat. Impressive. He loses his mind and all sense of dignity as he shakes out of control from this position. He's holding me tight and kissing me on the back once the shaking has subsided. We stop for a much-needed break.

This man has made me extra horny these last few days. I have no doubt I'll request another round of this. The sex is greater than me watching Serena winning her first Grand Slam, and I love Serena. She's the GOAT of tennis.

"So, just so we're clear, I'm staying tonight."

"Ok, I'm glad. I want you to stay," I speak slowly.

"Hmm, you're getting better."

"Is that right?"

"We're doing this, so I don't want you to push me away. We're done with that."

"You're bossy."

"Nope, I'm just assured about what I want, and I go after it."

"What do you want?"

"You."

"Well, what if I said no, you can't have me. What would you do then?" I smirk.

"I'll make you surrender."

He tickles me so hard I laugh uncontrollably, and I almost pee on myself. The laughter fades, and I relieve myself plus clean off the sex residue. He walks in to do the same. I have an extra toothbrush, so I give it to him to use. We head back to bed where we lay naked in each other's arms for some time. We're both grinning as we fall asleep holding each other.

I wake up amazed on Sunday morning that I didn't dream everything from Saturday night. The sun is shining brightly through the curtains, and I nearly fall out of the bed from jumping up so fast. I'm unsure of the time, but I planned to go to church and Sunday school. **(I know what you're thinking. YES, I go to church. And you're probably thinking after what I did last night, I need prayer. Well, I would need it even if I didn't do everything I did with that fine specimen of a man.)** He wakes and smiles at me.

"Good morning!" I cheerfully say to him in a mild tone since I'm unsure if he's a morning person.

"And a good morning it is. How'd you sleep?" he responds with a smile.

"Never better."

"I concur."

(I want to invite him to church, but it may be too soon in our relationship. Well, if it's too soon to ask him to go to church, I shouldn't have had sex with him.)

"What's wrong, sweetheart?"

"Nothing really. I usually go to church and Sunday school. I plan to go. Would you be interested in coming with me?"

"I would love to go with you on one condition."

"What's that?"

"You go to church with me next Sunday."

"Deal."

We get up and shower together. **(I know. Don't judge me. When it's good, it's good!)** Keith didn't have any clothes here, so he had to truck it back home to get dressed. He's dressed in a perfectly tailored pinstripe navy suit, with a light blue collared shirt, burgundy and navy geometric-shaped tie, and exquisitely shined Cole Haan pair of shoes. He's so fine, and I'm nearly tempted to take him back to bed.

(I said nearly, peanut gallery. I know I need to hear the word to keep me grounded and out of the gutter.) I'm wearing a dress with a boatneck and a flared skirt in pale blue, a burgundy wide belt, and burgundy wedges. I didn't plan for my outfit to compliment Keith's as well as it does.

"You're beautiful," he breathes out when I answer the door.

"Thank you, and so are you. Handsome that is."

The service at my church generally lasts one hour, and there's another hour for Sunday school. I would normally attend the eight o'clock service, and today is no different. Keith comments he loved the service and Sunday school class today. I'm proud knowing this is another thing Keith and I have in common. I'm looking forward to going to his church next Sunday. After church, we head to one of the brunch spots I frequent.

We spend Sunday together. After brunch, we hang out and play various strategic games with one another. We end up having a great time challenging each other. We're both super competitive and sometimes that's not a great advantage in a relationship. I can't believe I have a boyfriend again. I don't want to overthink anything anymore. My anxiety is at its highest when I'm not with him or pushing him away. Before I know it, Sunday night is here again. Keith and I don't want to part from one another. We spend the night together, and it feels so natural waking up in his arms. It's Monday morning, and I stretch out while yawning. Waking in

Keith's arms is more than I expect it to be. He moves slightly and holds me in an embrace.

"Morning," I cheerfully mouth at him.

"Good morning, I'm so happy to wake to your beautiful face."

"Aww. Thank you. Ditto. I'm glad you're here."

"Just so you know, this does mean something. You and me. We mean something. I haven't stayed the night with anyone in a long time."

"I figured it out. So, when you asked me to stay the other night, did you break your own rules?"

"There aren't any rules. It's just not something I wanted at the time. Now, I want it with you," he pauses, "There's something else. We need to talk about a few things."

"Yea, what's that?"

"A few weeks ago, I saw you dressed like you were going on a date. You asked me if I'd been mad at you. I didn't tell you the truth. Not about being mad at you. I didn't like the fact you were going out with someone."

"Thanks for your honesty. I hated you were with someone other than me the other night."

"I hated you being with your ex, too. When he kissed you, I nearly broke my drinking glass. I couldn't stand it. Well, you know this. I came over here like a mad man."

"Well, you don't have to worry about it. Isaac and I have been done for seven years. He destroyed any reunion the moment we broke up. He told me he didn't want to settle with me. He's been married, and he has a kid. So, nothing to worry about there."

"Wow, he told you he would be settling with you?"

"Yea, it happened back in college, and it hurt a lot at the time. I'm over it."

I check the time to gage how long we have to talk. Even though it's a workday, I love being here with Keith. I have a few things to handle at Food Will today.

"As much as I love being in your arms, we both need to get up now. I'll make us breakfast. Go get showered and dressed."

"I'd love breakfast. I think I can get used to this."

I take care of my personal grooming prior to making us a breakfast of champions. We enjoy some spinach, tomato, and cheese omelets, pancakes, and coffee. He finishes eating ahead of me, and it's certainly getting late. He jumps to leave, and he kisses me deeply.

"Thanks for this weekend," Keith remarks.

"You're welcome."

"I'll text you later today without being confusing."

"Ok, sounds good. Bye, babe."

"Goodbye, sweetheart. Have a great day!!"

He kisses me again as I follow him to the door. He leaves, and I stand in my kitchen blushing. It's hard to believe I'm moving on with Keith. I'm not quite dressed for work yet when there's a knock at the door. I wonder who this could be. I open the door to find Keith standing there. I find myself with a cheesy grin on my face. I'm ecstatic he's back.

"What brings you back this morning?" I cheerfully remark, "I thought you had to get to the office."

"I do, but I want this more," he zooms in on my lips as he pulls me in for a kiss. "I just needed this before I go to work. You have plans tonight?"

"I guess I do now. Have a great day!"

"Thanks, you have one, too. Do you want to go out to dinner?"

"I would rather Netflix and chill," I wink.

"I'm definitely down for it, sweetheart. Don't work too hard today."

"No, you don't work too hard. Aren't you the one whose super busy these days?"

"Yea, there's quite a bit going on there. It's nothing I can't handle. Let me go. I have an early meeting with one of the partners, and I don't want to be late."

He grabs and kisses me one more time, and he turns to leave. I'm not shy about staring at his perfectly chiseled ass as he goes in the opposite direction.

"Why do I sense you're staring at my ass, sweetheart?"

"Yep! I am! You have a great ass, sir."

He turns and laughs, "I'm glad you approve. By the way, I love you without underwear," he winks.

I dress for work and leave with a pep in my step. In the elevator, I run into one of my neighbors, Jerome. He's been trying to get at me for a long time, even pre-Jackson. Jerome had cooled off a lot when Jackson and I were living together. He must have found out we were no longer together. He's been circling around me like a lion searching for its prey. I've never been interested in him. My lack of interest hasn't stopped him from trying to change my mind.

"Hey, Lauryn. It's been too long. Jackson still yo' trade?"

"Hello, Jerome. Huh?"

"Is he yo' trade? Yo', dude?"

"No. Jackson and I aren't together anymore."

"Really?" he gleams excitedly, "Sorry. How about we go out for a drink sometime?"

How could this dude ask me on a date two seconds following his claim to be sorry about the end of my relationship? He is FOS. I swear. "I'm sorry. I'm not interested. I'm dating someone."

"I'm not asking for a date. I only hoped two friends could get drinks and talk, shawty."

The elevator opens to the garage. "I have to get to work. Have a great day, Jerome."

I shouldn't have to keep dodging him. Unfortunately, the alternative isn't promising. He's extremely persistent in his effort to break my defenses down. I simply don't feel him. I'm actually not physically attracted to him. He always appears to be overly nice. It's something about him. I can't put my finger on it. He's mad creepy. A door opens near the stairs, and a pissed-off woman comes out and starts yelling.

"Jerome! Where in the hell have you been? It doesn't take this long to get us coffee."

"Why you tripping, girl? Ain't been gone long."

"Long enough for me to miss you."

"Jerome," I interrupt, "you have your hands full. I'm going to go. Have a good one."

"Who in the hell is she, Jerome? Are you cheatin' on me and our son?"

"Wait a minute. Stop," Jerome looks guilty, "we ain't together, Aliyah."

"Like hell, we're not. Last night you made it clear that Aiden and I were your priority. Did you lie for some pussy last night? What's the truth?"

"Aliyah, baby," he squirms, "you and Aiden are my priority. I'm not ready to get married."

"I never mentioned anything about wanting to marry your squirmy ass, did I? You need so much more paper for me to consider marrying you."

As entertaining as this is, I have to bounce if I'm going to make it to work on time. I scan my wrist to gage the time. I'm surprised to learn I'm 15 minutes ahead of schedule. Do I continue to watch this train wreck? Do I want to go to work early? I could stop by Bucky to get some coffee if I leave now. Who am I kidding? I'm stopping by Bucky anyway. This trainwreck is pulling me in while making it impossible for me to turn away.

"Aliyah don't start it with me. This is the main reason why we constantly arguing. You always want money. Money. Money. Bukoo Money. Always money. I swear you're using me for money."

"I've never used you for money. It's your job to care of your family, and it's my job to take care of your needs. I'm damn good at my job. Why you frontin' like you're from New Orleans. You're from Boston, fool!"

"You don't know me like that. Damn, girl. If I didn't know better, I would assume you're pregnant again. You're acting mean as shit like you were with Aiden. Are you pregnant, babe?"

"Don't you fucking jinx me, Jerome! I'm late for my damn period. You saying I'm pregnant, will make me pregnant."

"I'm not jinxing you. Is the baby mine?"

(Wait a minute! She's pregnant because he jinxed her. I'm seriously not making this shit up. Typical man. Is it mine? Really now. Why did he have to go there? I'm finding it hard to hold a straight face without saying in my Maury Povich voice, "Jerome, you are the father?")

"How dare you ask me if it's yours?! Who else is in the equation, asshole? 1. I'm not sure I'm pregnant and 2. Fuck you 3. Of course it's yours, punk 4. Unlike you don't fuck around and 5. Sex is off the table forever. Aiden and I are leaving, Blake!"

"Why you gone use my government name?"

She ignores him and turns to leave. He runs behind her.

"Baby, I'm not cheating. It's my baby. Don't leave," he pleads, "I love you, boo. Come on!"

"Love isn't happenstance, fuckboy!" she yells at him before turning away.

Jerome grabs Aliyah by her arm and tugs her into his chest. He nestles his mouth against her neck and begins to systematically open-mouth kiss her neck until he could claim her lips. They begin what I consider to be sex with their clothes on right in the parking garage of our building. She struggles and abruptly pulls away. She turns to walk away, but stops.

"Stop, Jerome! I'm not doing this with you again."

"This is our thing, baby. We fight. We make-up. We fight. We make-up. I'm tired of fighting today. So, let's get to the making up part."

"No! Dammit! You've used me one to many times."

"Used you? When in the hell have I used you? I swear you're pregnant, woman."

"We have this same argument everyday, and I'm tired."

"I'm tired, too. Come here, baby."

"No," she pouts.

"Yes, come here. You know you want to come to me."

She shrugs and moves over to him slowly. He pulls her into a deep kiss. I feel borderline creepy staring at them. Well, only a little. She fights hard not to give in at first, but she relents after a few minutes. He must have touched her at just the right spot. She melts into him and allows him to continue groping her as she gropes him. They're both so caught up in each other to recognize more people are in the garage staring at them for their morning entertainment.

"Get a room, dammit, Jerome," an older gentleman croaks, "Some of us don't want to see young and hot bodied people go at it like a porno in the making."

"Darling, what are they doing?" an older gentile woman asks who I assume is her husband.

"They're fucking, darling," her husband responds, "You remember, something we used to do before you became all society and refused to utter the word 'fuck.'"

"Dick, do you have to be so crude?"

"Frannie, they're making love in the parking garage. Does this sound better to your virgin ears?"

"I don't know why I stay married to you, Dick. You're such a dick."

"Wow! Punch me in the gut. You called me a dick when my name is Dick. You need to learn how to insult much better, dear."

"I'm done looking at this freakshow. Dick, I'm going home. You better be right behind me if you know what's good for you."

"I better, Frannie. How's this tone work with your society folk? I don't recall any of your 'uppity friends' speaking in such a tone. Frannie, you should be ashamed of yourself. Acting one way in public and a whole different way at home. Go on, Frannie. This is the best entertainment I've had all year. I'd be damned if I walk away from it."

Another couple murmured to themselves, "How dare they? Isn't he on the HOA board?"

"Hmm, is it him? Didn't the HOA guy have blonde hair?"

"His hair could be dyed, or it could've been dyed then. This could be his natural-colored hair," a woman passing by informed them.

"I guess you're right, dear. Thanks."

"No problem. What's the problem here?" the same woman asks.

"Don't you realize this is public indecency?"

"Is it, though?" the woman cynically returned, "They're completely clothed and will probably do what comes naturally for all sexual beings in a less public setting."

"You millennials have no regard for decency."

Jerome and Aliyah broke away from their hypnotic state. The heat is still shining in their eyes deeply. They seem slightly embarrassed as they leave to finish what they started in a private place. The crowd disbands with the older folks grumbling, and the younger ones unfazed.

CHAPTER 32
Stranger

He watched Lauryn in awe as she conquered her volunteer mode. He loved this about her. It showed how much she cared about people. He stared at her as she embraced a woman who feared for her life. She spoke in a hushed voice like she didn't want others to hear. Her husband threatened to kill her and the children if he found them. The woman shivered. She'd been frightened to the bone. Her hopeless demeanor couldn't be ignored. Her gaze didn't make him doubt she believed her death would be eminent. She only wanted to save her kids. This broke his heart to witness. He knew a little bit about abuse and people often went too far. He wanted to help. He couldn't figure out how without revealing himself too soon. He would find a way. This woman and her kids deserved better. Nothing could justify domestic abuse in his point of view.

Lauryn only listened to the woman. She patted her arm in a consoling manner, so the woman and her son knew their importance. Their story mattered. She didn't pass judgement or try to tell the woman how to react. As the woman finished pouring her heart out, Lauryn hugged her tightly. He could tell Lauryn wanted the woman to feel supported. She wanted to give her some sense of stability. Witnessing this side of her only made him love her more. She'd been so compassionate to a complete stranger without caring who noticed her generosity. Her genuine empathy made her even more beautiful. She did the right thing. It didn't matter who observed it. He considered volunteering at the Domestic Violence Safe Haven, too.

He would be close to her even more this way. He loved she gave back to the community. He'd always given back to various organizations, but his passion involved helping the disenfranchised. The least of those who were economically disadvantaged and racially despaired were the people he desired to help the most. He knew all too well what living with the bare necessities did to a family, and he would do everything in his power to help others not to have those types of experiences. If he could dismantle homelessness and inequities, he would be over the moon. Humanity will be as it should be if equity is truly achieved. People's outcome would not be predicted by their race, gender, or economic stations in life.

He didn't like she'd been getting close to anyone. He assumed Alex, the trainer, could be a nuisance and a problem. He wanted to slash Alex's tires as he witnessed him kissing her. Things fizzled out with them, so he didn't have to worry. He noticed their body language didn't quite mesh.

They weren't on the same page or in sync. He figured the probability of those two being romantically involved couldn't be high. Whatever chemistry existed between them died on the vine. She began hanging out with her neighbor, Keith, a lot more. This upset him. Keith didn't deserve her.

He had to show her how much he loved her now. He had to claim what belonged to him. Keith could become too much of a problem since he distracted her with his handsome face. He had to figure out how to get Keith out of his way. He won't stand a chance if she fell for the ex-football player who could probably fit in any football team's starting lineup. He knew guys like Keith. The kind of guy who would only break Lauryn's heart. She won't deal with any more duplicitous men if he had anything to say about it. He didn't think she could take anymore after Jackson. She'd crumble if she were hurt that badly again. He couldn't allow this to happen.

He'd been considered a pretty decent looking guy by most. His physique didn't compare with Keith's. His stature resembled one of a runner. Not grotesque and thin but also not hugely muscular. He'd been fully aware his physical appearance didn't compare to those she'd dated. He didn't think Lauryn would be so shallow and allow something so minor to come between them. He had to get her attention someway in order to capture her heart. He'd been an introvert and quite shy most of his life. He relied on the long game. He would prove he'd always been the man she needed and deserved. He had to make things happen. Time stood still for no one.

With so many guys interested in making her theirs, he didn't have the luxury of sitting around waiting for the right moment. He had to figure out how to make the best impression on her and get it done soon. She's a hot commodity, and this didn't surprise him. He only hoped he'd have time to approach her correctly. He would make her love him once she viewed his heart and understood his complete devotion to her happiness. He would do anything for her.

Being deeply immersed in his own thoughts, he'd been unsure how he made it home. The day dragged on and on. He wanted to take a moment and chill without any worries. He sunk into the couch to relax. He barely noticed when someone entered the room. He wanted an hour to himself. **(Why couldn't he just have one damn hour without her bugging him? Was this too much to ask? If he wanted to be alone, she would bug him. That's her MO.)**

Without turning around, he knew it had to be Melanie. Anyone else would've given him space. She approached him. He didn't acknowledge her presence. He closed his eyes and pretended to be asleep. He hated her living with him. He wished he hadn't promised his mom he would care for her. Sometimes he wondered if this is what his mom meant. Melanie took everything literally, and she wouldn't let him forget his promise to his mother. He grew disgusted by Melanie and her lewd behavior. It took all his willpower not to kick her on the street where she belonged.

"Hey, lover. Are you still daydreaming about 'your woman?'" she asked air quoting the words "your woman" as she rolled her neck.

"How many times must I tell you not to call me 'lover?' What's on my mind is none of your business."

"Touchy! Well, have you checked out her new guy? I love you, lover. I do. I'm gonna be honest with you. If I ever have a chance to ride him, I'll take it."

"Why don't you occupy his time instead of always bothering me? If you love me so much, you'll distract him with all you got going on," he motioned by waving his hands to demonstrate the curves on her body. "Prove this so-called love for me."

"Baby, there's only one certainty in your life, and it's I love you. Loving you won't change if I'm not able to distract him. He's particularly enamored with her. Maybe even more than you are. Why do y'all have this broad on a pedestal? She's cute, I guess. Does she even have a personality?"

"She's more than cute. She's gorgeous and extremely enchanting. You're jealous of her."

"I'm leaving now. I wouldn't want either of us to do anything we'll regret. You'll be back. It won't work out. This I'm certain. No woman will ever replace me."

"It's impossible for any woman to replace something that never existed, Melanie."

"You'll regret being so mean and nasty to me. You'll never be happy with her. Do you hear me?!" she hisses.

"I'm not deaf. Of course, I hear you. Will I be happy with her? Absolutely. Is there a possibility it won't happen? Sure, there is. Will I ever be with you? Hell no, I won't!"

"You make me sick!"

"Good. Are you moving out?"

"Good try. I'm not moving out. Remember what your mom said."

"As if you would ever let me forget. Why do you constantly belabor the fact you'll always be here? As if I need to hear it repeatedly."

"I will. I don't understand why you fight me. You're aware I'm not going anywhere. Why are you constantly irritating me? How will Lauryn react to me living here and what about our past?"

"She won't ever experience your kind of crazy. You're sick, and I won't allow you to hurt her. You don't matter. She has her own place. I wouldn't bring her around you."

"Damn you! I'm leaving," she storms out of the room.

He blew out a sigh of relief as she left. He'd had enough of her today. She repeatedly busts into his places of sanctuary, or she appeared at places without an invitation. Luckily, she left without too much of a hassle, and he could resume relaxing as his mind lingered on the beautiful Lauryn. He knew his hand would drift to his happy place as he envisioned her naked. He had to figure out a way to show her why he's the man to make her happy. He'd never let Melanie's prophesy determine his destiny.

He tried to make sure he would casually be at the same places as Lauryn during the week. He obtained access to her calendar and used it to sync with his. He had to be where she would be if he wanted to win her heart. Planning for her schedule veered near impossible since her schedule changed on a dime. "It beat guessing where she would be," he mused. Having her by herself without a trace made him anxious. He needed her. She brightened his day. There are many days where she only had to be herself. He missed her the last few days. He hadn't gotten her schedule right. Today, she appeared out of nowhere. She spoke and he listened. He stuck to every word she vocalized as if he were a magnet.

He followed her making sure he never got too close. He wanted to avoid any suspicions she might have. He walked into a restaurant on the tail of Lauryn. He suspected she would meet someone. He didn't care who she planned to meet as long as it wasn't a guy. He only wanted to be in her world close enough to touch her. She happened to be meeting her girlfriend, Kennedy or Katrina. He couldn't be sure. He witnessed chill bumps on her skin as he breathed in her essence. He wanted to hold her in his arms.

He could smell her light-scented cologne, and the fragrance swirled around near his nose. He longed to smell her neck and subsequently kiss those luscious lips. He fantasized about her, and he almost got caught. He'd gotten too close to her. He couldn't help himself. She stood a fingertip away. This may have been too close. It seemed like she sensed him near. She turned around suddenly to search for something or someone. Luckily, the restaurant neared capacity, and he'd been able to blend into the surroundings. She didn't have a chance to detect his presence. She shook her head slightly and brushed off any odd notions of being followed.

On another occasion, she'd been within his reach. He couldn't do anything about it if he wanted to preserve his anonymity. She strolled from her car to volunteer at the domestic center. She brushed his arm as she passed him. She murmured, "I'm sorry," he turned the other way to avoid her recognizing him. He returned, "no worries," in a muffled voice to avoid any voice recognition.

Later, he witnessed her being a boss at her workplace giving directions to her team. She stood strong and confident in her element. He blended into the background performing his volunteer tasks he'd been given at the beginning of his shift. She hadn't been around on most of his other volunteer days. He'd been pretty bummed he missed her. One day his luck changed for the better. Her sweet melodic voice rang in his ears just as her angelic face appeared facing him.

"We actually must have a handle of our inventory in order to make any improvements to the system. It's important for us to determine what the current state is, what the WIP is, and find any gaps in the process," she spoke.

He didn't comprehend a word out of her mouth. He figured it inspired her team by their reaction. He loved how confidence exuded from every limb of her body, and she made him believe in every word she uttered. He found her to be extremely sexy. He couldn't stop staring at her as he pretended to work. Jim, a very hard ass, would tear him a new one if he circled in his direction. No one bothered, so he took the opportunity to gaze at Lauryn without any pretense. He focused on her delectable mouth prior to venturing downward over her body.

To catch her at work more, he changed the times he volunteered. He wanted to put his best effort to win her heart. He could sense the connection between the two of them growing stronger every day. Its strength lies in his ability to frame their future and ensure their connection nourished even though they hadn't spoken one word to each other. This happened to be just another day of volunteering which made these days extremely special for him.

He went to his normal spot where there were no obstructions. She generally conducted her business, like team pow wows, in the same place every day. He found a way to successfully follow her around without her knowledge. She'd been crying one day, and he wanted to comfort her so much. He didn't have a clue how he would help with her pain. It physically pained him to observe her like this. Her state of vulnerability beckoned him.

She needed him. He was certain, if he offered her his shoulder to lean on, she'd lay her head there. She'd literally examined him for the first time and allowed him to care for her. Did he imagine her staring at him? Could she be inviting him to comfort her. Her change of heart had been inevitable to him. She wanted him even if she didn't realize it yet. He knew it, and that's the only thing that mattered. He couldn't rush her. He had to be patient. Lauryn would be his one day.

"Hi," Lauryn whispers, "I couldn't help but notice you watching me. Am I intriguing to you?"

"Yes, you are. I haven't ever met anyone quite like you."

"Is that right?"

"Well, why would I lie about this?"

"What makes me so fascinating? If you utter anything about my body, I'll slap you."

"I wouldn't dare start with your body. Your ideas suggest your capability to process incredibly complicated issues. I listened to you earlier as you spoke to your team. I didn't understand a word of it. What struck me is how you drew me in with how knowledgeable you are!"

"Really? Now you're interesting."

"Why do you assume I'm interesting?"

"You listened to me talk about process improvement for half an hour. You admitted you didn't have a clue as to what it is. Who does that? Only someone who's interesting. People who love learning something new and are willing to absorb the information like a sponge."

"Yep, I'm your regular old sponge trying to soak in everything."

"Well, it's the one thing the man can't take from you. Education is an important currency, and most aren't utilizing this currency to its full potential."

"I never considered this concept at all."

"Well, now you have. No excuses moving forward. Education is currency."

"Yep, no excuses, Roy."

"Roy? Who's Roy?"

"It's a boxing thing about Roy Jones, Jr. Are you familiar with him?"

"Yea, I'm aware of who he is. I'm not a huge boxing fan, though. It's great chatting with you. I'm going to head back."

"Thanks for taking the time. I hope we'll meet like this again sometime."

"I don't see why not."

"Until next time then."

"Ok, have a good one."

He imagined his conversation would flow easily like this with her. No pretense nor frills. They'd simply have an easy conversation. He could tease her about not being a boxing fan or something else altogether. He continued to fantasize about how their relationship would grow from the simple conversation to full-fledged romance.

He didn't discover the footsteps behind him until she tapped his shoulder. He'd been busy imagining Lauryn barely dressed. He never registered when the female volunteer approached him. He figured she wanted to give him guidance or request his help for something. He'd been surprised by her brushing against him in a way that could be construed as sexual. He stared at her with raised eyebrows. For someone who hadn't met him, she's getting surprisingly familiar within his personal space. He didn't care for anyone invading his personal space unless he wanted them to do so.

"Hello, I'm Stacy. You're new here, right? Could you use some of my...special assistance?"

"Not really...kind of. I used to come here at a different time," he stated as he tried to dodge her. She continued to invade his personal space. He moved away slightly, and she came in even closer to him. He figured she didn't pay attention when he moved away or least she pretended not to notice.

"I've been volunteering for years. I love to give back to the community. This is for my peeps. Ya' feel me?"

"Mos def. I want to give back as well. I have such a sense of accomplishment when I'm done. Well, I have to get back. If I don't catch you again today. Have a good one."

"Okay. Nice to meet you."

He'd been extremely happy she left. He didn't normally like being around people. He did everything in his power to avoid her for the rest of the day.

As he left, he saw her occupied with someone, and he sneaked right past her. He casted a quick glance back to catch her scanning the room for something. He didn't stop. He sped up to make sure she didn't recognize him leaving out of the door. Lauryn happened to be leaving at the exact time, and his expression on his face changed from a grimace to an ecstatic gaze.

He stared as she strode to her car. He practically memorized her every movement from the way her hips swayed with each lifting motion of her legs to how her butt jiggled and bounced just a little with each step. Every prance brought him surges of joy. He admired how she could make simply walking incredibly sexy. She drove him crazy simply by parading around. How would he make it? He would die a happy man if he only got to observe her bouncing her ass like she were twerking on the table. He stayed in place staring at her until she drove off. He hadn't moved an inch when someone called out to him.

"Hey, there!" This voice annoyed him.

He considered ignoring her. He wanted to pretend he didn't hear what she yelled out. He constrained himself. He did everything is his power to avoid being rude. He turned towards her and shifted his lips into an unassuming fake smile.

"Stacy, hi," he answered, "Are you leaving, too?"

"Sure am, wait up."

He begrudgingly waited for her to catch up with him. He dreaded any conversations with her. He didn't want to associate with anyone. For now, he would grin and bear what came with whatever she wanted. He mumbled, "I could be at home drinking a cold one for as long it's taking her to get over here." Well scratch this idea. Melanie would ruin any good time he had in mind.

"So, hey Gary," Stacy greeted him.

He acknowledges her, but that's not his name. A group of other people around their ages come out to the parking lot giggling and whooping, "It's Friday."

"Stacy!" a guy yells. "Come with us. We're going out to happy hour."

"Edge, give me a minute!" Stacy returns his enthusiasm.

"You should go, Stacy," he encourages her. He doesn't like groups.

"Only if you come out, too. Gary, they're cool. It'll be fun," she chuckled.

"Ok, I'm only staying for an hour," he agreed. Maybe, he'd been too harsh previously.

For the first time in a long time, he went out with a group of people and things weren't awkward. They made him feel like he belonged. Stacy appeared to be an equal opportunity flirt. She spent a lot of time next to Edge. When he looked over at Edge and Stacy cozied up with one another, he felt relief.

"She does this all the time. You shouldn't let it bother you," a woman whispered to him.

"Who does what all the time?"

"Stacy! She's the biggest flirt ever. She won't back it up, though," she says with a tinge of anger.

"You're not Stacy's biggest fan, I assume?"

"You can say that. I'm her sister. My name is Stephanie. You can call me, Steph. Everyone does."

"Ok, Steph. Is it safe to assume you guys aren't close?"

"You can say that. Edge was my boyfriend. So, why would my sister be all in his face? Only because she wants to make you jealous."

"Why would she want to make me jealous? I just met her."

"She has to have all of the attention."

He had no idea how to respond to her. He didn't want to be anyone's pawn. Maybe Steph is being paranoid about her sister and her ex. Even he couldn't keep telling that lie. Stacy seemed close to dropping her panties for Edge. He couldn't figure what any of this had to do with him. Stacy wouldn't have a chance with him if she decided to sleep with Edge. Then he caught her looking over at him to ensure he'd witness her kiss Edge like her life depended on it. He stared at them kissing so indecently in public, and he frowned. He didn't know what was happening to him. He had no idea why. He didn't spend the night thinking about Lauryn, and that surprised him.

CHAPTER 33
Interloper

He had a hard time figuring out Lauryn's schedule. She hadn't been consistent, and he didn't like it one bit. His mode of operation tended to be methodic, and he thrived on order. Unbalances and changes often threw him off his game. He had to learn where she spent her time, day-in and day-out. This wouldn't normally be a challenge. He didn't particularly want to deal with any challenges. It annoyed him to make concessions for her. What made her better? Did she shit standing up or something?

He scouted for her on the job. There were moments at Food Will, the Adoption Family Center, and the Domestic Violence Safe Haven where her face appeared to display haunted images. He didn't like that he had to roam around these three different locations to figure out where she would be, and half the time his attempts failed him.

She should volunteer at a consistent time. She tended to do it as the mood hit her. There'd been no rhyme or reason to her schedule. She worked either crazy early or late. He got a headache thinking about it. He couldn't grasp why she pretended to be virtuous with this whole "volunteering act." It didn't change his opinion of her. Only fools would fall for her act.

It irritated him to follow Lauryn to learn about her life. Hopefully, he'll be rid of her soon. He felt like her life lacked meaning. She wandered about with a different man every day. What in the hell was she doing? Was she some kind of hoe? She pissed him off. He didn't like bullshit. He believed in controlling every aspect of things, and he demanded everything to go according to his plan.

Why couldn't she be boring and predictable like most people? Well, of course the almighty Lauryn couldn't be like most people. Proving his point, she lacked likeability. She commented once, "I'm too pretty to be bothered with bullshit." She pranced around with an air of superiority. Well, newsflash, he thought, "Her being pretty doesn't mean shit, and it doesn't pay the rent. Pretty women are a dime a dozen. She's no better than the rest of humanity."

Lauryn's choice to work at a non-profit didn't sit right with him. It happened to be the complete opposite of what she did when she chased the almighty dollar for so many years. How she could "so-called" work at the consultant firm for a couple hundred grand and turn around to work for a non-profit for peanuts? It confused him.

She'd grown up well-off. People like her don't become humble over-night. They don't stop caring about making money. He recognized the type of car she drove, and the type of clothes she wore. They weren't cheap. Poor people don't drive Jaguars.

He considered himself to be a simple man with simple desires. He didn't worry about petty things. He noticed her dressing casually at work or to volunteer. He'd been surprised she even owned clothes considered to be appropriate for "casual Friday." He should've known this, and that annoyed him. He needed all the intel he could get if he were to pull off a kill shot and destroy her. He pulled up his listening device to hear the details of the conversation. He bugged her office to gain intel.

A poorly battered woman with four kids wandered into the center. The older child, a boy, appeared to be no older than 12, and the other three children ranged from two to seven. The woman hobbled to Lauryn, and she barely spoke any English. Her oldest child translated the woman's need for protection. The child's words were bone chilling and horrific. He'd witnessed more than most in his profound young life.

"What's your name?" she asked the child.

"Enrique, and my mami is Marcella."

"Does your mom speak English?"

"No, ma'am. She made sure I did."

"Nice to meet you, Enrique and Marcella.

Enrique responds, "You, too, ma'am." Marcella nods.

"Have a seat. I want to ask you all a few questions. It may be hard for you to answer since you're so young. Why do you want to become an American citizen?"

"Mami has been threatened and beaten to within an inch of her life. The man's anger towards her became my horror. He raped and beat her. He only hit me a few times. We figured he would eventually hurt the others," Enrique spoke softly.

"Well, all except my little brother, Hector. You see, Hector is his bio-logical son. Mariana, Selena, and me all have the same papi, but he died before Selena was born. We had to get out of there before he hurt or killed us."

"Who did this to you?"

"I'm not allowed to tell you. We'll get killed."

"Don't worry. We'll protect you."

"Not possible. No one can. He has power. Please help Mami, ma'am."

A tear rolled down his cheek. His palms were sweaty, and he clinched his fist. His anger rose. Not again! This shouldn't happen. He turned away quickly to gain his composure. He couldn't forget why he'd been here.

Why did she volunteer with domestic victims? He didn't recognize anyone who could publish an article about her being philanthropic. What did she get out of "helping" victims? He didn't buy it. Her having the gall to volunteer struck a chord with him, and he found her behavior strange. She must be doing it for attention. He knew she didn't care about anyone other than herself. Was it for social media? These people really needed help.

How could her priviledged ass even relate to someone who has suffered this way? She never had to struggle a day in her life. She didn't have to worry about where her next meal would come from. Did this make him jealous? Hell, yea, it did. He hated her in that moment.

Images of her flashed through his mind, particularly of her wearing that nude thing at the STU event. He could still envision every curve and angle of her body. He didn't want to feel anything, but his body had been betraying him lately. His body wanted what it wanted. He could envision her as Ciara sang, "Body Party," as she gyrated her hips in the same way as Ciara did.

He'd be damned if he didn't admit she reminded him of sex on a stick. His manhood betrayed him every time he caught a glimpse of her sweet ass. He loathed her. She drove him insane. He wanted something dangerous, and something he shouldn't. He had to get her out of his mind.

Damn his libido, and damn her, too, for being too damn sexy. He never wanted to have a reaction to her. He only wanted to hate her, but his damn body had a mind of his own. His body wouldn't stop veering in the absolute wrong direction. He wouldn't allow indecent thoughts of her to ruin what he planned to do to her. She had to suffer, and he would see to it.

He could imagine her bowing down on her knees satisfying his every desire. Would it be so wrong to live out this fantasy? What would it hurt? She proved she'd been a dirty slut. She would want it. It would only be fair to give her pleasure then apply pain. These unsensible desires must cease. He had to forget the urge his body craved. Lauryn reminded him of a Belle Guinness in the making. Her evil would transcend and live on for the rest of time. She would be known as the one of the worst women to have walked this earth. She'll become infamous amongst mankind. Pondering deeply, he didn't hear the waitress address him. He raised his head to be stunned by the vision before him.

"Sweetheart, would you like something to drink?"

Her calling him "sweetheart" would normally irritate him, but it didn't this time. He let it go and beamed at her anyway. He placed his meal and drink order since he knew what he wanted. Dining alone could get lonely, and he didn't want to sit at this "table for one" for too long.

"Ok, I'll get your order started and come back to check on you soon," she stated before she shifted to leave him to fill the order.

The waitress lingered a bit and took her time leaving his table. She watched him like she wanted something else and suddenly decided against it. He turned in time to check out a couple seated across the room. He didn't need them recognizing him prematurely. He sat near a potted plant, and it hid him from their view. He had a clear view of the room.

He couldn't linger in this restaurant. He wouldn't be discovered. Not yet anyway. He would only reveal himself when he wanted to do so, and only at the right time. He turned away immediately since he didn't want to be caught here. He sighed a breath of relief for several moments after the couple left without noticing him. He had to be particularly careful moving forward.

The waitress returned to give him a bit of sugar and a lot of spice. She openly flirted with him. As he left to pay his bill, he added an extra tip for a job well done.

Maybe the little waitress could calm his nerves. They both could get what they clearly wanted and be done with it. He had nothing to lose by asking for her number. He pondered for a minute, and the perceived orgasms he'd have nearly surpassed any doubts of being discovered. She could help him to eliminate the illicit visions he'd had of Lauryn, and it would be worth it. She's not Lauryn, but she'll do. The way the waitress responded to him seemed like he would be pounding something very soon. This notion brought an instant smile to his face.

CHAPTER 34
Lauryn

After spending a long and productive day at work, it's time to go to the gym. I leave to go workout. I totally forgot I'm supposed to chat with Alex today. He wants to talk about something, and I'm fairly certain I'm aware of what he wants to discuss. From the way he's staring at the new client, they may be more than friends. It's cool with me if he doesn't want to hangout anymore. Keith's a reasonable guy, but I'm not certain he would be comfortable with our friendship since things transpired between us.

The new client is probably more Alex's type anyway. They both seem to have this easy-going zen-type energy. I beam as he admits he loves having me as a friend, and I concur. He's nervous as he admits we shouldn't hang out as much as we've been moving forward. He's interested in pursuing something deeper with the client named, "Sexy Tiger," her fighter's name. It takes a lot of confidence to pick a name like Sexy Tiger in a kickboxing gym.

He didn't want to give her any reasons to mistrust him. I tell him it's cool. I'm involved with someone, too. I wish Alex the best with her. I hope none of this jeopardizes him from being my trainer. Replacing Alex will be difficult. It'll be hard for me to find someone who'll kick my ass in shape just like I need it. He assures me our client/trainer relationship won't change. I'm cheerful watching Alex approach her, and she smiles at him like he's the man for her.

Driving home, I'm excited for a night of chillin'. **(Hmm, I got a man now)**. I need to shower and change right away. I jump in and take care of business quickly. I go to my closet and pull out some cute shorts and a nice t-shirt to wear. I elect to wear my flat gladiator sandals. I pull my hair into a ponytail and put on some lip gloss. As soon as I'm finished getting dressed, there's a light knock at the door signaling its Keith.

I reach to open the door and greet him with a kiss. He flashes a grin me and speaks, "Hello."

"Hello, you. Come in."

"We should probably do this at my place. Your media room is okay. If we're watching something cinematic, we should do it right."

"So, you gone diss me?"

"Nah, baby. Mine's just better. Come on, you'll have time to enjoy it later."

He grabs me in his arms and lifts me to face him. He kisses me deeply as I wrap my arms around his neck. This is my happy place. I didn't imagine I could be this happy again.

"Wait, I need to get my purse."

"Your purse? Why? I live down the hall."

"Keys, phone. A girl's gotta have her purse when leaving home." As I turn to grab my purse, he slaps me gently on the ass. I yelp in surprise from the impact.

"Dang, just a sec. It won't take me long."

"Better not. The clock is ticking, sweetheart."

"I'm on a clock now? I figured we were chillin.'"

"We are. Hurry!" he lifts me as I automatically put my legs around his torso.

"You absolutely don't have to carry me."

"I know. I like carrying you."

We arrive at his place, and he proceeds to order pizza on an app on his phone. He orders the same type of pizza I love to eat. I'm impressed he remembers what I like. It could be a coincidence. I like to tell myself he remembers this about me. It sounds better in our narrative.

"Did you remember I like thin sliced beef pizza?"

"Well, it wouldn't be hard to remember since it's my favorite, too."

"Ha! And here I gave you so much credit."

"Credit? What do I get?"

"You'll just have to wait for it."

The pizza will arrive in about 30 minutes. In the meantime, we joke and dance to some music playing in the background. It's nice slow dancing with him. I deeply inhale his clean scented cologne from being so close. My senses are overwhelmed as I breathe in all his good arousing aroma in slow long breaths. We stare intently into each other's eyes as his phone buzzes.

He doesn't seem compelled to leave me even though he's only going downstairs and retrieve the pizza. I don't want this moment to end either. I'm being silly. He's only going downstairs. I give him a nudge once my stomach growls. He kisses me on the cheek and leaves to get the pizza.

Until my stomach growled, I didn't realize I was even hungry. He sweeps back in with the hot piping pizza in his hands. The aroma is making my mouth water. I consider grabbing the box from him.

"What would you like to drink, sweetheart?" Keith asks as he places the pizza boxes on the counter. "I have Angry Orchard, Coke Zero, lemonade, wine, water, and maybe something stronger."

"Give me an Angry Orchard please. Thanks."

He hands me the bottle, and a plate for my pizza. I prepare my plate, and he indicates for me to join him in the great room.

"Is this it? Your media setup seems standard to me."

"Well, if this was my media room, I would agree with you, but it isn't. We'll check it out later. Let's eat and talk some."

"What should we talk about?" I ask in between bites.

"World peace, gun control…just kidding. We need to talk about you not running away from this because you're afraid."

"I'm sorry I avoided you from the moment we kissed. I have major trust issues after Jackson."

"Well, I'm not him. I haven't been in a relationship in years, but when I commit, I commit. I want to be with you. We're in a relationship now. We didn't talk much over the weekend. Other things were a priority for both of us. I think we need to have a clear understanding about us now. Do you like what's going on between us?"

"Yes, I like you a lot. Unquestionably, I like what's happening between us. I guarantee if I didn't like you, we wouldn't have done all we did over the weekend." I declare emphatically.

"Well, that's good to know," he beams. "So, we discussed us being exclusive, but everything happened fast. Have you been dating anyone else?"

"Well, not really. We probably should've had this discussion before all of our intimate moments over the past week."

"You're probably right. What does not really mean?" he asks.

"I have gone out with a few people (Isaac, Jeremy, and Alex), and they're all friends."

"And you called me a playa."

"I'm no playa, sir. It's been nice to hang out. Honestly, Jackson and I were together for nearly three years. My definition of friendship doesn't involve any intimacy. Well, in most cases."

"Most cases?"

"Alex and I had a moment, but we both decided we're better being friends."

"Hmm. Okay. So, you think the others are cool being your friend?"

"Yea, why wouldn't they be? I didn't lie. I'd been upfront and truthful." I'm seriously interested in his point of view.

"A man who wants you doesn't want to be your friend, even if those words come out of his mouth."

"Okay, what about you? You assured me we could be friends."

"Truth to point. I never planned to be your friend long term. If things hadn't evolved like it did, I would've always wanted more."

"What about you and your situation-ships? It sounds like 'it's complicated' to me. Do I have anything to worry about?"

"Not at all. I only hung out with Sabrina. That ended."

"This won't be a situation-ship," I cock my eye at him.

"You're different. First, we have in depth conversations. For the longest time, we didn't even have sex. You've been slowly creeping into my dreams and into my heart. I want you more than your body. I want everything with you."

"As much as I've tried to fight everything building between us, it's impossible. I want you this. Just be patient with me, especially if it seems like I'm holding back. It'll take me some time. I promise to try."

"I trust you will. That's why I'd been willing to be your friend. Not forever, though."

"Thanks for being patient. Every part of me is "Team Keith," and fighting my inner voice is too much of a struggle. One I'm not going to win. I don't even want to win. I'm happy with you."

"So, to be clear. We're in a relationship. You're my lady."

"Am I now?"

"Yes, you are."

"Well, I don't remember you asking me to be your lady."

"Oh, I did. Earlier I mentioned we're exclusive."

"Um, no. That's not asking."

"Please, sweetheart. I want you to be mine."

"Just giving you a hard time. I'm yours."

"You remember what happened the last time you gave me a hard time."

"Is this a threat?"

"Nope. I'll never threaten my girlfriend, but it doesn't mean I won't pay her back with tickles."

"You win. I don't want any of that."

Once we finished eating, my stomach grew noticeably bloated. I ate and drank way too much. YOLO! I'm happy to have one day where I'm not counting calories. We grab a few Angry Orchards from his fridge and head to watch a movie in his "world-renowned" media room. I actually figured, "he's being kind of extra," bragging about his great media room. I couldn't have been more wrong. In his media room, he has an 84" TV and some comfortable theater seats to view the screen. It's like being at our own private movie theater. His media room is indeed the perfect setup to view any film.

We watch the latest Captain America movie on Netflix. Since Keith is a true Marvel fan, I don't want to interrupt the movie by asking questions. I like Marvel movies, but I'm not an aficionado or anything since I didn't read the comic books. We don't talk at all during the movie. It's such a good film. I figured we'd have to debate its merits once it ends.

We discuss how the emergence of the Black Panther will be epic for Black America. We debate how the many mind games are played in the movie from Bucky to Captain America are legitimate. It's Monday night, and I want to spend the night with him, but I don't want to appear presumptuous. I don't have anything for tomorrow, so I get ready to leave.

"Are you leaving me again?" he asks sincerely.

"Nope, I need clothes for tomorrow. That is if it's okay that I stay."

"It's more than okay. I want you to stay."

"I need to go home and pack a bag?"

"Sure, let's go. It's time to chill, baby."

"We'll chill alright. You're going to have to catch me first," I laugh and break out into a run.

I'm still fast. Apparently, not fast enough. He catches me before I make it out of his living room. We're both laughing as he lifts me to carry me on his shoulders.

"Nice try, sweetheart. You got out there, though."

I chuckle, "I couldn't make this easy for you."

"I definitely love a challenge."

"I aim to please."

"Well, you definitely do your job well."

After Keith and I solidified our relationship, I called Isaac to let him know I'm with Keith. He didn't take it well, but he's not trying to cause any issues. In the end, he decided he wanted to be in my life as a friend.

It's hard to believe it's been a few months already. Keith and I have been together a lot , but I still find time to hang out with friends. Sometimes work has us tied up, but other than that, we've been connected as tight as a rope. Most nights, we're in my bed or his. We're taking everything at our pace by genuinely learning more about each other while appreciating one another, too. It alleviates us from having any pressure with our new relationship.

We haven't hung out with friends or family as a couple yet. I undoubtedly want to be sure this is going somewhere first. I don't go around introducing randos to my peeps. Only permanent fixtures get the introduction. I guess we're on the same page about this. We love frequenting the movies, dinner, lounges, spoken word, and escape rooms, just to name a few.

If we don't go out, we either chill at his or my place. Some nights we have sex, and others we'll lay in each other's arms content to be held. I'm not pressured with Keith. We genuinely enjoy each other's company. We make each other laugh. I'm starting to fall harder than I should, and it scares me.

I'm falling in love with him a little more every day. Did the word love pop in my head? Not today, not yet. It's too soon. We're not in love yet. Something tells me we aren't far from it, though. Am I ready for this? He's my perfect match. I'm excited every time we spend time together. Why can't this be love? What's this arbitrary timetable we need to follow?

At times, we're both busy and unable to get together. I miss him tremendously during those times. My heart still skips a beat admiring him as he strolls into any room. Its electrifying being near him. Keith makes it hard for me to remember life prior to him. The pain and despair I once felt no longer dominates my world.

I'm free to have the happiness I deserve. He's been my beacon through the darkness and storms. I haven't felt this comfortable and natural in such a long time. I'm falling hard for this man, and nothing will stop its impact. I hope I don't hit the pavement and shatter. I hope there is a soft pillow to catch me as I fall.

Tonight, we have plans to go to open mic at this cool, chic place downtown. Keith has no idea I spit. Well, I used to get on the mic. I want to surprise him tonight with a performance. I hope he likes it. I created a new piece I'm dedicating to him. He's made my life so much brighter these last few months. I imagined it would always be gray.

Now, my vision is filled with hues of bright colors in my orbit. I want him to share what he means to me in a different form of expression. I hope he likes this piece. I'm anticipating the moment he first spots me approaching the mic to gage his reaction. I'm wearing some distressed skinny jeans, a halter top, and 5-inch stilettos. This is the perfect date night outfit. I leave him seated claiming there's someone from work I have to speak with quickly. I only use this as a distraction to sign-in for open mic. Lady J is sitting at the table, and we go way back.

"Lola, are you coming out of retirement to grace us on the mic?"

"Yea, I wanna do something new here tonight."

"Do you want to go first?"

"Nah, it's a surprise for my boyfriend. I would like to go third."

I return to my seat and talk to Keith. The show will start soon, and I'm excited to witness these new poets. They're inspirational and thought provoking. The crowd's applause is deafening following the second poet. Lady J returns to the stage to introduce me.

"Yea, yea. It's so hype up in here. It's going to get better and better, ya hear me? I have a very special guest coming to the mic tonight. She used to spit all the time. Subsequently, life happened, and she got busy. You guys know her, and for those who don't, you're in for something lit tonight. Welcome Lola to the stage. Come on up here, girl."

"Excuse me," I whisper shyly towards Keith, "I'll be right back."

"You're going to miss the next act."

"No, I'm good."

I stroll onto the stage, and his reaction is as expected: shocked and awed. Which in turn allows me to easily transform into Lola, the poet. The nickname Asia pinned me with freshmen year works when I pull out my inner diva.

"Hello, everybody!! I hope everyone's good. I've been working on something new, and I want to dedicate this to someone deeply special to me. I hope he likes this."

"Life was a walking conundrum | Conundrum without any foreseeable solution | Solutions make sense to me | Feeling despair unsure

when this feeling would end | I had no idea life would change for the better | Meeting you wasn't planned | Meeting you wasn't expected | Meeting you changed my life forever | The fear surrounded me, and I couldn't let you know that I wanted more | A guy like you would surely hurt me | At least that's what I told myself | I had to forget about you | Forget about this strange tingling that sprouts whenever you're near me | I can't let that feeling rule me | In fact, I avoided it like the plague | The uncomfortable feelings when you're near | Why is my body betraying me? | Wanting you | Needing you | Wishing, hoping you're my ever after | The feelings that I have aren't foreign, but they weren't wanted | Every time I pushed you away | My body yearned for you | Driving me crazy with need and want | The urge was overwhelming | I need you | I want you | Fighting the urge to stop my wandering hand | With thoughts of you erupting all of my fantasies | Damn, boy, how can I stop having these elicit thoughts about you | Those hands of yours roaming over each and every one of my curves | Your lips succulent tasting | Travel from here to there to the wonderland | My body tingles with anticipation | Wanting you | Needing you | Wet dreams engulf me | Waking up in cold sweats | Thoughts of you disturbing my sleep | Be the end of my conundrum | Be my fantasy"

The room explodes with applause and snaps. I'm happy with everyone's response. Honestly, the only response I want is his. He keeps his eyes on me as he smiles the entire time. His gaze indicates he's proud of me. I exit the stage, and I rush into his open arms. He kisses me on the forehead.

"Sweetheart, you were amazing. You blew me away with the poem."

"You liked it, huh?"

"Yes, I loved it. So, is the conundrum over?"

"Hmm, you tell me."

"I believe it is. Tell me more about these wet dreams."

"Cocky! How you know I'm talking about you?"

"Because you wouldn't dedicate a poem to another guy. Not on a date with me."

"You're so sure?"

"Of course. Tell me I'm wrong."

"You're not wrong."

"So...how about we umm leave a little early?"

"You're not enjoying the open mic?"

"I am. I'd like to do what I have in mind a lot more," he winks at me.

"We'll go in 15 minutes."

"I have you on the clock."

"Aye-aye, sir."

I give him my sexiest come-hither gaze. Well, it probably didn't come off as sexy. More like goofy. Especially when I'm striving for "sexy goddess." My seduction game needs a little work. I want to get in the sheets with him. This has been fun and all. I'm so ready to blow this joint. He nods while acknowledging we're on the same page. I jump out of my seat to leave.

In my eagerness to start the next part of our evening, I invertedly brought attention my way. Some of the patrons stopped me to discuss my future open mic plans. They regaled me with praise, accolades, and how much they missed me. For a minute, only a minute, I get caught up in the adoration of the crowd. I found it hard to believe my following had been awaiting my return for three years. I stopped spitting as my schedule changed to traveling every week at STU.

"Hey, Lola," a spunky lady in her early twenties greets me. "I'm so glad you're back. You inspire me. The poem you wrote and recited, 'You Complete Me,' resonated so much with me. I initially put it in the sappy love poem bucket until you broke it down for the crowd. I love how you made me, the listener, understand that no one has the power to complete me or make me whole. It's my job to complete myself. A complete me will be open for love. Thank you so much."

"Wow, you are a fan. 'You Complete Me,' is one of my earlier works. I considered myself a novice and still trying to find my voice."

"Your voice has always been above everyone else's."

"Thank you. What's your name?" I ask her, "You don't mind me asking your name, do you?"

"Of course not. I'm Mykala."

"Mykala, it's so nice meeting you."

"Tell me you're writing again."

"The piece I did tonight is brand new and only heard by this audience."

"Wow, just wow!! I'm going to cry. I'm so excited. May I have your autograph?"

"Sure, this is a first. I've never been asked to autograph anything."

She hands me a piece of paper. I decide to write something personal to her because apparently, she's my number one fan. *"Mykala, my biggest fan, thanks for supporting me, and I'm grateful you're still a fan with all these turbulent times. I hope you're successful in whatever you choose to do." XOXO Lola*

"Here you go, Mykala."

"Thanks, Lola. Omg, I'm still shocked that I, Mykala Jenkins, met you."

"It's okay, Mykala. I'm a normal girl who writes and participates in open mic sometimes. I'm definitely not a star."

"You're a star, Lola. Well, simply a star in the making. Your time to shine will come," she gawks at me like I'll disappear if she blinks her eyes.

"Well, it's nice meeting you, Mykala." I'm trying to be polite. I'm done with this conversation. My mind is filled with images of getting naked with Keith. "I hope you're here the next time I grace the stage."

I blow out a sigh of relief once I'm able to move past my number one fan. I don't want to disappoint her, but I'm focused on completing my mission with Keith tonight. I want to sprint to him so we can get out of here. I almost make it when someone taps me on the shoulder. "Damn," I think, "are there special hexes on me that won't allow me to get out of here?" I turn shocked to see it's Isaac waiting, and he's not alone. Good for him. Moving on ain't easy.

"Lauryn, or should I call you Lola? You were so good, tonight! I'm glad to see you back on the mic. You were always so amazing."

"Thanks, Isaac. How have you been?"

"I'm great. Lauryn, this is Nat —"

"Natasha," Keith interrupts, "How are you?" I didn't realize Keith walked up to us.

"Oh my God, Keith!! It's been so long," Natasha releases Isaac's hands and hugs Keith. **(Yes, they were holding hands. I'm not sure what's going on.)**

"You two know each other?" Isaac and I ask at the same time.

"Sweetheart, I need you to hear me out," Keith admits. Why do I need to hear him out? Is she someone that I need to be worried about. We're still relatively new.

"Keith and I dated," Natasha admits.

"In college," Keith clarified.

"Oh, not a big deal," I admitted, "Isaac and I dated in college, too. Keith is my boyfriend now."

"Wow, does this seem like 'Wife Swap?'" Isaac jokes.

"Nope, none of us are married, buddy," I laugh. "It's nice to meet you, and it was good seeing you, Isaac. Thanks for your support. I hate to dash, but we have somewhere we have to be."

I turn and walk away with Keith in tow. In more like 30 minutes and not a second to spare, we discreetly leave the venue to head to paradise. On the way home, I'm confident, strong, and empowered. I want to try something different with Keith tonight. I'm unsure if he'll accept his role. He's strong-willed, and he likes to be in control. I want him vulnerable. How will he react when I'm in control? Would he allow me to set the pace? Will he like the freak in me tonight? I don't want to go too far. We haven't been dating too long. He's self-assured enough to allow me to be the boss in the bedroom tonight. Something tells me he will be turned on by me.

I don't want to push things too far. I want him in a whole different way. I want him to trust me in the good and bad times. There is so much more I need to learn about him. I turn to study his profile, and I'm still awe struck at how handsome he is. I'm close to drooling with saliva pooling out of my mouth as I admire him. Now, I'm acting like the nerdy teenager who had a crush on the quarterback. Why am I acting like this? This man is mine. Tonight, will be a night he won't forget.

CHAPTER 35
Keith

'm in awe of the poem she's reciting for me. It's sexy as hell. She's putting everything out there, and any doubts I've had about the depth of her feelings for me are melting away. She's commanding the room with her sultry voice. The sensual flow is beckoning everyone to her.

The way she sways her hips and moves the rest of her body during this performance makes me pay attention. I'm itching to get her home and do unimaginable "things" to her.

Luckily, we're on the same page, and we aren't going to make it to the end of open mic. I'm not disappointed. Despite running into a few surprises, we're able to leave expeditiously. I drive faster than I normally would. I want her bad. As soon as the door closes to her place, she changes. She shows me a different side of her. Her true alpha comes out, and she commandeers me in a way that's unexpected and welcomed. I'm generally the one in control. Some part of me wants to be handled by this woman. I want her to grab what she wants and impose her will on me. I'm not at all ashamed to admit it.

"Do you have problems with restraints?" she asks. More like demands.

"It depends on what we're doing with these restraints."

"I won't hurt you. Well, only unless you want me to. I want to be in full control of what happens tonight. Is this okay with you?"

"It's more than okay. Where do we begin?" I utter as I start to undress. When I say I need her now, I'm not exaggerating.

"No, no, no. I'm in control now. You won't undress until I allow you. Do you understand?"

I figure this role play requires some obedience on my part, so I respond, "Yes ma'am. May I ask you a question?"

"Questions are permittable. Proceed."

"May I remove my clothes?"

"No, you may not. Not yet. You may follow me to the bedroom, and I will strip completely naked. When I'm done, I want you to lay down on the bed."

"No problems here."

"Silence!"

"May I ask another question?"

She sighs like she's annoyed, "Go ahead."

"Is there a safe word you'd like to use in case things get out of hand?"

"I know what a safe word is, and you're right. What is your safe word?

"Barney."

"Like Barney from our childhood? The purple guy," she laughs.

"Yea, Barney helped me through a lot as a kid."

"You're aware we won't be doing anything kid appropriate, right? "All kidding aside you won't need a safe word. I'm not into pain."

"What a relief!"

"You started to wonder about me, didn't you?"

"I did."

"Seriously, Barney. That's a mood killer. A kid's show. Talk about a cock block."

"Oh, I guarantee nothing about tonight will be kiddie-related."

"You're not in control of what will occur remember. I don't want to punish you, but I will."

"A punishment," I squeak out trying my best to hold back my laughter. I could be in deep shit. "Maybe a punishment is exactly what I need."

"Silence! You have spoken out of turn enough. The next time you do it there will be consequences. You may or may not enjoy those consequences. I guarantee you, I will."

I want to see where this goes, so I choose to obey what my queen demands. The new side of Lauryn has me super intrigued. I follow her silently on a very slow and long ascend upstairs to her boudoir. Why is it taking an infinite amount time for us to get there? She's torturing me with each sensual step. It's like she's moving in slow motion with her hips gyrating to its own tempo rivaling the slow drum beat on the Conga. It's sexier than a woman twerking. These moves are deliberate and will drive a sane man crazy. She grasps my forearm and gestures for me to sit on her bed. I don't waste anytime following these directions.

She begins to remove everything from my body one piece at a time. It's done in slow motion. She's not rushing anything. She caresses my skin as she removes each item of clothing. It's like she's memorizing every muscle, angle, blemish, and scar gracing my body. She begins teasing me with her lips and tongue causing every part of my body to be on alert. She's getting more intimately familiar with me than anyone ever has. She pushes me back on the bed and requests that I close my eyes. It doesn't take long for me to figure out she's restraining me. I want to kiss her and touch her, but my hands are restrained by the headboard. I'm at her mercy. Only what she wants to happen will happen.

Her tongue is roaming down my body. She's maneurving every nook, crevice, and slope of my body. I'm about to cum, and I haven't even stroked anything yet. She demands that I open my eyes. The vision before me is volumptious. Her breasts are so close to my tongue but just far enough away to prevent a taste. She keeps teasing me this way. Bringing her succulent breasts close to my mouth to suck and taking them away before I get a taste. She's driving me mad. At the same time, I'm excited for what's to come. She teases me for what feels like eternity. I really want out of these restraints. Finally, she releases me from my confines.

I immediately try to jump into action. It's my turn to play. I want to make her cum like no one ever has. Make her forget her name. This night will be filled with ecstasy.

"Not so fast," she murmurs seductively.

"My queen, I only want to please you."

"Oh, you will."

She lays down spread eagle, and I don't wait for instructions. It's only nine o'clock, and I love a challenge.

"Damn right, I will!"

"Don't get so cocky. I'll be the judge of my pleasure attainment."

"It's not cocky, baby. It's confidence."

"We'll see. I expect to be pleased the rest of the night."

I won't lie. I haven't ever been pressured to satisfy a woman for a constant three hours. This is a challenge I don't plan on losing. I do everything to make her body quiver. I'd bring her to climax and stop her right as she's about to release. I did this repeatedly. Watching the agony on her face at times is worth it as she finally comes like there's no tomorrow.

At the stroke of midnight, her body is quivering uncontrollably. Her breathing is heavy, and she's smiling at me like someone whose won the lottery. I hold her in my arms and stroke her hair as she relaxes. I didn't figure sex between us could get any hotter. I admit I may have been wrong. This is more than sex, and its greater than my mind will initially comprehend. We fall asleep entwined in each other's arms content with everything that has transpired between us.

I didn't get out of line anymore, so I didn't get punished. Part of me wish I had, but (consequently) I enjoyed every moment tonight. We don't normally role play. We may have to make some exceptions moving forward. I'm secure in my manhood and proud to admit I don't mind my bossy temptress making her demands. She constantly makes me even happier. I didn't imagine it could be possible to surpass the level of happiness I sustained with her. I'm enjoying this ride. I'm glad her walls have started to crumble some, so she could allow herself to be happy with me.

It's a couple of weeks later, and I love how things are going with Lauryn. Tonight, I'm taking her to hang out with my friends. She met them during our we're "just friends" phase. Now that things have changed between us, we'll hang out with them as a couple. I haven't brought anyone around since Courtney. Both Jason and Sam knew Courtney from Vanhogen. They never did jive with her. Well, I guess that's not totally true. Jennifer has been around. It doesn't count since we weren't together, and she's friends with Erica, Sam's girl. It will be the exact opposite with Lauryn. She's a natural fit with my crew.

With Lauryn's love of sports, she'll click with the guys and the girls easily. Finally, I'm with someone who fits in all aspects of my life, professionally, personally, and socially. I meet Lauryn at her place following work, and she is as beautiful as always. She's dressed in skinny jeans, the Atlanta Falcon's t-shirt I gave her for her birthday and sandals. She's wearing my gift, and this makes me smile. Her style is simple and laid-back today. Those jeans hit all her curves in just the right places. She doesn't have on a lot of makeup which I like.

"Why are you even more beautiful today than you were yesterday?"

"Thanks," she blushes, "You don't have to lie."

"Never lies, sweetheart."

I grab her near to kiss those tantalizing lips. I thrust my tongue deeper into her mouth and savor every last bit of her flavor.

"We absolutely need to get going. You're wearing more lipstick than me now," she chuckles as she pulls some tissue out of her purse and wipes my lips.

Her touch is so tender I want to kiss her wrist. I groan and agree she's right. She reapplies her lipstick, and we head for my car. I open the car door for her as a gentleman should. She removes her shades from her purse and puts them on looking fly as hell. I still don't have any shades, so I have to use my handy visor to stop the sun from completely skewing my vision. I'm not being cheap. I just never think about buying shades until I have to pull my visor down.

We arrive at the pub at the same time as Jason and his fiancée, Jasmine. Jason proposed to Jasmine last weekend in Barbados. I'm sure it'll be the highlight of this evening's entertainment. The women will definitely want the details. Jasmine is absolutely beaming from head to toe. She's extremely excited to become Mrs. Jason Smith. Jason and I do the "man" hug greeting, and I hug Jasmine as well. I'm happy Jason is marrying Jasmine. She makes him happy, and he deserves this. He had a hateful ex, Carmen. Carmen played him like a fiddle, stole $10,000 from him, and left like a thief in the night. That's another story for another day.

"Hello, all. You remember Lauryn," I announce.

"It's good you could make it," Jason responds.

"Thanks! Congratulations! Keith told me you were recently engaged," Lauryn exclaims.

"Thanks. We're so happy," Jasmine says gleefully staring happily at Jason.

"Thanks. I'm a lucky man," Jason comments.

"Whew, it's hot as Hades out here!" Jasmine exclaims.

"Sure, babe, let's get inside," Jason suggests. We go inside where Sam and his girlfriend, Erica, are already seated.

"Sam and Erica, this is Lauryn," I introduce her to them.

"I remember you from brunch, right?" Erica asks.

"Yes, it's nice seeing you again," Lauryn returns.

Sam raises his eyebrow after checking out my gift to Lauryn. He jokingly asserts, "Hey, I hope you're into fantasy football. We need some more women to play. I can't get past this shirt, though. You were a cool chick before I realized you have poor taste in football teams."

"Why is it poor taste?" Lauryn asks. "I'm from Atlanta."

"You live here now. Get with the Titans," Sam retorts proudly.

"I like the Titans, too. It's possible to like more than one team. My sports knowledge has never failed me in my fantasy football leagues."

"Oh, so you DO play fantasy?" Sam asks intriguingly.

"Yep, I have three championships under my belt. How many you got?"

"Well —"

"Like none," I butt in before Sam answers.

"Whoa, Sam. You asked for it," Jason jokes.

"Sam always bites off more than he can chew. He talks a lot of shit with no backup," Erica adds.

"Wait, baby," Sam starts, "aren't you supposed to be on my side?" Sam pouts and appears wounded. We all get it's all in fun.

"Well, don't start nothing, won't be nothing," I note.

Jasmine changes the subject to start talking about the trip she and Jason took to Barbados. It took less than ten minutes for the conversation to shift to the engagement. I wish I bet someone on the odds the engagement would be mentioned within the first ten minutes of arrival. I would make a killing. Jasmine is a great woman, and Jason is fortunate to have her. She deserves this time to shine. I just like a great bet.

"Jason shocked me by getting down on one knee to propose to me. I had no idea it would happen on this trip. Of course, we talked about getting married in the past. I thought for sure he'd be ready in another year or so." She passes her phone to show pictures of their trip, specifically the moment Jason popped the question.

"The water is breathtaking. I imagine it's incredibly peaceful and relaxing," comments Erica.

"It's heavenly," Jasmine sighs, "I could stay there forever. We're definitely going back one day."

"Have you guys set a date yet?" asks Lauryn.

In unison, both Jason and Jasmine respond, "Not yet, but soon."

"I'm patiently awaiting the day I become this man's wife," Jasmine admits cheesing like a small kid watching the movie Frozen.

"Me, too, baby. I'm ready to be your hubby," Jason beams at her like she's the only woman on earth. "Your baby daddy and all that."

Jasmine blushes while Erica uses this opportunity to change the conversation. I have a strong inclination she doesn't want to discuss weddings anymore since it's a long way off for her and Sam. I could be wrong, but her eyes convey envy.

"Lauryn, how did you and our favorite bachelor over here meet?" Erica asks pointing at me while I glare at her.

"Well, Keith and I met a several years ago. We're neighbors," Lauryn answers.

"Oh, wow. You guys are neighbors. How long have you all been dating?" Jasmine asks.

"I guess it's been about a year," I respond.

Lauryn gives me the side-eye, and I'm clear on what she's thinking. We became official a few months ago. I've been counting the entire time we've been going out, and it's well beyond a year plus some, too.

"Really? A year? I didn't realize you were 'on lock' so long, Keith," Sam jokes.

"Wow! 'On lock,' baby? You're in a relationship, Sam, or do you want to reconsider your stance?" Erica asks.

"No, baby. I'm just kidding," Sam counters sheepishly.

"We've only been exclusive for a few months," Lauryn clarifies.

"What do you do, Lauryn?" asks Jason. I'm sure he wants to redirect this explosive conversation.

"I work for a non-profit in continuous improvement."

"Where did you go to school, Lauryn?" asks Sam.

"I graduated from NTU for undergrad, and I went to Vanhogen for my executive MBA."

"Tigers!" the guys exclaim.

Jason inquires, "I got my MBA from Vanhogen, too. When did you attend?"

"I finished two years ago. I went through the program on the weekends."

Jason says, "Sometimes, I wish I had gone the executive route. I didn't have the work experience at the time, unfortunately."

"Yea, you're expected to have some work experience in the executive program," Lauryn validates.

Sam asks, "What did you study as an undergraduate?"

"Mechanical engineering."

"Wow, smart and beautiful," Sam comments. "You hit the jackpot this time, my friend. She's definitely a keeper. Way better than —"

"Don't even do it," Jason interrupts.

I'm grateful for Jason's interruption because I know Sam is about to say Courtney, and this isn't the time for that at all. I look at him sternly. There is no point ruining our night talking about an ex that doesn't matter anymore.

"The only problem I have with you, Lauryn, is the Falcons t-shirt you're reppin,'" Sam continues.

Lauryn returns, "This again. You won't let it go."

Jason asks, "Lauryn, will you join the fantasy league? We need a few more women players."

"I would love to play. I'll warn you now. I'm confident in my skills as a GM. I may talk a lot of shit. I also win, too."

"This doesn't surprise me. I remember that from when we were shooting pool, and you weren't even winning," I joke.

"I don't like to lose, and I'm awfully competitive. Sue me," Lauryn returns.

"Funny, in the company of lawyers, you should never ask to be sued," Sam retorts. "You're perfect for Keith. A competitive woman who just may whoop his ass in fantasy football," everyone laughs.

"Now, let's talk about this draft. I want to wrap my head around the specifics like when, where, and how," Jason mentions. "It's about time someone knocks this one off his thrown," he points at me. "Haters gone hate," I comment.

I like how Lauryn is getting along with everyone, and she's basically holding her own. Not that I had any doubts she would. She's an all-around super star, and I'm blessed to be in her presence. I have a sudden urge to go to the bathroom. Yea, no surprise there. Drinking beer is a sure-fire way to having to piss. This guy nearly runs me over on the way to the bathroom.

"Sorry," he mutters.

"No worries, my brother."

My arm hurts slightly from the impact with a guy who ran into me. He hadn't been paying attention as he passed. I shrug it off since he apologized, and I'm positive it had been only an accident. The rest of the evening we talk about the fantasy football draft logistics. Sam mentions several people from the DA's office are interested in playing this year. He wants to at least one more woman to play for even distribution. The ideal number of people to play fantasy would be ten. We choose to have the draft on the Sunday before Labor Day. I'm ready to claim another victory. Who could stop me? Playing fantasy football has kept me connected with the game I love so much.

As Lauryn and I step outside, I notice one of my tires is flat. I don't need this now. It's already late, and we both have an early day tomorrow. I change the tire in no time flat. I don't want my lady out here longer than necessary.

"You deserve a reward for this fast tire change," she states.

"Hmm, collecting this reward may be worth this hassle."

Collecting had been certainly worth it, even though she didn't owe me anything. She has to be the most giving woman I've ever dated. Her selflessness is another thing I find attractive about her. I'm feeling a rush of emotions for her that I'm positive are too soon to feel. What can I do about it? Who's to say what I'm feeling for her is too soon? There's a risk with falling hard for her, but there's also an opportunity to gain a love I've never known before. I'll tread lightly, but I have a feeling I won't have to do so.

It's finally draft day, and I'm ready to get another "W" for the year. Lauryn agrees to get into the action. I don't doubt she'll handle her own. I had to learn the hard way to challenge her about sports, but this is my domain. I don't lose. It's like the DJ Khaled song, "All I Do is Win." Yep, I'm confidently cocky about winning another year.

Who goes into any bet or battle thinking, "I'm gonna lose?" All I can say if you do, you're going to lose. Confidence (or dare I say cockiness) is one component to winning. It's not like I run around throwing my wins in everyone's faces all the time. I don't. I'm humble, but sometimes (when warranted) I get my brag on. You just have to understand who's in this league. A little trash talking has never hurt anyone.

You get my drift. I dominate, and I hope she'll handle this "L" okay. Again, she's impressive. Her winning isn't an option. Her knowledge of the game is top notch. The guys were shocked to learn about Lauryn's football IQ.

Last week, Jennifer texted me to get her into the league. I hope Lauryn is cool with a girl I used to date being in the league. She probably will be. There's nothing between Jennifer and me. This could work out, right?

Jennifer knows enough about sports to be dangerous, and she could help with the total number of women the league needs. I inform Sam about Jennifer wanting to play in the league. Sam doesn't care. He only wants to fill the quota. One of the ladies in the ADAs office is joining the league, which makes the number of players right with ten players. I never like to play in leagues with more than ten players. Your players options for players are just too slim.

The draft day details are finalized. There'll be a live draft with someone typing in the roster as the GM officially picks their players. It resembles the NFL draft, and it's decidedly lively. I'm glad we chose to have this format. I'm in another league at work where we draft online, and it doesn't compare to this one. People chat their trash talk. It's not nearly as fun. We also have a huge party celebrating the big draft winners.

The day has finally arrived for us to have the fantasy football draft. I'm excited to get this one started. Lauryn and I head to the draft party. She's more confident than normal as we approach the bar where the draft is taking place. As soon as I park, I establish some ground rules regarding our interactions for the season. She side-eyes me with a warning not to "mansplain her." She didn't need my help. Of course, I'm simply being a great boyfriend. This is war even with her being in the league.

"So, I'm not sure if this season will put a strain on what we've built. I hope you're prepared to take the 'L,'" I state.

"Why would I be prepared to lose this season? I'm prepared for this draft today. Are you nervous, babe?" she asks me teasingly.

"Why would I be nervous? I'm the reigning champ."

"So, you have reminded me. Reigns aren't guaranteed to continue. Plus, they rarely last. I hope you don't take your ball and go home following your loss, babe."

"It depends on which ball you're referring to."

"Well," she pauses to ignore my pun, "let me rephrase. Just take the loss like a man."

"Ok, we'll see what happens."

We enter the bar and mingle amongst the groups of people already gathered. Nearly everyone (including Jennifer) is already here as we make our entrance. Everyone's hype and ready for the draft. I go to the bar to get drinks for Lauryn and me. Someone approaches me from behind. It's a woman from the way her delicate hands and arms glide over my shirt to wrap around my waist for a quick embrace. Thinking it's Lauryn, I turn around to give her a kiss. Noticing it's Jennifer, I release her arms from my waist. Clear boundaries need to be set with this woman.

"Jennifer," I note surprised she would try to hug me intimately in public.

"Hi, Keith. I'm so happy to see you," she smirks. Then all of a sudden, she leans towards me like she wants to kiss me. I move to my left to put some distance between us.

"Jennifer, I'm here with someone," I assert strongly.

"I heard you were dating someone. Are you trying to say things are serious with this woman, Keith? You never wanted to take things to the next level with me," she whines.

I search for Lauryn to make sure she isn't upset before responding, "Jennifer, I'm sorry things didn't work out for us. I'm here with my girl-friend. I hope you'll respect my relationship."

"Whatever, just remember, I'll be here once this so-called relationship of yours fails. You'll soon realize she won't do it for you."

I don't want to continue this unproductive conversation with Jennifer. We were never in a relationship, so what's her problem? The bartender places the drinks on the counter. I retrieve them and head back to our table where Jasmine is talking to Lauryn. I'm uncertain if I'm in trouble or not. I hope not. I place the drinks on the table, and I'm fully prepared to explain everything. I want transparency in this relationship. Lauryn has been through so much with Jackson, and I don't want to give her any reason to mistrust me. Jasmine could sense something, so she leaves to presumably find Jason. I'm grateful. I don't want an audience for this conversation.

"So, who's the girl who put her arms around you?" Lauryn asks.

"Her name is Jennifer."

"Is she one of your situation-ships?"

"Sort of. Not really."

"What do you mean? Oh, don't tell me! She's a jump-off?"

"Jump-off, no, not really. I dated her for a couple of weeks. Nothing serious."

"Okay, so no need for me to worry?" she asks.

"No reason at all. She's in my past. We went out a few years ago."

"Okay Keith, we're cool."

"I'll always be upfront with you."

"As long as you are, we're good. Everyone has a past. Just to be clear, I'm uncomfortable with women putting their arms around my man."

"I agree. I'm uncomfortable with it, too. I don't want you to be disre-spected. I told her about you. I hope she'll respect we're together. If not, I'll handle it. Don't worry."

There is someone knocking or beating a drum to gain everyone's at-tention. Sam gets on the microphone to announce the draft will be starting in five minutes.

"We're good. No need to talk about this anymore. We need to focus on what's important. You need to get prepared for being destroyed," Lauryn conveys confidently. "I'm in this to win it!"

Other than Jennifer being extra, the fantasy draft is a total hit. Lauryn has the number one pick. As predicted, I have the 10th pick. She's been pretty secretive this week. I didn't have a clue if this draft would be serious for her or not. I'm surprised me by how die hard she is. I'm a tad worried she might be some true competition in this. She's been legitimately strategizing on how to make her picks. She appears to be in her element never wavering when it's her turn. I wouldn't be surprised if she did several mock drafts.

I simulated several mock drafts in the 10th position to determine what options I could potentially have on draft day. This year's draft isn't disappointing either. I'm glad Lauryn gets to experience our fantasy football league with its hype and party atmosphere. She's fitting right in, and I'm here for it. Lauryn mentions she's highly impressed with the setup. Prior to the actual draft, there's a lot of trash talking. She talks a big game, and I hope she comes through on delivery. Our matchup will either cause issues between us or a rivalry. I'm voting for the ladder. It'll be memorable. She'll probably ban me from her bed when we face each other.

She picks Todd Gurley as her number one pick. The league is a PPR which is short for points per reception for those of you whose vernacular doesn't involve fantasy football. It's a great pick. Todd Gurley is a running back. He also has just as many receiving yards. By the end of the draft, her roster is so impressive I'm slightly nervous about this season. I won't ever let her know it. I have a rep to protect. I didn't win the championship two years in a row being shook. I got this. I inform Lauryn she should make sure her lineup is set on time. This week the first game is Thursday night. "Don't get caught slipping," I warn her. "You should set the lineup Wednesday night to avoid any issues on Thursday night." I guess I'm mansplaining again since she rolls her eyes at me. The week we battle, I'll be sure to distract her on Wednesday night. Does she have a shot to win? Sure, she does. Do I want to exploit all my advantages in order to win? Damn right, I do. Did I mention that I love to win? I do what it takes to make it happen except cheat.

Once we arrive home, specifically her place tonight, I'm not sure if we need to talk about Jennifer anymore. I'm willing to put forth the effort to ensure this relationship is built on trust. I want to make sure our foundation is solid. I'm fully aware of how important it is for Lauryn to trust I'll be faithful to her. I convey how honesty is eminently important to me, and I'll always be honest with her no matter how hard things become. I won't break her with cheating. If things start going sideways with us, I'll break things off before hurting her like that.

"Lauryn, I won't cheat on you, ever. I'm committed to our relationship."

"Keith, I don't doubt you. I get you aren't Jackson. If you would've lied to me about Jennifer and your past, we would have a problem. I won't deal with lies."

"I'll never lie to you."

"I appreciate it more than you know."

"Well, I would like to make a request?"

"Sure, what is it?"

"I want to go to bed now," I utter seductively.

"I'm happy to honor your request."

Since the time she took control, I've wanted to relive what we shared. I desire to slowly explore her entire body once again. I crave to reacquaint each part of her body to memory. I covet her by savoring every taste and every touch. She begs me to pleasure her. This is surprising since she tortured me so much previously. She screams how much she needs me. I caution her to be patient by guaranteeing it'll be worth it. I slowly navigate every curve and shape of her body with deliberate kisses and strokes. Suddenly, I thrust into her hard. Our bodies move together in great harmony. Her moans exhilarate me to give her more at a faster pace. She's keeping up with every motion, and the vibration that results between the both of us is incredible. I'm on a high like one I've felt after scoring the game winning touchdown in a bowl game. Afterwards, we lay in each other's arms blissfully with satisfied expressions on both of our faces.

"You were so worth the wait," Lauryn breathes out heavily.

"I'm glad. You were, too. Memorizing and delighting every inch of your body is more than I'm able to adequately verbalize right now."

"So, it's possible for you to differentiate every nuance of my body now?"

"Sure, plus this," I tease as I tap her head. "This is something I'm dying to decipher and learn more about. Plus, I plan on learning a lot more about you in and out of bed."

"Well, I'm glad to hear it."

"Are you tired?"

"Not really."

"Do you want to do this again?"

"Hmm, yea. I thought you would never ask."

We spent the rest of the day in bed, and no complaints here. My phone has been buzzing all evening. It's not like I'm going to stop consuming Lauryn's essence to answer it. Whoever this is will wait. Well, they had to wait anyway. I wasn't at a stopping point.

"You're going to be the death of me," she exclaims as she smiles at me.

"Well, you're gonna die happy," I joke.

"Smart ass," she yawns.

"I'm glad you noticed," I smirk at her. "In all seriousness, rest baby. Tomorrow's a holiday and if you think today wore you out, give me a whole day to devour your sexy ass."

She chuckles, "What makes you think you'll be the one doing the devouring?"

"Well, I'm here for that, too."

"Okay, I just need a short nap."

"Sweetheart, go to sleep. I'm not kidding about you needing your energy."

"Ok, sleep's calling me," she drags out as she yawns.

I hold her in my arms as she starts to drift. My phone dings again. I can't imagine whose blowing up my phone. I realize I can't ignore the dings anymore since I'm still wired. Suddenly, something races through my mind. I shouldn't ignore the calls. I panic, "What if something happened to my parents?" I feel an immediate sense of guilt for ignoring my messages. I hope it's not them. Lauryn has fallen asleep, so I gently remove my arm from beneath her head to place her on the pillow. I reach to retrieve my phone and learn there isn't an emergency. It's Jennifer texting. She texted me more than 50 times. What's up with her? Clues nor blatant facts work with her. I blame myself for getting involved with a clingy woman who's oblivious to the obvious. The last few texts concern me.

Jennifer: You'll never be happy with her. She won't have you, Keith. She won't. You'll never be with her, Keith. Not like we were together.

Jennifer: You better answer me, Keith.

Jennifer: I'm the woman for you, and I'll always be there for you.

Jennifer: She won't please you sexually like I will. She won't do the things I'll do to you.

Jennifer: I love you, Keith. Why don't you love me? Why her?

Jennifer: Answer me, Keith.

Jennifer: I know you love me.

Jennifer: Why her? What does she have that I don't?

Jennifer: I'm compliant. All of my other boyfriends told me I'm good in all areas that count.

Jennifer: Why r u ignoring me?

Jennifer: Would u prefer sexts?

Jennifer: Would my tits make you respond?

In the next text string, an image of Jennifer's bare breasts appeared, she licked out her tongue, and used her pointer finger to try to pull me in. She sent another picture that revealed her naked and masturbating. I had no idea this girl, who I now consider as unhinged, would go ham and crazy on me. I only had sex with her a few times. Not enough for her to go all *Fatal Attraction* on me. Maybe she had too much to drink. These texts seem a lot like drunk texts. Hopefully, she'll be embarrassed and try to forget this all happened.

Yea, she's over the top because she's two sheets to the wind. I'm hoping this will just die down tomorrow, and she'll go back to our non-existent acquaintance relationship. I reread her texts to confirm the drunk test theory. There is a theory you are bolder and do things when you're drunk you wouldn't do sober. This girl acts like we're together. I've been involved since her, and I didn't get hassled like this. I wonder if it's because I've labeled Lauryn as my girlfriend. I guess that's making her go mad. She wanted to be my girl. Well, two years later, Lauryn didn't hurt her chances for becoming mine. She did it all on her own.

I don't answer her. She's delusional. I'm saving her text messages in case I need evidence she's crazy one day. You never know, and I won't be caught slipping. I'm blocking her number before glancing at Lauryn's angelic face. These messages aren't worth sharing. I'll share if I need to, but she sounds like a harmless desperate woman. I'll soon forget I ever spent time with her. I'm getting tired finally. I settle into bed and move close to her. She's my happy place. I make sure her head is relaxed and adjusted before I slink down into the sheets. I'm happy to be with her in my arms. I haven't ever been this happy. I deluded myself with previous relationships. No one compares to her. The last thing I think about before I fall asleep is I'm falling in love with her. Sometime ago, this would've frightened me, but today I'm exhilarated about our future. She's like home to me, and I don't intend on leaving it.

CHAPTER 36
Lauryn

So, it's been a few weeks since I've hung out with my girls. It's Saturday morning and time for my weekly brunch/gab session with Kennedy and Tonya. We're trying a new spot, and I hope it lives up to its hype. It's beginning to get cooler since it's early fall. I decide to breakout a light sweater, skinny jeans, and ankle boots. As I approach the table, I see them engrossed in a conversation. I sure hope I'm not interrupting anything private.

"Hello, ladies," I say enthusiastically as I pull out my chair to sit down.

"Hey, girl," Tonya said, "We've missed you these last few brunches."

"So, what's up?" I ask.

"I guess you haven't heard about Kassidy and Derrick, have you?" Tonya asks sneakily.

I look at Kennedy, "Your sister and Derrick?" I ask. "As in a couple?" Kennedy nods. "I guess it makes sense oddly enough."

"What do you mean by that?" Kennedy asks.

"I can kind of see them as a couple. That's all," I respond.

"I've been trying to get those two together forever. Kassidy would act like it was weird. I don't understand why. I think Derrick has always had a thing for her," Kennedy says.

"Well, I can see why," Tonya says.

"Why?" I ask.

"Well, let's see. Eric and Derrick are twins, and she's Kennedy's sister," Tonya says giving me an "Isn't it obvious look" and "You know that's weird" at the same time.

We all laugh, and Kennedy says, "They may be identical in looks, but they're so different. Eric is so focused on building his empire, and you know I think money-driven men are sexy. Derrick is more of a humanitarian. That's cute, but Kassidy is like that, too. I swear Kassidy has found her match, and they're both doctors. Can you imagine what their kids will be like?"

"Aren't you getting ahead of yourself?

"Nope, not at all. I bet you all that Derrick's going to be my double BIL."

"Your what?" Tonya asks confused.

"Brother-in-law," Kennedy and I say in unison.

"Oh, that must be some couple speak. Who knew there was an acronym for that?"

"Anyway, I was wondering why Kassidy doesn't join us. Is she working most weekends?" I ask.

"Girl, yea. Her schedule is so crazy," Kennedy says, "She barely gets one weekend off a month. When she does, she spends it with Derrick if he isn't working."

"I bet they have hot *Grey's Anatomy* sex," Tonya says.

"I wouldn't know. She's super tight lipped about her and Derrick. I didn't even know they were together until the gender reveal party," Kennedy says.

"What! Are you kidding?" I ask.

Kennedy reveals, "Yea, after you all went to the hospital. Derrick and Kennedy were attending to you guys, but there was a moment when they disappeared. I walked up on them inadvertently. I saw Derrick put his arm around Kassidy, and they looked comfortable.

She was reassuring him, so I thought. Later, Kassidy must have thought we left, but I saw her and Derrick kissing. Not just a peck on the lips but full tongue. When I asked her about it, she was cagey about them, but she finally admitted they were together. She swore me to secrecy that day. She's open about their relationship now that she's confident they're the real thing. She was apprehensive at first in case they didn't work out. They've been together for two years. I'm so happy that I was right about them. When I told Eric, he didn't seem shocked. He always thought they wanted each other, but they were too stubborn to admit it."

"So, when will I find my man? All of you have found someone. It's Tonya's turn."

"Now, Tonya, do you really want to be settled down with one guy?" I ask.

"Nope," she says, "I just thought I would complain about it," we laugh.

"Kennedy will you have a gender reveal party with this baby?" I ask.

"No. Do you remember the shock that we had with the twins? I swear Eric and I wanted to pass out when the pink and blue cake was cut. I would rather not find out in a room full of people if I'm having twins again. We're just having a good old fashioned baby shower. Luckily, we still have a bunch of stuff from the twins, so we won't need much. It'll just be a celebration of the baby."

"That's understandable," I say.

"I know that's right. What's going on with you, Lauryn?" Tonya asks.

"Nothing much. Enjoying Keith and working at Food Will."

"Kudos on enjoying that fine ass man!" Tonya exclaims. "I'm surprised you're still at Food Will, though. No offense, but you've always been more leadership focused."

"None taken. There's a lot to do there now, but once things are stable, I think it may get boring."

"Well, I'm just glad to see you so happy. My boy, Keith, gets a fist bump from me," Tonya says.

My phone vibrates with a text message, and I look to see who it is. It's Jeremy, and he wants to go out. I hadn't talked to him in a while, so he didn't know my relationship status had changed. I didn't want to break this to him over the phone, but I do owe him the truth. I plan to meet him next week to let him know about Keith and me.

"That looks serious," Tonya says.

"Not really. Just a friend I have to break the news about my relationship status with."

"Who? Isaac? I heard he was back."

"No, he knows my relationship status. We've had some moments."

"So, what's he been up to?" Tonya asks.

"He's been living it up in New York. He's been married, and he has a very cute little girl named Bella. She's super adorable."

"Wow, I always thought you would be the mother of his kids," Tonya says and laughs.

"Didn't we all!" Kennedy joins in.

"Girl, everybody can't be you and Eric. Plus, I think he's moved on now."

"Really? With whom?" Kennedy asks.

"I don't remember her name, but she and Keith used to date in college."

"Wow, he's dating your man's ex and vice versa," Tonya burst out laughing.

"Well, it's not like we met at a swingers' bar and switched partners. It's a small world when it comes to dating and love connections."

"Say that girl!" Kennedy chimes in.

"I have to go to the ladies' room," I say. "I'll be right back."

I'm refreshing my lip gloss when another lady enters. I'm not really paying any attention to her until she begins speaking to me. She's a thin woman with blond hair and blue eyes who looks vaguely familiar.

"You know, Keith will never be faithful to you," she says.

"Do I know you?" I ask.

"No, not really," she says, "I just remember when Keith told me you were his girlfriend. I'm Jennifer."

I take a deep breath before responding, "Is there anything specific you want to say?"

"No, I just want you to know that he isn't the relationship type. I know that. As much as I gave myself to him, it just didn't matter. He wouldn't or couldn't commit to me."

"So, are you saying that you were his girlfriend, and he cheated on you?" I ask trying to stay calm as well as figure out what her point is.

"He said we would be together, too, and he lied. I thought he would fall in love, like I did. What makes you so special? Is it because you have an ass? Does that ass of yours make you special? I could get butt injections if it's your ass."

This chick is crazy, but I remain calm. I really don't want to bring out her single white female. I'm being cautious with her. I want to get out of this bathroom unharmed. At the very least, I want to leave this bathroom without having to snatch her ass up. She looks wild-eyed, and maybe a little high. So, it's clear I need to handle this very carefully.

"Look, I don't know enough about what you and Keith had before. I know that it may seem strange that he's in a relationship with me, but that's what it is. I need to know that you can accept this and not cause any scenes or outbursts."

"Me?! Cause a scene?! Never! I just thought you need to know who your boyfriend is."

"Thank you for the information," I say a little sarcastically. "I need to return to my friends now."

I hurry away from the bathroom confused about the encounter. I don't want to get stabbed in the back by some rejected fatal attraction moniker. I return to the table, and Kennedy sees the look on my face.

"What's wrong, girl?" Kennedy asks.

"I'm not sure. Just something I need to talk to Keith about later."

"Are you sure, lady?" Tonya asks.

"Positive," I affirm. "I need the facts before I talk about it. I'll tell you guys once I know more. Don't worry."

"Alright, girl," Kennedy says, "Whatever you need."

I'm not ready to discuss this with them in case it's not a big deal. If you tell your girlfriends something negative about a guy, they'll hold it against him forever. I don't want to give them any reasons to hold grudges against Keith. It's best that I keep this to myself for now. I'm sure my instincts are right about this crazy girl, but I want to talk to him first.

All throughout brunch, I couldn't stop thinking about the crazy look in Jennifer's eyes. She looks like she's still in love with Keith or rather obsessed with him. She seems like she would do anything to get him back. In a way, I'm sad for her because she has an unrequited love for him. He said he made it clear that he hadn't been interested in her long before I came into the picture. I guess there's a possibility that he played or misled her. I don't see him doing that. I believe he's honest and straight up with people. That's one of the reasons why I love him. Shit, I said I love him again. Could I really be in love with him? There's only some many Freudians slips I can have before what I'm saying is the truth. I'll get to the bottom of this Jennifer situation when I get home.

After having our prerequisite number of mimosas minus Kennedy, filling up our bellies, and gossiping like there's no tomorrow, we leave brunch. I can't stop thinking about what Jennifer said in the bathroom. Is she going to be a problem? First, she put her arms around Keith, and now she approaches me with some lovesick crap. Did Keith drive her crazy? Keith and I will talk. He is hanging out with Jason and Sam until later, and I have errands to run.

I don't want to be weird about Jennifer, but I'm kind of pissed. Not at Keith. I'm pissed about how she approached me. She has some nerve. Keith comes by the house after he's done hanging out. He pulls me into his arms for a kiss. When I don't open my mouth to accept his tongue, he just pecks me on the lips and looks at me.

"What's wrong?"

"I honestly hope nothing, but I can't help but be concerned."

He looks worried as he comes into my great room and walks to the couch to sit down. I follow him and sit down next to him.

"I ran into your friend, Jennifer, today. She had quite a bit to say about you."

"What? At your brunch?"

"No, not at my brunch. She was at the same restaurant. That crazy girl followed me to the bathroom."

"Wait, what? She followed you to the bathroom?"

"Yea, she wanted to tell me how you did her wrong, and how you would do the same to me. I don't think she got the memo that you weren't a couple."

"I'm really sorry about her, Lauryn. I knew that she had feelings for me, but I ended things so long ago. Way before you and me. I never wanted a relationship with her."

"Look, I'm not holding your past against you. I have people coming out the woodwork, too, but I don't think she has a clear understanding about you and her. She thinks she has a chance with you now since we're together."

"Yea, I didn't want to be an asshole. I guess, 'it's not you, it's me' didn't work, and she needs some real direct truth. I thought I could spare her feelings by not telling her, she's as 'dumb as a box of rocks, so it wouldn't work out.'"

"Yea, that could hurt," I giggle.

"She sent me some crazy text messages the night of the draft, but I honestly thought she was drunk. I blocked her number."

"Why didn't you tell me about the text messages?"

"I honestly thought she was drunk texting and that would be the end of it."

"Okay, that makes sense. So, what are we going to do about her?"

"Not 'we.' Me. I need to be clear with her about us, and how she will never be my girl. I think I need to do this now." Keith calls Jennifer, and he has her on speaker.

"Hey, Keith. It's nice to hear from you. I guess your friend told you I saw her today."

"Yes, Jennifer, my GIRLFRIEND told me she saw you!"

"Girlfriend! Hmph! We'll see how long this lasts!"

"Look, Jennifer, I'm really sorry. I've never been interested in a relationship with you. I naively thought that we could be friends, but that wasn't fair to you. Your feelings for me will never be returned. You'll never be someone I want to be in a relationship with. I don't appreciate the unwarranted texts you sent nor ambushing my girlfriend in the bathroom. This ends today."

"Keith, how can you be so cruel? This is about her, isn't it?"

"Well, of course it has something to do with her. She's my girl, and we have something real. We have something that could grow into much more."

"How can you, Keith! You told me you weren't interested in a relationship with anyone."

"I wasn't…two years ago, Jennifer. Things change."

"I didn't think you would ever throw away your black book. What the hell is wrong with me?"

"Look, Jennifer. We weren't meant to be together."

"Why? Why her?"

"I don't have to explain to you why I picked Lauryn or why we're together. This will be our last conversation. We can't be friends. You disrespected my girl, and I won't tolerate that."

"Fuck you, Keith! You're a damn asshole! I never should've gotten involved with your ass. You're such a dick! Don't ever call me again in this lifetime. I will get someone to replace me in the fantasy football league. I hope you and that bitch rot in hell!" She yells and hangs up on Keith. I feel bad for Keith because I know he wanted to do the right thing.

"Well, I guess she told me," he chuckles.

"I guess she did. Well, hopefully that's the last time we have to worry about her interference."

"From your beautiful lips to God's ears," he murmurs as he leans in and gives me a kiss.

Later in the week, I decide to meet Jeremy at a coffee bar. I know this guy loves to drink coffee. I don't feel guilty because I've never wanted anything with him, but after witnessing how Jennifer reacted I want to be cognizant of his feelings. I'm planning on breaking this to him gently. I arrive before him, order my coffee, a chocolate-filled croissant, and await his arrival. I find a cozy section with two armchairs for us to sit. After taking a bite of my croissant and a sip of my coffee, Jeremy walks in looking sheepishly at me. He strolls over to take a seat.

"Hey there, Lauryn. How have you been?"

"I'm doing well. I got here a little early, so I went ahead and placed my order. Why don't you get yours then we can catch up, yes?"

"Sounds good.

He does just as I suggested and places his order. After a few minutes, he returns to the table to await his order. He has a wide grin on his face.

"I have some exciting news!" he exclaims.

"Yea? Do share?"

"I've been doing really well in school, and I've applied some of the principals I've learned at work. They've taken notice. This summer I've been offered an opportunity to join the management rotation at the corporate office in Atlanta."

"That's awesome news. Congratulations!!"

"Yea, this could be a great opportunity for my career. They're paying for school, and if things work out, I could be moving to Atlanta after I graduate next year. I've always wanted to live there."

"Atlanta's great. You'll love it there."

"You're from there, right?"

"I am. I'm so happy for you, Jeremy. I told you good things payoff if you're determined and focused on your goal. Way to go!!"

"All I'm missing now is you in my life," he looks at me seductively.

I nearly spit out my coffee and cough a little. When I gain my composure, I ask him, "Wait! What do I have to do with this?"

"You know how I feel about you. I know you were in a bad situation before, and the timing wasn't right, but I think we could be great together. You're from Atlanta. Things could be perfect for us in the future. I could really love you the way you deserve."

Wait! Pump the brakes! What in the hell is wrong with this guy? We've never dated, and he wants to build a life with me. Delusional much? I have to break it to this guy the hard way. Being nice to unrealistic people isn't doing them any favors. If I didn't learn anything else from Keith's situation with Jennifer, I learned that.

"Look, Jeremy. There is no us. We're not a couple, nor will we ever be one. I did have a bad breakup, and you've been a great friend. Emphasis on friend. We don't have any type of future."

"I know you're still feeling some kind of way from your —"

"A cappuccino and a banana nut muffin for Jeremy!" the barista yells.

"I'll be right back to finish discussing this," he remarks as he walks over to retrieve his order. He's back before I could get my thoughts together. "Yum, I love this place. The coffee and pastries are the best," he comments as he sits down. "Where were we? Yea, I apologize if I came on too strong. Rushing things. It's not my intent. I'll wait for you forever, Lauryn."

"Jeremy, we're only friends. We'll never be a couple."

"Give us a chance, Lauryn."

"I'm sorry, Jeremy. I'm not attracted to you. I only see you as a friend. I didn't want to hurt your feelings, but I can't let you keep thinking there's a chance for us. I'm dating someone, and we're committed to each other."

Jeremy's expression goes dark, "You're just a little bitch, aren't you?" he sneers. "Leading me on. Telling me you're just not in the right space for a relationship. Giving me hope."

"Excuse me! I never led you anywhere. I have never given you hope. We're done here."

I get up, grab my coffee and pastry, and prepare to leave. He tugs on my arm before I can get out of his reach. "You're gonna regret this!"

"Let me go, asshole. The only thing I'm going to regret is helping you out at all. Don't ever call me again!" I snatch my arm away.

"You don't have to worry about that. You fucking tease! You give women a bad name!"

I hurry to the front to exchange my coffee cup for a to-go one. I should've just ghosted this fool. He didn't deserve a clean break from me. I glance back to make sure I won't have another encounter with him. He shoots daggers my way, and I'm glad I found out about his fake ass. He pretended to be the helpful friend until he didn't get his way. What a jerk! Good riddance! To think I cared about his feelings. Well, that's over. I'm headed home to my man.

I soon forget about my nasty encounter with Jeremy and get back into the swing of my life. It's Sunday Funday. Keith and I are having brunch with his friends. There are several couples here including Sam and Erica along with Jason and Jasmine. The trash talking from the fantasy match-ups begin as soon as we sit down. Sam and I are going head-to-head. He has 20 points from the Thursday night's game, and that has given him confidence. I didn't have any players on Thursday, so I just let him have this moment.

"Are you afraid you're going to lose to me this week, Lauryn?" Sam asks.

"Not at all. It's still early, and I only have two players in the noon game. Most of my team is playing this afternoon and later tonight. I also have two players going tomorrow. I'm not worried. I just want to see how well you do after these first games. It looks like you'll only have one more player going tonight."

"You're going down, Lauryn!!" Sam shouts.

"Enough, Sam!" Erica scolds him. "You can't get too cocky. You're only ahead by 20 points."

"Ok, ok," Sam says. "Jennifer called me to say that she was quitting the league. She got her roommate, Zach, to play in her place. Does anyone have a problem with one of the female players changing to a male player?"

"Nope! I'm going to win either way. I don't care if it's a woman or a man! It doesn't matter to me!" Keith boasts.

"I wouldn't be so sure, babe," I counter.

"I love it! Keith's finally met his match," Sam jokes.

"I agree! We love her for you!!" Erica grins.

"I do, too," Keith smirks at me.

Jason and Jasmine have been really quiet most of the day. I don't know them well enough to determine if they're having issues. I may ask Keith if everything's okay later. They exchange a look at one another where their love can't be denied. Whatever their issue is I don't think it's about them. I won't be nosy. I do hope everything's okay with them. They're becoming my friends, too. I love that Keith's friends are becoming my friends and vice versa.

"Guys," Jason breaks the silence. "Jasmine and I want to invite you all to our wedding/reception in Barbados. All of your expenses will be paid. Lock the date. December 14th – December 21st. I hope you all can take off work and celebrate with us."

"Wow! Congrats! I had no idea you guys were getting married so soon," Keith comments.

"This wasn't our initial plan," Jasmine starts, "I wanted the big wedding, but the only thing I really want is to become Mrs. Smith. Now, I want to elope and get our lives started."

"I'm excited for you guys," I state.

Jasmine's phone buzzes, and her mood changes when she looks at the message. It seems like she may break down in tears.

"What's wrong, baby?" Jason asks, and she hands her phone over to him. "Damn, them!" Jason hisses. "I'm sorry guys, but we need you guys to be discreet about our wedding plans. No social media post, please. My mom and her dad will try to do something to destroy our day. I hate them!"

"Baby, we said they can't do anything to us. They can't destroy us. Everyone we want with us will be there. No one will ruin our wedding. They, for damn sure, won't ruin our marriage."

Would you like the backstory? Keith broke it down for me. Okay, here's the tea. Later when we're alone, Keith breaks it down for me. It seems that Jason's mom, Kathleen, knew Jasmine's dad, Matthew, years before she married Jason's dad, Julian. Matthew was Kathleen's boyfriend in the past. They messed around early in their respective marriages before Jason and Jasmine were born. After the kids, they tried to make their marriages work. Adultery wasn't the reason why both sets of parents divorced, but Jason and Jasmine found it hard to believe after Matthew and Kathleen ended up back together.

Matthew and Kathleen continue to cause all types of drama for Jason and Jasmine. Julian has found love again and has married Jason's step-mom, Evelyn. Jasmine's mom, Theresa, has married her stepdad, Thomas. For some reason, Matthew and Kathleen have been against them being together. Jason wondered if Matthew could be his biological father since they're so adamantly against them being together, and Kathleen began treating Julian like he disgusted her before their marriage ended.

Jason demanded a paternity test, and both Julian and Matthew refused to provide a sample. Julian knew in his heart Jason was his son, and he didn't need a test to prove it. Jason decided to work around this by testing himself against Jasmine. He hoped and prayed that he hadn't falling in love with his sister for the entire waiting period. He had a sneaking suspicion that he hadn't because their parents would been more fucked about them being together if that had been the case. Waiting for the results turned into a very long wait. It was confirmed by 99.4% that Jason and Jasmine weren't related. Both of them were incredibly relieved knowing their love would survive.

Jason continues, "So, our ideal guest list wouldn't include my mom and Jaz's dad."

The problem now is they didn't want to deal with any surprises that could pop up from Matthew and Kathleen to ruin their wedding. They only wanted people they cared about with them on that special date. Keith and I would talk about it later, but I would love to celebrate their wedding in Barbados as well as have a nice little vacation with my man. December in Barbados will be very nice. I can't wait to lay out on the beach when it's freezing cold back here in Nashville.

When we're alone, Keith asks me, "Do you want to go to Barbados with me, babe? I know this will be a huge step in our relationship."

"I would love to go, but I don't want to be pushy. These are your friends."

"He's giving me a plus one."

"I'm so in if you're inviting me."

"You're invited," he clarifies as he kisses me.

It's been wonderful since we've become "official." I'm getting into the groove of having a boyfriend and a well-balanced life. Keith has changed my viewpoint on being in a commitment by only being himself. I'm enjoying this ride with him. Plus, I'm not second-guessing myself by wondering if I'm ruining things. This man (I'm sure I shouldn't mention this out loud) is the best thing that's ever happened to me. I know, don't jinx it, yet he is. I won't be telling him this too soon. I don't want him to get a big head or anything.

Being in the fantasy football league has been a lot of fun. It's early in the season. My team is killing it. If I don't have any major injuries, I could seize the championship. Keith may not accept losing well. He's likes to rub it in my face that he's won the championship two years in a row. Well, boo, there's always this year for you to lose.

I hope he isn't a sore loser. I don't like sore losers, or people who can dish it out but can't take it. Our first matchup is this week. He's been trying to distract me. Does he seriously believe I'm going to bungle this matchup? He couldn't possibly have it in his head I wouldn't set my lineup in time. I'm not a rookie in fantasy football. I guess he needs to learn the hard way because I don't play. I'm going to squash him like a bug.

Part of his devious strategy to get me off my game is to plan a surprise for me. He won't discuss any of the details with me. I don't care what his plans are. He's still my nemesis this week. I'll keep my emotions under wrap. I have a thing about surprises. I like them for other people. Not so much for me.

My curiosity is getting the best of me. I want to know what the surprise is, and he's not budging. He seriously won't even give me a minute hint. I have no idea what I need to pack or if I need to pack at all. How long will we be gone? I tried to find out if it's a day or night surprise. He's giving me nada. He's assured me he has everything under control. I don't have to worry about anything. He's only requested that I'm present. I won't stop trying to figure out where we're going.

I'm beginning to question if he's the best thing that's ever happened to me? Nah, I'm kidding. He's still incredible even if he won't tell me what we're doing. He only mentioned I should get off early on Friday and be ready at my house at precisely two o'clock. He's being oddly specific, and I have no way to figure out what we're doing. Yea, I'm a control freak, and this lack of control is jarring. Precisely at two o'clock on Friday, my doorbell rings. I answer it with a sense of anticipation and joy.

"Well, hello there," I express coyly with a hint of a smile.

"Hello, sweetheart. I hope you're ready to go."

"As ready as I can be with the limited amount of information you've provided."

"Well, prior to leaving, I have to do something," he reaches into his pocket and pulls out a scarf.

"What's that?"

"Oh, this? It's to prevent you from figuring out where we're going. I'm going to blindfold you."

"This could freak me out. I very well could be claustrophobic."

"Well, I'm not putting you in a small space. You probably mean merinthophobia. Considering your alter ego, Lola, didn't mind binding me, I don't imagine this blindfold will be a problem."

"Well, what if I have agoraphobia?"

"A fear of places and situations that might cause panic, helplessness, or embarrassment? Really? You're not going to give me this."

"Okay. I'm giving you a hard time to make you fold and tell me. It would be nice if you'd tell me where we're going."

"Soon enough, baby," he imparts as he loosens my tightly wound hands, "If you're unhappy with the surprise, you can make me do three things I'll hate without protests or questions from me."

"Three things, hmm? Intriguing."

"Now, trust me."

"I do trust you."

"Prove it."

"Okay." I give up and let him blindfold me.

He escorts me out of my condo to only God knows where. I'm honing in with my other senses to get an idea where we could be going. I'm not having much luck unless the sound of a car door shutting is a good indicator. I wouldn't make a great detective. I can't even figure out if we're traveling east, west, north, or south. Where is he taking me? I guess the signs are telling me to sit back, relax, and enjoy the ride. I'll stop guessing, but I won't make this car ride a joy for Keith. He blindfolded me and kept me in the dark. I definitely won't give him the pleasure of my gift for gab. No chatty Kathy tonight. Hmph!

"Your body language is screaming uptight and tense. Are you angry? Does the baby need some food?" he croons in a baby voice.

"No, I don't. Thank you."

"Wow! You're mad for real. Weren't you supposed to trust me? I won't do anything to disappoint you or make you unhappy. I guarantee as soon as we arrive at our final destination you'll be pleased, and you're going to regret sulking."

"I guess we're going to have to see about this, won't we?"

"Okay. How about we play a game?"

"A game. You want to play a game?"

"Yea. Like an icebreaker."

"Okay. Fine. Whatever."

"Have you ever played, 'Never Ever Have I?'"

"The drinking game?"

"Yea, the drinking game. Hmm, it's more fun with drinks. Ok, yea, we should play it later. Let's play, 'Would You Rather?'"

"Okay, I'll probably forget about being blindfolded."

"Would you rather walk through a muddy pit with snakes or eat slimy worms?"

"This is not even a choice. I don't want either."

"Come on. It's a game."

"Alright, the worms. Yuck," I gag. "They won't kill me. The snakes could be poisonous."

"Yep, I probably would have to tolerate the snakes. Worms and the texture. Nope."

"Who's the baby now?" I laugh.

"Not a baby. I'm all man."

"We'll see. Would you rather live the rest your life rolling around as a pig or live the rest of your life in a cage as a parrot?"

"I'd pick the parrot as long as you're my owner."

"Hardy har-har."

"What? I could talk sexy to you all the time. It would be hot. Instead of Polly want a cracker, I would ask you to rub my tail."

I chuckle, "Only you would think a life inside a prison would be great. I guess those tail rubs could be worth it, huh?"

"Yep, definitely worth it. Plus, I like to consider the glass as half-full rather than half-empty. Would you rather compulsively wink following every word you utter or speak every sentence in the form of a question?"

"Winking following every word would be a challenge and annoying. I don't think I want to be on Jeopardy for the rest of my life. The struggle is real. I guess it'll have to be speak every sentence in the form of a question. Would you rather be on the Harlem Globetrotters or in the American Idol tour?

"No brainer. I love sports so Harlem Globetrotters."

"I guess. I could imagine you trying to be one for real."

"Would you rather have your favorite celeb as your personal assistant or have $100K."

"No brainer. $100K. Give me the moola. I don't have a celebrity crush I would want or need in my life in a personal capacity."

"Yea, I would pick the money, too," he laughs. "You're having fun, right?"

"I have to admit I am. Would you rather never be able to use deodorant or use a fork?"

"The fork most definitely. I refuse to go around being stank."

I laugh, "Yea, I would have to dump you if you had body odor. That's a deal breaker."

"Yea, I must concur. Would you rather have all your singing-in-the-car moments shown on TV or have all your arguments with your family shown on TV?"

"Well, this a tough one. Not really. I don't sing not even a little bit, and I rarely argue with my family. If this is ever on TV, it would be boring and get cancelled immediately. I'm not the 'throw the drink in your face' or 'flip tables' type of chick. I would never be picked for the RHOA cast even if I happened to be with a baller."

"Did you honestly state the acronym from *Real Housewives of Atlanta*?"

"It's a hot show. I don't watch it, though. Wait, do you?"

"Nah, I know people."

I laugh, "Really?"

"Yea, it's not my thing.

"Hmm, something tells me you might, Keith."

"Huh? What you trying to say? It's my guilty pleasure?"

"I won't judge you if it is."

"Nah, it's not me. My ex obsessed over that show, and she hung out at my place a lot. She would get mad if I didn't sit down to view it with her."

"You were a great boyfriend and looked at her show with her or did you pretend?"

"At first, I would start off trying to watch it. Like you asked, I tried to be a great boyfriend. The shows had too much drama. I would always get an 'urgent call' during the show and ask her not to wait on me. The call would last until the show ended."

"That's quite manipulative and conniving, ole boyfriend of mine. I'm impressed."

"Yea, I'll admit it, but in my defense, I hated the show. She knew it and didn't care."

"I'm sorry. It sounds like your breakup caused you a lot of pain."

"Thanks. I'm not the least bit sorry we broke up. If we hadn't ended, I wouldn't have met you. I wouldn't be exactly where I want to be."

"Such a charmer," I blush.

We continue playing a few more rounds, and I have to admit I'm no longer dreading not having knowledge of where we're going. Soon enough the car stops, and my anxiety to be in control comes rearing back. I've learned not to ask any more questions. I hear him exiting the car and opening the passenger car door. He gently guides me out of the car and holds my hand to guide me to wherever we're going.

"I still need the blindfold?"

"No, I'm going to remove it now."

He unties the blindfold to release it from my face, and it's a minute or so before I've adjusted to the lighting. As I adjust my eyes, I have a magnificent view of a beautiful cottage and garden. I have no idea where we are. I admit, at least to myself, I love this surprise. The goldenrods and chrysanthemums have bloomed perfectly for this time of year. This resembles our own personal oasis. I begin breathing in the fresh flowers' aroma with deep, controlled breaths. I savor this moment. It's like home. I'm beginning to relax. I want to remove my shoes and run around in the garden. This place makes me happy, and I can't contain the smile that's peeking out. I refuse to admit it, but this is the best.

"Someone's happy with my surprise," he teases me.

"Who?" I pretend to be confused.

"You won't admit you like this surprise, will you?"

"I'm not petty. I love this surprise."

"I'm glad to hear it, beautiful."

With a cheeky expression, I ask, "Whose house is this?"

"Ours for the weekend. I wanted to get you away all to myself."

"I hate to admit this, but I love this idea. Thank you for surprising me, and I'm sorry for acting ungrateful. I'm super nosy, I guess."

"It's fine. You're going to make it up to me."

"Oh, I am, am I? How do you propose I'll do it?"

"Oh, you'll see," he grins and throws me over his shoulder as I burst out laughing.

"Wait, wait. What about clothes? I didn't prepare for a weekend away."

"Well, there are reasons why your boyfriend is not only a great catch, but he's actually industrious. Your clothes are packed in my trunk."

"What clothes did you pack?"

"None you would recognize. I bought you stuff for this weekend."

"I'm impressed. Well, I probably should wait until I see what you picked out for me."

"You will soon enough. Let's go into the house." He carries me into the house and places me on the couch in the living room while informing me, "I'll be right back. I'll get our bags."

"Okay, I'll check out the rest of the place."

I wander around admiring the updated modern cottage, and it's perfect. It has the outdoor feel I love with the garden and updated modern conveniences. The kitchen is state-of-the-art, and it has a double oven. I doubt we'll be using both ovens this weekend. If we ever wanted to come out for a small gathering this place would be perfect. I check out the entire place quickly and methodically. It's about 2500 square feet with four bedrooms and three bathrooms. It's a ranch-style home. I'm standing in the doorway of the primary when I sense Keith's arms around my waist.

"Hmm, you found exactly the place I want to venture into first."

"Here? Hmm, one track mind?"

"Never, baby. I want you in every room in this house. As you can tell, my mind has several tracks."

"What am I going to do about you?"

"You know what you're going to do with me."

Not having time to respond, he turns me around to engulf me with his tenderness. Suddenly, we're knee-deep entangled with one another. It's hard to tell where I end and he begins. We make love until we're both overcome with ultimate climatic pleasure. This man is going to be the death of me; I'm certain. I guess, if this is the case, I'll die a genuinely happy woman. I'm overwhelmed with joy as my stomach growls. I would normally be embarrassed. I'm not with him. I don't get anxious about around him. I have no idea what this means because I'm oddly comfortable with him. I know what it means. I'm not sure if I'm ready to face it.

"Oh, somebody's hungry. I guess we did work up quite an appetite. I'll go get us a snack. You should stay here and relax," he suggests.

"Wait, there's food here? How did you have time to get this place stocked with food?"

"Well, there's this thing called a packaged deal where you can pay extra to have the owner go grocery shopping for you prior to your arrival. It's well worth it if you want to be occupied doing other things."

"Aren't you smart. I love how prepared you are."

I throw on his t-shirt, and he puts on boxers as we head to the kitchen to discover what goodies we have. The sun is setting and there is a bay window where the view is breathtaking. I'm captivated by the view, and I would love to read by the window. I prefer hardback books, but I didn't bring any with me. I doubt I'll have time to read around this insatiable guy anyway. If there's any downtime, I have my tablet with me. I'm in the middle of this mystery novel I must finish prior to the next book club meeting. Luckily, it's two weeks away.

"This view is beautiful," I observe and turn to him.

"I agree. Simply beautiful," he murmurs as he gazes at me, "Maybe, we should have breakfast on the deck tomorrow."

"I didn't get a chance to check out the deck," I grin at his innuendo.

"We will. Let's grab something to eat."

"Then, I would love to see what you arranged for me to wear this weekend."

"I got you."

Opening the suitcase, I could cry with joy. The outfits and shoes he purchased for me were perfect. It's as if he were my personal shopper. I had no idea he liked shopping. I pick up the shoes, and I'm flabbergasted the shoe size is correct. Is this Freaky Friday, or does he truly have skills to decipher and acknowledge my short comings?

"I could cry. These clothes are perfect."

"Wait, baby. This is supposed to make you happy."

"I'm happy, extremely happy. These are happy tears. You took everything into consideration this weekend."

"Why don't you model a few outfits for me?"

"Okay. I'll channel my inner Tyra the entire time."

I put on the plaid tweed hip-hugging skirt, the cream cashmere sweater, and brown riding boots. I twirl around and gaze in the mirror slightly surprised with how stylish the outfit is, and the size is right. "He's good," I whisper to myself. I kidded previously about him being able to be my personal shopper, but he does rival me when it comes to outfitting me.

(I'm falling harder for this guy with everything he does. Why, oh, why? I'm unsure about me being strong enough to fall in love again. Whoa! Love? Where did that come from? Who said anything about love? I like him a whole lot. That's all. Love is extreme. You don't fall in love with someone this quickly anyway. He would probably hightail it out of here if he thought for one second I loved him.)

"Sweetheart," Keith yells out, "what's taking you so long?"

"Coming."

I strut out with my best impersonation of a model stance while Keith whistles at me. I'm failing to keep the stoic model expression. I burst out laughing as he changes from whistles to howls.

"Nice," he flirts, "I knew this would look incredible on you the moment I saw it."

"You did a great job. If you ever want to quit this lawyering thing, you could always be my personal shopper."

"No offense. I doubt you'll be able to afford me. Correction, I doubt you'll be willing."

"Whoa, touché, my friend."

"Well, I would have to make way more than I do now, and I wouldn't undercut myself. Even for someone I'm —" he trails off, "Yea, even if I care about you."

"Not even a girlfriend's discount?" I jokingly ask since I'm unsure of what he almost said.

"Well, I could give you a discount in other ways. You can't mess with my paper." We both laugh.

I wonder about what the other discount could be. I have a sneaking suspicion it's something sexual. I don't and won't pay for it.

"It's not sex. Stop those wheels spinning up there in your head at a rapid speed. You're probably cursing me out. It's not hard to imagine you ranting, "I don't pay for sex. Who does this asshole think I am?""

"You're making a huge assumption like you know me or something."

"Better than you think."

The next morning, I smell something fantastic, and it draws me out of what resembles a memory than a dream. I'm sure all the vivid memories bombarding my brain actually happened last night. Remembering every moment is making me want to drag my fine ass specimen of a man my way. I reach out for him only to grasp some sheets. My eyes pop open, and I notice his side of the bed is empty. Duh, the smell isn't in the dream or memory, I suppose. There is something cooking in the kitchen, and it smells wonderful. I yawn and stretch as I make my way to the bathroom to welcome my morning ritual before going to seek out the scintillating aroma from the kitchen. Keith has outdone himself. The spread looks amazing. He's prepared apple cinnamon pancakes, spinach quiche, mimosas, and coffee, too. He has all the food and drinks on a tray.

"Is there some way for me to help you? You should've woken me up. I would've helped somehow."

"No, I'm good. You may open the door to the patio for me. Everything else is done."

"Why didn't you wake me? I'm not holding up my end. I feel bad."

"Don't. You needed your rest. I gave you a great workout last night. I always planned to make you breakfast today."

"Another check in the pros column for you."

"Pros column, hmm. Tell me more."

"Well, you're gonna laugh."

"I won't I promise."

"I'm a checklist, girl. I developed a pros and cons list about you to determine if we should date or not."

"Okay. How are my pros compared to my cons?"

"Obviously, you have way more pros than cons."

"How is this obvious to me, 'girl' with the list?"

"We're together, aren't we?"

"Good point, but I would like more information about my pros. I guess I want to know my cons, too. I could always improve, right?"

"How about I share your pros and cons with you later? A girl can't share all of her secrets right away you know."

"Well, I'm gonna hold you to it. I'll be waiting to hear those pros."

We go out to the patio, which is just as cute as the house, and have breakfast. The sun is rising, and it's not too cold out for this time of year. I enjoy brisk weather. Just not too much of it. The temperature today is perfect. The food is as mouth-watering as it's presented. I'm moaning like I'm having an orgasm. This food tastes like heaven on earth. I guess I'm having a foodgasm. He glances at me with a curious expression every time I moan.

"If you keep moaning, I'm going to have to do something about it."

"Well, you might. I can't stop enjoying this breakfast. This food is delicious. What did I do to deserve you?"

"Being you, baby."

"Well, I guess I'll always get breakfast since I'll always be me."

"I'm glad. I wouldn't want it any other way. You get breakfast anytime you want it."

Later in the evening, we relax on the couch. I'm laying back on Keith with my backside against his chest. We had steak, baked potatoes, and salad for dinner. We're drinking an after-dinner glass of wine when I get a bright idea.

"Why don't we play, 'Never Ever Have I' now?"

"Drinking wine?"

"Well, do you have something stronger?"

"Vodka."

"Well, I'll need a chaser."

"I'll get the bottle of vodka and cranberry juice. You're about to be wasted, and I would never do anything sexual without your consent. Drunk girls can't consent. I'm honorable."

"I give you honorable permission to have all of my body tonight. Consent granted ahead of time."

"Oh, you're giving me pre-consent. What if you change your mind?"

"I guess I could. I'll verbalize with a 'no,' okay? Plus, you're going to be drunk, and I'm a good girl. I won't get the goods when you're drunk."

"Oh, you have my permission, too. You won't ever hear me utter the word 'no.' Drunk or not."

"I guess I should be glad you won't turn me down. Let's play."

"Never ever have I flashed a stranger," I begin, and Keith downs a shot. "You're starting off with a bang. I'm going to win."

"Hey, I played football. We did crazy stuff."

"Umm hmm."

"Never ever have I wanted to date one of my friend's sisters or siblings in your case unless —," he comments, and I do my shot. "Do tell?" His eyebrow spikes upward.

"It's not a woman. Not that I have anything against people who like girl-on-girl action. I'm just strictly dickly." He burst out laughing, and it took a minute for him to calm down. I continued with the tale, "I wanted to date Asia's brother our freshman year. We kissed. We both decided not to pursue it. If it ended badly, Asia would be in the middle."

"Wow, you were very mature. Should I be worried about him being your unrequited love?"

"No, he died tragically in a car accident with a drunk driver."

"I'm sorry. That's horrible."

"Yea, horrible," I pause and ponder memories of Anthony for moment. I jump back into the game. "Never ever have I had sex in a public place," I declare with confidence figuring without a shadow of a doubt neither one of us would drink. Keith took a shot. "What? You got down in public?"

"Yea, once in the stadium after practice, and I'm pretty sure it was deserted. My girlfriend at the time wanted to try something she fantasized about, and hey, I was a guy in college whose girlfriend wanted public sex. Hell yea, I did it. My only defense is I experienced some stuff in college. I'm much more laid back these days. Never ever have I had a one-night stand," he pronounces, and I drink. "What? You?"

"Well, I guess it's not completely a one-night stand. I knew the guy and we were friends. It only happened one time. Like one and done."

"Nope, it doesn't count. It had to be with a stranger you hadn't met prior and haven't seen since the deed. I guess I got a free shot from you."

"Never ever have I slept with a co-worker," I affirm, and neither one of us drink.

"Never ever have I slept with someone of the same sex," he asserts, and neither one of us drink.

"Never ever have I sent a nude to someone," I avow, and he drinks. "Back on track now. I'm taking you down."

"There are plenty of opportunities for me to corrupt you," he jokes and winks, "Never ever have I shoplifted." Neither one of us drinks.

"Never ever have I joined the mile-high-club," I chirp on my turn, and neither one of us drink.

We play the game for a while longer and I'm tipsy or possibly slightly drunk. He's not faring better than me. As for him not taking advantage of drunk girls, that's a negative. We're in the midst of having drunken sex, and we're louder than normal. I don't regret this at all. My inner Lola is heightened with all the alcohol I've consumed. She's been the primary player with the flirting and the risky questions. Sometimes, you need to flip the script to keep a man interested. I wake extremely early and without a hangover. Considering the night we've had, that's astounding. I'm rather sluggish. I could stay here longer than this weekend getaway. I gaze lazily at Keith, and he's pretending to still be asleep. I drag my fingers to caress his lower abs, his ticklish spot, to lightly brush the area. His breathing hitches prior to him laughing. I keep moving my fingers over this area. I dig in further into the spot, and he's whooping out of control.

"Payback" *laughter* "will be a" *laughter* "a bitch!"

I'm probably being too confident with my tickle game. I fail to recognize Keith turning the tables on me. He flips me on my stomach and immobilizes my arms and hands. **(Whoa! I'm in trouble because I'm four times more ticklish than he is.)** He doesn't show me any mercy. He tickles me so hard I nearly pee on myself.

"I give up! I give up! I'm extremely sorry! Please stop!"

"Do you solemnly swear to obey future tickle rules and commands?"

"I do. I do," I'll profess anything to stop this tickling torture.

"I'm aware you're only doing this because it's what I want to hear. I shouldn't stop tickling you."

(And, what's wrong with that?) "Why" *laughter* "would you assume I wouldn't" *laughter* "honor" *laughter* "my word?"

"Okay, I'll stop for now. There's something else I want more than this from you," his tone becomes serious as he laser stares at me.

"I shouldn't even ask what."

"You're right you shouldn't," he winks.

As the tickle fest ends, he glances at me with an unadulterated, yet hungry expression which I'm certain I'm mimicking. I don't grow tired of being with him. I'm certain I'm in love with him. I also realize it's too soon. I have to keep my growing emotional developments to myself at least in the immediate future. I don't want to ruin what we have by making a declaration of love too soon.

"Sweetheart, I want you," he declares in a seductive tone.

"I want you, too. I can't get enough of you."

"You took the words right out of my mouth. Now, come to me. I want to collect."

"Collect what, sir?"

"You owe me a little something since you were crabby about coming here, remember?"

"Oh, you were supposed to forget about that."

"Nah, I never forget. You're going to give me what you owe me."

"Whoever mentioned what the reward would be?" I ask coyly.

"Well, since I'm the collector, I get to make the call."

"Do you?"

"I certainly do."

"What if I want to make a slight adjustment to things?"

"I'm listening."

"Why don't we kill two birds with one stone?"

"I'm intrigued."

"Meet me in the shower. You won't regret it."

I jump up and sway my hips from side to side luring him into the shower with me. I plan on riding him every way possible and getting clean all in one fell sweep. I reach the door to the bathroom and swing my head over my shoulder towards him. To incentivize him, I tug the t-shirt off and drop it on the floor. I give him my sexiest glance.

"Are you coming?"

"Yep, and you will, too, soon enough."

"Well, you better hurry before I get started without you."

"No starting without me," he yells out and chuckles at the same time.

We dry off and get dressed. It's nearly ten, and we have to check out by 11:00 AM. Leaving this house will be bittersweet. I hate it's time to get back to our reality of work and other obligations. Having Keith to myself has been extremely nice. I'll never act like a selfish brat if he has a surprise for me in the future. I have to trust Keith only has my best interests at heart. He's going to put in great effort to ensure I'm happy. Why did I suddenly doubt he would and have a lack of trust? Are my control issues this much out of whack to drive me to make the decision to discard someone who's so right for me? I have to get a handle on this. I could've ruined our weekend with my bullshit. Well, I'm going to work on letting go. I don't have to be in control of everything.

"Sweetheart, I don't want this to end, but we should probably get a bite to eat and pack up. It's nearly time to go."

"Yea, I guess you're right."

This weekend has been everything. I'm extremely happy we got away. We eat a light breakfast and then we pack our things to go home.

"Thank you for surprising me with this time away together. I didn't realize how much I needed to be alone with you. I've learned a lot about you in such a creative way this weekend."

"I had a great time. Thank you for coming."

We're walking out to the car, and I remember I left my charger in the bedroom. I motion to Keith I need to run back into the house for something. It's almost 11 o'clock, and I don't want any problems. I hurry back into the house to get the charger and rush back out. "I got it," I run out to him. I didn't get a moment to utter another word as a car comes barreling towards us.

The car is coming directly towards me, and it's not stopping. I'm frozen in place. It's like I'm paralyzed or in shock possibly. Keith knocks me out of the way and the car hits him. Everything happens faster than I could blink. It's also as if time stopped. Everything's happening in slow motion. I scream bloody murder. The car keeps driving and never stops. I reach for my phone to call 911 and run next to Keith to make sure he's still with me.

"911. What's your emergency?" the operator asks.

"There's been a hit-and-run accident. My boyfriend is injured. I need an ambulance right away."

"Where are you located?"

"Umm, yea," I search around for the street address, "It's 2047 Swimberly Way."

"Can you tell me if your boyfriend is breathing?"

I check his pulse, and there's a heartbeat. Thank God. He seems to be breathing, too. I respond to the operator, "Yes, he's breathing. He isn't awake."

"Is he bleeding anywhere?"

"Yes, there's blood," I answer.

"Try to put pressure on the wound. Don't move him. He could have internal injuries. The ambulance is on its way. I'll stay on the line with you until they arrive."

"Thank you," I sob. "Keith, baby, the ambulance is on the way. You're going to be okay. This isn't the end of our story. I need you to know I'm falling in love with you. You'll open those gorgeous eyes of yours and stare back at me soon. Just rest now and take care of yourself." He opens them, peers at me, and smiles before closing them again. "I love you," I repeat. "You have to be okay. I don't want the only time you to hear 'I love you' is before you leave me. Don't leave me!!! I have a whole list of pros to share with you. I keep my promises. You better keep yours." I cry like I haven't in a long time. He has to be okay. I can't survive this if he doesn't.

Epilogue

The person driving the car had been extremely angry, and the anger grew more by the second. The couple in the cottage were engrossed with themselves and were oblivious to the danger around them. They didn't deserve to be happy. They rubbed their joy in the faces of just about everybody. Neither deserved the happiness exuding from every fiber of their beings. Being miserable seemed like it suited them more. How dare they assume they could ride into the sunset without a care in the world? Things didn't go as planned. No one should've been hit. He better make it. This better not become a casualty. There will be hell to pay for such recklessness. He had to make a full recovery. The perpertrator shouldn't have left the post?

An idiot could've executed this simple plan. Even simple plans fail sometimes. It would only be a matter of time before the police discovered the car. It had to be chopped and destroyed. This incriminating evidence had to disappear. Who could be trusted with this task? It had to be dealt with like yesterday. Things had to move extremely fast to make the call to destroy the car. There could be DNA on the car from the impact. No more than an hour and half following the accident, the car met its fiery end with an accelerant and a match. It didn't take the fire trucks any longer than 30 minutes to begin rushing to the scene. They rushed into rescue mode to stop the fire and assess if there were any people trapped inside the vehicle. The firemen concluded there weren't any passengers in the car. The fire had been deemed suspicious. The "what, when, why, and how" still had to be determined. The firemen neutralized the blaze within 10 minutes of their arrival. Two of the firemen speculated the fire's origin.

"This screams good old arson to me," one of the firemen stated.

"I don't disagree. The question I guess is why?"

"Well, that's for those good old detectives to find out."

"It's a pretty expensive model, isn't it Harry?"

"Well, I only like American made vehicles. I believe this is a Porsche, Bentley, or one of those fancy cars. Why would anyone torch a car like this?"

"Only someone whose got something to hide, I suppose."

"Hide indeed. Well, the station is calling."

One of the fire fighters answered the call and informed the station about what occurred. The fire fighters would have to wait until the police arrive on the scene since the fire would now be classified as a suspected arson. The cops arrived shortly. The fire fighters discussed their assumptions with the policemen as they arrived on the scene.

"This reminds me of a cover up, Jack," one of the fire fighters mentions to the officer.

"Give me your opinion, Charlie," stated Jack.

"Check out this car. Some expensive shit, like what, Porsche or Bentley."

"It's a Porsche, Charlie."

"Well, you know me and that foreign shit. They're all the same to me."

"Yea, I know, Charlie. Give me the rest of your theory."

"Look, Jack, there's no accident. The car is expensive. Whoever did this used an accelerant. Why?"

"Good theories, Charlie. The why is for me to figure out, but everything you speculated is solid."

"Well, we're going to head out. Duty calls!"

"Great, buddy. Let's get some beers later this week."

"Yea, beers are my language. None of that foreign shit, Jack."

"Charlie, there's nothing wrong with a Dutch beer."

"There's nothing right with it either. Well, catch your Dutch drinking beer ass later."

Jack walked around the scene searching for more suspicious clues. Charlie theories were initially what he concluded as well. Why the cover up? Why would someone torch a Porsche? Someone who didn't care the car cost over $100K. Jack feared he'd be dealing with some rich people and their games. The last thing he wanted to deal with happened to be some rich kid who figured it would be funny to torch his friend's Porsche because he messed around with his girlfriend. Yea, something like this has happened to Jack before. Rich people and their games. He didn't want or have the time to deal with their shit.

As much as Jack wanted to chalk this up as a prank, he had to complete a proper investigation. He had to start asking questions. If this hadn't been a prank, then what was it? Charlie's theory of a cover up could be accurate. Now, he had to deal with the why and the what. Could there be evidence on or in the Porsche that had been destroyed after the car met its demise through incineration? This didn't sit right with him. What were the culprits trying to hide? He wouldn't find out much here on the scene.

This car or what's left of it had to be sent to forensics. Something bugged Jack about this whole thing. Why did the culprit allow the automobile to be so easily found by the cops? Were they simply sloppy and in a rush or were they trying to make a fool out of the police? If the ladder happened to be the case, he would make those punks pay for wasting taxpayer funds.

The perpetrator who had a clear interest in this case spied on the scene of the crime nearby. The person remained inconspicuous where the cop wouldn't be able to notice someone else in his vicinity. It would great if the cop maked a false judgment about the fire and close the case. The sooner this thing closed the better it would be. The cop didn't need to put two and two together connecting the car with the hit-and-run two counties away. The problem remained. This cop wanted to figure things out. This could become problematic. What if some of the evidence could be found on the car to link the perpetrator to the accident? No, not possible. This cop wouldn't find any evidence to link this to the accident. The cleanup had been extremely careful. The car hadn't been registered to anyone. The physical evidence had been destroyed in the fire. The car probably should've been disposed of somewhere else, perhaps, in the woods where it wouldn't have been discovered so quickly. That had been really the only mistake made. If discovered, it would be a costly one. Normally, something like this wouldn't be discovered for days or even weeks. Trying to get rid of the evidence fast caused the pertrator to make a series of questionable decisions like torching the car right off the highway where the flame would be detected in less than 30 minutes.

The cops were supposed to be lazy and blow it off. The best-case scenario would be that this unfortunate incident became a cold case never to be solved. Without evidence relating this car fire to a crime, the case would be dropped. It would be imperative for the perp to stay ahead of the cops to ensure the case is dropped. Absolutely nothing could come out of the forensic report. It must corroborate the prank theory. There couldn't be anyway the cops could put this together. The hit-and-run and this incinerated car cannot be linked in any way. The perpetrator wouldn't go down for it. The perp got into an unmarked car to travel away. Nothing good ever came from hanging out at the scene of the crime.